CRAWSHANKS GUIDE TO THE RECENTLY DEPARTED

DEAD SERIOUS

CASE #1: MIZ DUSTY LE FREY

VAWN CASSIDY

Crawshanks Guide to the Recently Departed
Dead Serious
Case #1 Miz Dusty Le Frey

ISBN: 979-8-7543137-5-0

This is a work of fiction. Names, characters, businesses, places, events and
incidents are either the product of the author's imagination or used in a
fictitious manner. Any resemblance to actual persons, living or dead, or actual
events is purely coincidental.

Please note this book contains adult situations, graphic language and explicit
sexual content, and is intended for mature and adult audiences.

Cover design by Natasha Snow @NatashaSnowDesigns

Stage I

Denial

1

Tristan

"There we go, Mrs Felton, all done." I roll my shoulders and crack my neck.

The air is cool in the sterile room with a faintly clinical scent to it, but it's so familiar I barely notice. A tired sigh is hovering on the edge of my lips, but I hold it in.

It's been a long day and stifling a yawn, I glance down at the old lady laying serenely on the stainless steel drawer. The pristine white sheet covers her bare chest modestly, barely revealing the edges of the 'y' incision in her weathered skin. My gaze migrates to her wrinkled face. I'm certain I can see a faint impish cast to her thin lips, and I swear she looks almost amused, which is a ridiculous conclusion considering the woman is clearly as dead as disco. If her cold white skin and lack of a pulse didn't give it away, the fact that I'd just spent the last four hours performing her post-mortem would have done it.

Shaking my head, I pat her cold, hard shoulder almost comfortingly. It's a strange habit I picked up somewhere along the way. As if somehow they still require a soft bedside manner and warm reassurance despite the fact that they have definitely checked out of existence.

Ignoring that sardonic expression permanently etched into the late Mrs Doris Felton's delicate, bony features, I pull the sheet up and cover her fully until all that's left is a small tuft of grey hair poking out the end.

"Rest well, Mrs Felton. They'll be along to collect you in the morning," I mutter softly.

And this is why people think I'm weird—talking to the deceased as if they're still here. With my lips curving self-deprecatingly, I slide the drawer in, and the steely hiss of the runners echoes in the cavernous tiled room followed by a soft clunk as I close and latch the small square door.

Crossing the room toward the now empty table, I scoop up the folder containing Mrs Felton's notes and remove a pen from the breast pocket of my lab coat, clicking it absently as I sign off on her post-mortem with a barely legible scribble.

That's me done for the day. The silence of the room is suddenly broken by my stomach giving a surly growl of protest, and as I glance up at the large round clock mounted on the wall, I realise it's gone eight. I was supposed to be finished hours ago, but we're already getting backed up, and with one of the pathologists out on leave, we're short staffed. Add into the equation that we're now heading through October and firmly into flu season, I know from experience it's only going to get busier. It's a sad but immutable fact that we're going to see a lot more senior citizens passing through the mortuary before spring.

Shaking off that morose fact, I take a deep breath. Sometimes it makes me feel sad, but death is just a part of life, one I can't change. Being a pathologist suits me. I don't have great people skills, and more often than not, I just feel awkward and out of place. There also seems to be some kind of continuous miscommunication between my brain and my mouth, often leading me to blurt out an embarrassing amount of word vomit.

As a person, I know that I'm somewhat of an acquired taste. There are very few people who can speak fluent Tristan, as my dad calls it, and even fewer people I feel comfortable enough to call friends. My world may be small, but it's quiet and peaceful, just the way I like it. The deceased don't talk back, they don't have any expectations of me, and they don't make me feel bad about myself.

My thoughts scatter as the door opens abruptly, and a familiar mop of red curls peeks around the corner followed by a pair of merry hazel eyes, a slim face, and a cute button nose.

"Hey, Tris." Henrietta, one of my co-workers grins at me. "Are you done hiding out in here?"

"I'm not hiding out, Hen." I roll my eyes with a small, resigned sigh. "I was working."

"Really?" She raises her brows slowly. "Because I could've sworn you've been avoiding us all day so you don't have to come to the pub with us tonight."

"Well, I haven't," I deny innocently.

I totally had.

"Tris, come on." She flutters her eyelashes at me. "Jesus, hun, you're only like what, twenty-five?"

"Twenty-seven," I correct absently.

"Exactly, you're young and hot."

"And you need a trip to Specsavers," I snort quietly.

"Uh, have you looked in a mirror lately, Tris?" She steps more fully into the room and lets the door bang shut loudly behind her. "You're a fox and should have blokes lining up for you. You're way too young to lock yourself away in a cold, dark room with a bunch of corpses."

"It sounds really disturbing when you say it like that." I can feel the smile tugging at the corner of my lips. "Besides, that's what I'm paid for." Henrietta, as annoying as she is when it comes to my non-existent love life, is one of the few people that I can not only tolerate but consider a friend.

"You still need a life, hun." She fists one hand on her cocked hip. "You're coming down The Crown with us, and I won't take no for an answer. It's Seamus's retirement do, and he's been here thirty-five years wheeling corpses back and forth, so the least we can do is get him pissed on his last day."

"I signed his card and gave, I might add, very generously toward his leaving present." I frown. "Although, what he's planning to do with a Segway is beyond me when he's on the waiting list for a hip replacement."

"It's what he wanted." She shrugs. "If you can't live a little at his age what's the point?"

I blink at her slowly.

"Anyway," she continues. "At least we got him one with the safety handlebars."

"Hen, the guy's pushing seventy, we should've got him a mobility scooter."

"Don't be so stuffy." She pokes her tongue out. "And don't think arguing will distract me. You're coming to the pub whether you like it or not. It's for your own good."

"Hen." I sigh tiredly, my plan of a long indulgent soak in the bath with bubbles and a glass of wine is rapidly disappearing like smoke through my fingers. "I've just signed off on Mrs Felton, and I'm satisfied her death was of natural causes, but we still need to call the funeral home to come and collect her first thing in the morning. We're running low on space. Plus, I'll need to be in early to cover Alan while he's off."

"Excuses, excuses." She rolls her eyes and gives a dismissive wave of her hand. "And none of them valid. It'll take you five minutes to call the funeral home." She glances down at the brightly coloured bubble gum pink watch at her wrist. "Besides, they probably won't even be there at this time, you'll have to leave a message. Oooh, in fact..." She brightens. "If they

4

do pick up, you can always invite Tony. He's a gorgeous hunk of a man, and he's totally got a thing for you."

"I am not inviting Tony anywhere." I frown.

"Why not?" She tilts her head. "He's always been sweet on you."

"He's not anything on me," I protest nervously. It's not that Tony isn't a nice guy, he is. He works at the funeral home, so our paths cross several times a week. The problem is, as nice looking as the guy is, I don't get involved with co-workers or colleagues. Besides, if I'm being completely honest, Tony makes me nervous in all the wrong ways. He's got such a big, booming personality that it just blankets everything and everyone in his path. He's too forward, too loud... just too overwhelming for an introvert like me.

"What's wrong with Tony?" she asks.

"He's a bear," I reply. "He'll probably snap me like a glow stick."

She chuckles affectionately. "Tris." Her voice is low and soft. "Just one drink, that's all I'm asking. I'll even pay for your Uber home."

"Fine," I relent with an eye roll. "But you don't need to pay for an Uber for me. I mean it though, one drink and only because I like Seamus, and the truth is I'll miss his gruff voice and inane love of pointless trivia."

She smiles widely. "Call the funeral home for Mrs Felton's collection. I'm locking up and heading out in twenty minutes," she informs me before disappearing back through the door, leaving me once again alone in the stark room.

One drink, I think to myself, feeling nerves dancing the full-on Rhumba in my stomach. *I can do one drink... what's the worst that could happen?*

Following Henrietta out of the room, she disappears down the corridor, I head into my small office and set the folder down on my untidy desk. Sliding off my lab coat and absently hanging it on a nearby hook, I turn and catch my reflection in the window. It's dark outside now, and I can clearly see myself reflected back against the cold glass of the brightly lit office.

Cocking my head unconsciously, I study myself meticulously for a moment trying to see what Henrietta does. She's insisted on more than one occasion that I'm hot, coupled with the fact she seems convinced that Tony is desperately attracted to me, but I just don't see it.

I'm skinny and at roughly five seven, not particularly tall. My eyes are grass green and hidden behind thick black framed glasses. My skin is pale and smooth with a light dusting of golden freckles across my cheekbones and the bridge of my nose, which more often than not makes me appear younger than I am. Seriously, you don't want to know how often I get ID'd when buying alcohol.

My hair is a dark non-descript brown and has an alarming tendency to do whatever the hell it wants no matter how much I try to ruthlessly style it into submission. It just has a mind of its own.

My gaze trickles down my body to the dark blue fitted V-neck sweater over a white t-shirt that clings to my petite frame, past my skinny jeans to the plain black Doc Martens loosely laced at my feet. I'm really nothing to write home about, so no wonder I'm still single. I mean don't get me wrong, I'm no virgin, but even if I'm not completely unfortunate looking, I seem to have a personality that's just not compatible with finding and keeping a boyfriend.

I huff out a laugh, ruthlessly squashing the small pang of longing in my chest. Nope, not going down that particular rabbit hole tonight. I do not need a man, I am not lonely, and my life is just fine the way it is.

Straightening my spine, I pull on my navy blue pea coat and wrap my favourite scarf around my neck loosely a couple of times. It's a deep aubergine colour, as soft as a cloud, and decorated with little white dancing skeletons. It was a birthday gift from Henrietta, who's always been good with gifts. Although I really am still debating the wisdom of her buying a seventy year old with a dodgy hip a Segway.

Shaking my head softly in mild amusement, I slip my keys and wallet into my pocket and head out of the office, flipping off the lights as I go and locking the door firmly behind me.

Heading through the silent, deserted corridors I find Henrietta standing alone by the main entrance, glancing down at her watch impatiently. Her garish lime green jacket clashes with her purple beanie and violently red hair, but it's so perfectly her that I can't help the affectionate smile I feel creeping over my lips.

"There you are," she huffs, rolling her eyes as she grabs my arm and tows me toward the door. "They'll be wondering where we've got to. I thought I'd have to come searching for you again."

"Nope." I give a slightly pained smile. "I'm here, as promised. Young, single and ready to mingle."

"If only that were true, Tris," she laughs as I step through the door, and she turns to set the alarm.

Heading out of the main door I step onto the pavement as a gust of wind rushes past me, sweeping a pile of dry, dusty leaves over the toes of my boots in a mad tumble of red and gold. The temperature has dropped sharply, and my breath expels from my lips as a diaphanous mist. A shiver runs down my spine as I jam my hands in the pockets of my coat, lamenting the fact I have once again lost one of my gloves. I tuck the lower half of my face into the curve of my scarf, allowing my breath to warm my jaw as I stare up at the sweet, little two storey Victorian stone building that houses the Hackney Public Mortuary.

Henrietta is locking the door, which is painted a bright fire engine red and to the right is a huge set of double gates painted in the same hue, through which our charges are delivered or collected. Three white framed sash windows dominate the front of the building, one on the lower level and two dormer windows on the second floor with little pitched roofs, which oddly enough look like a pair of quirked eyebrows, and the two chimneys either side of the main roof jutting up into the night sky like feline ears.

All in all, it's a cute, homely sort of building despite what goes on behind its hundred year old walls, and I find I infinitely prefer it to the cold, impersonal sleek glass buildings, which are so often characteristic of modern architecture.

"Okay, all done. Let's go before you change your mind." Henrietta joins me on the pavement and links her arm through mine.

We amble companionably down the empty back street arm in arm with the stars above us twinkling like little silver pin pricks in the indigo sky. Turning left at the end of the road, we head toward the main high street and toward the warm, welcoming glow of The Crown. Another cute little Victorian building, a main staple of London's East End, the exterior is painted a deep midnight blue in contrast to the bare brickwork and warm walnut coloured bay window and doors. Fairy lights twinkle in the windows like tiny fireflies, and as Henrietta purposefully strides up and yanks the door open, I'm hit with a blast of heat and noise.

I can do this.

I step into the bustling space behind Henrietta and follow along obediently in her wake. Music is drifting in the air, but I can't make it out over the low hum of animated chatter. Brick columns are scattered through the space in front of the bar, each with a polished wooden skirt mounted around it to serve as a standing table. The rest of the columns are wound with more white fairy lights. It's a pretty and inviting space I have to admit, with only one downside. There are way too many people for my comfort level.

I can already feel the scratchy edge of discomfort dancing around me, my shoulders tensing slowly and inching up toward my ears defensively. I have to remind myself to relax my posture and take a breath.

Just one drink...

My gaze scans the bar and snags on a small group of people gathered at the end of the bar. There's nothing exceptional about them other than the absolutely gorgeous man standing with them. He's tall, over six feet at least, with broad shoulders and a narrow waist. He's wearing a suit with the jacket unbuttoned. His collar is open, and his tie stuffed into his jacket pocket. I drift along absently, watching in fascination as he lifts his pint to his lips, his exposed throat rippling as he swallows. His hair is short and golden blonde, hanging just slightly in his eyes, the colour of which I can't make out from this distance.

Christ he's delicious, and way out of my league, I think to myself as he smiles and laughs at something one of his companions says. He looks away from his friend, and his gaze scans the room until it locks on me, tracking me across the room and all the breath leaves my lungs.

"Oofph." I stumble back a step as I accidentally collide into the back of a short, plump man as he turns around and glares at me. "Sorry," I mumble an apology for bumping into him. "I didn't see you there."

He huffs at me dismissively and turns back to his companion. God, my cheeks flush as I send up a silent prayer. Please don't let the insanely hot guy have seen that. I risk a glance back across the room, and yep, he's still watching me, only now his mouth is curved into an amused smile as he lifts his pint back to his mouth and takes another sip, watching me unhurriedly.

"Damn it." I flush, feeling my ears heating up and my cheeks glowing in embarrassment.

I cross the rest of the distance toward my co-workers resolutely ignoring the appealing stranger at the end of the bar, but it's like I can still feel the heat of his gaze tickling the back of my neck.

"Tristan!" Seamus calls out to me.

He's planted at a small, round table surrounded by the rest of our colleagues from the mortuary, nestled among them like a little wiry steel grey flower. He's all wild tufts of hair and ruddy cheeks. He beams up at me through slightly bleary eyes with a beatific smile plastered across his round face.

"Seamus." I smile genuinely as I lean across the table reaching out to shake his hand.

"Tristan!" he repeats, his lilting Irish brogue wraps around every bubbly syllable as he grasps my hand and tugs me forward and off balance into a hug over the table.

Unable to do anything but follow my momentum, I stumble forward awkwardly, banging my knees against the table and causing everyone to reach frantically for their drinks to stop them spilling. A small tsunami of peanuts washes up and over the side of the heavy glass dish in the middle of the table, sending them skittering in every direction.

"Hey, Seamus," I chuckle fondly. "Are you having a good time?"

"I am now you're here." He smiles drunkenly, and I absently glance down at the empty pint glasses lined up in front of him, which I assume at some point contained Bitter. "You don't get out enough." He waggles a stumpy chipolata of a finger at me. "You spend far too much time locked in a room with dead people."

"So I'm told." I glance across at Henrietta at the bar as she shoots me a wink.

I straighten up and unbutton my coat, unwinding my scarf from my neck, which is now starting to feel a little sweaty as it's so warm in here. I stand watching Henrietta as she pays the bartender and picks up two glasses of a dark pink liquid, which

I can only assume are cocktails of some description. I'm trying desperately not to look back across at the hot blonde guy, but thanks to my sterling display of grace, surely he's lost interest by now.

"Here, Tris." Henrietta hands me a glass. "Get this down you."

"What is it?" I take the glass and sniff experimentally. It's our thing, and whenever she actually manages to drag me out, she makes me try all sorts of weird flavoured cocktails.

"It's a Woo Woo," she informs me. "It's Vodka, Peach Schnapps and cranberry juice."

"Doesn't sound too bad." I quirk my lips curiously.

"Down the hatch." She taps her glass against mine.

"Bottoms up." I raise the glass to my lips and taste, feeling the heat of the vodka, and the peach and cranberry notes dance across my tongue as I hum in appreciation. "It's nice." I decide.

"I know right?" She beams.

She turns toward Seamus and strikes up a conversation as I absently scan the room again, conspicuously looking everywhere but the end of the bar.

Don't look... don't look... don't look... dammit...

I can't help it as my gaze once again sweeps over to Mr Gorgeous Suit, and he looks... amused. Like he somehow knows I was trying not to stare at him. I can feel the hot blush creeping up my neck as we watch each other. Then he smiles at me, and it kicks my heart into overdrive.

Suddenly, I'm a bundle of sweaty nerves. He obviously thinks I'm interested. What if he comes over here to talk to me? Oh my god, what am I going to say? He's going to expect me to be all witty and flirtatious, but in reality, he'll be getting Forest Gump. Awkward as fuck. Oh my god, what do I do? He's setting his drink down on the table. I think he's coming over. No. No, no, abort, abandon ship, mayday, mayday!

As the panic and social anxiety begin to bubble up, my

stomach twists into a big knot. I lift my glass without thinking and take a huge glug. The liquid hits the back of my throat like a tidal wave and bringing with it a huge chunk of ice, roughly the size of the iceberg that sunk the Titanic. I give an automatic splutter and an involuntary cough, spraying a mouthful of my drink, but it's too late I realise in horror as the iceberg is firmly wedged in my throat.

My mouth is flapping open and closed like a fish stranded on dry land as Henrietta's eyes widen in realisation. She grabs my glass from my hand and begins thumping me on the back mercilessly.

I can't breathe, and the panic is almost overwhelming as little black spots begin to swim in front of my eyes. The last thing I see is the alarmed expression of the gorgeous stranger before my eyes roll back in my head and the ground is rushing up to meet me.

Am I dead?

Wherever I am, it's dark, and I can hear a low hum of noise, voices... that seem familiar. I blink slowly a few times, and my eyes are assaulted with a blurred kaleidoscope of colours and shapes I can't quite focus on.

I take a slow breath and open them again, and as my vision shifts into focus everything seems a little clearer.

"Take it easy," a low voice rumbles.

I don't recognise the voice, but it's the most comforting voice I've ever heard in my life. It calms me, sweeping over my body and filling all the little spaces inside me I didn't realise were empty. Maybe it's the voice of God... I wonder absently, although... why would God have a northern accent? Odd choice...

There's a low amused chuckle beside me. "No, I'm not God."

My eyes snap open, and I find myself staring into the face of the handsome stranger I'd been ogling since the minute I walked through the door. His large, warm hands are cradling my face and neck gently as he watches me.

Blue... his eyes are blue, I register the thought. They're intense and filled with a mixture of amusement and concern.

I glance around and realise two things. One, I'm lying on the floor like an idiot and two, everyone in the room has formed a circle around me and is staring.

Oh, sweet baby Jesus, this is literally my worst nightmare. It's like that dream when you walk into a room filled with people only to realise you're stark bollock naked... I feel my eyes widen in panic as I lift my head and glance down at my prone body.

Nope... not naked... okay, small mercies... I draw in a shaky breath and try to sit up.

"Hold on there a minute," the man beside me mutters. "You shouldn't try to move just yet."

"What? Why?" I croak realising my voice sounds a bit weird, like a I have a cold.

"Just humour me, okay?" He smiles.

It's not fair, I muse as I stare at him, no one should be that good looking and have a voice like that too—the whole sexy package.

Okay, Tristan, there's a roomful of people staring at you do not think about sexy packages.

Even as I mentally admonish myself, I can feel my cheeks flushing.

"Good, you've got some colour back in you." The man nods. "You gave us quite the scare."

"The paramedics are here." Henrietta suddenly appears at his side.

"Why?" I croak. "Who needs a paramedic?"

"You do, hun." She drops down on the wooden floor beside me with a clunk, her large brown eyes filled with worry and relief as she grabs my hand. "You technically just died."

"Um, sorry, what?" I blink slowly.

"Just for a minute," she amends. "A cup of hot water to melt the ice cube and some CPR, and you were incredibly lucky."

"Excuse us, make some space," a firm authoritative voice cuts through the low murmur of the crowd, and I see the dark green uniform of the paramedics cutting through the mass of gawkers. "Have a little class, man," one of them growls at a young guy who has his phone out and is filming every moment of my utter humiliation.

They clear everyone out of the way, shunting Henrietta aside, although she still hovers over me like a little mother hen. I lose sight of Mr Blue Eyes, but it's probably for the best. I really don't think my self-confidence can take much more of a battering tonight. I literally want the ground to open up and swallow me.

The two paramedics are brisk and professional, flitting around me asking questions, poking, and prodding me before deciding a trip to the hospital to get checked out is definitely in order as my heart did in fact stop for a total of fifty-three seconds according to Hen, that is, before Mr Sexy Northern Accent got his mouth on me and apparently saved my life.

My current condition is not considered life threatening, but they didn't want me walking out to the ambulance until I'd been thoroughly assessed, so I had to suffer the further indignity of being strapped into an emergency chair. It wasn't even a wheelchair but some weird metal contraption with a harness and two wheels at the back only.

Man, just when I thought my night couldn't get any worse, they cross my arms over my chest, strap me in, tilting the chair back and wheeling me out like I'm Hannibal bloody Lector.

Seriously? Why me?

2

Danny

I watch the cute dark-haired guy being wheeled out on one of the most uncomfortable looking emergency chairs I've ever seen and feel a wince of sympathy. He looks absolutely mortified, and it's easy to tell he doesn't enjoy being the centre of attention. In my line of work, I'm constantly surrounded by people who live for drama, but honestly, the poor guy looks like he wants the ground to open up and swallow him whole.

Damn, this wasn't how I envisaged my evening going. When I'd first seen him enter the pub, I thought my luck had finally changed. He's not my usual type. I don't usually go for petite and twinky. But he is just so pretty with the cutest nerdy glasses, and all that mass of dark, shiny, wavy hair, which obviously refused to be tamed. My fingers involuntarily twitched as I recall how silky and smooth it felt at the nape of his neck as I'd held him gently while he came to.

I didn't even get to ask him his name, although I did hear someone call him Tristan. My mouth curves as I roll the name around on my tongue, and I wonder if he's local? I've got a place over in Whitechapel, not too far from here, only a couple of stops on the tube. This is the first time I've been to this particular pub, then again, I've only been in London a month. New city, new job, same old me.

I never thought I'd leave my hometown and head down south, especially not to London, but when the job offer came up, I knew I wasn't going to turn it down. Putting some distance between me and my family seemed like the right thing to do at the time, and I hope that if distance doesn't make the heart grow fonder, it'll at least make it more tolerant.

My thoughts once again stray back to the pretty guy, Tristan. His glasses had fallen from his face as he hit the ground. After I'd revived him and he'd come to, I'd found myself staring into the most vivid pair of green eyes I'd ever seen. They were like a cat's as they locked on me in confusion. He has an adorable little dusting of golden freckles across the bridge of his nose and the softest looking lips. I hadn't really registered them while I was performing CPR, I was too focused on getting him to breathe, but as I'd held his face and he'd watched me, I had the craziest urge to lean down and brush my mouth against his. Talk about bad timing.

Just thinking about him is giving me a nice, warm little hum in my belly, and I know I really want to see him again. Something I'm not willing to leave to chance. I glance over to the table where his friends are still sitting, slightly subdued with varying expressions of shock at what had happened.

I head over with my most comforting smile, something else I have to use in my line of work more often than not.

"Is everyone okay?" I ask gently. "It's been a hell of a night."

"Seamus Gallagher." The burly Irishman clambers to his feet, knocking the table abruptly and filling the air with the sound of clinking glasses as he holds out his plump hand. "I can't thank you enough for what you did for our Tristan. We're very fond of the lad, and it hurts my heart to think of what might have happened if you hadn't acted so quickly."

"It's no trouble, honestly." I reach out to shake the offered hand and feel my fingers crushed in his grip as he pumps my hand so enthusiastically that I hear my wrist crack. "You know him well then?"

"Known the boy for years. We all work together, or rather did." Seamus releases my hand and settles back into his seat and chugs the dregs of his pint glass. "I retired today."

"Congratulations," I murmur automatically.

"I feel bad." Seamus frowns into his empty glass as if he's not quite sure why it's empty.

"Why?" I can't help but ask.

"We knew he didn't want to come out tonight, but we strong-armed him. We just care is all. He doesn't get out enough. We've told him dozens of times he can't just spend all his time cutting up dead bodies, it isn't healthy."

"Cutting...up...dead...bodies?" I reply slowly, certain I've misheard or perhaps misunderstood.

"Oh, hush now, Seamus." A middle aged woman with ash blond hair and pale green eye shadow tuts good naturedly before turning to me. "Don't pay any attention to the old fool, he does it for dramatic emphasis. Tristan isn't a serial killer. He's a pathologist. We all work around the corner at the Hackney Public Mortuary. I work in the office myself, but Tris is very good at what he does, treats the dead with the respect they deserve. Not everyone can stomach the job."

"I see," I reply, slightly intrigued.

A pathologist... I muse internally. Performing post-mortems for a living is certainly not what I would have pictured him doing, in fact it probably wouldn't have even made the top ten if I'd had to guess.

I suppose some people would be put off by his profession but me? I'm not squeamish, not after some of the things it's been my misfortune to witness in my line of work. In fact, it makes me more curious to unpick this man stitch by stitch. He's like a fascinating puzzle, and my fingers are itching to pick up the pieces.

Suddenly, I feel my phone vibrate in my pocket. "Excuse me." I smile at them politely as I see the caller ID and step away to take the call. "Hayes," I greet briskly as I head to a quieter corner.

"Didn't get you out of bed, did I?" the DCI murmurs gruffly down the line.

"No, sir," I reply easily. "I'm not home."

"You sober?" he asks suspiciously.

"As a judge."

"Clearly you don't know Judge Cleaver then," he huffs. "Where are you now?"

"The Crown in Hackney," I answer honestly.

"You sure you're sober?" he asks suspiciously.

"Two sips of a pint, sir," I admit. "Barely enough to wet my lips."

"Yes, well, I know you're technically off duty right now, but we've got a suspected homicide at a club in Shoreditch, and I don't have anyone else available right now."

"No problem, sir," I reply easily. Although I'm tired and was looking forward to heading home to bed, I know there's no chance of that now. As one of the newest detectives at Scotland Yard, I've yet to prove myself to my colleagues and superiors, despite my stellar reputation from my time on the force at West Yorkshire Police. I'm certainly not going to be a primadonna over out of hours cases. "I'll head over now."

"Good," he rumbles. "Place is called The Rainbow Room, and I'm sure you'll have no trouble finding it. Keep me appraised of the situation."

"Yes, sir," I agree, disconnecting the call as the line goes dead. Pulling up the Uber app on my phone, I arrange a ride to Shoreditch and grab my coat, heading out the door without a second thought.

. . .

The Rainbow Room had looked innocuous enough from the outside. The exterior had been painted a matte black with gold edging and above the double doors, The Rainbow Room flashed brightly in multicoloured neon, but it wasn't until I stepped inside that I really got a feel for the place.

It was an explosion of glitter and colour. Filled with gauzy curtains in a myriad of hues, ostentatious light fixtures, and chandeliers. A brightly lit bar dominates one whole wall on the main floor with raised dancing platforms either side. Tables and chairs are scattered around the edge of a dance floor and directly ahead of it a wide stage backed with heavy red velvet curtains and gold fringed sashes.

I can only imagine the ambience when the lights are down and the spotlights on, but right now, the whole space is flooded with bright overhead lights. People are gathered in small groups speaking in hushed tones, some are giving statements, but I bypass all of them and head toward a uniformed officer guarding what I assume is the entrance to backstage, the dressing rooms, and the staff only areas.

"Inspector Danny Hayes, Scotland Yard." I flash him my ID.

"They're expecting you." He nods, stepping aside and opening the door. "Carry on straight back, last door to the left, you can't miss it."

Tipping my head in acknowledgement, I slip past him and enter a long dark hallway. The carpeted floor beneath my shoes makes no sound, and there's soft light spilling in intervals from the wall sconces giving the corridor a strange kind of phosphorescent glow.

I bypass closed and unmarked doors, which could be anything from dressing rooms to storage, but my gaze is firmly fixed on the one door open to the left at the end of the dim corridor, which is spilling bright light over the worn carpet.

As I approach, I catch a whiff of perfume that is so faint I wonder for a moment if I'd imagined it, but it's suddenly smothered by the smell of vape smoke, something sickly and cloying with a fruity undertone that burns the back of my throat as I stop in the doorway and scan the room.

It's a small room, obviously a dressing room. There's a star mounted on the door with the name 'Dusty' scrawled across it. To the left of the room are racks of costumes in an array of bright colours, beads, sequins, and feathers. Above, is a shelf with a neat row of polystyrene heads each mounted with an elaborately styled wig in a different colour, from bright electric blue to murderous red, all except the last head, which is conspicuously bald due to its missing wig.

There are rows upon rows of shoes, including platforms so tall you'd need scaffolding to climb into them and spiky heels that could double as lethal weapons. In the centre of the back wall is a huge vanity with a large mirror edged in brightly lit spotlights. Photographs and notes also adorn the edges and the wall surrounding it.

But it's the people congregated in the room I turn my attention to. Another uniformed police officer is standing beside an open door that leads, from the looks of things, into a built-in cupboard, but I can't see it very clearly from the doorway.

There are three others in the room, two of which are in drag. The taller of the two, clearly about six two even with the added five inches of strappy heels, decorated with thin metal spikes, is dressed in a tiny and tight leather dress with a metal link choker. Her wig, a sleek, dark cherry-red, is cut into a severe bob, and her make-up is fierce. I watch as her dark violet coloured lips pucker as she sucks on a vape viciously before exhaling a sickly sweet cloud of smoke.

The smaller of the two is wearing a rather frumpy, misshapen dress, which reaches her knee and flares out into a large ruffle. It's obviously too big for her five four frame even with what I would deem beginner heels in a conservative three and a half inches. The straps of her dress keep sliding off one thin shoulder, and the plastic bangles at her wrist jangle as she constantly shoves it back into place. Her wig is a bright, curly, orange monstrosity, and her make up a little over done, which is saying something for a drag queen, or possibly a drag intern by the looks of her. She look's young, really young I realise as I look beneath the caked layers of foundation. She can't be much older than eighteen maybe? I've got to admit that the longer I look at her the more tempted I am to ask for ID. Surely, she's too young to be in a place like this?

Standing between them is a short, slightly stocky bloke in tight leather pants. His black satin shirt is unbuttoned at the collar revealing tufts of wiry grey shot hair and ruthlessly tucking his middle-aged paunch into his leather belt, which is mounted with an ostentatious silver buckle. He has a bushy moustache, the likes of which I haven't seen since my junior school PE teacher, Mrs Holland, and a round bald patch at his crown surrounded by a thick halo of salt and pepper hair.

Ignoring the mismatched trio for a moment, I step further into the room and glance into the cupboard beside the officer and get my first glance at what he's guarding. Curled up in the bottom of the cupboard, perched on a plastic storage box, is the body of a woman. She's wearing a rouched gold lamé dress that clings to her killer body and rides up her slim thighs, revealing long and shapely legs. One foot is bare with painted toenails and the other is still wearing a tall gold, glittery stiletto. I can't see her face because her head is hanging forward, the thick wavy curls of her blonde hair obscuring her features, but there's a huge blood stain at the crown of her skull, leaving not much guessing when it comes to the possible cause of death.

"What do we have here?" I ask the officer, even though the body and corresponding injury are pretty self-explanatory.

"Drag queen, Inspector." The officer nods. "Blunt force

trauma killed her, I reckon, then someone shoved her in a cupboard."

"Drag queen?" The small man with the 80s porno moustache sputters, his thick cockney accent indignant. "She was a fuckin' star. Show some respect, PC Plod."

I turn slowly and study his pink face. "And you are?"

"Roberto Caligliari," he replies as his eyes narrow.

I blink slowly, the name is so at odds with his East End accent I find myself wondering if it's some kind of stage name, after all, he kind of looks like one of those 1980's one hit wonders who should be reclining on an album cover wearing a medallion nestled amongst his copious chest hair.

"I know what you're thinkin', son," he answers. "The name's legit, my old man was Italian. Knocked up my mum over 'ere on a student exchange back in sixty-two then fucked back off to Calabria or wherever the fuck he was from. Can't blame 'im much though, my mum never shut up, could talk the hind legs off a fuckin' donkey..." He clears his throat. "God rest 'er soul," he adds almost as an afterthought.

"Very well, Mr Caligliari," I reply politely, my eyebrows raising slightly as I retrieve my notepad and pen from my jacket pocket as I thumb through to a fresh page.

"Ari," he corrects. "Most everyone calls me Ari, and this 'ere is Brandy." He turns to the tall woman standing next to him. "For god's sake put that fucking thing down, show some respect for the dead."

"It's only a vape for fuck's sake, Ari," she hisses in a low baritone. "It's not like I'm smoking a real cigarette. This has all been a terrible shock, and I just need something to take the edge off."

"That's all very well but does it 'ave to smell like fuckin' strawberry cheesecake?"

Brandy shrugs and takes another defiant pull, blowing out a thin stream of smoke before shaping her lips and letting loose a perfect circle of smoke as she winks lasciviously at me and runs her tongue suggestively over her shiny lips.

Ari rolls his eyes and tilts his head toward the smaller one absently. "This one 'ere is Ginger." He turns his head to look at her. "Love... fix yer tits, they're wonky, one's bigger than the other."

She flushes in embarrassment and discreetly adjusts the padding in her bra.

"Don't mind 'er," Ari continues. "She's new."

"And the victim?" I glance back at the woman folded into the cupboard at an awkward angle.

"Dusty," Ari replies quietly. "Er name was Dusty, and she was the brightest light in 'ere. She was a star. Everyone knew who she was. Voice like a fuckin' angel she 'ad. The rest of these girls don't have a scooby."

"Scooby?" My brow wrinkles in confusion.

"You know... a Scooby doo..." Ari replies staring at my blank expression before sighing. "A clue."

"Oh." I nod, my knowledge of cockney rhyming slang begins at apples and pears, and ends with dog and bone, anything else is white noise.

"Anyway, like I said," Ari continues. "Dusty was different... special, not like most of these no talents. They maybe be pretty to look at but they all mime. Not Dusty though, she outperformed all of them."

"So would you say they were jealous of her?" I muse.

"Jealous of her," Brandy snorts. "Pur-lease." She rolls her eyes.

"Oi." Ari glares at Brandy.

"So, you're the proprietor of this establishment?" I ask Ari.

"I am, son." He nods.

"What can you tell me about what happened here tonight?"

"Dusty came in earlier than usual, about six-ish," Brandy answers, as she takes another puff on the disgusting vape. "She holed up in her dressing room in a mood, getting ready so we left her to it."

"Why was she in a mood?" I question.

"She just was." Brandy shrugs nonchalantly. "Wasn't unusual for her, so like I said, we left her temperamental arse to it. She was due on stage at nine, but at quarter to, Ruby came to find us saying she couldn't find Dusty and that her dressing room was empty. We figured she'd flounced off in a strop, so Ruby covered her number instead."

"Was it usual for her to just walk out?"

Brandy shrugs again, attitude leaking out of every pore.

"Nah, it wasn't," Ari butts in, glaring at Brandy. The two of them exchange a look before he turns back to me. "Dusty was many things, but she was a professional, she wouldn't walk out if she was supposed to be performing, but we didn't have time to look for her. I'm running a business 'ere. So, we moved the line-up around and some of the others covered, but by eleven, we still hadn't found her, and she wasn't answering her phone."

"Who found her then?"

"I did,'"Ginger speaks up timidly beside Ari, her voice sounding like it had not long broken. "Dusty was always good to me, and she had a lot of patience when the others didn't. She was teaching me to be a performer."

"She was mentoring you?" I clarify. "How old are you?"

"I'm twenty-one," Ginger replies. "But I came from a very strict religious upbringing. My family wouldn't accept that I was gay."

I know that feeling, kid, I think absently to myself.

"My family would never have understood that I wanted to wear make-up or dresses or be on the stage. So, when I came here, I had no experience. Dusty took me under her wing, she let me try on her stage costumes and started teaching me how to apply make-up."

Brandy snorts silently.

"She was teaching me how to dance." Ginger breaks into a little sob. "And to perform. She was the best person I've ever known, and now she's gone."

I gaze at the young kid in sympathy, watching the streaks of mascara roll down her cheeks as she cries in earnest for her friend.

"How did you find her?" I ask gently.

"Ruby uses a huge feathered fan for one of her numbers and it broke." Ginger hiccups. "So, I went to get Dusty's one from her storage cupboard, and that's when I found her, like that." Her tear-stained gaze locks on Dusty's corpse.

I drop to my haunches in front of the cupboard, and with the edge of my pen, I carefully sweep a lock of hair away from her face so I can see her properly. She was a beauty alright I muse, staring at her face. I take in the streaks of mascara trailing down Dusty's face almost to her jaw. For a second, my gaze flicks back to the kid and her own smeared mascara. Dusty had been crying before she died. Had she begged for her life, I wonder with a heavy heart. Had she known her killer? Chances are, she did.

I look up once again, and this time I see Ari staring at Dusty, his eyes unreadable.

"Brandy," he calls. "Why don't you live up to your name an' go get me one. I need a fuckin' drink."

"Fine," Brandy huffs. "One brandy coming right up."

"And take little orphan Annie wiv you." He rubs his forehead tiredly as they both exit the room. Once they're gone, he fixes me with a hard stare. "Find out who killed 'er," he says quietly. "Whatever you need, it's yours, statements, searches, employee records you name it, but I want to know who did that to 'er."

. . .

I watch him carefully, his eyes are dark and glinting, his mouth a thin, grim line as he stares at the body in the cupboard, his expression almost unreadable... almost. He's hiding something, it's sitting like a rock in my gut, but whatever it is, he cared about Dusty that much is true. Still, it won't rule him out as a suspect. Chances are Dusty knew her killer, and I wasn't going to stop until I'd figured it out.

"You have my word, Mr Caligliari." I nod professionally as I turn back to Dusty, studying her sagging head for a moment.

"I'll find out who killed you, sweetheart," I mutter under my breath. "I promise."

3

Tristan

I breathe in a sigh of relief as my feet cross the threshold into my small upstairs flat. It's three in the morning and I'm shattered. I've been poked and prodded, I smell like a hospital, and I may never get over the utter humiliation of almost choking to death on an ice cube of all things, and worse still, in front of the best looking guy I've seen in months. Just when I think my life couldn't get any more pathetic.

"Stop it," Hen's voice says firmly behind me.

"What?" I turn to face her as she hovers in the hallway just outside my door. Bless her heart, she'd not only insisted on going with me in the ambulance, but she'd stayed by my side the whole time we'd been at the hospital, which really just involved watching me laying on a hard bed with a thin blue blanket staring at the wall studying a chart on resus methods for hours on end while we were waiting to be seen by a doctor who didn't look much older than me.

"I know what's going on in that brain of yours, Tris." She frowns. "I know you too well."

"Thanks for being a good friend, Hen." I smile at her affectionately.

"I really wish you'd stayed overnight for observation at least," she says, blowing out a frustrated breath.

"They didn't have any spare beds and it really wasn't necessary," I reply. "They were satisfied that I haven't suffered any lasting damage, and there's nothing wrong with me, except for a terminal case of bad luck."

"Tris, you technically died." She scowls.

"Only for like a minute." I frown. "There's no permanent damage done. I was lucky and I'm grateful. Plus, I'll be drinking all my beverages through a straw from now on to avoid choking hazards."

She huffs out a small laugh. "You sure you don't want me to stay? I can sleep on your sofa."

"Even your tiny arse wouldn't fit on that sofa, its practically hobbit sized." I smile. "Go on, your Uber's waiting for you outside."

"Fine." She drops a sisterly kiss on my cheek. "Try not to injure yourself further."

"Going straight to bed, I swear." I cross my chest and smile.

"Fine, night, Tris." She waves as she heads down the stairs.

"Night, Hen," I whisper as I close the door and lock it.

Slumping against the door, I draw in a long, tired breath. I'm exhausted, and I've only got a few hours before I need to be up for work. There's no way I'm not going in, not only is there, technically, nothing wrong with me, unless you count a terminal case of mortification at my perpetual crappy luck, but it doesn't change the fact we're understaffed.

I blow out a tired breath and push myself away from the door, traipsing through my tiny flat toward my bedroom not even bothering to switch on the lights. I hear a soft thud to my left, followed by a soft mewl and pause briefly. Feeling something rub against my ankle and twine around my legs I reach down, my fingers connecting with soft, warm fur.

"Hey, baby," I croon quietly. "I'm sorry I was out so late. It's been a long night."

I'm rewarded with a loud meow as I start walking once again, this time feeling him padding companionably along behind me. I hate to admit it but it's kinda comforting. Although, I wouldn't admit it, what happened tonight scared me. I nearly died, for no good reason, not that there's ever a good reason for dying, but I'm forced to confront the uncomfortable truth. What would happen if I died? Who would look after my cat? And most importantly what would happen to my dad?

My chest feels heavy with anxiety as I plod into my room toeing off my boots and dumping my coat and scarf on a nearby chair, which is piled so high with laundry that my heavy coat simply slides off and hits the floor with a muted thud. I strip off my skinny jeans and thin jumper before climbing onto my bed in my t-shirt and boxers. I know I smell like hospital, and while it's not particularly pleasant, working in a mortuary I have smelled way worse. I'll have to remember to strip the bedding tomorrow morning after my shower.

I lay plastered to the bed on my stomach, arms and legs splayed like a starfish, staring at the tiny sliver of moonlight filtering through the gap in the curtains. It's a weird feeling. I'm exhausted but I feel wired. My skin's tingling as if static electricity is making the tiny hairs on my arms rise, and there's an uncomfortable prickle at the back of my neck.

A sudden cold breeze washes over me and I shiver. My head darts up as a shadow passes by, skimming the periphery of my vision. I fumble for my glasses, knocking a paperback novel from my nightstand to the floor, and shove them on, staring into the deep shadows of the room, my eyes narrowing. I can't see anything but darkness. It's funny because it's never bothered me before. When most kids were complaining about monsters under their beds and in their wardrobes, I always found the darkness to be very soothing. In a world of bright noise and colour that all too often overwhelmed me, the darkness was a soft, warm blanket that lulled my mind into rest. Not now... now the darkness feels full somehow. There is no other way to describe it. It's the weirdest sensation. It feels like I'm standing in a crowd of people, only there's no one there.

I feel a sudden weight land on my back, and I jolt in shock, my heart pounding and my vision dimming slightly. I suck in a sharp breath, trying to calm my racing pulse as a soft purr rumbles in my ear, and a tiny cool blunt nose nudges my cheek, his whiskers tickling my ear.

"Holy shit, Jacob Marley." A weird sound escapes my lips, a cross somewhere between a huff of a laugh and a sigh of relief.

Oh, and yes, by the way, my cat is called Jacob Marley. In my defence, I was slightly drunk when I named him. He's a grey tortoise shell, and the patterning of his fur makes it look like he's wrapped in chains. He even has a light-coloured banding around his head, which looks like a bandage. I know it's stupid, but the problem was that once I'd sobered up, he'd decided he liked the name and literally wouldn't answer to anything else.

Swamped by another wave of exhaustion, I pull my glasses off and set them down on the bedside table, burying my face into the pillow. Jacob Marley kneads his soft paws into my back right between my shoulder blades, purring loudly before settling down on my back to sleep.

I don't want to admit it but I'm grateful for the comfort. Usually, it doesn't bother me that I live alone, but I have to admit, tonight it would have been nice to come home to someone. To have slipped into bed and have them wrap their arms around me, but still, I know better than most, you can't always have what you want. With a deep bone-weary sigh, I close my eyes slowly, and I don't even notice when I slide into a deep, dreamless sleep.

· · ·

"What on earth are you doing here?" A loud voice startles me from the chart I'm holding onto, causing it to wobble in my hand as I attempt not to drop it.

I glance up to find Judy, from the office, standing by the door staring at me with a kind of stern maternal disapproval.

"Morning, Judy." I yawn.

"Don't *morning, Judy* me, young man." She purses her lips tightly as she folds her arms across her waist. "As if I wasn't there at The Crown last night."

I wince slightly, feeling a flush of embarrassment heat the tips of my ears. "Do we have to mention that," I mutter. "I was hoping we could just forget about it."

"Forget about it?" She frowns. "Tristan, why aren't you still in the hospital?"

"Because there's nothing wrong with me," I reply. "Judy, I know you care, and I appreciate it, but the doctors wouldn't have let me go home if they weren't satisfied that I was in no danger. It was just an unfortunate accident and I got lucky."

"Thank God," Judy adds.

I frown and shake my head. "After last night, I'm not so sure there is a God."

"Why?" Her thin lips quirk. "Didn't see a bright light?"

"No," I mumble. "A gorgeous man had his mouth on mine for the first time in I don't know how long, and I was technically dead at the time."

"That was unfortunate," she chuckles.

"Yeah, sucks to be me," I reply tiredly. "Now, if you don't mind, I'd like to move on and not think about it."

"Hmm," she hums non-committedly. "I still think you should've taken the day off."

"And do what?" I ask. "Sit around and stare at the walls all day."

"You need a hobby."

"I have one." My mouth curves slowly. "It's called cutting up bodies and trying to figure out how they died."

I wasn't kidding either. As sad and as morbid as my job is, I love a puzzle, and there's nothing more complex than the human body. There must be a billion different ways to die, and for me that's the draw. The science of it fascinates me, which is why I branched out into forensic pathology. I've never been able to resist a riddle.

"Tristan." Judy frowns.

"I know." I shake my head. "But honestly, I'm fine. Just a little tired. Alan is still out for a couple of days, and there's a back log to catch up on. Ted tells me we've got a suspected homicide arriving in the next half hour, and as I'm the only forensic pathologist we've got right now...."

"Fine, fine," she huffs. "The suspected homicide is already here as a matter of fact. They're just unloading her now."

"Thank you, Judy."

"Don't thank me," she sighs. "We were just going to put her in the cooler until tomorrow, but as you insist, go right ahead. If it's too much and you need to go home..."

"I know." I nod. "I'll let you know."

Giving a sharp nod, she turns and sails out the door, letting it swing back and forth behind her. She's firm but fair. She likes to tell people she works in the office, but the truth is she pretty much runs this place. Especially, considering the actual manager, Mr Clarence Baxter, does nothing but sit around with his feet on his desk reading the Angling Times or napping.

I toss the chart down on the counter and grab my white lab coat, sliding it on over the top of my scrubs. I'm just reaching for a pair of disposable gloves when the doors once again bang open and Ted, Seamus's replacement, wheels in a trolley upon which is a body bag.

He parks the trolley beside the table, and I grasp the end of the bag as he grips the top. "On three," I tell him, and he nods. I count down, and we heave the dead weight onto my table.

"All yours, Doc." He grins as he throws me a mock salute and heads out the door.

Shaking my head, I turn toward the body bag. I miss Seamus already. I don't do well with change. I like routine as opposed to chaos. I like to have a meticulous plan in place for everything from my education to cooking dinner, no one could ever accuse me of flying by the seat of my pants.

The room stills, once again silent, some people would think it a little creepy, but I've always found it quite peaceful. I stare down at the zipped bag and feel a strange kind of prickling at the back of my neck that skitters down my spine on sly, spindly fingers, making my skin pebble, and a low hum begins to buzz in my ears.

Shaking off the odd feeling, I automatically reach for the zip and lower it with a creak, folding back the sides to reveal a young woman in her late twenties I'd say. Beneath the heavy make-up and thick black streaks of mascara staining her skin, it's easy to see she was beautiful. She had a slim chin, high cheekbones, and smooth flawless skin. Her inky black lashes are long and thick, and probably not real. Her lips full and pouty, painted a deep crimson, which is slightly smudged on her lower lip.

Reaching out carefully, I sweep the bright blonde hair from her face to get a better look and feel it shift under my hands. Looking closer, I can make out the silk mesh around her hair-line, and I realise it's a wig, an extremely high quality one from the looks of it. Dried blood has congealed obscenely at the crown, which had obviously seeped through the fine weave of the skull cap. I won't be able to see the wound until I strip her down and remove the wig. Whether or not that particular wound has proved to be fatal has yet to be determined, and I'm not one for jumping to obvious conclusions.

My gaze tracks down to her throat, and I notice a very definitive Adam's apple. I glance down at the skin-tight rouched gold lamé dress she's wearing and the heavy make-up, possibly a drag artist.

I tilt her head slowly to the side and notice a thin red line scored across the back of her neck. Leaning closer, I realise it's not deep, more like a very thin friction burn, as if something was torn from her neck... a piece of jewellery maybe? If it had been a ligature mark it would have been much deeper and would also have encircled her whole neck, not just the nape. I take a quick look at her eyes, no petechial haemorrhaging, which means death by asphyxiation is unlikely.

Suddenly, I feel the strange prickle from earlier flare at the back of my neck, only ten times stronger, as static electricity ripples along my skin causing me to shiver involuntarily, and once again, that low pitched hum buzzes in my ears. My hair feels like it's standing on end, and there's a peculiar metallic taste in my mouth.

I blink slowly as I become aware of a presence, and from the corner of my eye, I see someone leaning in alongside me to stare at the body, mimicking my stance. Wandering who'd managed to sneak into the room without me hearing the door, I slowly turn my head, my eyes tracking to the person leaning down next to me. I blink again, and for a long, slow minute my brain can't quite seem to process what my eyes are seeing.

I can't even explain it. There, standing right next to me is the woman who is currently lying dead on the table, a doppel-gänger? A twin? My brain is desperately grasping at straws trying to figure out what I'm looking at when I register the woman standing next to me doesn't just look the same as the person on the table, she's exactly identical right down to the blood stained blonde wig, the mascara tracks down her cheeks and the gold rouched dress.

She looks up at me, her wide brown eyes locking on mine,

mirroring my shock. She glances back at the corpse and then back to me, panic and disbelief swirling in her eyes. She lets out an ear-piercing scream, which jolts through my system like a thousand volts, and I'm ashamed to admit that I let out my own startled scream, which is surprisingly high pitched and with all the style and finesse of a cheerleader about to be murdered in the opening scenes of a B rated horror movie.

I stumble back instinctively and slam into the table of surgical instruments sending them crashing to the floor as I clutch the table behind me so tightly my knuckles turn white.

I watch in profound disbelief as the woman in front of me sucks in a loud breath, and as her eyes roll back in her head, she drops to the floor in a dead faint.

My heart is pounding in my chest so hard I can feel it in my ears, and I'm breathing heavily as my eyes flick between the body on the table and the one on the floor, unable to come up with a logical explanation.

There's only one thought flickering in my brain like a broken neon sign...What the fuck is going on?

Stage 2

Anger

4

Tristan

I glance up, my heart still hammering as the door opens and Judy appears, her eyes wide with concern.

"Tristan?" She hurries over to the table. "Are you alright? I heard an almighty crash and thought you might've collapsed or something. You look really pale and shaky. I knew you shouldn't have come back to work so soon."

Judy rounds the table, and I expect her to see the body passed out on the floor, but to my utter confusion, she steps right over her as if she's not there.

"Tristan?" She reaches for me, fussing in concern. "Are you alright? Do you need a doctor? Or to lie down?"

I open my mouth to speak, but a weird little squeak emerges instead of actual words as my eyes once again land on the unconscious heap on the floor.

"What?" Judy follows my gaze, looking behind her, and her gaze sweeps across the floor, obviously seeing nothing amiss. "What?" she asks in confusion

I kind of nod my head inarticulately in the direction of the person on the floor, my eyes almost popping out of my skull.

"What?" Judy says again completely bewildered by my odd behaviour.

"Can't you see that?" I answer shakily, my voice manifesting as a hoarse whisper as I force the words past my numb lips.

"See what?" She goes back to staring at the floor.

I raise my trembling hand and point.

Judy frowns and turns her attention back to me. "Tristan, I really think you should go home. A day's rest after what you've been through won't kill you."

She couldn't see it; the body on the floor. The one that looks suspiciously identical to the one on the table about to undergo a forensic post-mortem. Judging from the blank look on her face, I'm forced to conclude only I can see it, which can mean only one thing.... Holy shit... I'm obviously hallucinating.

"Tristan." Judy shakes my arm to drag my attention from the floor and to the slim shapely body sprawled out next to us. "I'm sending you home. I'll see if Mr Baxter will drive you, otherwise I'm ordering a taxi."

"Nobody gets a taxi these days," I say randomly, as I stare at her, my mind a jumble of confusion. "We Uber."

"Yes, well." Judy's lips purse. "I'm clearly old school. I still remember the days the TV remotes were attached to the telly by a wire and there were only three channels."

I can't help it, and snort quietly, and Judy smiles at me.

"There that's better," she coos. "Your colour's coming back. You went very white there for a moment. I really think you should go home and rest, dear."

I shake my head. "No, honestly I'm fine. I don't want to go home, but as a compromise I won't stay late. I'll complete this one then I'll call it a day."

She stares at me, her eyes narrowing suspiciously.

"I promise," I say earnestly.

"Well." Her lips thin again as she contemplates my sincerity. "Just one?"

"Just the one, I swear." I nod.

"Fine, I'll be checking back in with you in a couple of hours," she replies, studying me curiously as once again my gaze deviates to the floor.

The person in the gold dress and blood-stained wig is still splayed out on the floor, with ridiculously long, smooth legs and wearing only one glittery stiletto.

"Tristan." Judy frowns. "What are you staring at?"

"Oh—" I blink back at her, as I tear my gaze away. There's no way I can admit I'm seeing things that aren't there, so I plaster on an amiable smile, which probably looks quite pained judging by the crease between Judy's brows. "A spider," I answer impulsively. "Huge spider..." I double down, spreading my hands wide to indicate some kind of man eating arachnid. "That's what the scream was all about, it startled me. It was huge. You know how they get in these drafty old Victorian buildings."

"A spider?" Judy yelps, her wide eyes scanning the floor in panic. "Nope, sorry you're on your own, Tristan. Call up to the office if you need anything or you're feeling unwell."

She turns and scurries out of the room. This time instead of stepping over the body on the floor, she inadvertently walks straight through it, as if it were an insubstantial as mist.

I hear the door bang loudly, signalling Judy's hasty exit, but my gaze is firmly rooted on the floor. Dropping slowly to my knees on the cold, hard tile, I reach out, my hand hesitating for a moment. Swallowing hard, I move to lay my hand against the woman's shoulder, and I gasp out loud when my hand passes right through and lands on the floor beneath her. I snatch my hand back, cradling it against my chest as my heart pounds.

This can't be real, it has to be some sort of hallucination. Maybe my brain was starved of oxygen too long last night before I was revived.

I shake my head, no, it was unlikely. According to Henrietta,

I was only down for maybe forty seconds. Probably not long enough to cause any serious damage. Maybe I hit my head when I dropped to the ground, and I'm suffering from some sort of delayed concussion.

I shake my head again. They thoroughly checked me out at the hospital before discharging me, and I showed no signs or injuries that would suggest a concussion. So, what the fuck is going on?

Before I can ponder the question further, the unconscious and apparently insubstantial form on the floor shifts and groans.

I scuttle back in panic, falling flat on my arse and pressing myself up against the cupboard behind me as she blinks and sits up.

"Urgh, my head." She raises a slim hand to her rather lopsided wig, her fingernails like talons and painted a murderous crimson. "What the hell did Ramone put in that cocktail. I'm having the weirdest hangover."

"Uhhhhhh." I open my mouth, but once again, my voice seems to have deserted me.

She turns her gaze on me, and when she continues to speak, her voice, despite her beauty and femininity, is a deep male baritone.

"Who are you?" she asks in confusion, glancing down at my scrubs and white lab coat.

"Tristan," I manage to squeak.

"Tristan?" she repeats slowly. "Well, honey, I'm Dusty," she introduces herself, looking around in confusion. "Where the hell am I?"

"Hackney," I answer, apparently I've graduated from no voice to one-word answers.

"Hackney?" Dusty frowns. "What the fuck am I doing in Hackney? Must've been a hell of a night because I literally cannot remember a damn thing." She squints down at her body. "Where's my other shoe?" She glances around the floor. "Shit, Ari's going to be so pissed when he finds out I went on the lash in one of my stage outfits."

'Uh," I manage to utter, not entirely sure what to say.

"Where about's in Hackney am I?" She pushes herself to her hands and knees, searching underneath the table for, presumably, her other shoe. "And where's my bag? I need my phone. Can I call for an Uber? What time is it? DAMN IT, I'm supposed to be in a rehearsal with Ginger this afternoon. I'm teaching her the Shirley Bassey number."

"Uh, Miss... Dusty... ma'am." There, almost a full sentence, progress at last. "You're in the Hackney Public Mortuary," I tell her, not sure if I should really be engaging with my hallucination or seeking immediate medical intervention.

"The Mortuary?" She pauses and stares at me. "Is that a new club?"

"No," I reply slowly. "It's an actual mortuary."

"I don't understand." She pushes herself to her feet. "What would I..." Her words trail off into a horrified and confused silence as her gaze falls on the open body bag on the table. The bag containing her body. "What the actual fuck?" She breathes heavily as she flaps her hands, clearly on the verge of hyperventilating. "OHHHH... I am tripping so damn hard. What the fuck did Ramone put in my drink... Oh my god, I've been roofied, and I'm stuck in the middle of a really lucid nightmare."

"You and me both," I mutter under my breath. "And I'm pretty sure you haven't been roofied. My guess is a severe subdural haematoma caused by a massive blunt force trauma."

"What?" she replies dryly, as she blinks at me.

"You got hit in the head with something heavy," I supply helpfully, ironically trying to soften the blow so to speak.

"Sooooo... I'm in a coma?" she replies slowly. "And this is some weird arse dream?"

I glance down at the cold, dead corpse in the bag. "Uh, I'm pretty sure you're not in a coma."

"No." She shakes her head in denial. "No, that would mean I... that I'm..."

"Dead," I say, wincing at how blunt that sounded. Even if she is some weird figment of my repressed brain trauma, I kinda feel bad for her.

"Oh my god," she whispers, as she reaches out toward the bag, obviously intending to see if the body in the bag is real or if it is all some kind of elaborate prank, but as her fingers connect with the bag, her hand passes straight through it.

I watch as she stumbles back, holding her hands up and staring at them with a mixture of panic and disbelief. They looked solid enough, and it's only when she tries to touch something, or someone tries to touch her that it becomes clear there is no actual substance to her form. Hell, if I didn't know better, I'd say she was a ghost or a spirit or whatever, but that's impossible. Everyone knows ghosts aren't real.

As Dusty backs up to the counter, still staring at her hands, her gaze snags on the mirror mounted on the wall. Breathing heavily, she turns toward it, her eyes tracking over her mascara-stained face and smudged lipstick before settling on her blonde wig, or more specifically the unmissable blood stain, which begins at her crown and trickles down the back of her head, matting the human hair weaves into dark red clumps.

"No," she whispers in horror. "This is just a bad dream. I can't be dead."

I jerk my head around as the door once again opens with a loud bang. I really do need to get the hinges tightened on that thing so it doesn't swing open so wildly, constantly clattering against the wall. Still, it doesn't stop the insufferable sigh from hovering on my lips. Seriously, it's like bloody Piccadilly Circus in here today.

I open my mouth to tell whoever it is that I'm fine, I don't need a lie down, I don't need a break, I don't need to go home, and I don't need a doctor... well, actually the jury's still out on that one considering my very lucid hallucination freaking out behind me. But it's not one of my well-meaning but interfering co-workers coming to check in with me, instead I find myself staring at Mr Blue Eyes from the night before.

He's wearing another suit that, god help me, clings to every inch of a six three body, which has clearly been hand carved by the gods while angels harmonised in the background. His suit jacket is unbuttoned, his white shirt stretched across a broad and obviously well-toned chest, his tie is loosened, and his top button undone.

Jesus holy moly Christ, the man is nothing short of tempta-tion incarnate. All he needs is a trench coat and I'd have my very own spank bank version of Constantine. He lifts his hand, raking it through his dark blonde hair, and I swear it looks like he's in slow motion. I almost reach up to check my chin in case I'm accidentally drooling.

He turns, his gaze sweeping the room, and as his piercing blue gaze lands on me, his mouth breaks into a smile, causing his eyes to crinkle slightly and revealing, not dimples exactly, but fascinating creases either side of his mouth that I find myself desperately wanting to trace with the pads of my fingers.

He crosses the room in smooth confident strides until he's standing on the opposite side of the table to me, with Dusty's body between us.

Great, I realise with a sinking feeling. I've now added my hot crush to my rapidly expanding list of hallucinations. There is no way he's really the guy from last night. He didn't even know my name let alone how to find me. At this rate, I'm going to have to check myself into a mental hospital.

"Tristan Everett?" He smiles as he holds out his hand.

Without thinking, I reach out and grasp his hand, ignoring the little zip of electricity and letting out a startled gasp. When

I'd tried to touch Dusty, my hand had passed straight through as if she weren't there, but Mr Blue Eyes' hand is warm and his grip firm.

"You're real," I whisper as he studies me, slightly puzzled by my response. "Uh, I mean." I clear my throat and offer him a polite, professional smile. He really doesn't need to know how much I'd like to lean forward and press my mouth to those soft looking lips of his, especially considering I'd missed out last night as I was unconscious when he had his mouth on mine, while he was busy saving my life. "How did you find me?" I ask curiously, momentarily forgetting everything in the room but him.

"Serendipity," he replies softly, his mouth curving as he watches me.

"I'm sorry?" I blink owlishly in confusion.

"Inspector Danny Hayes, Scotland Yard," he introduces himself, as his gaze flickers momentarily down at Dusty's body. "That's my case you're about to post mortem."

"Ohhh," I reply slowly as his words sink in. My mouth forms a small, silent 'o' as I stare at him, lost in his denim blue gaze, only marginally aware of the soft smile playing on my lips.

"Oh my God, are you two seriously eye fucking each other over my dead body?" a dry voice interrupts. "Er...rude..."

I jolt out of my trance, my cheeks flushing with embarrassment when I realise that I'm still holding his hand over the top of Dusty's corpse. I quickly let go and step back, clearing my throat once again.

"Um, sorry," I apologise with a small shake of my head. "So... you're here about Dusty?"

It's only as the words leave my mouth that I realise what I've said.

"Dusty?" he replies. "Did you know the victim then?"

"What? Er... no, wait a minute... is that her actual name? Dusty?" I ask in confusion.

'Actually, his name was Dustin Boyle, Dusty Le Frey was his stage name. He performed as a drag artist at a club called The Rainbow Room, in Shoreditch," Inspector Hayes replies watching me curiously. "Did you know him?"

"No." I shake my head, frowning in confusion and wondering if Dusty was a hallucination my brain had conjured up, what are the actual odds of my subconscious guessing his name.

"Then how did you know his name?"

Good question...

"Uh—" Fuck, how am I going to explain this one when I wasn't entirely sure of the answer myself.

"Tell him you didn't know me personally, but you must've seen me perform." Dusty appears next to me as she studies the gorgeous inspector.

"I didn't know her personally," I repeat dutifully, grateful for the direction. "She looked familiar. I must have seen her perform somewhere."

Actually, that really was quite a plausible explanation. Maybe I really had seen her perform somewhere and my mind had subconsciously retained the memory of her face and attached the name to my hallucination.

"I got the impression from your drinking companions last night that you didn't go out much," Inspector Hayes replies in amusement.

"I don't," I answer truthfully. "I'd rather a hot bath, a glass of wine and a good book with the company of my cat."

"Honey, that's just sad." Dusty shakes her head pityingly.

"I don't usually go out unless my friends decide to interfere in my non-existent social life and drag me somewhere." I keep my gaze on the gorgeous police inspector and purposefully ignore Dusty's commentary, especially considering she isn't actually real, just a figment of my imagination.

"That's what friends are for." He grins.

"That's what Hen says," I admit ruefully.

"Hen?" he muses thoughtfully. "Would that be the same Henrietta from last night, wearing a jacket the exact shade of Kermit the Frog?"

"That's the one," I chuckle. "Some days I think she might actually be colour blind, but I think the truth is she does it on purpose so we won't lose her on a dark night. You've got a good memory for names."

"She leaves quite the impression," he replies with a laugh. "Besides, being good with names and details is kind of a prerequisite for this job."

"I guess," I murmur as my voice trails off, and my mind goes blank. His lips really do look really soft.

"Seriously?" Dusty interjects dryly. "Are you two just going to stand there making moony eyes at each other or is someone going to actually figure out what the hell happened to me?"

"Um." I break away from his eyes and stare down at Dusty's body. "What can you tell me about Dusty?"

"Well." He reaches into his pocket and pulls out a small black notebook, flipping through the pages until he reaches the notes he was looking for. "Dusty was in apparent good health, not into drugs from what I understand, thirty-one years old."

Dusty inhales a loud indignant gasp, and unable to help myself, I turn to discreetly look at her.

"Twenty-six," she corrects as I stare at her wryly. "Fine..." she huffs with an eye roll. "Twenty-eight." I raise a brow. "Okay." She throws up her hands dramatically. "I'm thirty-one, but only just, and you're not supposed to discuss a lady's age, that's just rude."

Shaking my head in bewilderment, I turn back to Inspector Hayes.

"I'm sorry, what were you saying?" I shake my head, realising he'd been speaking at the same time as Dusty.

"I said." He smiles. "That we really need to know the C.O.D as soon as possible."

"What's a C.O.D?" Dusty wrinkles her nose.

"I suspect the *cause of death*," I say pointedly in Dusty's direction in answer to her question. "Was due to the blunt force trauma, at least that's how it presents on initial examination," I tell the inspector. "But I really don't like to speculate until I've concluded a full post-mortem. I'll send blood samples to the lab to test for any of the usual suspects when it comes to drugs or poisons. I'll also swab the body for any trace. I'll bag and tag everything she's wearing and send those over to be tested for trace too."

"Thanks." He nods.

"You should have the full report in the next couple of days," I add.

"Okay then," he says softly. "I guess I should—" He kind of nods toward the door. "I should let you get to work."

"Oh, um, yeah," I reply. "Work, right..."

We stare at each other for another few moments.

"Christ, it's like hippos slowly circling each other in the middle of the Serengeti." Dusty's dry voice intrudes. "I'm surprised I can't hear David Attenborough's voice over... *And having made his overture, the male stares slowly at the female trying to gauge her interest in the beginnings of the mating ritual...*"

Inspector Hayes' phone rings, and as he pulls it from his pocket glancing down at the screen, I take the opportunity to shoot a look in Dusty's direction.

"Shut up," I mouth at her silently, my head snapping back as the Inspector looks up, and I smile innocently.

"I really should go," he tells me softly, as he silences his phone, his gorgeous northern accent a low rumble that warms my belly in a way I don't want to examine too closely at the moment.

"Sure," I reply politely. "I'll have the report over to you as soon as I can."

"Appreciate it." He nods as he turns and heads toward the door.

"Inspector," I call out, cringing slightly as my suddenly loud voice ricochets around the cavernous tiled room. "Um." I round the table and cross the room until I'm standing next to him by the door. "I just wanted to say thanks, you know, for saving my life last night."

"You're welcome." He smiles and once again I'm fascinated by those creases at the sides of his tempting mouth. "I'm glad you're okay."

"Me too," I reply.

"Oh, for the love of Christ will you just ask him out already," Dusty yells across the room in exasperation. "I swear to god this is painful to watch. He's hot and he's totally into you. He's practically undressing you with his eyes. Do you need a written invitation?"

I try to ignore Dusty, but I can feel my cheeks heat.

"Here." Inspector Hayes reaches into his jacket and pulls out a business card. He plucks a pen from the breast pocket of my lab coat and scribbles something on the back before tucking both the pen and card back into my pocket. "Give me a call sometime and let me take you for coffee." He smiles easily.

"Oh, um." Dammit, I can feel myself blushing again, and the awkwardness factor cranks up to a level 6. "Thank you, Inspector Hayes."

"It's Danny," he says softly with a smile as he slips out of the door.

"Holy shit, that was smooth." Dusty grins. "You are one lucky little Twink."

"I'm not a Twink." I turn to her with a frown.

"Sure you're not, honey." She shakes her head.

With a long-suffering sigh, I head back over to the table. I still have a job to do, and if Dusty really is just a figment of my imagination, wasting time arguing with her is unproductive as I'm technically just arguing with myself.

She watches me silently as I stop beside the body grabbing a pair of latex gloves and slipping them on. With the ease of experience, I grasp Dusty's body and roll her over, slightly tucking the body bag underneath her, then rolling her the other way and pulling the bag out from beneath her.

I quickly and efficiently strip off her personal effects, earrings, and a flashy rhinestone bracelet. I remove the one shoe she's wearing, not sure what happened to the other, and cut away her dress as she watches what I'm doing wordlessly, her dark eyes unreadable. As sensitively as I can, I remove her bra and padding, but when I remove her underwear and bag them with the rest of her clothes, I pause when I find what looks like duct tape. I know exactly what it's for, it's common amongst drag performers to tuck and tape their genitals flat to give them a smoother, more feminine contour beneath their revealing outfits.

Avoiding Dusty's gaze, and as politely and professionally as I can. I carefully peel the tape away, pausing for a second and blinking slowly before my wide eyes raise to meet Dusty's.

"What?" She shrugs. "It's cold in here."

"No." I shake my head, glancing down again.

"You never seen a bejazzle before?" She smirks.

"Uh." I clear my throat and try to avoid that area as I continue stripping the body down. It's not like I don't see naked bodies every day, both male and female, but trying to be professional while that person is standing over you and watching your every move is a little disconcerting whether Dusty is a figment of my imagination or not.

"Oh, sweet child, you're not a virgin, are you?" she chuckles.

"No, I am not," I reply stiffly, my cheeks once again flaming, and I know the heat coming off my face right now would be enough to toast marshmallows.

Trying to ignore Dusty, the last thing to be removed is the blood stained wig. I carefully bag it, also removing the clips, tape, and mesh skull cap. His real hair is short and mousy brown, kinked at weird angles from being crushed beneath the wig. I carefully search through his hair, but the dried blood and matted hair is making it almost impossible.

Retrieving a set of clippers from a drawer, I expertly shave away the hair, leaving his scalp exposed. I can see the wound much clearer now, but there's still a lot of blood and loose hair concealing what looks to be a quite distinctive shape. More often than not with a head wound, it's just a mangled, bloodied mess, but every now and then, we get lucky, and the wound has specific edges that are often helpful in determining the murder weapon.

Dusty is quiet, hovering on the periphery of my vision, but I tune her presence out. Once I have the body stripped and swabbed for trace, I gently clean peel off the false eyelashes and gently clean away the heavy make-up before washing the body to remove any remaining blood.

I pause for a moment and just stare at him. The young man laid out naked and still on the cold stainless steel table is a million miles away from the flamboyant and colourful woman brought in. A slim, pretty young man in his early thirties, he looks like someone who would've blended into a crowd. Someone quiet and introspective. I look up and find Dusty watching me with that unreadable expression in her eyes.

"You're very gentle," she says finally, her deep voice echoing in the stillness.

I glance across at the small tray sitting nearby on a tall slim trolley, upon which is a neat uniform row of surgical tools before turning back to Dusty, and in that second, I'm not thinking about whether or not she's real, or if I'm hallucinating, all I know is I don't want her to witness this.

"Dusty," I whisper.

She stares at the corpse for a moment longer before her large, dark eyes rise and lock on mine. I can see a fine sheen of tears that make them look fathomless like deep, dark galaxies, infinite and filled with secrets.

I blink slowly, only to find myself suddenly alone, and my only company, the cold corpse laid out before me.

5

Tristan

"I don't know what to tell you, Mr Everett, everything looks fine to me." My consultant, Mr Fitz-Williams, squints through his half-moon spectacles as he studies the scan of my brain.

"So, there's nothing that would cause delusions or hallucinations?" I ask casually, picking at an imaginary piece of lint on my jeans.

"What was that?" he hums non-committedly as he sets the scan down and picks up an expensive looking fountain pen and begins to scrawl something completely illegible in my notes.

"There's nothing that could potentially cause hallucinations then?" I say a little louder. I'm surprised he can hear anything through the little tufts of grey hair sprouting from his rubbery looking ears.

"What? Oh, no, nothing like that." He waves a hand and leans forward scribbling something else in the notes, and I almost squint at the sudden reflection of light bouncing off his shiny scalp, which looks a little like a liver-marked oasis surrounded by a small halo of wiry grey hair. "Why?" He looks up, his wild bushy brows wrinkling as if my question has only just registered. "Have you experienced any symptoms like that? Paranoia, delusions, hallucinations.... Voices?" he asks almost hopefully, as if my potential brain trauma would somehow break the monotony of his day.

"No," I reply carefully.

It's kind of the truth, I haven't seen anything out of the ordinary. It's been two days since Dusty's post-mortem and there hasn't even been a sniff of anything weird. After the strange hallucination of Dusty disappeared that day, I completed the post-mortem, concluding, as I suspected, that she was killed by a severe subdural haematoma caused by massive blunt force trauma to the skull. I sent the report over to Inspector Hayes office at New Scotland Yard opting to keep our interaction purely professional as tempting as his offer for coffee was. There is one immutable fact about me that is as absolute as the sun rising in the East and setting in the West, and that is... that I am absolutely 100% hopeless at dating. It's like watching a slow moving car crash watching me attempt to socially interact with a man I'm attracted to.

There's no doubting that Inspector Hayes is like a shiny new Christmas present with my name on, and I'm desperate to open it. He's made it perfectly clear he's interested but... I don't know... there's something holding me back. The card he gave me with his number on is burning a hole in my pocket. I almost don't want to admit that I don't even need the card anymore, I've already memorised it, but I still haven't called him. I don't know what's stopping me, but every time I think about his gorgeous face and those blue eyes, my stomach swoops like I'm strapped in a rollercoaster and just cresting the top of a hundred foot death defying plunge to the ground.

"Well, Mr Everett." Mr Fitz-Williams clears his throat, closing up my file and tapping it against his desk a couple of times. "Despite your unfortunate incident, you're as fit as a fiddle. I'm completely discharging you, but if you have any further worries, please feel free to address them with your GP."

I stand slowly as he offers his hand.

"Thank you." I nod, shaking his hand.

I leave his office and make my way out through the maze of corridors in the huge hospital. Although I'd initially been seen in A&E at Homerton Hospital in Hackney, for some reason my follow up outpatient appointment had been moved to The Royal London in Whitechapel, probably because they're under-staffed.

When I finally step out of the main entrance and into the crisp autumn air, there's a slight bite to the wind. Looking up, I can hear the rustle of the dry leaves in the trees as I set off along the path, trudging through waves of red and gold leaves, which roll and tumble in front of me like breaking waves. I inhale deeply and feel my soul settle for the first time in days.

I'm in no particular rush to head back to the tube station as I wander aimlessly down the street, heading wherever my feet decide to take me. I don't find myself in Whitechapel often, there's really no reason to. Although it's famous for the Jack the Ripper murders, there's not much here that interests me, but still, it's nice to have a change of scenery, especially after the stress of the last few days.

A weight has definitely lifted from my shoulders now that I know there's nothing medically wrong with me. What happened the other day was probably just a weird after effect of the accident. Seeing Dusty, or rather me thinking I'd seen Dusty, was obviously just a one-off hallucination brought on by stress and lack of sleep.

"It's just as well I can't feel the cold, it looks chilly out here today," a familiar voice interrupts and I freeze. "Give me tropical beaches, Mai tai's and a gorgeous bronzed waiter in tiny pants any day."

Swallowing tightly, my heart pounding, I turn my head

slowly to find Dusty standing next to me, looking decidedly lop sided as she's still only wearing one glittery platform stiletto and the other foot bare.

She looks the same as the other day, in her tight, short gold dress and her huge blonde blood-stained wig. As she fixes her mascara streaked gaze on me, her expression is dry and resigned.

"No," I breathe in denial. "You're not real,"

"Sorry, honey." She shrugs. "Turns out I am real, just lacking a pulse."

"What?" I squeak.

"I think I'm a ghost." She pouts, her hands fisted on her hips.

"That's not possible." I shake my head emphatically. "That's crazy." I turn away from her sharply.

"Hey!" I hear her call out behind me. "Wait!"

I don't stop, hurrying along the street blindly as the anxiety builds in my chest. I can feel a lump building in my throat as the panic claws its way through my insides. Oh my god, am I actually having some kind of psychotic break?

A huge, old familiar looking building appears as I cross the street, nipping between the traffic accompanied by a cacophony of blaring horns and a rather irate man in a brightly coloured Fiat flipping me the finger. I pay no attention as my mind is filled with horrifying images of me in a padded room wearing a straitjacket. Damn it, I shouldn't have watched *One Flew over the Cuckoo's Nest* the other night. Stupid Film Four and their cult movies fest.

I hurry into the tall, imposing building and hopefully toward salvation, despite the fact I'm not in any way religious. The air is cool and smells like every other church in the history of ever. Slightly dry and stale, old, I guess. I wander a little way down the aisle and slide into a hard wooden pew, drawing in a breath.

I'm safe, hallucinations can't cross consecrated grounds, can they? No, wait a minute... spirits can't cross consecrated grounds? Fuck, I don't have a clue. I only know the very idea of ghosts is insane. They're not real, and what's far more likely is that I'm just manifesting early signs of paranoid schizophrenia. Christ, what a cheery thought.

I hear a slow, uneven clicking behind me and my heart sinks. I don't need to look to know what that sound is, but I shift in my seat anyway. Dusty is walking as dignifiedly as possible down the aisle, well... as dignified as one can get limping along wearing only one shoe, a glittery showgirl dress, wrecked make-up, and a bloodstained wig.

She pauses in the aisle next to me, looking up at the large Christ on the Cross near the altar and crosses herself. I say crosses herself, but I use the term very loosely. I would bet money she's no more religious than I am, and her act of piety is less warding off potential evil and invoking the lords blessing, and more a weird little squiggle in front of her body followed by a curtsey... almost as an afterthought before she slides into the pew alongside me.

"I've never cared for churches much," Dusty remarks casually, looking around, her nose wrinkled in distaste. "They smell like Christians and judgement."

I stare at her mutely, my brain unable to formulate a response to that statement.

"Look, Timothy," she sighs.

"Tristan," I correct automatically.

"Tristan." She sucks in a breath. "Look, I realise this is all a bit..."

"Crazy?" I burst out, my voice obviously louder than I intended as an older woman four pews in front of me turns around and scowls at me.

"Sorry," I mouth contritely, as she huffs and swivels back indignantly in her seat.

"I'll admit," Dusty concedes. "This is not an ideal situation."

"Not an ideal situation?" I whisper harshly under my breath. "Not an ideal situation? Ghosts aren't real, and I'm clearly having some kind of mental breakdown."

"Honey, I hate to break it to you, but ghosts apparently are a thing, and I'm pretty certain you're looking at one."

I close my eyes and take deep calming breaths. Trying to find my balance. Dammit, why didn't I ever bother to learn meditation? Surely it can't be that hard. I mean, it's just thinking tranquil thoughts, right? I blow out another slow breath, in through the nose, out through the mouth.

It's not real, it's just a figment of my imagination. I just need to calm down, find my happy place... and breathe...

I peek one eye open to find Dusty still sitting there watching me dryly.

"Feel better?" She raises a brow slowly.

"Will you just go away," I hiss under my breath.

"I can't," she snaps back.

"Why?" Wow, that totally came out as a whine my seven year old self would have been proud of back in the day.

"Because for some reason you're the only one who can see me," Dusty snaps in frustration.

"What?" I blink. "Why?"

"Do I look like a magic 8 ball?" She scowls.

"But ghosts aren't real," I protest stubbornly. "This is impossible."

"What about the Holy Ghost then?" she asks pointedly.

"Huh?" I frown in confusion.

"You ran straight into the nearest church," she continues. "Clearly you believe in God."

"I don't believe in God." I shake my head. "I believe in science."

"Then why are you in a church?" Dusty frowns.

I shrug. "I panicked when I saw you, and it seemed like the thing to do at the time."

"Charming," she replies faintly.

"This is ridiculous." I shake my head. "I'm going home."

I stand up, pausing when she looks up at me with those big brown eyes streaked with mascara.

"Excuse me." I frown.

"I'm not moving." She shakes her head stubbornly. "Not until you listen to me."

I don't know why the hell I'm entertaining my delusion; this is all in my head, it has to be. Shaking my head in annoyance, I step straight through her and into the aisle letting out a short, shocked gasp. As I passed through her, it felt like I'd stepped through an icy cold waterfall. My body shudders violently, and I have to suck in a sharp breath.

What the hell?

Steeling my spine, I march purposefully out of the church, but I can hear the uneven clicking of Dusty's lone stiletto, and I know she's following me.

"Tristan, wait." She scrambles after me.

"No," I mutter crossly. "I don't want this, this isn't my life. I just want my life to go back to normal."

"And you think I don't want that?" she yells angrily, and I stop sharply in the middle of the street turning to face her. "You think I want to be dead? That I wouldn't give anything to go back to my life? To my friends? To my family? But I can't. I know because I've tried, but none of them can see me. Only you, you're the only one I can talk to."

Her words shame me. I've been so wrapped up in myself that I haven't even thought about what this must be like for Dusty. Although, I still think I'm suffering from some kind of psychosis and that she's not real. But, in this moment, with her standing in front of me on a freezing cold street wearing nothing but a gold spangly costume and her own blood, her eyes filled with pain and frustration, she feels real to me, and the beginnings of a seed of doubt are planted.

What if she's telling the truth? What if she really is a... a... I can barely bring myself to think the word, let alone say it.

"Please, Tristan," she says softly, her deep voice so low its almost snatched away by the wind. "I don't have anyone else."

I see people glancing at me and hurrying past with their heads down avoiding eye contact as if my craziness is somehow catching. I need to get off this street and away from prying eyes. I glance back at Dusty who's watching me intently before heading down a small, winding side street and tilting my head to indicate for her to follow me.

"I'm sorry, Dusty," I tell her quietly. "I don't know how to do this, it's so far out of my comfort zone. I'm a scientist. I believe in the physical world. I believe in what I can see and touch. There's just no concrete proof to support the theory of life after death."

"I'm your proof," she replies, as we wander slowly along the narrow back street. "Okay so you can't touch me, but you can see me, you can hear me. I'm sure there's some way I can prove to you that I'm real."

"I don't see how?" I frown.

Dusty looks up and sees a rickety sign a short way down the street.

"I've got an idea." She grins. "Come on."

"What?" I follow along behind her until she comes to a stop in front of a tiny little shop tucked away.

I glance up at the cracked and peeling paint on the wooden sign as it bangs in the wind.

"*Whitechapel Occult Books and Curiosities.*" I read aloud turning to look at her as she points to a sign in the window. "*Madame Vivienne's spiritual readings for those who wish to commune with the dearly departed.*"

"Seriously?" I reply dryly.

Dusty shrugs. "You wanna get rid of me or not?"

"Can't you just go into the light or something?" I can feel my brows crinkling, and at this rate, I'm going to end up with premature wrinkles.

"I didn't see a light," Dusty states emphatically. "Which means I need to figure out why I'm trapped here."

"But a medium?" I reply unconvinced.

"It worked for Patrick Swayze." Dusty shrugs.

"Does that make me Demi Moore then?"

"No, it makes you the Oda Mae Brown to my Sam Wheat." Dusty's mouth curves.

"Why am I Whoopi Goldberg?" I blink.

"Because you're the only one who can see me, and you have to help me solve my murder," Dusty replies matter-of-factly.

"I never said anything about helping solve a murder." I frown.

"Potato, potahto." She shrugs.

"I must be mad for even considering this," I mutter under my breath.

"Please?" She flutters her heavy false lashes and makes big puppy eyes at me.

"Urgh." I roll my eyes. "Fine," I concede. "But if I hear the opening bars of *Unchained Melody*, I'm outta here."

She grins as I reach for the brass door handle, gripping it firmly, I open the door into the dim shop accompanied by a merry tinkle of bells.

"This is completely pointless," I grumble. "I don't need a bloody medium. I can see you just fine, that's the problem."

"But you don't believe it," Dusty points out. "You need a second opinion. If she can see me too, then it must mean I'm a real boy, and you're not on track for the psych ward, plus proving the afterlife does, in fact, exist."

I shake my head in resignation. "I'm sure there's some sort

of convoluted logic in there somewhere," I mutter as I step fully into the shop.

6

Tristan

The old, scarred wooden floorboards creak beneath my boots. I close the door behind me with a hard push and it rattles in protest. Taking a moment to gauge my surroundings, I'm not surprised or otherwise impressed, it looks like every other old second-hand bookshop I've ever been in, but it has a nice warm feeling to it.

There's a low, sagging sofa that may have started out its life as a cream colour, but I'm not sure I can correctly identify its current shade, however most of it is covered in a hand crocheted, multicoloured blanket, which hides the worse of the wear. Directly in front of it is a polished, if not slightly scuffed, coffee table.

Behind the worn sofa and table is a solid oak counter upon which sits an old-fashioned till with brass keys and pop-up sales. The rest of the surface is filled with small bowls of crystals, candles, and a small carousel of bookmarks, one of which catches my eye and I edge closer. It reads '*It's not my fault, I was left unsupervised during the full moon...*'

Behind the counter is an opening concealed by a rather ancient looking brown beaded curtain, which probably dates back to the late seventies. The rest of the space is dominated by walls filled from floor to ceiling with bookshelves, most of which are sagging in the middle due to the weight of the books and look as if they haven't been dusted any time this century. My gaze briefly scans the spines of the worn second-hand books and note it's an eclectic mix of esoteric and practical with a little whimsy thrown in for good measure.

The sudden rattle of the beaded curtain draws my attention, and as I glance over it's to find a short and rather kooky looking woman standing in the doorway, her hands braced against the doorframe either side of her and holding back the long strands of the beaded curtain. She's wearing some kind of billowing robe with dozens of strings of beads and crystals hanging from her neck. The fingers of each hand are decorated with rings inset with crystals and moonstones, making it look like she's wearing new age knuckle dusters. Each wrist jingles with thin metal bangles as she steps up behind the counter, letting the curtain fall closed behind her in a jangle of clinking beads.

Her long, curly grey hair is pulled back from her face beneath a tie-dyed silk scarf, and she's wearing a pair of purple round plastic framed glasses with lenses so thick they look like old fashioned milk bottles. For a second, I almost want to laugh because whether it's by design or happy coincidence, she looks exactly like Professor Trelawny from the Harry Potter films.

As Dusty shifts impatiently beside me, I remember why I'm here in the first place, and I approach the counter with a healthy amount of suspicious reservation.

"May I help you?" the woman asks.

"Madame Vivienne?" I hazard a guess.

"I am." She waves ostentatiously. "Purveyor of otherworldly knowledge to the weary soul. How may I be of help to you, no wait." She holds up a hand. "Don't tell me." She holds her fingertips to her temples. "I'm getting something."

"It's not a migraine, is it?" I reply dryly.

"The spirit world is restless, and they wish to speak." She rolls her eyes, her voice dropping half an octave. "Yooou..." She drags the word out, and I can only assume in the name of showmanship. "...have recently suffered a bereavement."

"Hmm," I hum. "I'd say it was less a bereavement more a potential brain injury."

Choosing to ignore my last comment, she pushes her glasses up the bridge of her nose, and I watch as they slide back down again. Either her glasses need tightening or they're all wrong for the gradient of her rather beaky looking nose.

"A reading is it then?" she asks, cocking a thin grey brow. "Or did you just want to browse a bit? Are you looking for something in particular? *A Beginner's Guide to Wicca*? *How to Dance Naked under the Full Moon with Friends without making it Awkward*? That book was really quite informative, not sure why it didn't sell more copies," she muses.

"Um." I glance around, and that's when I notice Dusty has once again disappeared. I spin around, leaning forward and peering around the nearest book display.

"Lost something, dear?" Madame Vivienne asks.

"My marbles possibly." I sigh. "I can't believe I'm actually going to do this, but I'm after a reading."

"Splendid." She claps her hands together. "That'll be fifty pounds."

"Fifty?" I reply incredulously. "Seriously?"

"Communing with the other side is, after all, a highly specialised skill," she replies earnestly.

"I don't have that much cash on..." Before I've even finished my sentence, she plonks a small portable card machine down in front of me.

"We take all forms of credit card including Visa, MasterCard, American Express and Apple pay." She beams widely.

"Of course you do," I mutter sourly as I pull out my wallet.

She completes the payment quickly and hands back my card before beckoning me around the counter toward the beaded curtain.

"Come, come, dear, I don't bite... that costs extra." She winks at me, and I edge around her uncomfortably. "Go on in. I'll just put the sign up."

I watch as she pulls a tatty piece of A4 paper from under the desk, which reads 'Communing with the spirit world back in twenty minutes...' in bold red marker pen. She stalks briskly across the shop and tapes it to the glass before flipping the lock on the door. Turning back in my direction, I see her making shooing gestures toward me, and with a heavy and reluctant sigh, I step through the jangle of vertical beaded strings.

Now, I'm not sure what I expected exactly, but I step into a room that looks like it belongs in a Miss Marple mystery. It could've been pulled straight from a 1940's post war suburban parlour.

Polished walnut cabinets and side boards are lined against two of the walls along with a tall standing lamp with a pink shade and tasseled fringe. Spaced at intervals along the wall are mounted light sconces with frosted tulip shaped shades. A tall wing backed armchair with a delicate flowered pattern is positioned in one corner, and a pale green chaise lounge in the other. The walls are papered with faded floral silk, which clashes horribly with the violently patterned olive-green carpet. A beige tiled fireplace containing an old gas fire dominates one wall, above which a hexagonal bevelled mirror hangs on a chain, and beside it sits an old wireless radio in a cherrywood cabinet with a record player on top and looks as if it hasn't been operational in years.

Dead centre of the mismatched room is a fair sized round table covered by a dark blue cloth embroidered with half-moons and stars, the fringed edges bald in places. On the table, sitting in pride of place, is an honest to God crystal ball, and beside it a dog-eared tarot deck.

"Come along, dear, don't dawdle." Madame Vivienne appears behind me in a clatter of swinging beads. "Take a seat. You only paid for twenty minutes, so if we over run it'll cost you extra."

Frowning at the audacity of the old woman, who I'm already firmly convinced is a fraud, I nevertheless take a seat at the table. Madame Vivienne slides onto one of the chairs opposite me and places her hands, palm down, on the table, closing her eyes and taking a breath.

"I'm just going to begin by taking a moment to tune into spirit," she intones.

I suspect she'd have more luck tuning into Greatest Hits Radio, I thought morosely, trying not to ponder the bottle of wine and Chinese takeaway I could've bought with that fifty quid and still had change left over.

"Is there anyone there," Madam Vivienne speaks loudly. "Spirit, reveal thyself."

"Did you know she's got a weird kind of foot pedal under there," a familiar voice answers as I glance across and see Dusty climbing to her feet and dusting off her dress. "She's also got a switch on the underside of the table."

"Where have you been?" I hiss quietly.

"I assure you, my dear boy," Madame Vivienne responds. "I'm still here"

Ignoring her reply as she continues to sway in her seat with her eyes rolling theatrically, I fix my attention on Dusty.

"Sorry," Dusty replies blithely. "I'm still not quite used to this whole dead thing. I was just thinking about the sofa out there in the shop, or more specifically the blanket, and it made me think of my grandmother. The second the thought popped into my head, I found myself standing in the middle of the living room of my Grandparents old house in Tottenham, which is now owned by an Indian family. They were just sitting down to dinner, and oh my god, it looked so good. I literally would have killed for a samosa."

I'm just mulling over Dusty's words when I hear a strange kind of tinny conversation behind me. It's distant and kind of drowned out by white noise, but it captures my attention enough for me to turn in my chair and look, wondering if the radio did somehow work and was picking up a random channel, but the dusty old wireless remains dormant, the dial dark and the needle still.

There was no one there... bit odd.

Shaking my head as if to clear my thoughts, I turn back to Dusty in time to see her leaning down in front of Madame Vivienne, waving her hand in front of her face.

"Huh," Dusty remarks. "Guess she can't see me."

Suddenly, I find myself shivering involuntarily like a cat that's been stroked the wrong way. All the tiny hairs on my arms are standing on end, and there's a cold feeling trickling down the back of my neck. Embarrassingly enough, my nipples pebble beneath my clothes. I've got a very strange feeling, and it's not altogether pleasant.

It reminds me of the night I came back from the hospital and although I was alone, in my room in the dark, it felt full, like I was standing in a crowded room of people. That's exactly what it feels like now, but Madame Vivienne, Dusty, and I are the only ones in here.

"Spirits, come forth. I summon you, speak!" Madam Vivienne entreats, throwing her hands up into the air wildly, so her arms form a 'V' shape, and I roll my eyes. She looks like she's dancing along to YMCA.

"Call me crazy but I'm starting to think she may not be legit." Dusty pouts solicitously as she shakes her head.

"Yer think?" I reply flatly, trying to resist tacking on a "Duh" to the end of that statement.

Suddenly, the table starts banging and rattling violently. I watch as Dusty dips back down under the table, only to reappear a few moments later.

"Bah, she's pushing the pedal. It must be some kind of mechanism to move the table," she snorts.

"I could've told you she was a fake and saved myself fifty quid," I mutter out the corner of my mouth, and as I do, Madame Vivienne flicks open one eye and squints at me.

I open my mouth to say something when another snippet of conversation echoes in my ear so close to my face that I almost jolt in my seat. I whip my head around to stare at... nothing! I could've sworn there was someone standing behind me, but there's nothing there except a tasteless watercolour of some cows grazing in a field.

"Hey." Dusty scowls as she stumbles forward. "Quit pushing."

I watch as she turns to glare at something I can't see.

"What's going on?" I ask.

"The spirits are feeling a little shy tonight," Madame Vivienne replies, not realising I wasn't actually talking to her.

"Can't you see them?" Dusty turns to me curiously.

"See who?" I whisper.

"The Others?"

"Wasn't that a Nicole Kidman film?" I frown thoughtfully, snapping my fingers. That's what this room reminds me of. The seance scene with the banging table.

"Tristan, the room is packed with spirits," Dusty replies a little nervously, glancing over her shoulder. "I'm not sure what's going on exactly, but there was only a couple of them milling around in here when I arrived but more just keep showing up, and— 'Oofph...'" She wobbles precariously on her lone heel before turning sharply. "Do you mind," she snaps indignantly.

"Are they here to talk to her?" I whisper, nodding in the

direction of Madam Vivienne, wondering if I hadn't misjudged her on the whole fraud front.

"No, lad, we're here to talk to you," a gruff male voice speaks up next to me.

I turn to look and find an old man in a beige cardigan and checked shirt staring at me.

"What?" I squeak, blinking rapidly, but as I do, my vision wavers slightly and my heartbeat picks up. One by one more people suddenly appear in the room... people... that I can see. "What the f..." My voice trails off breathlessly as a large woman with iron grey hair and a knitting bag appears in the chair in the corner. Next to her is a young man dressed like a hippy, wearing floaty harem pants, a linen tunic, long hair, and John Lennon glasses. Old, young, male, female, of every ethnicity and personality type just keep appearing in the room, making it feel more and more claustrophobic, as if I'm crammed into a tube carriage at the height of rush hour and worse still, they're all talking at once.

I'll give you three guesses who they're talking to, but you aren't going to need them.

The chatter is almost indistinguishable, rising and rising in volume and desperation as they try to make themselves heard. I cover my ears, feeling my anxiety building and panic clawing its way through my chest. I can't breathe, it's too tightly packed in here. I can feel the mood of the room shift from desperation to anger.

Suddenly, a picture frame containing what looks to be a rather generic field of hay bales somewhere in Shropshire, flies across the room, smashing against the opposite wall. I'm guessing it's no real loss to the art world, but Madam Vivienne's eyes widen in shock.

"What was that?" she asks wildly.

"Uh," I reply, but my mind is blank, watching in a kind of muted horror as the table levitates... honest to God, actually levitates. The heavy glass crystal ball in the centre of the table starts bouncing up and down like a ping pong ball, and the tarot cards begin fanning around the room in graceful arcs like the Queen of Hearts soldiers from Alice in Wonderland.

Madam Vivienne lets out an almighty ear-splitting screech and flees the room, leaving me sitting there open mouthed as I watch the impossible carnival show.

I duck down, flinging myself off the seat and onto the floor, protecting my head as the glass wall sconces detonate one by one, flinging glass in every direction. I look up and see the old fashioned wireless radio come to life, despite the fact it's not even plugged in, which I can see from my vantage point sprawled across the hideous floral carpet. The dial lights up, the needle going haywire as it cycles through the different stations, giving a strange compilation of Irish folk music, Metallica, Dolly Parton, followed by what I'm pretty sure is Churchill's address to the nation announcing we're going to war with Germany before finally settling on the 1966 world cup coverage.

"What the hell?" I gasp as Dusty drops to the floor, lying next to me as chaos swirls around us.

"I think they're a little pissed off," Dusty deadpans.

"You think?" I yell, ducking down as another picture sails across the room.

"I think we need to get out of here." Dusty's eyes widen as a loud cracking and wrenching sound fills the air.

We both look up to see the table levitate even higher, ripping the mechanism from the floor that allowed Madam Vivienne to give the impression the table was moving. My mouth hangs open as it hovers somewhere near the high ceiling.

"Tristan!" Dusty shouts above the din. "What are you waiting for? A personal invitation from Mary Poppins and Dick Van Dyke to tea party on the ceiling? MOVE!"

Realising I'm now directly under the heavy dining room table, which should it decide to plummet to the ground like a loony toon's piano would not work out in my favour.

Ridiculously, a scuffle has now broken out between the spirits packed tightly into the room, and as knitting needles and punches fly, I can barely see through the packed crowd to the exit. Opting to stay as close to the ground as possible, I crawl commando style on my belly and elbows toward the beaded curtain while Dusty crawls along next to me.

We make it out into the main shop, but Madam Vivienne is nowhere to be seen. I haul myself to my feet and round the counter, stopping and leaning forward, pressing my hands to my knees and breathing heavily.

I look up to say something to Dusty when I feel a thump against the side of my head, and a loud thud as something hits the floor.

"Ow," I complain, rubbing the side of my head with a wince. Bending down to pick up the item, I realise it's a book. "*Crawshanks Guide to the Recently Departed by Cornelius Crawshanks.*"

Dusty opens her mouth to say something, suddenly pausing, her eyes widening as the sofa in front of us starts rattling violently. Books start spewing from every single shelf, arcing over our heads and crashing into walls and furniture like a flock of demented pigeons.

"Run!" Dusty lunges for the door, and I follow closely behind, ducking down to avoid the literary missiles being launched at my head.

So focused on Dusty's back, I forget for a second that she's non corporeal, and as she disappears straight through the locked front door, I collide with it spectacularly. The impact throws me off my feet, and as my back hits the floor, the oxygen whooshes from my lungs like a deflated bagpipe. I glance up at the door, slightly dazed, to see Dusty poke her head and shoulders back through.

"This is no time to take a break, Tristan. Move!" she shouts.

I growl as I push my body up and turn the lock, tripping over the raised doorstep and stumbling out into the street. The door slams shut behind me and locks. Suddenly, there's a loud screech of protesting metal as the shutters slam down.

Dusty and I stare at each other for a millionth of a second before bolting down the back alley, attempting to run. I'm still badly winded and Dusty is hampered by the fact she's still only wearing one shoe. I want to ask her why she doesn't just take it off, but I don't have the oxygen to spare. By the time we reach the end of the alley, we're both laughing hysterically, but as I round the corner, I collide with a solid body, and I feel myself once again falling back, bracing myself for the inevitable impact.

After a moment, I notice I'm still more or less upright and being held carefully by a pair of firmly muscled arms. I peek an eye open tentatively, opening the other when I recognise the deep blue eyes of my rescuer. I'm sure my mouth is open, but for some reason, I can't seem to make legible words come out of it as I stare at the gorgeous Inspector Danny Hayes of Scotland Yard.

"Tristan." His voice is low and delicious, and I'm pretty certain my insides have just turned to jelly, not just any jelly though, jelly with ice cream and sprinkles... rainbow-coloured sprinkles. "You're the last person I expected to run into in a dark alley." His mouth curves in amusement.

"Oh, well, you know." I clear my throat. "That's me, I do like to keep the local constabulary entertained."

Yes! I mentally high five myself having managed an entire sentence, which, admittedly, is slightly dorky but intelligible at the very least.

"Hello." Danny smiles softly.

"Hello," I echo back quietly.

We stare at each other for another long moment until a deep familiar voice intrudes.

"You're totally Meg Ryan to his Tom Hanks right now." Dusty smirks. "You do know that right?" My gaze flicks over to Dusty for the barest hint of a second. "Seriously?" She fists a hand on her hip, waving her other hand in disbelief. "*Sleepless in Seattle*, ringing any bells? *'And all I could do was say hello...'*" she quotes in a querulous imitation.

I'm pretty certain that should be my Deborah Kerr to his Cary Grant, as that scene was originally from the film *An Affair to Remember*, but I'm not about to argue semantics with Dusty, especially not in front of the mouth-watering police inspector who probably already suspects I'm a sandwich short of a picnic basket.

"Are you okay?" Danny asks after a moment, and I realise he's still holding onto me, and neither of us have noticed.

"Oh, um." I give what can only be described as a cross between a giggle and a laugh, one that immediately makes me think of Rowan Atkinson as the awkward vicar in *Four Weddings and a Funeral*. That's pretty much me on a good day and why I don't get why this intelligent, funny, and insanely good looking man would be into me, unless it's for entertainment purposes.

I pull back, stepping out of his warm embrace and immediately feel the loss. He looks down and sees something I've dropped, and I watch as he scoops it off the ground and looks at it. It's a book, one I didn't even realise I was still holding when I fled the bookshop.

"*Crawshanks Guide to the Recently Departed*," he reads thoughtfully and glances up at me enquiringly.

"Uh, gag gift," I reply quickly as I reach out and take the book back. "For um... someone at work."

Great, I think sourly. I've just accidentally shoplifted for the first time in my life, and the first thing I do is run smack dab into a police inspector. A really hot, blonde, blue eyed... shit what was I saying again?

"Well." Danny smiles. "Seeing as we're both here and neither of us seems to be working, how about that coffee?"

"Sure," my mouth supplies before my brain has a chance to wade in with an opinion. I'm pretty sure he could've invited me on a donkey ride in the middle of the Outer Hebrides and I still would've said yes to anything that came out of his mouth.

"Great." He smiles again, his blue eyes filled with all kinds of delicious mischief and invitation. And that wet splatting sound? I'm pretty sure that was my heart rolling over and flopping out of my chest before hitting the ground.

Oh boy, I'm in so much trouble...

7

Danny

I glance over at Tristan sitting by the window as he mumbles to himself, and I smile. He's fucking adorable. Totally not the type I usually go for, not that I dated much back home, after all I was mostly half in, half out of the closet. Don't get me wrong, I still went out and picked up men, hooked up when the mood struck, but I wasn't able to have a relationship, not with my already strained relationship with my family and certainly not with the attitudes of the guys I worked with. I'd always had to be so careful who knew about my sexuality, and while things aren't always perfect down here in London, I have a hell of a lot more freedom than before.

Not that I'm looking for a relationship. I'm not sure that's entirely feasible at the moment. I'm not saying never, but I've only just moved South, and I work long hours trying to prove myself at The Yard. Not only that, doing what I do, investigating violent crimes, can take me to a pretty dark head space sometimes, and there's no way I'd want to put someone else through that. It wouldn't be fair.

I step forward a pace in the queue as it slowly shuffles

toward the counter, but my gaze is still firmly fixed on Tristan. He's so pretty and so vibrant with all that wild dark hair, his vivid green eyes, and nerdy black framed glasses. His face is fascinating to watch, and right now, he seems to be having a slightly heated argument with himself. I chuckle slightly, shaking my head.

I always thought I had a type. The men I'd end up taking to bed were of a similar height and build to me, broad shoulders and tight muscles, someone I could wrestle with in bed without worrying about hurting them or going too far. I may not have been in a relationship before, but I love sex and the dirtier, the rougher, the better as far as I'm concerned. I think rolling around in bed with someone should be fun, and I don't want to have to hold back.

My gaze roams over Tristan's lean frame, taking in those long legs encased in skinny jeans, which I could all too easily imagine wrapped around my hips as I pound him into the mattress. I suck in a sharp breath and exhale slowly counting to ten. The last thing I need is to be queueing in a coffee shop with a blatant hard on bulging through my jeans.

Trying not to think about getting him naked, my gaze skims up his body to his pretty face. His cheeks are still flushed from the cold outside, and I find myself still trying to figure it out. The men I've been involved with are usually confident and with similar interests to me, but Tristan is completely the opposite. He's slim and willowy like some kind of fae creature, and he's nervous and slightly awkward, as though he doesn't quite fit in with the rest of us mortals, yet so utterly charming I find myself captivated by him. I don't know what it is, I just know that there's something about him that grabbed me from the second he walked into the pub that night.

"Can I help?"

I turn around and find that while I've been studying Tristan the queue has moved, and there's now two feet of space between me and the empty counter. I shake my head lightly and chuckle again. For someone who's career depends on expert observational skills, I'm failing abysmally here, totally caught up in a pretty young man and blind to everything around me.

"A flat white, a pumpkin spiced latte and two cinnamon rolls please." I smile at the girl behind the counter. She blinks up at me slightly dazed for a moment before sending me a flirtatious smile, but I barely notice, my gaze once again drawn back to Tristan who's still talking to himself, and I wonder if he does that all the time or whether it's just a nervous thing.

I pay quickly, tucking my wallet into the back pocket of my jeans before lifting the tray and heading back toward Tristan, who stiffens in his seat, his cheeks flushing shyly.

"Here we go." I slide onto the stool next to him and set the flat white coffee in front of him, handing him a couple of packets of sugar. "I didn't know if you wanted white or brown sugar," I say as I lift one of the plates and set a cinnamon roll in front of him.

"Oh, uh, either, thanks," he replies, picking up a packet at random and emptying it into his coffee, followed by a second packet.

He sneaks glances in my direction and seems so preoccupied that I wonder if he's noticed he's actually mixed up the sugars and added one of each or whether it's just another quirk of his.

"What's that?" He moves a little closer and sniffs lightly.

"A pumpkin spiced latte." I grin. "It's nearly Halloween, and they do an absolutely amazing black forest gateaux one at Christmas."

"Fancy." His mouth curves slowly.

"You want to try some?" I offer as he wrinkles his nose.

He eyes it suspiciously for a moment, then gingerly raises it to his lips, taking a small sip. He pulls back and grimaces, poking his tongue out like a kid who's just been served sprouts.

"Not a fan then." I grin as he slides my latte back toward me.

"I don't like pumpkin," he replies.

"Then why did you try it?" I laugh, feeling my belly warm as he watches me.

He shrugs. "To see if it actually tasted like pumpkin. Some-things don't actually taste like the something they're supposed to taste of but taste of something different."

"Huh?"

He smiles and huffs a laugh. "Sorry, I'm probably speaking Tristan again."

"Speaking Tristan?" I repeat curiously.

"That's what my dad always called it. My dad and a couple of my friends are the only ones who can speak fluent Tristan. When I wander off down a conversational tangent, my mouth tends to follow my thought process, but apparently, it doesn't always make sense to the unfortunate person on the receiving end."

"I like it," I say softly, thoroughly enchanted by him.

"Uh, well." He flushes. "What I meant was that artificial flavourings don't always taste like the thing they're meant to be re-creating. For example, I like bananas, but I hate anything banana flavoured."

"Makes sense." I lift my latte and take a sip as I watch him, wishing I could press my lips to his and taste the adorable babble of words tipping out of it, but instead contenting myself with placing my lips where his had been on my cup.

"So, what brings you to Whitechapel?" I ask conversation-ally, wanting to know everything about this complex and fasci-nating man, and this seems as good a place to start as any.

"That sounded like a professional enquiry, Inspector." He smiles in amusement.

"Just a conversation starter and slightly less pedestrian than the obligatory 'do you come here often?'" I grin.

"I had a follow up appointment at the Royal London, and good news... turns out I do have a brain even if I did try to choke myself to death using an ice cube as my weapon of choice."

"Are you okay though?" I ask in concern. "There's no lingering problems?"

"Nope, I'm fine." He shrugs.

"Yes, you are," I mutter against the rim of my cup, and his cheeks flush prettily again.

"What brings you here then?" he asks as his restless fingers tear at the edges of the cinnamon roll. "More death and mayhem?"

"I live just around the corner, and contrary to popular belief, working at The Yard isn't all preventing the theft of the Crown Jewels and high-speed chases through winding London streets."

"That's totally what you were picturing when you applied wasn't it?" Tristan smiles behind his mug as he takes a sip of his flat white coffee.

"Maybe," I hedge, laughing in response. "The very unglamorous reality really just involves stacks and stacks of paperwork."

I watch curiously as he glances over his shoulder, almost listening intently for a moment before rolling his eyes.

"How's the case going then?" he asks after a moment.

"Which one?" I reply.

"Dusty's murder." He frowns. "Am I allowed to ask about the case?"

"Sure you can," I answer easily. "I can't discuss details of an active investigation, but you can ask in general."

"So..." He tilts his head consideringly as he watches me. "How's the case going?"

"We're pursuing leads," I answer evasively.

"Isn't that the company line for you've got nothing?" His mouth curves.

"More or less," I snort quietly. "It's still early days, and it's a difficult case."

"Why difficult?" he asks in genuine interest.

"Because it occurred in a public club, during the busiest period, and they were at maximum capacity. That's a very large suspect pool. Not to mention the general lack of security and plenty of high traffic areas with cross contamination of evidence."

"I see." He nods.

"They're holding her funeral the day after tomorrow," I tell him, not sure why I'm mentioning it, but there's something about the Dustin Boyle case that tugs at me, the same way Tristan does, and it's an itch under my skin I can't quite reach.

"Oh." His brows wrinkle slightly as he stares down into his cup.

"But the post-mortem report you sent over was very helpful," I tell him genuinely. "I've worked with a lot of pathologists, and believe me, none of them are as meticulous as you. The photos you sent over of the head wound should help us to identify the weapon used."

I'm not kidding either. The photos he sent of Dusty's head wound after he'd shaved away her hair and cleaned the blood had revealed a very distinctive shape, a row of three triangles lined up, almost like a little princess crown.

"Thank you." Tristan nods. "I hope it does help. I'm not sure exactly what it is you're looking for. I think it's probably a case of Miss Scarlett in the Ballroom with the lead pipe... or candlestick, either way you're looking for something large and heavy."

Despite the seriousness of the topic, I can't help laughing lightly, not even trying to hide my enjoyment of him. "What made you want to become a pathologist in the first place?" I ask curiously.

"I like puzzles." He shrugs. "And I don't like families not having answers to how their loved ones died."

"Sounds like there's a story to go with that," I reply quietly.

He watches me thoughtfully. Behind us I can hear the odd clang of plates and cups, and there's a low, hushed hum of conversation surrounding us in the little coffee shop. Directly outside the window in the fading light, the rain has begun to drizzle, and every now and then a gust of wind blows wet leaves past, leaving an errant leaf or two stuck to the glass. It's warm and cosy in here, like a little nest weaved around us as we watch each other. Finally, after long pause, he draws in a slow breath.

"When I was thirteen," he says quietly. "My mum died."

"I'm so sorry," I murmur softly.

"She..." He swallows painfully, and I can tell even after all this time that the pain for him hasn't dulled. "She sat down in the front room in her favorite chair with a cup of tea to watch Coronation Street and never got back up again."

"What?" I breath heavily.

"It's called S.A.D.S," he clarifies. "Sudden adult death syndrome, it's basically the adult version of cot death. You're there one minute and gone the next, no warning, no reason."

"Tristan," I murmur, wanting to reach for his hand, my heart hurting for him.

"I suppose it doesn't take a genius to figure out why I chose the career path I did." He shrugs, glancing out of the window as he continues to speak. "She was great, my mum. My parents were older, and I was a miracle, a change of life baby, or whatever... call it what you will. They were told they couldn't have children, and after years of trying they had given up when I finally decided to show up."

He turns back toward me with a small smile playing on his lips.

"I bet you were spoiled rotten." I smile.

"You'd be right," he sighs sadly. "I never got enough time with my mum, but my dad was great. He was always figuring out crazy adventures for us, and even when I came out at seventeen, he accepted me without question."

"You're lucky." I nod slowly. "It's not like that for everyone."

"Yeah, I was lucky, and even with my dad being part of that older generation, he never minded that I'm into guys. He loves me, I know he does. He took such good care of me after Mum died, even though he was grieving himself, but the situation with my dad is... complicated."

"They often are." I nod in agreement.

"What about you?" he asks.

"Me?"

"Let's start with the accent, Leeds?" He tilts his head thoughtfully as he studies me.

"Yep, Yorkshire boy born and bred," I confirm. "I was born in a small rural village called Allerton Bywater, it's just southeast of the city of Leeds. My dad was a seventh-generation coal miner, but when the colliery closed in '92, we had no choice but to move closer to the city so my dad and my older brothers could find work."

"Brothers?" Tristan queries curiously. "How many do you have?"

"I'm the youngest of eight."

"Eight?" he repeats back incredulously. "Eight children? Was your mum perpetually pregnant."

"Pretty much." I nod. "Not much to do in a tiny rural village in West Yorkshire. I've got five brothers and two sisters. You don't even want to attempt to count how many nieces and nephews I have now." I chuckle.

"You must miss them," he says contemplatively. "I'm the only child of only children, so I didn't even have aunts and uncles and cousins, so it was always me and Dad after mum passed. I can't imagine what it's like to have such a big family."

"It's... difficult," I sigh. "I love my family, but it's hard to miss them when it's a relief to not be around them."

"I don't understand." Tristan studies me.

"Three of my brothers and one of my sisters aren't talking to me," I admit. "The rest of the family are cautiously ambivalent to my existence."

"Why?"

I shrug. "You have to understand what it was like growing up the way I did. It was a small village run by a bunch of stubborn old men, some of them up to eighth generation miners. It was a hard life, and they didn't like change. When all the collieries began to close, they lost their livelihoods, their identities, their homes. We moved closer to the city, and my father and brothers took work wherever they could get it, which mostly meant the factories and foundries. I was the only one in my family to go to college and then to university. I worked myself into the ground to pay for it myself. Then I went on to train with the police and made it up the ranks. I never stopped pushing myself. I didn't want to just exist, scraping by on minimum wage and living on the very edge of the poverty line the way my parents did, but my brothers didn't see it that way. They resented me and always felt like I thought I was better than them, which I didn't. They thought I was keeping secrets from them, and I guess I was, well, a big one anyway."

"They didn't know you were gay," Tristan guesses.

"I didn't hide it exactly, but I certainly didn't come out and say it. I knew they wouldn't take it well, especially not on top of the resentment they already felt toward me. I was discreet, even as part of the police it wasn't something I felt I could share openly."

"What changed?"

"An officer I worked with... a friend," I tell him quietly,

feeling the familiar pulse of regret and pain. "He was attacked and beaten very badly."

"Because he was gay?" Tristan asks gently.

I nod. "Everyone was talking about it, and I mean everyone, my family, my brothers, my parents, the whole community. It seemed everyone had an opinion on it." I scowl thinking back to that painful time. "He was my friend, but it was like the gossip mill completely stripped him of his identity. He was no longer a good man, a good friend, a loving son and an accomplished and decorated officer of the West Yorkshire police. He became that gay policeman that got attacked for misreading a situation and hitting on a straight guy. That's what he was reduced to, and it gutted me."

"What did you do?" Tristan asks softly.

"I came out, very publicly. I wasn't going to hide behind closed doors feeling ashamed of my sexuality or afraid I'd be attacked for making an honest mistake. I came out very publicly and made a statement about hate crimes because it was something I felt so strongly about. My family were not happy about my newfound notoriety, as you can imagine, that went down with them about as well as a dose of the clap. My sexuality was something to be hidden behind closed doors and never spoken about."

"Danny," he says softly, reaching out and placing his hand on mine, gently squeezing. "That was really brave."

I shrug, focusing on his warm hand covering mine. "Anyway, the chance to work in London came up and I jumped on it."

"Are you still on speaking terms with your family?"

"More or less," I murmur. "In that, the more I speak the less they listen," I elaborate. "They haven't outright disowned me, but I'm not really welcome back home, maybe..." I shrug again. "I don't know, maybe in a few years when the dust settles."

"There shouldn't be any dust to settle. They're your family

and should be proud of you." An adorable scowl pinches his brows together, and my belly warms at his obvious outrage on my behalf.

Unable to help myself, I turn my hand over, so it fits palm to palm with his. I hear him draw in a slow breath as our fingers entwine and fold together like the closing petals of a flower hidden in shadow.

"Thank you." I give him a small smile. "But you and I both know people aren't always kind when it comes to sexual orientation, even if they are related to you by blood. Acceptance isn't always a given."

"How long has it been since you moved to London?" He looks up at me, and I'm pleased to note he doesn't withdraw his hand, seemingly content to sit with our fingers wound together like vines.

"A little over a month and a half," I reply.

"Are you settling in okay?" He frowns, and it's so cute. "Have you made friends?"

A small smile tugs at my lips as I squeeze his hand gently. "I'm getting there," I respond and he flushes, his gaze turning toward the window and the rain-soaked street, now almost fully dark and lit by passing double decker buses and street lamps.

"I... don't have many friends either," he admits quietly. "But..." He swallows shyly as he turns back to look at me. "I've enjoyed this."

"I'm glad," I tell him, my fingers twitching with the need to gently slide the pads of my fingertips under his jaw, lifting his chin so I can lean forward and brush my lips against his, but I don't. Whatever this is between us, I don't want to rush. He's unlike anyone I've met before, and I don't want to risk scaring him off. As much as I want him naked beneath me, wound around my body until I don't know where I begin and he ends, this isn't about just tumbling him into bed. For the first time in my life, I think I might want more.

"I've enjoyed this too." I patiently pull back and offer him an easy smile. "I was kind of hoping you might like to do this again. Maybe dinner next time? You could pick the place and show me what you love about London."

"I'd like that." He smiles widely, and something deep inside me that I didn't even realise felt so empty begins to fill.

Stage 3

Bargaining

8

Tristan

Yawning widely, I trot across the kitchen, my eyes bleary from lack of sleep. I'm not sure what the hell I was dreaming about last night, but my sleep ended up being very disjointed. Every time I'd drop off, something would wake me, and consequently, I'd spent all night tossing and turning. It's my own fault, I suppose. I'd stayed up later than I should've reading that stupid book I'd inadvertently stolen from Madam Vivienne's shop. I suppose I really should have returned it with an apology or at least offered to pay for it, but the truth is I'm in no rush to set foot back in that place. Plus, to be fair, the old fraud had already swindled me out of fifty pounds, so I consider the book fair game.

I should've just tossed it on the bookshelf in the lounge, but for some insane reason, I'd crawled into bed and picked it up to idly leaf through the pages. Call it curiosity I suppose, but the more I read, the more I couldn't put it down. I mean, the guy who wrote it was quite clearly absolutely bonkers. His name was Cornelius Crawshanks, and from what I can gather, the man was a Victorian medium, quite a well-known one at that. A brief internet search on my phone had revealed, well, that and the fact it said on the inside cover, written by world renowned expert medium and spiritualist Cornelius M Crawshanks, although he could've just been blowing his own trumpet, after all you know how authors are.

But despite his Victorian idioms and his very strange ideas, I found myself helplessly caught up in the pages. So much so that it's now currently sitting next to me on the kitchen side while I wait for the kettle to boil.

My gaze is just skimming down the page when a ball of grey fur launches itself up onto the counter and head butts me. I smile softly as I lift my hand to stroke him, but I barely need to do anything as he arches his spine and undulates his body stroking himself from head to tail with my palm. "Morning, Jacob Marley."

"You named your cat Jacob Marley?" a deep voice rumbles from the opposite side of the kitchen.

"I was drunk." I shrug, turning toward Dusty. "Apparently, a name given under the influence has no take backs because now he won't answer to anything else. You can't even call him Jacob. He doesn't like it and hisses and lifts his tail to show you his bum hole on the way out the nearest door."

"Well, if that isn't just the best fuck you to people who get your name wrong," Dusty laughs in delight.

I watch in fascination as Jacob Marley abandons me and the promise of breakfast and struts regally along the kitchen side with his chin held high until he reaches Dusty. She reaches her hand out, and he lifts his little, blunt pink nose toward her fingertips scenting the air as he stares at her and meows loudly.

"I think he can see me," Dusty whispers in pleasure. "Hello, beautiful boy," she croons. "Can you see me?"

He rewards her with another loud mewl before settling in to purr loud enough to drown out a tractor.

"Did you know that in ancient Egypt cats were considered

the Guardians of the dead?" I muse absently as the kettle clicks off, and I pour boiling water into my instant coffee.

"Maybe the Egyptians were onto something if he really can see me." Dusty lifts her hand as if to stroke him. "Is that right, JM? Are you a guardian of the dead?"

He purrs even louder and lifts his head toward her palm, overbalancing and nearly falling straight through Dusty's hand, which is as insubstantial as Vapour.

"I can't believe he let you call him JM," I say as Jacob Marley turns his head to hiss at me. "Oh what?" I whine. "That's really unfair."

"What can I say?" Dusty grins. "All the pretty boys love me."

I stare at Jacob Marley, brows lifting. "If that's how fickle you are with your love, don't think I'm getting you any Catnip any time soon, you little stoner."

He bounds back along the counter and begins rubbing his head against my arm, purring as I lift his food dish onto the side and begin to fill it.

"No, don't go buttering me up like I'm your dealer, Jacob Marley." I place the dish down on the floor and watch as he leaps down nimbly after it and shoves his face in with no finesse. "There's just no loyalty." I shake my head morosely. "Maybe I should've named you Judas."

Dusty chuckles in the corner and I turn my attention back to her.

"Where did you get to yesterday anyway?" I ask her. "One minute you were sitting next to me in the coffee shop, badgering me to ask Inspector Hayes about your case and the next you'd disappeared again."

"I don't know." Dusty frowns thoughtfully as she shakes her head. "I told you, I still haven't got this whole afterlife thing figured out yet, it felt like my batteries drained or something. I was sitting there watching you two when suddenly everything faded, and next thing I knew I was here in your kitchen."

"Oh," I reply, not really sure what the correct response to that is. Up until recently, I didn't even think there was an after-life, so I don't have any more insight than she does... although... my gaze tracks over to the open book on the counter.

"I was sorry to hear about your mum," Dusty says so quietly I almost miss it.

I stare at her quietly. "Thanks," I mutter, feeling the familiar sadness in my heart that always accompanies the thought of my lovely mum.

"I lost my mum too," Dusty adds softly. "When I was eight... cancer."

"I'm sorry too," I reply, feeling a strange kinship to the dishevelled drag queen leaning against my microwave.

"Well, aren't we just two little lost boys." She smiles and its bittersweet.

"Dusty?" I muse as my gaze travels over her lopsided wig, sparkly dress and single shoe. "Why don't you just take that shoe off? It looks kind of silly with only one, and it can't be comfortable to walk around like that."

"It's not," she replies.

"Then why..." I duck as she yanks the shoe off and flings it across the kitchen toward my head, although it probably wouldn't have hurt me even if it had hit me squarely between the eyes being as incorporeal as she is.

I watch as she executes what can only be described as a high kick worthy of the Moulin Rouge and settles her slim shapely leg on the small dining room table. I blink slowly, twisting around to glance behind me and then back to her foot again. The stiletto she'd hurled toward my head was once again firmly fitted on her foot.

"What the?"

"Why?" she repeats my earlier question, her voice laced with frustration. "Because I can't take it off, and it's the same with the wig, and the eyelashes. I'm stuck looking exactly as I did the moment I died, and nothing I do will change that, believe me I've tried."

"I'm sorry, Dusty." I wince. "Um, it's really not that bad."

"Not that bad?" she retorts as she turns her head to look in the hallway mirror studying the dark black streaks of mascara running down her cheeks. "That's easy for you to say, you're not the one who's destined to spend eternity looking like Alice bloody Cooper."

"Maybe there's something in here?" I turn back to the book and flip through the pages until I come across a heading that piques my interest.

How to return restless spirits to the afterlife...

To dispel and disincorporate a troublesome or restless spirit to the afterlife requires a substance of impeccable purity and a strong will. Pure salt can be dispersed with firm instruction to return to their place of origin delivered with great conviction by the practitioner.

I scan through the passage as Dusty crosses the kitchen to stand in front of me. Tossing the book down on the counter, I impulsively grab a nearby metal canister and yank off the lid, tossing its contents directly at Dusty, but they merely pass straight through her, scattering across the tiled floor.

There's a moment of utter silence as Dusty stares at me before slowly tilting her head down to look at the heap of white granules piled around her feet.

"Sugar?" she states dryly. "What are you trying to do exorcise me or bake a cake?"

"I don't have any salt." I grimace sheepishly.

"Sam and Dean would be so ashamed of you." She shakes her head tutting.

"Who's Sam and Dean?" I reply in confusion.

"Are you seriously telling me that even with your obsessive love of Netflix you don't know who Sam and Dean Winchester are?"

I stare at her blankly.

"The TV show *Supernatural*?" she adds expectantly.

"I tend to watch more movies than TV shows."

"You've never watched..." She clasps her chest and sways slightly, resting her hand on the counter to steady herself. "Oh, Tristan, my darling, darling boy. You have got such a treat in store for you. It's the only TV show where I not only desperately dream of being sandwiched between the two brothers, but I'd totally have the dad too."

"The dad?" I repeat.

She closes her eyes, drawing in a deep breath on a little hum of pleasure, her deep voice dropping lower if that's possible and holding up her finger to stop me from talking. "Mmm... Jeffery Dean Morgan. I can just picture him now with that dirty smile, those deep creases in his stubbled cheeks, that hairy chest."

"Do you need a moment?" I ask diffidently.

She blows out a breath and smiles at me. "We are so having a Supernatural fest the first chance we get, but for now, I have an idea." She claps her hands in excitement.

"What?" I ask suspiciously.

"I think we should go to my funeral," she declares.

"What?" I blink slowly. "Sorry, that sounded like you just said I should go to your funeral?"

"That's right." Dusty nods. "Think about it, it's perfect."

"I fail to see how going to a complete stranger's funeral will be perfect in any way." I frown.

"People do it all the time," Dusty replies, "and besides, it's not a stranger's funeral you know me."

"Yeah, now I do." My voice rises incredulously. "Just how am

I supposed to explain that we didn't meet until after you were dead?"

"Well, obviously, don't do that." Dusty snorts. "Just tell them we were friends. Trust me no one will question it. I know a lot of people."

"I can't." I shake my head. "I'm sorry, Dusty, but going to your funeral would just be weird."

"Tristan, honey, you are weird..." she replies, looking immediately contrite when my face falls, backtracking and looking genuinely worried she'd hurt my feelings. "But only the best kind of weird... like adorable-weird," she insists.

"No, Dusty." I stand firm. I'm not going to her funeral, no way, no how. I struggle to deal with people on a regular day to day basis, so the last thing I need is to be stuck in a crematorium with loads of them, especially loads of them I don't know."

"Tristan, please?" Dusty whines. "I need to know what happened to me."

"What do you remember?" I ask curiously.

"Nothing." She shakes her head. "That's the problem. The last thing I remember is leaving my flat and arriving at The Rainbow Room. I had a cocktail at the bar with Ramone, he's one of the bartenders, and that's it. Everything else is a big fat blur until I woke up on the floor in the mortuary."

"Dusty." I shake my head. "I wish I had answers for you, but I don't think you're going to get them from witnessing your own funeral. Don't you think it will be too hard for you to watch? They're going to burn your body to ashes."

"Yeah, okay, that part isn't great," Dusty admits. "But, honey, I know every single one of those lying, conniving divas, and trust me, if one of them killed me then you can bet your Louboutins I'm going to figure out which one."

"Well, good luck with that." I shake my head, then look up

at the clock on the wall. "I'm going to shower. I need to be at work in an hour."

"But..."

"No, Dusty," I say firmly as I head into the bathroom and shut the door behind me.

Stripping off my PJ's and old t-shirt as the water warms up, I climb over the lip of the bath and slip behind the shower curtain, sighing in pleasure as the warm water hits my body and relaxes all the muscles in my body that seem to be in a constant state of tightly coiled tension. I'm just lathering up my hair when I hear a cross sigh.

"You know it really wouldn't kill you to do me this one tiny favour." Dusty's voice echoes through the small, steamy room, and I shriek in surprise, followed by a pained yelp as the shampoo burns my eyes. I shove my head under the shower-head, practically drowning myself as I try to get the Pantene out of my eyes. Shoving the wet, heavy mass of my hair off my face as best I can, I peek around the edge of the shower curtain, blinking through bloodshot eyes as I try to focus and clutching the shower curtain to my wet body like I'm a slightly despoiled virgin.

Dusty is perched on the top of the cistern, with one foot propped on the closed toilet seat and her legs crossed sassily as she points one of her violent red talons in my direction, her eyes flashing with annoyance.

"You know that doesn't make a difference, honey." She smirks sweetly. "The shower curtain is completely transparent. I can see everything. Good job on the manscaping by the way, very neat."

"For fuck's sake, Dusty." I half turn and cup my hand over my dick and balls behind the curtain. "Get out!"

"I don't see what the big deal is." She rolls her eyes in exasperation. "Darling, it's not like you haven't seen mine."

"That doesn't count," I reply indignantly. "It was my job. I didn't walk in on you in the bloody shower. This is a blatant invasion of privacy."

"Stop being such a prude, Tristan." She flips the locks of her wig sharply over one shoulder and fixes me with a flat expression.

"This isn't a case of you show me yours I'll show you mine." I scowl. "Now, get out!"

"Not until you agree to go to my funeral!"

"I said no," I reply stubbornly.

"Then I'm not leaving." She folds her arms resolutely and leans back against the tiled wall, tapping her nails repetitively against her arm.

"Fine," I grate between clenched teeth. "Then I'll leave." I shut off the water and yank the towel off the rail, wrapping it around my waist and climbing over the edge of the bath before storming righteously into my bedroom. I yank a pair of boxers from my underwear drawer, turning around and jumping when I find Dusty perched on the edge of the bed in front of me.

She draws in a breath and opens her mouth to speak.

"No," I say firmly and pull my boxers on roughly underneath my towel before turning my back on her deliberately. I dry myself off quickly, scrubbing my hair before tossing my wet towel in the laundry basket.

"You should hang that up and let it dry first or everything in there will smell damp."

I ignore her as I pull on the rest of my clothes and head out into the living room to find Dusty now sitting on the arm of the sofa.

"No," I state before she can say anything.

I can feel her eyes burning into the back of my neck as I pull my boots and coat on, winding a scarf around my neck as I drop my keys and wallet into my pocket. Without another word, I head out the door locking it behind me and stepping onto the tiny landing with a dark, narrow staircase leading down.

I trot down the stairs briskly. My flat is part of an old Victorian terrace, which had been converted to a one up one down. I'm not sure who my downstairs neighbour is, some gruff older man who's been there since before I even signed my tenancy agreement, but he doesn't seem any more inclined to be sociable than I do. The sum total of our interactions being nothing more than a brisk nod in greeting if we unfortunately find ourselves on the doorstep at the same time. Something we both tend to avoid at all costs.

I step out of the main front door and turn to make sure it's locked securely, turning back around to find Dusty standing in front of me on the doorstep.

"Nope." I shake my head, deliberately shoving my earbuds in and skirting around her to head down the street with a loud medley of Girls Aloud blaring in my ears.

She clips along lopsidedly, keeping pace with me, and every now and then, I catch her glare. I genuinely do feel bad for her. I'm not being obtuse on purpose, but showing up to her funeral on my own, surrounded by a bunch of strangers is literally my worst nightmare.

Fortunately, the mortuary isn't far from where I live and before long, I'm heading inside out of the cold early morning air and run straight into Judy.

"Morning, Tristan." She looks up from her clipboard.

"Morning, Judy." I pull one of my earbuds out and leave it dangling from my neck.

She casts a quick and surreptitious glance at what I'm wearing before clucking her tongue thoughtfully. "You might want to grab some scrubs."

"Oh?"

"Your first one of the morning wasn't found for a few days, and he'd left the heating on," she replies casually. "Could get messy."

"Great," I mutter, just what I need this morning.

She disappears through one of the doors and up the stairs toward the office as I slip through into the locker room, quickly changing into a pair of scrubs and pulling on my lab coat. Leaving my earbuds hanging from my neck, I slip my phone into my pocket and head into the main room.

The smell hits me before I've even stepped foot inside, and I try to breath shallowly through my mouth. Nothing like the smell of advanced decomp first thing in the morning to have you on the verge of re-evaluating your career choices.

I step into the room and see Ted, the new orderly, standing by the table with a file for me.

"Morning." He nods. "Got a ripe one today."

"Thank you for stating the obvious." I grimace as I reach up and pull a small pot of Vicks down from the shelf. I smear some on the inside of a medical mask before covering my mouth and nose. It doesn't completely cover the stench of the corpse, but it at least reduces the worst of it.

"Got another one coming in." Ted hands me the folder. "They're just unloading him now. Some guy drowned in his tub. We'll put him in cold storage."

"Okay." I nod, opening the file and beginning to read as he heads out the door.

"Are you going to ignore me all day?" Dusty huffs as she stomps across the floor to stand next to me.

"It depends," I reply as I continue to read through the notes. "Are you going to keep asking about your funeral?"

"Yes," she states stubbornly.

"Then, also yes, I will be ignoring you." I smile pleasantly, although it's lost on her as I'm still wearing the light blue surgical mask.

"This isn't fair." She stamps her foot, fisting her hands on her hips.

The door bangs open loudly, drawing my attention as Ted backs into the room pulling a trolley containing what looks like a rather large body bag. I can only assume there's a rather portly individual inside as the plastic is almost pulling tight.

"Sorry," Ted calls out as Jonas, one of the other orderlies, pushes the rest of the trolley through the door. "We'll be out of your way in a moment. This one's a two-man job. Big guy, drowned in the bath."

"Dusty," I whisper before they get close enough to hear. "I ..."

My voice trails off, and even Dusty falls silent as they wheel the body past us, but it's not the trolley that has our attention. It's the very fat, very wet and very naked guy trailing along behind it calmly as if this sort of thing happens to him every day, and as he passes us, he nods politely.

"Morning," he greets and continues to follow the trolley.

Dusty and I stand watching with our mouths hanging open as Ted and Jonas open the door to the walk in cold storage we use when the deceased are too large or too heavy to fit in the wall units. They wheel the trolley in, and as the door closes behind them, the naked guy walks straight through it as if it wasn't even there and disappears.

"Did you just see that?" I mutter faintly.

"I really wish I hadn't." Dusty swallows faintly. "There isn't enough eye bleach in the world to erase that image."

A moment later, Ted and Jonas reappear nodding to me as they pass, heading back out of the main door, leaving Dusty and I once again alone.

I turn back to Dusty, but as she opens her mouth and draws in a breath, I pre-empt what I know is going to come out.

"No," I repeat.

"Urgh," she growls, stamping her foot again. "This isn't fair. You're acting like I asked you to rob a grave with me."

Opting for avoidance, I place my earbuds back in my ears and hit play on my phone, letting the loud, upbeat pop drown out her tirade. I know she's now saying several probably very uncomplimentary things about me, accompanied by some quite wildly over embellished gestures, but I calmly pull on a pair of latex gloves.

"I can't hear you," I yell loudly, tapping my earbuds. "It's Britany, baby!"

Her face flames pink as she screeches at me, but ignoring her completely, I turn to the body bag in front of me and steel myself for a very unpleasant morning.

The day passes fairly quickly. Dusty disappeared pretty much as soon as the contents of the body bag were revealed. I don't know if spirits can actually vomit, but she looked pretty green. She never returned throughout the day. Every time I turned around, I expected to see her, but she stayed away for which I was grateful. After all, I did still have a job to do.

At the end of the day, I'd taken a long and very vigorous shower at work before changing back into my own clothes. After that advanced purification case this morning, I'd needed it. Fortunately, cases like that didn't come up often. In fact, the mortuary rarely smelled bad at all. We kept it well ventilated and meticulously clean.

But I'm exhausted, right down to my bones. I'd managed to grab a sandwich at work, but after the day I'd had, I didn't have much of an appetite, as you can imagine. By the time I arrive home, I barely have the energy to strip my clothes off and crawl into bed, flopping onto my back on top of the bedding, wearing nothing but my boxers and t-shirt.

I close my eyes and let out a long, slow sigh, already sliding toward sleep.

"Are you ready to talk to me now?" a stubborn voice demands imperiously, and I groan.

"Dusty, I'm too tired to argue with you." I yawn, barely able to keep my eyes open.

"I'm not here to argue," she replies determinedly. "All you

have to do is say you'll go, otherwise I'll be forced to... persuade you," she adds ominously.

I'm not really worried, after all, she's about as dangerous as a light breeze being an incorporeal spirit, and I doubt there's anything she can do to me physically.

"The answer's still no, Dusty," I mumble, unable to keep my eyes open.

"Don't say I didn't warn you," she replies coolly.

"Whatever..." I mumble, already so far into the land of OZ at this point that I'm practically already snoring, and I'm not sure whether I actually said that last word out loud or had only answered in my head.

There's a blessed silence and warm, inviting darkness enticing me to sink into it like a puffy raincloud. I can actually feel myself sliding into sleep, my limbs twitching slightly as they relax.

I can feel my brow furrowing. That's weird... why am I dreaming about Gloria Gaynor and why does she have such a deep voice?

It takes a moment but I slowly begin to realise I can actually hear someone singing.

"What?" My eyes open as I lift my head, and sure enough, there's Dusty in all of her fabulous glory with her arms raised and spread wide.

She lifts one leg, propping her foot on the end of the bed and pointing one dark red talon at me as she continues to sing.

You've got to be fucking kidding me, I think to myself as I groan loudly.

She climbs onto the bed, strutting along the mattress until she is standing over me with one foot either side of my waist.

"This isn't going to work," I tell her flatly.

Her voice gets louder as she picks up the beat.

"Seriously?" I scowl. "You're being ridiculous."

Her voice is building, getting louder and matching the

tempo of the song. Thank God my neighbours couldn't hear her.

"Oh, for the love of God!" I cry out, as she launches into a full on, stand in place version of Gloria Gaynor's *I Will Survive,* which I assume is one of her stage acts, and was, no doubt extremely popular as I'm forced to admit she's got a great voice and a hell of a presence. However, the slight drawback is that she's wearing a very short dress and is standing straddled over my prone body, giving me a rather uncensored view.

Jesus, she is really hitting her stride now as her voice builds to a crescendo.

"Just so you know, I can totally see right up your dress," I inform her primly as I cover my eyes with my hands as she hits the main chorus line at the top of her voice.

"Alright, alright!" I yell, moving my hands from my eyes to my ears.

"Honey, I can keep going all night." She smirks. "In fact, I'm known for my stamina."

I groan. "Are you seriously just going to keep singing all night long until I agree to go?"

"It worked for Patrick Swayze in Ghost." She shrugs.

"What is it with you and Patrick Swayze?" I frown.

"The man is fine as hell. Didn't you see his arse shot in Roadhouse?" She raises her brows.

"As a matter of fact, I did," I concede. "But this is not about Patrick's arse no matter how stunning it is or was. I mean it, I'm not going to your funeral, and that's final," I state emphatically, as her eyes narrow. "No," I protest firmly. "Absolutely not."

9

Tristan

"Dearly beloved, we are gathered here today to celebrate the life of Dustin Boyle or as she was more commonly known amongst those who knew her best, The Fabulous Miz Dusty Le Frey."

I shift uncomfortably in my seat, resisting the urge to tug at my clothes. I feel like I should be wearing a suit. Isn't that what people do at funerals after all? But Dusty had taken one look at the only suit I actually own, which has been shoved at the back of my wardrobe since well, forever, and stated in no uncertain terms that there was no way I was attending her funeral looking like a waiter.

To be honest, I don't remember buying it, let alone ever having occasion to wear it. Dusty had more or less had me empty the entire contents of my wardrobe and finally settled on black skinny jeans, my trusty and ever-present Doc Martens, a dark blazer and a deep purple shirt with tiny little colourful Mexican sugar skulls printed on it. It had been another of Henrietta's gifts, and one I'd never worn or had any intention of wearing and had shoved so far in the back of the wardrobe it was practically in Narnia.

Dusty had loved it. I'd put up a protest, but she simply launched into a rather enthusiastic rendition of *It's Raining Men* without missing a beat, followed by Anita Ward's *Ring My Bell*. She'd just reached the first chorus of Olivia Newton John's *Xanadu* before I finally gave in. I'm beginning to think she's got a penchant for disco. I'm also pretty sure I've screwed myself irreversibly because she now knows exactly how to get me to do what she wants.

I'm not saying she can't sing, just the opposite, she's amazing, and I have to admit the accompanying dance numbers, even executed in one shoe with a lopsided wig, were pretty entertaining. I'm sure on stage she was incredible, but in my bedroom, or living room... or, yes, even in the bathroom in such close proximity it's a couple of hundred decibels too much for my poor ear drums.

So, here I am, sat on an uncomfortable plastic chair in a crematorium staring at a bald-headed man wearing false eyelashes and a lurid lime green suit with plump purple marabou feathers decorating the collar and cuffs as he reads Dusty's eulogy in a soft effeminate voice.

I needn't have bothered worrying about looking out of place I think to myself as my gaze migrates across the room. It's a kaleidoscope of eye popping colours, patterns and textures and holy crap the hats! I've truly never seen anything like it. Hats and fascinators as far as the eye can see, some so large they're like sombreros and almost all of them decorated with dramatic chiffon and netted veils.

Dusty hadn't been exaggerating when she'd said she knew a lot of people. The whole crematorium is packed wall to wall, and there are more people outside who haven't been able to squeeze in.

I try to turn my attention back to the short man speaking up front, but his voice is so monotonous, it's hard not to let my mind drift.

"Who do you think wrote your eulogy?" I mutter under my breath to Dusty.

"Well, it certainly wasn't Ari," Dusty snorts. "He wouldn't have made it two words into the first sentence without inserting the word fuck at least three times."

"Who's Ari?"

"See for yourself." She nods toward the small podium.

The man in the lime suit, having finally talked himself out, produces a tissue from his breast pocket and dabs the corners of his eyes, careful not to disrupt the enormous fan-like fake lashes, which are so thick I wonder how he can keep his eyelids open.

He shuffles off the small platform and another man takes his place. This one is wearing all black and his shirt is unbuttoned just enough to reveal a heavy gold medallion nestled amongst thick greying chest hair. I watch curiously as he clears his throat, and when he begins to speak it's with a thick, slightly nasally cockney accent.

"Twinkle, Twinkle, little fuckin' star," he begins to read from a slightly crumpled piece of paper.

"Jesus, Ari." Dusty lifts her hand, rubbing her forehead as she chuckles under her breath.

"That's what she was to me," he continues. "She was a star, gone too soon, taken from us, and it ain't fuckin fair and it ain't right. She didn't deserve the way she was done in, but we're gonna make sure she ain't never forgotten. In the words of Lulu, my days are just an endless stream of emptiness to me, filled only by the fleeting moments of her memories. Sweet memories, sweet memories."

He nods as if he'd just made a profound point and then climbs off the platform and moves back to his seat. He's replaced at the podium moments later by a tall red head, wearing a very short leather dress, black stockings and vicious looking six inch platforms with thin needle like heels and a row of steel spikes decorating the toes. Her make-up is dark and fierce beneath a huge fascinator, which could have doubled as the Trafalgar Square fountain, and from which a black net veil hugs her face.

"Urgh, Pleather." Dusty looks at her disdainfully. "Brandy's as classy as ever I see."

When the red head opens her mouth to speak, her voice is even deeper than Dusty's, but there's a calculated coolness to her tone that Dusty doesn't have. Dusty is warmth and humour with a hint of wickedness.

"Stop all the clocks, cut off the telephone," the red head begins loudly, lifting her hands as her eyes widen melodramatically.

"Isn't this poem from *Four Weddings and a Funeral*?" My eyes narrow as I study her.

"What did we say about your ridiculous film obsession?" Dusty sighs.

"Prevent the dog from barking with a juicy boner," Brandy intones deeply.

"I'm pretty sure that's not how it goes," I mutter to Dusty, who is glaring at the one she called Brandy.

"Silence the pianos and with muffled drum," Brandy continues, the rise and fall of her voice, her wide eyes, and her exaggerated hand gestures, more suited to telling ghost stories around a campfire. In fact, all she needs is a flashlight pointed at her chin. "Bring out the coffin, let the mourners come."

"Bitch, please." Dusty rolls her eyes, crossing her arms over her chest.

"Let aeroplanes circle, moaning overhead. Scribbling on the sky the message. He is dead!" Brandy cries out, lifting her arms and fisting her hands.

"Oh my God, dramatic much. It isn't bloody Shakespeare!" Dusty curls her lips in contempt. "Talk about milking it. She's always been a complete attention whore. I mean, God forbid the attention should be on me at my own fucking funeral."

"I take it you two didn't get on?" I whisper quietly.

"Brandy doesn't get on with anyone. She's a complete narcissist. We only got stuck putting up with her shit because she had her mouth around Ari's cock seventy percent of the time and being dicked down the other thirty."

"He's sleeping with her?" I ask inquisitively.

"Yep." Her lips pop around the word. "And I know the last thing anyone wants to be thinking about is his cock in her arse, but actually, it's the other way around, it's more like her dick in his arse."

"Really." I blink at her. "He's a bottom?"

She nods salaciously like she's about to impart a delicious morsel of gossip as she leans forward and whispers in my ear. I can literally feel my face burning all the way from the tips of my ears to the roots of my hair and I choke a little.

"No," I breathe, utterly scandalised.

"Uh huh." She grins. "Giant ostrich feather... swear to God."

My cheeks are still flaming as I turn back to the small platform. Brandy has now finished her recounting of the poem with all the authenticity of an Oscar acceptance speech. I fully expect her to take her seat but instead she continues to speak, and I sigh, shifting again because my arse cheeks are starting to go numb.

"Those of us who knew poor Dusty best, might say she was impetuous, that she liked to take risks, that she often made shockingly bad decisions... some might even say she was almost asking for such a grisly end..."

"That bitch," Dusty growls, leaning her head toward me while keeping her narrowed gaze firmly fixed on Brandy. "Put her on the suspect list."

"No," I hiss quietly. "We're not here to solve your murder. We're here to pay our respects."

"Which seems oddly self-serving on my part." She rolls her eyes and glances over her shoulder toward the back of the room, her mouth curving into a knowing smirk. "Don't look now, but Inspector Easy on the Eyes is here."

"What?" I jerk in my seat, immediately turning around to see Inspector Hayes standing respectfully at the back of the room, once again wearing one of his mouth-wateringly fitted suits.

"Why is it whenever you say don't turn around, people immediately turn around?" Dusty sighs loudly. "Although not that I can blame you. I'm so jealous of you right now."

"What? Why?" I blink in confusion.

"Seriously?" She nods toward the back of the room. "Like you and Inspector Massive Cock haven't been eye fucking each other since day one, and it's only a matter of time before you get to sample the goods."

"Dusty," I hiss in embarrassment.

"What?" she replies innocently as her eyes run over him, and she sucks her teeth speculatively. "I bet he has got a massive cock, you're so lucky."

"Will you stop talking about his cock," I whisper harshly, my face burning like I'd spent midday in the Sahara without sunscreen. "We're at a funeral for God's sake."

"So? It's my funeral, and I can do what I want."

"Stop staring at him," I mouth silently, as if from this distance he could somehow hear me.

"Why?" She blinks. "It's not like he can see me, besides I'm trying to figure out who he reminds me of." Her eyes narrow thoughtfully as she purses her lips. "An actor." She decides after a moment. "Young, blonde, played some sort of British agent."

"What? James Bond?" I reply, wrinkling my nose in disagreement, narrowly resisting the urge to turn around and stare at Inspector Hayes gorgeous face. "He looks nothing like Daniel Craig, although I wouldn't say no to Daniel Craig."

"Preach, sister." Dusty nods enthusiastically. "And, no, not Daniel Craig. I meant the other one, the one who had a pug dog."

"Ohhh," I reply in realisation. "You mean Taron Egerton in the Kingsman movies?"

"Darling." Dusty blinks at me, "You know way too much movie trivia for your own good, it's not healthy. You're too young and pretty for your social life to be deader than I am."

"What?" I frown. "I happen to like watching movies."

"Yes, but there has to be more to your life than just cutting up dead bodies and working your way through the entire listings of Netflix."

"I bet Ed Gein would've disagreed," I mutter.

"He didn't have Netflix," she replies primly. "And you need to stay off the crime channels too," she adds almost as an afterthought.

As Brandy brings her condescending diatribe to an end, I lift my gaze to the casket on the raised dais behind the podium. Rather than plain glossy oak, it's finished in a metallic glittery pink and covered in sprays and sprays of rainbow-coloured flowers. The Master of Ceremonies, or whatever he's called, steps back up to the platform and folds his hands respectfully in front of him.

"If you would all be upstanding as we say our final goodbye to our beloved friend and sister," he intones, formally eliciting a small whimper of distress from Dusty.

There's a load of shuffling and noise as everyone stands, culminating in several minor collisions as numerous people accidentally headbutt each other with their giant and elaborate hats. Eva Cassidy's cover of *Somewhere Over The Rainbow* pipes out loudly from the speakers, and the rollers beneath the coffin begin to spin, moving it slowly back toward the curtained alcove.

Dusty makes another small sound of anguish, and I turn to her, my voice low.

"Dusty, meet me outside," I say gently. "You don't need to see this."

She swallows hard, her Adams apple bobbing convulsively before she winks out of sight. I carefully shuffle my way through the press of people, some of which are sniffling and some outright sobbing. I try to shut out the painful sound of their grief as it reopens old wounds of my own that I'd thought long buried.

As I reach the back of the room, I glance across, and my eyes momentarily lock with Inspector Hayes. His eyes widen in surprise, and I give a small, slightly uncomfortable smile as I slip out of the door and wonder how the hell I'm going to explain my presence at his murder victim's funeral.

I push carefully through the throngs of mourners gathered outside, and once I'm able to break free of the crowd, my gaze searches the grounds until they land on a familiar figure. I head toward the display courtyard at the entrance to the memorial garden where the funeral directors have set up all the arrangements of flowers for viewing, each with sympathy cards attached. I stop next to Dusty as she stares down at a large arrangement of pink carnations designed in the shape of her name.

"I know this is probably a really stupid question," I say softly, wishing that I could reach out and touch her in comfort. "But... are you okay?"

She swallows again, and when she turns to look at me, her eyes are red rimmed and glazed with a fine sheen of tears.

"It's really real, isn't it?" she whispers hoarsely.

I nod slowly. "I'm so sorry, Dusty."

She blows out a breath and looks up blinking rapidly.

When she turns toward me, the hint of pain and vulnerability she'd shown me is gone, and in its place is her showstopper smile, even if it didn't quite reach her eyes.

"Woo." She waves a hand nonchalantly. "Where's a Martini extra dirty when a girl needs one, huh?"

"Dusty," I say in concern. "It's okay to be upset."

"Oh, look." She wiggles her brows, avoiding the subject altogether. "Here comes Inspector Hot Lips."

I turn to look and see him striding toward me purposefully.

"Shit, shit, shit," I mutter in panic.

"What?" Dusty frowns. "I thought you liked him."

"I do," I reply without thinking. "I mean—" I shake my head. "How am I going to explain what I'm doing here?" I whisper harshly under my breath as he approaches.

"Don't worry." Dusty smirks. "I got your back, boo."

"Tristan," he greets as he stops beside me.

"Inspector Hayes." I nod politely.

"That's very formal." He smiles softly. "What happened to calling me Danny?"

"Oh, um." I tug at my blazer, slightly flustered. "I just thought... um, you know that you were here in a professional capacity."

"I am," he replies easily. "But then again, aren't you?"

"Aren't I what?" I frown in confusion. "Oh, no," I reply without thinking as comprehension dawns. "If I attended the funeral of every person I post-mortemed I'd never get anything done."

I laugh nervously and hear Dusty groan beside me. Shit... why the fuck did I just say that? He'd just handed me the perfect excuse for my presence here, and I went and babbled like a complete twat.

"Then why are you here?" His head tilts a fraction as he studies me.

"I...um... um..." Floundering helplessly. "Because I know

Dusty," I blurt out unintentionally. Fuck, I really don't hold up well under intense scrutiny. It's a good job this isn't five hundred years ago because I'm pretty sure the Spanish Inquisition would have broken me like a cheap vase. "I mean...I knew Dusty." I backtrack.

"I thought you said you didn't know her?" Danny asks as his gaze narrows slightly.

"Tell him it was a conflict of interest or something," Dusty says next to me.

Shit that could work I think quickly.

"I couldn't really say anything," I explain. "Although it's not an actual rule, the mortuary don't like us working on people we have a personal connection to. Especially murder victims."

"I see." Danny frowns in concern. "You know you really should've said something. What if we arrest someone and their defence uses your connection to her to challenge the findings of the post-mortem?"

Fuck, I hadn't thought of that.

"Um... I didn't think of that," I say honestly. "But I had Henrietta double check everything I did and documented, which is standard practice for us in cases of homicide. If you check, you'll see she signed off as a second signatory."

Thank God, for Judy instituting the second opinion protocol I think to myself.

"I see," Danny replies as he continues to watch me thoughtfully.

"I'm sorry," I say genuinely. I hate lying to him.

"How did you know Dusty then?" he asks.

"Is that a professional inquiry?" I reply.

He fixes me with a look that has me immediately capitulating. How does he do that? One look from him and he has me wanting to spill my guts... Shit... someone hand me a shovel, I'm about to dig myself deeper.

"We met a few years ago." I decide on the spot. "Uh... I'd been dragged along to a club. We hit it off."

"Was it an intimate relationship?" He asks with a small frown, and I flush.

"No." I shake my head. "We were friends. I don't know if you've noticed, but I'm not really a people person. I don't have that kind of skill set, and I don't particularly enjoy the club scene. Dusty and I would meet up for coffee sometimes. Although, I did know she was amazing at performing, I didn't have much to do with the drag side of it, so I've never been to The Rainbow Room, and I don't personally know the people she worked with, but she talked about them. Sometimes I think I'm the only one she could be real with."

"Damn, girl." Dusty gives a slow clap, and I daren't turn toward her. "You certainly know how to spin a yarn."

Hopefully, that should do it. It kind of explains my intimate knowledge of her but also why I don't know any of her co-workers.

"Inspector." A loud, brash voice startles us both, breaking our staring contest as we turn to see Ari strutting toward us with Brandy hot on his heels, tottering along in her vertigo inducing platform stilettos as she puffs away on a vape.

"Mr Caligliari." Danny nods as he greets them with professional politeness. "Miss Butter."

I blink. Butter? Her name is Brandy Butter? I cough slightly as I'm shrouded in a thick cloud of Pina Colada scented smoke.

"It was good of you to come," Ari tells Danny gruffly, more or less ignoring me as if there are far too many people here for him to bother asking names. "We're having the wake at The Rainbow Room if you want to come. I've got somethin' I want to show you."

"Alright." Danny nods. "I'll meet you there."

Ari nods and walks away abruptly.

"Don't mind him, he's in a mood." Brandy takes another

suggestive suck on her vape pipe, and I wonder if she actually thinks that's sexy because she looks like someone who's trying to suck a MacDonald's thick-shake through a straw that's too small.

"I imagine it's quite a difficult day for him," Danny replies stoically.

Brandy huffs. "Whatever."

I hear Dusty growl next to me.

"I'll look forward to seeing you at The Rainbow Room." Brandy lets her gaze roam over Danny's body before switching to me. "And make sure you bring the pretty little twink with you." She winks suggestively at me.

I see Danny's jaw tighten and is the only outward display of emotion as I edge slightly behind him and using him shamelessly as a human shield. I have no doubt Brandy is an aggressive top, and she'd eat me up and spit me out like a chicken bone.

I watch as she pivots expertly on her heels and struts off.

"Are you coming to the wake?" Danny looks at me and his expression has softened.

"Sure," I reply.

Dammit... engage brain before answering the hot policeman I silently scold myself. Now I'm stuck having to converse with people at a wake that's being held at the scene of Dusty's murder, which, call me crazy, I think is in a bit of bad taste.

"I can give you a ride if you want?" Danny's mouth curves, and I hear Dusty mutter something that sounds suspiciously like, *lucky, bitch* behind me.

"Okay." I swallow nervously.

I can do this. I can make polite conversation with a room full of flamboyant drag queens about my fictional friendship with their murdered friend. Fuck, I breathe slowly. How is this my life?

I turn back to Dusty, only to find her staring down at an arrangement of black calla lilies, her expression unreadable. I glance down at the card pinned to the flowers, but instead of a message, there is only the initial 'R'.

Dusty looks up at me slowly.

"What?" I mouth silently so Danny can't hear me.

She shakes her head and walks away, and unable to ask her anything else, I fall into step beside Danny as we head toward his car. After a while, the strange card and the Calla Lilies slip from my mind.

10

Danny

Tristan is quiet next to me on the drive to Shoreditch. I'm not sure what's on his mind, but he seems deep in thought, although every now and then he glances strangely at the empty back seat of my car. I find myself sneaking glances at him while still trying to watch the London traffic and turning over his words in my mind.

He says he's known Dusty for a least a few years, but he showed no signs of shock at her death when she was wheeled into his mortuary. In fact, he'd showed no signs of grief or distress at all, despite that his friend was in a body bag.

I don't know, maybe he's just a hell of an actor. After all, he did say he'd had to keep his personal connection to her a secret or he wouldn't have been allowed to be involved with her post-mortem at all. Maybe he concealed his pain from me that day, maybe... just maybe, he was telling me the truth, or maybe he's lying to me, and I'm too personally invested in him to want to see the truth.

He's the first man I've ever met who I've been interested in for more than a tumble in the sheets with. I'd thought I could keep my work and personal life separate, but now the one man

I want is tangled up in my murder investigation, and I know he's keeping something from me. I don't know what, but he sure as hell isn't telling me the whole truth. He wants to tell me; I can see it in his eyes. It's right there on the tip of his tongue, but he's holding back, and I can't help wondering why? Is it fear? Or worse, is it guilt?

The smartest thing right now would be to slam on the brakes, not literally, I might add. I can't imagine the guy in the flashy dark green Jag behind me would appreciate it if he ploughed into the back of my little Peugeot 308. No, I mean slamming on the proverbial brakes with whatever is going on between me and Tristan. That would be the sensible thing to do, and I always do the sensible thing.

Except, I glance back over at him, there's something about him. My head is telling me to step back, get a healthy distance between us and just work the case, but as I look at that beautiful, delicate profile, the light dusting of tiny, faint freckles across the tops of his cheekbones and those gorgeous green eyes that have turned to catch my gaze, I don't see deceit or cool calculation, I see vulnerability and beneath it, loneliness.

Dragging my eyes away from him before I crash the car and end up killing us both, I turn down a side street and pull the car into a small carpark behind the club, which is marked for staff. We both climb out of the car as I turn to lock it. Tristan edges around the car and stands a distance from me, waiting patiently as I join him, and we begin walking.

"Are you okay?" I ask after another moment's silence.

"I suppose." He shrugs. "There's been a lot to take in since Dusty's death." He blows out a breath as he looks ahead.

"I can imagine." I nod, and the silence continues.

"Danny," Tristan finally says, his tone betraying a hint of uncertainty. "Can I ask you something?"

"Sure," I reply easily as we turn the corner and head down the side of the building.

"Do you..." He pauses, and I get the feeling he's trying to figure out how to best phrase whatever question he has for me. "Do you believe in an afterlife? I mean... do you believe in ghosts."

At first, I think he's joking. Whatever I thought he was going to ask me that question takes me by surprise, but one quick, surreptitious glance at his earnest expression tells me he's serious. I give his question some consideration. I don't think it's something I've ever been asked before.

"I don't know," I answer honestly. "I don't suppose I've ever really given it much thought. My family's not overly religious. My parents are Methodists, so we were all dragged to church on Sundays, but the topic of ghosts never really came up in our house. I don't think there's any concrete evidence either way. I don't think we're meant to know, but I guess we'll all find out when our time comes. What about you?"

"I never used to," he replies, his dark brows marred by a thoughtful frown.

"But you've been thinking about it recently?" I guess.

"I suppose." He shrugs.

"Let me guess," I say quietly. "Since Dusty was killed?"

"How did you know?" He looks up at me, his frown deepening.

"Believe it or not, it's more common than you think," I tell him. "When someone dies unexpectedly, especially in violent or suspicious circumstances, it's common for the loved ones and friends of the victim to start questioning their beliefs. Did they suffer, were they aware? Did they know they were dying? Do you think they're at peace?" I list a mere fraction of the questions I've been asked over the years when I've had to speak to the friends and relatives of a victim.

"I suppose that's to be expected." He sighs. "It's a natural human state to seek comfort."

"Tell me about her," I ask impulsively. Maybe I'm subconsciously testing him, or maybe I'm just genuinely curious about the drag queen who'd had near on five hundred people turn up at her funeral and that was a conservative estimate.

"Dusty?" Tristan smiles, and I relax, happy to see the confusion in his eyes replaced with amusement. "She's a character." He chuckles. "She's got a really dry, understated sense of humour, and she's really quite sarcastic too, but she has this hint of sweetness beneath the layers of snark. She likes to get her own way, and her voice is incredible. She has an annoying love of seventies disco anthems, which she will belt out at a moment's notice without warning, and she has a high kick that would make Dita Von Teese weep with jealously."

I listen to the genuine fondness in his voice, and I wonder if he's even noticed he refers to her in the present tense like she's still alive. I stop him gently, my hand on his arm, and it feels like lightning has shot through my palm.

"I'm sorry I never got to meet her," I tell him sincerely. "But I will find out what happened to her, I promise."

He stares at me silently for a moment, his eyes searching mine, and whatever he was looking for he must've found because he nods slowly.

I let go of him reluctantly, puzzling over the sudden urge I have to slip my fingers into his and hold his hand. I've never been a hand holder in my life and certainly not in public, but everything about this man has me wanting to throw all my caution out the nearest window.

We approach the main entrance of the club and slip through the doors to be greeted by a large, solidly built man who I can only assume is one of the bouncers.

"You Hayes?" he asks gruffly as he eyes up Tristan next to me, and I have the unfamiliar urge to pull him in closer to my body and wrap my arm around him so everyone knows he's taken.

The sudden and possessive thought takes me by surprise.

Although I'm more than interested in him, we've only had a handful of conversations and one impromptu coffee date, that doesn't mean he's taken. Although I secretly admit to myself, I'd very much like him to be. I shake my head at the thought. I can't even think about starting something with him until I figure out what it is he's hiding and have it clear in my mind just how involved he is in my case. I really should take a step back or at least wait until the case has been resolved before I try to pursue anything with him.

"Yes, I am," I tell the bouncer, answering his earlier question.

"Ari's waiting for you in his office." He nods his head toward the entrance into the club. "Head backstage and hang a left, end of the corridor next to the fire exit."

"Thanks." I nod, placing my hand on the small of Tristan's back without thinking and guiding him toward the main section of the club. I pull my hand back quickly, admonishing myself for my uncharacteristic lack of control, but every time I resolve myself to take a step back from Tristan, I'm pulled back toward him.

He turns to look at me, and in that one brief second, I know that he feels it too, and just like me, he's at a complete loss as to what to do about it. It's like we're the sun and the moon, pulled back and forth by each other's gravity and creating the ocean waves. Only the rise and fall of the waves are an unruly dichotomy of desire and uncertainty.

Pushing all inappropriate thoughts of the beautiful and timid man next to me aside, I lead him into the club and sternly remind myself that I'm here to do a job and catch a killer. Not flirt with Tristan.

We step inside the club, it's not anywhere near filled to capacity yet as most of the mourners are still at the crematorium but it's pretty full. The sound of chatter and music fills the wide open space, the main lights are on, and the bar is open.

Along one wall dozens of tables have been uniformly lined up and covered with crisp white linen. Caterers are currently filling the table with platters of sandwiches, sausage rolls and all manner of other buffet finger foods. Up on the stage, a huge screen has been erected, and a projector is playing a continuous show reel of Dusty's on and off stage antics.

I feel Tristan tense up beside me, and I remember he doesn't like being around large groups of people. I narrowly resist the urge to put my hands on him in comfort as I lean in a little closer and he shivers.

"I have to go and speak with Mr Caligliari, are you going to be okay by yourself?"

Tristan looks up at me and gives me a slightly uncomfortable smile. "I'll be fine."

"I won't be long," I tell him.

"It's fine, Danny," he says with a more sincere smile. "You're here to do a job remember? Not babysit me. I'm good."

"Okay." I nod, feeling a curious reluctance to leave him. Jesus, the feelings he stirs in me are so unfamiliar I have no idea how to deal with them. Turning around I head to where I know the backstage entrance is, determined not to look back even though I want to.

I slip through the door and turn left, continuing on down to the fire exit where I find a plain black door beside it. I knock firmly and turn the handle when a familiar voice invites me to enter.

Ari is sitting behind a heavy desk piled high with stacks of paperwork. There's an inch of dust over everything and an overspilling pencil pot with half chewed pens. The filing cabinets and shelving propped against the walls aren't in much better shape, and I cringe at the chaos and disorder. The whole room is so against the deeply ingrained nature of my tidy soul it makes my skin prickle.

"Inspector." Ari nods and indicates the chair in front of the desk. It's a low leather bucket chair, and a quick glance reveals it's at least clean.

"Mr Caligliari." I nod, taking a seat opposite him. "You said you have something to show me?"

"That's right." Clearly not one to make idle chit chat, he gets straight to business and pulls his phone from his jacket pocket, which is slung over the back of his chair. He taps the screen a few times and a video clip starts playing. "Ramone took this at the bar the night Dusty was murdered," he explains.

I turn my attention back to the screen, the camera angle is all over the place for a moment then it settles down, and Dusty's smiling face comes into view. She's sat at the bar laughing at something Ramone has said to her as she tilts her head back and tosses back a shot of something before picking up a cocktail glass and sipping.

She laughs again, and there's some banter between them until her phone rings. The camera angle switches to another drag queen sat next to her, and this one takes her shot and gags a little, laughing and shooting Ramone the finger. Dusty leaves her bar stool, and I can see her just behind them in the background as she answers the phone. I can't hear what she's saying, but it's clear from the expression on her face that she's really upset. Then she turns and disappears out of the camera shot.

"Is this all of it?" I ask as I watch the clip back again.

"That's all of Ramone's footage," Ari replies. "I know we've already turned over our internal security cam footage, but we went back and looked at our copies and found this."

He takes the phone back and brings up another clip. This one is from the inside of the entrance to backstage and shows a drag queen slipping through the door and closing it behind her before setting off down the corridor and out of the camera shot. I move the slider back and watch the clip again, pausing it. You can't see her face clearly, yet there's something about her that seems out of place, but I can't quite put my finger on it. I look up at Ari.

"Who is she?" I ask.

"Dunno." He shakes his head. "Never seen her before, but I can tell you, whoever she is, she ain't one of mine."

"She doesn't work here? You're sure?"

"She don't work 'ere," he confirms. "Which means she had no business backstage. This clip was taken about two hours after the one on Ramone's phone."

"Is there anything else?"

"Yeah, this." He shows me another clip, taken around fifteen minutes after the mysterious drag queen entered the backstage corridor that leads to Dusty's dressing room. Only in this clip you can see the back of her quite clearly, until she pauses by the door and glances back, as if she heard something. For a second, we catch a glimpse of her heavily made up face. It's not that clear, and I'm not sure if it's enough to get an ID but it's something.

"Can you forward the footage to me, and I'll have our team go over it closely." I hand him back his phone.

He nods and I stand.

"Thank you again for your cooperation." I hold out my hand, and he shakes it, his dark eyes watching me closely and it raises the hackles on my neck. "I'll be in touch."

I step out of his office closing the door behind me and note that the fire exit, which had been closed, is now open with a drag queen propped against it. She's wearing a long, straight red wig, which hangs almost to her buttocks and a tight-fitting black dress that moulds to her slim, padded hips. Her shoes are glittery fire engine red platform pumps, which match her glittery red lips.

"You the cop?" she asks as her gaze trails over me slowly.

"Inspector Danny Hayes." I hold out my hand. "Scotland Yard, and you are?"

"Ruby." Her warm hand grasps mine, grazing my skin with her long acrylic nails, which could have doubled as ice picks. "Ruby Slippers."

"Ruby Slippers?" I smile as my brows rise. "If it's not a rude question, why Ruby Slippers?"

"Because if you click your heels together three times, handsome, I'll take you home." Her smile is warm and teasing with a hint of wry amusement, unlike Brandy who gives the impression that if you were on a plane that crashed in the middle of the frozen Andes, she wouldn't think twice about eating you to stay alive.

Ruby's gaze flicks to the door to Ari's office and then back to me.

"Don't let Ari's heartbroken employer routine fool you." She lifts a cigarette to her lips and lights it with a cheap plastic pink lighter, which she tucks back into one of the padded cups of her bra.

"Oh?" My brow quirks questioningly.

"He was majorly pissed when he found out Dusty had been offered a spot on Drag Race."

"She was offered a place on Ru Paul's Drag Race?" I repeat in some surprise.

"Oh yeah." Ruby nods. "But Dusty made Ari a lot of money, especially when she did her old Hollywood starlet shows. She was famous for her Marlene Dietrich and Marilyn Monroe performances. In the last year, her shows would literally bring people in from all over, and they would come to London just to see her perform. You should've heard the crowd when she did *Happy Birthday, Mr. President*. She was practically a legend in our world. There was no way Ari wanted to give that up."

"I see." I scratch my chin, feeling the five o'clock shadow starting to show. "What about Brandy?"

"Brandy? Brandy's a survivor." Ruby flicks the ash from her cigarette absently. "None of us had it easy growing up. Being gay was hard enough but being a boy who liked to wear dress-es?" She shakes her head, "But Brandy came up through the system and had it particularly rough. It taught her only to rely on herself, and she's never changed. Brandy only cares about Brandy."

"And Ari?" I ask. "Does he care about Brandy? I see them together a lot."

"He's her meal ticket, darling." Ruby blows out an elegant stream of smoke. "And he puts up with a lot of her shit because he has a type, and there aren't too many queens or fems out there willing to top a middle-aged man who looks like Mussolini and sounds like Ray Winston."

"I see, and what exactly is it that Brandy gets in return?"

Ruby shrugs. "Who do you think is headlining now our beloved Dusty is out of the way?"

"So, she had a lot to gain from Dusty's death?" I muse.

Again, Ruby shrugs. "Maybe, maybe not," she replies thoughtfully, taking another long, slow drag of her cigarette, the cherry tip glowing in the dying light as evening approaches. "I'm not Brandy's biggest fan. I think she's a selfish bitch who'll stab you in the back so much as look at you but murder? She didn't need to kill Dusty to get her out of the way. It was no secret around here that Dusty had an offer from Ru Paul, but what's not common knowledge is that Netflix was sniffing around after her, some sort of reality series with her as the star. Dusty was always meant for bigger things than The Rainbow Room."

"I see." I nod.

"Look, Brandy's a class A bitch who only looks out for number one. Ari's a balding middle-aged man who has a predilection for queens and fem boys and Ginger is a timid little mouse who wouldn't say boo to a goose, but the rest of us..." She looks away as she blows out a thin stream of smoke and stares at the rapidly filling car park but not before I catch the hint of genuine sadness and grief in her eyes. "We all loved Dusty," she murmurs softly. "We were her family." When she turns back to me, her eyes harden. "Whoever did that to her, I want them to pay."

"I'll do my best," I reply. "You have my word."

She nods sharply, and I feel myself dismissed. Leaving her to her thoughts, I turn away, pausing and looking back when I hear her voice once more.

"If you haven't already," she tells me almost as an afterthought. "Make sure you speak to Chan. She was Dusty's best friend in the whole world. They came up together, known each other since they were kids. No one knows what went on in Dusty's life like Chan."

"Thanks," I reply. "I will."

She nods again, and this time when I turn to head back down the hallway, she doesn't stop me.

11

Tristan

I stand there staring into the rapidly filling space and swallow hard, my stomach giving a long slow roll. My palms are sweaty, and my shoulders are so tense I'm practically wearing them as earrings.

"Relax, boo," Dusty says next to me. "You look like they're going to eat you alive."

"Sooooo many people," I mutter, my eyes wide.

"You can do this," she says softly as she looks at me. "Come on, you don't have to stay for long, but there's a couple of people I really want you to meet."

"Why?" I ask curiously.

"Because..." She pauses. "I just want to make sure they're okay," she finally says. "There are two people who were very important to me, and I never got the chance to say goodbye."

I stare at Dusty, seeing past the demanding attitude and smudged make-up to the vulnerable person beneath. Ever since I've met her, I've been witness to a myriad of emotions from her, from sarcasm to outrage, to annoyance, to frustration, but now I see a quiet sadness and a deep sense of loss. These people aren't just mourning her, she's mourning them.

"Okay, Dusty," I say gently, pushing back the slightly panicky feeling of being around so many people in an unfamiliar place and focusing instead on her.

"Come on." She leads me through the crowds searching for two very specific faces.

Eventually, she leads me to the very edge of the room, and in a quiet secluded corner at the end of the buffet tables, I see a young man in a smart black suit sitting all alone. I draw closer, and when I see him more clearly, I realise he has Down Syndrome and looks to be in his early twenties maybe, with mousy brown hair and a pensive expression as he holds a plastic cup of punch and stares out into the room.

"That's Benny," Dusty says softly, her voice filled with affection and worry. "I just want you to check in with him and make sure he's okay."

I nod and head toward him, stopping close by as he looks up at me curiously.

"Hi." I smile. "Do you mind if I sit next to you?"Indicating the vacant seat beside him.

"Okay," he replies, watching me.

"Thanks." I settle beside him. "My name's Tristan," I introduce myself.

"My name's Benny," he returns. "I like your shirt." He eyes the little day of the dead skulls decorated with swirls and flowers.

"Thank you." I stare out into the room, much as he's doing. "I always get nervous at things like these," I tell him honestly. "There are so many people. It feels overwhelming."

"I like watching people," Benny replies, sipping his drink. "Their faces tell stories."

"Really?" I tilt my head as I turn to look at him. "Does my face tell a story?"

He studies me. "You feel sad," he says after a moment.

I search my feelings and realise that he's right. It's not just that I'm uncomfortable in large crowds of people. It's that deep down I feel sad. It reminds me of my mum's funeral. She was a big part of our community and so well loved, and her death was so sudden and shocking that her funeral was packed. Afterward everyone had crammed themselves into our tiny mid terrace two bedroom house.

Huh...

I think I'm having an epiphany, and the more I think about it the more I'm convinced that was the actual moment that started my aversion to crowded spaces and large amounts of people. I was this tiny, skinny kid who didn't understand why his mum was suddenly not there anymore. My home was filled to the rafters with strangers who kept squeezing my cheeks or petting my head in sympathy like I was a dog that needed stroking and soothing, and I'd hated every minute of it. I'd squirrelled myself away in a corner sitting all by myself, much as Benny is doing now, wearing my grief like a magic cloak and trying desperately to make myself invisible so people wouldn't talk to me.

"I guess I am sad," I tell Benny honestly.

"It's okay." He pats my shoulder. "I feel sad too. Do you want a sticker? Whenever I feel sad, I pick a sticker."

"I'd love a sticker." I smile genuinely. The kid's a sweetheart, no wonder Dusty wanted me to check in on him.

Benny reaches into his jacket pocket and pulls out a slightly crumpled, half used sheet of stickers. He sets his plastic cup down on the edge of the buffet table to his right and unfolds the sheet showing me my options. There are rainbows and hearts, stars, and smiley faces. I point to one, and he meticulously peels it from the backing paper, the tip of his tongue peeking out as he tries to get his short fingernails under the edges of the sticker. Finally, he pulls it free and sticks it to the collar of my blazer, patting it a few times to make sure it is stuck firmly.

"Do you want one too?" I ask and he nods. "May I?" I point to the small, tatty sheet.

He hands it over, pointing to one of the stickers, and I peel it off with ease, sticking it to the collar of his suit jacket the same way he did with mine before handing back the sheet of stickers, which he folds carefully and tucks safely back in his pocket.

"Are you here with someone?" I ask him as he picks up his cup of punch.

"I work here," he tells me.

"You do?" I reply curiously. "What do you do?"

"I'm the cleaner." He smiles. "I keep everything tidy."

"And do you like it here?" I tilt my head as I watch him.

He nods enthusiastically. "I love it. Dusty and Chan and Ruby are my friends. They take care of me, and I take care of them."

"That sounds lovely," I murmur, my heart aching for him as he mentions Dusty's name and his face falls. "Benny, are you okay?"

"They said something bad happened to Dusty," he tells me, and the look in his eyes nearly breaks my heart. "Is it true?" he asks.

I can't lie to him, so I answer as honestly as I can. "Yes, something bad happened to her, but my friend, Danny, is a policeman, and he's going to do everything he can to catch the person who hurt her."

"Will they go to prison?" he asks.

"I hope so." I nod as he lets out a loud sigh.

"I miss Dusty," he replies miserably and stares down at his plastic cup.

I watch silently as Dusty kneels down in front of him, her face filled with sadness. I watch as her hand hovers just above his knee, wanting to give him comfort but unable to touch him.

"Oh, Benny," she says, her voice a deep murmur. "My sweet,

sweet boy. I miss you too, but I'll always be watching over you, I promise."

"Benny," I say quietly. Knowing he can't hear Dusty's words of love. "You know Dusty has gone to heaven."

"I know." He nods.

"Well, I know for a fact that she can see you from heaven," I tell him. "Even though you can't see her, she'll always be watching over you."

"Like an angel?" Benny replies curiously.

"Something like that." I can't help my lips curving into a smile as I try to picture Dusty with wings sitting on a cloud plucking at a harp.

"Benny," a voice intrudes, and we both look up.

I find myself staring at the face of a stunning drag queen. Her delicate Asian features are almost doll-like, her eyes, highlighted by understated eye make-up, are more grey than blue. Her cheekbones high and mouth delicately painted a deep blushing pink. She's wearing a rather conservative black body con dress with a slashing neckline from one slim shoulder to the other, and rather than the customary platform heels so many others are wearing, she appears to be wearing classic black suede Louboutins. Her long nails are painted a deep plum and her shiny straight hair flows down her back in shiny waterfall, the colour so black it almost has a blue hue to it, and I somehow doubt that it's a wig.

"Benny," she says again, her voice deep but not as deep as Dusty or Brandy.

"Hello, Chan." He looks up.

"Ruby's looking for you," Chan says with a sympathetic smile. "She thought you might like to help her arrange the cupcakes since they were your idea."

"Okay." He gets up, and I watch as she wraps him up in her arms affectionately and hugs him tight, adding a little sway of comfort before he sniffs and pulls back.

"Alright, darling boy?" She brushes his hair back from his face and he nods.

"Bye, Tristan," he says, turning to me.

"Thank you for the sticker," I call out as he disappears into the crowd.

I look back to find the one he'd called Chan studying me curiously.

"He gave you one of his stickers?" she asks blankly after a moment, and I nod in confirmation. "He doesn't usually do that with people he doesn't know."

"He said I looked sad," I murmur, a little touched he'd deemed me special enough for one of his prized stickers. "I guess I was thinking about my mum's funeral."

"That'll do it." Chan nodded. "He's always been sensitive to the moods of others even when he's hurting."

I see Dusty rise slowly from where she'd been kneeling, and her face when she looks at the other drag queen is filled with equal amounts of intense love and utter devastation. Not knowing what else to say, I stare, I can't help it, Chan's incredibly beautiful.

"Well," Chan says politely. "Be sure to try the punch, but if you want something a little stronger, Ramone and Damien have just opened the bar. Damien makes a hell of a cosmopolitan."

She turns to walk away and Dusty's face morphs into panic.

"Don't let her leave," Dusty says quickly. "She's the other one I needed you to find."

"Chan!" I blurt out, and she stops and turns back toward me questioningly. "That is your name, right? I'm Tristan."

"My stage name is Chan-dee-lerious, but mostly I go by Chan," she says musingly as she studies me. "I saw you at the funeral. You're the odd little duck who talked to himself the whole way though the service."

"Um, nervous habit," I reply with a tight swallow.

"And how did you know Dusty?" Her eyes narrow suspiciously.

"I er... um..." I fumble as my brain draws a blank.

"Tell her the truth," Dusty says, and I jump, not expecting her to be right beside me. Unable to help myself, my gaze flicks briefly to Dusty in alarm. Surely, she can't mean tell her about the whole ghost thing?

"Trust me," Dusty says, her expression serious. "Tell Chan the truth. Tell her I'm here, please."

I mutter under my breath. She's going to get me committed one of these days if I can't find a way to send her into the light. Taking a deep breath, I turn to Chan who's watching me expectantly.

"Um, the thing is..." I begin, trying to figure out how best to phrase my particular brand of crazy. "Dusty, she... well, she never fully checked out. If you know what I mean."

I watch as Chan's perfectly arched brow wrinkles in confusion as Dusty moves to stand beside her.

"What?" Chan murmurs and I sigh.

"She's standing right next to you," I state, bracing myself for her reaction.

Chan blinks slowly. "I'm sorry, say that again?"

"She's... standing right next to you," I repeat hesitantly.

"Who?"

"Dusty," I answer simply.

"Dusty," she repeats slowly.

Dusty quickly limps over to my side on her one remaining shoe and whispers in my ear. My eyes widen, and I pull back casting a horrified glance at her. "I'm not saying that," I hiss quietly.

Instead of slapping me, or yelling at me, or flouncing off in denial, Chan simply stands there, her head tilted slightly as she studies me like I'm a mildly entertaining dinner theatre performance.

"Tell her," Dusty urges me.

"No," I whisper harshly.

"Tell her," she insists.

"Shut up." I pinch the bridge of my nose. "Don't you dare start singing again," I warn, almost forgetting Chan is there. When I risk a look over at her, Chan's eyes have widened and her mouth parts on a slow breath.

"Singing?" she says quietly.

"I didn't even want to come to the funeral," I explain. "But Dusty spent all night standing over me on my bed singing Gloria Gaynor's *I Will Survive* until I gave in."

Chan's eyes widen, and she suddenly laughs loudly. "That's how she got me to go out with my first boyfriend, only in that instance it was CeCe Peniston's, *Finally.*"

"Nineties pop? So, she knows more than seventies disco?" I say sourly. "Good to know."

"Oh, she has an extensive repertoire, be warned." Chan sobers slightly. "What is it she wants you to tell me?" she asks skeptically.

"She wants me to tell you something personal to prove she's real," I sigh. "Something that only you and she would know."

"Okay." Chan watches me curiously as she steps over to the neat row of chairs lined up against the wall and lowers herself elegantly into the one Benny had vacated. She crosses her legs smoothly and pats the seat next to her with long purple coloured nails. "You have my attention."

I sink into the chair next to her and draw in a breath, fighting the blush I know is already staining my cheeks. "You're taking this a lot more calmly than I thought you would."

"I'm Chinese, darling, we believe in the Shen."

"Shen?"

"Benevolent spirits. Traditionally we're taught that its possible to contact the spirits of our deceased relatives and ancestors through a medium. We believe the deceased will help if they are properly respected and rewarded," she explains.

"Okay then, so um..." I blow out a breath, glancing up at Dusty who is hovering over us, her expression a mixture of embarrassment and glee. "Dusty tells me you've been friends since pre-school and that you grew up together, living in houses opposite each other on the same street and went to all the same schools. She said that you both figured out early on that you liked wearing feminine clothes, and as it was just Dusty and her dad in their house, you two would often take things from your mum's and older sister's wardrobes to try on."

Chan sits quietly watching me, her eyes unreadable, so I continue with Dusty chattering in my ear the whole time, filling in specific details, which I dutifully repeat to Chan. "When you both were fifteen, you stole a pair of lace panties each from the lingerie department in Debenhams. You said that there was no way you were trying on your mum's or your sister's knickers."

"Oh my god," Chan chuckles, shaking her head.

"Dusty decided that if you were going to try on lace knickers for the first time that you should try taping too." Chan is already laughing, clearly remembering how this story ends. "You took some duct tape from your dad's shed, but because he was a plumber it was the industrial grade stuff that he used to lag pipework with."

Chan is openly laughing, tears streaming down her cheeks and it's infectious. I can't help the smile breaking across my face as I continue to speak.

"Dusty announced she was going to go first, but she forgot one very specific step... she forgot to shave first. When she tucked and taped herself up for the first time, the tape ended up almost welded to her skin, and in the end, you had to rip it off for her, taking a rather tear inducing amount of hair with it."

"Oh my God." Chan holds her stomach tightly as she

continues to laugh. "I can still remember the look on her face. I'm surprised she didn't lose her foreskin along with her pubes. That stuff was like Gorilla Glue. She made me swear on a spit pact that we'd never tell another living soul."

I look up at Dusty who is smiling down at Chan. After a moment, Chan's laughter dies down, but the tears remain, sliding down her pale porcelain cheeks as I root around in my pocket and hand her a clean tissue.

"Thank you," she whispers as she wipes her tears. "I bet my make-up is toast right now."

"You're still beautiful," Dusty rumbles in her low voice, watching her best friend, and I can hear the painful longing in her voice. I know she wants nothing more than to wrap her arms around Chan and hold her. I can see the bond between them as clearly as if it were made from golden thread.

"Dusty says you're still beautiful," I repeat.

"She's always been biased." Chan swallows convulsively as she fixes me with a penetrating tear-stained gaze. "She really is here? You really can see her?"

I nod.

"Is she...okay?" Chan wipes her nose daintily.

I shift my gaze to Dusty and see her face fold into a frown as she watches Chan.

I shake my head. "No," I tell Chan honestly, despite Dusty glaring in my direction. "She's not alright, she's stuck here. Trapped in some kind of limbo. She can't move beyond the point of her death. She appears to me exactly how she looked the moment she died."

"God." Chan sniffs. "She hated that dress too," she mutters, which earns a small snort of a laugh from Dusty. "Does she remember?"

I shake my head again. "The last thing she remembers is arriving at The Rainbow Room that night, then nothing until she woke up in front of me."

"Why you?" Chan frowns in confusion.

"Because," I tell her reluctantly. "I was the one assigned to perform her post-mortem." I hear Chan's sharp intake of breath, and I continue, "I'm a pathologist. I work at the Hackney Public Mortuary."

"And you're also a medium, you see dead people?" Chan blinks "Like for real? See their spirits, I mean."

"I'm not a medium, actually, this has never happened to me before," I admit. "Dusty's my first."

"That sounds deliciously dirty." Dusty grins at me with a wink. "I totally popped your cherry, boo."

"You did not pop my cherry, Dusty," I whisper as I roll my eyes, and Chan laughs again.

"Tell me what I can do to help." Chan sobers.

"I honestly don't know." I shrug helplessly. "I'm kind of floundering here. I've never had to deal with anything like this before. I'm having to lie to the police inspector about how I know Dusty."

"What? Why?" Chan asks.

"He wanted to know why I was at Dusty's funeral, and so I told him she and I had been friends for a few years, but that I wasn't into the club scene. She and I would meet for coffee. I figured it was the best way to explain my knowledge of Dusty's life but the fact I didn't really know anyone from The Rainbow Room."

"Clever," Chan muses, puckering her lips thoughtfully. "Did he believe you?"

"I'm not sure." I shake my head. "I hate lying to him."

"This police inspector?" Her eyes narrow. "Is he like a sexy blonde version of Constantine?"

"Um, yes, why?" I frown. "How did you know?"

"Because, honey, he's heading this way," she croons. "Oh Mama, he looks like he wants to eat you for breakfast, lunch and dinner."

My head spins around so sharply, I almost give myself whiplash, and when my eyes lock on Danny striding purposefully through the crowd towards us, my heart gives a helpless little shimmy.

"Looks like the feeling's mutual." Chan's mouth curves as she studies me in interest.

"Oh my god, what am I going to say to him?"

"Relax, honey." Chan smiles. "Auntie Chan has got your back."

"You sound like Dusty," I murmur as Danny stops in front of us.

"Inspector—" Chan rises gracefully and holds out her hand, giving Danny no choice but to take it.

"Hayes," he supplies as he shakes her hand. "And you are?"

"Chan," she answers. "I was just catching up with Tristan here, we haven't seen each other in a long time, what with him being so busy at the mortuary. I joined him and Dusty for coffee a time or two. Dusty just adored Tristan, and she talked about him all the time."

"She did?" Danny replies and something in him seems to relax.

I glance at Chan gratefully and then to Dusty who winks at me.

"I was just speaking with your colleague, Ruby, and she tells me you knew Dusty very well."

"We grew up together." Chan nods.

"I was wondering if I could have a moment of your time to ask you some questions," Danny asks. "Obviously, not today, but maybe we could arrange a suitable time?"

"Sure." Chan slides a card from the slashed neckline of her dress and hands it to Danny. "Give me a call, but for now, there are some people I need to say a quick hello to. Why don't you take a seat next to Tristan?"

I watch as Chan wraps those long, elegant talons around Danny's bicep and expertly steers him into the seat beside me.

"Tristan, darling." She air kisses my cheeks as if we're old friends. "We'll talk more soon." She winks and disappears into the crowd.

"How are you doing?" Danny asks as he turns toward me in his seat.

"I'm okay, I guess." I rake my hand through my hair, no doubt making it look even wilder than it did. I wrap my hand around the back of my neck and roll my shoulders. "It's been a stressful week."

"I'll bet." He watches my hand, and I swear I see his fingers twitch, like he wants to reach up and rub my neck for me. I have to admit, I wouldn't put up much of a protest. My muscles feel like knotted steel.

My gaze gravitates over to the massive screen playing clip after clip of Dusty, and I see Dusty watching the reel of herself. The expression on her face, I'm not sure I can put a name to, but it hurts my heart.

"It's not fair," I mutter quietly. "She had such a bright future ahead of her."

"I know." Danny nods, looking up as someone approaches us.

I turn my head and see Benny wandering over with two loaded plates.

"Chan asked me to bring some food over for you both before it's all gone. She said you look like you need something to put in your mouth," he says innocently, and I hear Dusty bark out a laugh nearby.

"Thank you, Benny." I take a plate, and Danny takes the other one with a smile of thanks.

Benny grins again and disappears back into the crowd.

"You know," Danny says ruefully as he lifts a vol-au-vent from the nest of carrot sticks, sausage rolls and tiny triangular ham sandwiches. "When I asked you out to dinner, this wasn't exactly what I had in mind."

I can't help it, I laugh, and he looks up at me and smiles.

"Guess we'll just have to try again," I say shyly, my heart pounding in my chest.

"I guess we will," Danny replies softly.

Stage 4

Depression

12

Tristan

"Dusty." I fold my arms and stare down at her as she lays flat out on her stomach on the sofa, one leg dangling over the side and one hooked over the end. She has one arm skimming the carpet with the other tucked under her head as she ignores me and continues staring at the mindless daytime TV. "It's been three days already, are you going to move at all?"

She gives a non-committed grunt.

"Dusty, seriously, come on." When I say she hasn't moved, I mean she literally hasn't moved. She doesn't need to eat, drink or pee. She just lays there staring at the screen. I know I haven't known her long, but I'm worried. I've never seen her like this. It's as if she's lost all her sparkle. Everything fabulous and totally extra about her, that made her... well... Dusty... is just A.W.O.L.

"Dusty!" I try again, wishing, and not for the first time, that I could touch her, if only to shake some sense into her, or at the very least knock her out of this funk she's settled in.

"Leave me alone," she finally answers.

I reach for the remote and switch the TV off, knowing damn well she can't switch it back on again, but she simply turns her head and stares at the back cushion of the sofa instead. I suppose I shouldn't be surprised that reality has now come crashing in on her. I knew going to her funeral was a bad idea, yet on the other hand, I do think she needed to see Benny and Chan for her own peace of mind. Unfortunately, the fact that her body has now been cremated and her ashes scattered over the same rose bush as her mum is a bitter pill to swallow. She can no longer convince herself she's just trapped in some weird dream. It's all real and she's dead.

"Dusty," I say more softly. "Talk to me, please."

"What is there to say?" she says quietly. "At least you've still got a pulse. I'm stuck looking like an extra from a B rated horror movie. I was offered a Netflix deal!" she bursts out angrily. "I was going to be on Drag Race! I was going to be a star! Now..." Her face falls, and I can feel her deep pain. "Now, I can't even hug my best friend."

"Dusty," I whisper, my heart aching for her, but I have no real comfort to offer. All my words seem so empty, but it doesn't stop me from trying anyway. "I'm going to find a way to help you, I promise. I know it doesn't seem like it now, but you will find your peace, it's just going to take time."

"Time?" she scoffs. "Seems like time's all I've got now."

"That's not true," I tell her fiercely. "You've got me."

She turns her head, and for the first time in days, she really looks at me.

"I have, haven't I?" she murmurs thoughtfully as she rolls onto her back, propping her feet back up on the arm of the sofa, which is way too short for her.

I can't tell what's running through her mind as she reaches up, and her fingertips trail absently over the hollow at the base of her throat. I've noticed her doing that a few times. I open my mouth to ask why when I'm startled from my thoughts by a sudden and loud banging on my front door. Even Dusty lifts her head and frowns.

"Are you expecting someone?" she asks. "Because I'm not in the mood for company."

"Oh, no problem," I say wryly. "I'll just tell them to come back later because my ghost is in a mood."

For the first time in days, I see the corner of her mouth twitch into an almost smile.

"I'd love to see their face if you did that," Dusty muses. "I wish I could move stuff, at least then I could have some fun. Being dead is boring and just plain depressing."

"This is all still new to you," I ponder thoughtfully. "Maybe it's one of those things where you get stronger as time goes on, or maybe it's something you have to learn how to do. I hate to hold up Patrick Swayze as an example but in *Ghost* he had to learn how to move things from that angry ghost on the train."

"AHA!" Dusty exclaims triumphantly. "So, you have watched it."

"What part of me being a gigantic film nerd don't you get?" I smile. "Of course I've watched it. I've also seen *To Wong Foo*, and I have to admit, Patrick looked fabulous in drag."

"I know, right?" Dusty beams. "And Wesley Snipes? Oh my god, it was worth watching it alone to see one of the biggest action heroes of the nineties in a fringed dress. I loved it."

The banging comes again, this time almost laced with an edge of frantic desperation. Giving in, I wander through the apartment and open the door blinking in surprise to find Madam Vivienne, the fake medium from the occult book shop in Whitechapel, standing on my doorstep looking a little wild eyed.

"Madam Vivienne?" I state in alarm. "How?" I poke my head out the door and glance down the stairs to the main front door, which should have been locked.

"Your neighbour let me in." She waves her hand dismissively before I can ask the question.

"Did he?" I reply evenly. "Well, I shall be having words with him about... wait...' The sudden thought occurs to me. 'How did you find out where I live?"

"I tracked you through your credit card payment." She looks around agitatedly.

"I'm pretty sure that's illegal." I frown as she steps past me and hurries into my apartment. "By all means, come on in," I mutter under my breath, closing the door behind her as I follow her into the lounge.

"Oh god, what's she doing here?" Dusty sulks as she stares at the ceiling.

I stop abruptly when I realise Madam Vivienne is standing staring wide eyed at Dusty, and it's clear she can see her. When I take in her appearance, I realise she's not quite as put together as the last time I saw her. Her long flowing dress is rumpled and judging by the label poking out of the neck, inside out. Her hair looks as if it hasn't been brushed in days, and she's wearing odd shoes.

"Can you see her?" I ask my eyes flitting between Madame Vivienne and Dusty.

Madame Vivienne nods mutely, her gaze a little wild.

Dusty's head snaps up in her direction, and her eyes narrow slightly, but she drops her head back on the sofa. "Maybe not such an old fraud then." Her gaze flicks over to Madam Vivienne. "Take a good look, Viv, honey, this is what eternity looks like. Nowhere to go, nothing to do, all your hopes and dreams crumbling away like dead leaves."

"Don't mind Dusty," I tell Madame Vivienne. "Her glass is very much half empty right now."

"The glass isn't just half empty." Dusty stares vacuously at the ceiling. "There is no glass," she says blankly as I turn back to Madame Vivienne.

"She's also clearly having some sort of existential crisis." I wince. "This really isn't a good time."

"No, no." Madame Vivienne turns to me. "You have to help me."

"Me?" My voice comes out as a squeak. "You're the medium here. What happened to all that purveyor of otherworldly whatnot?"

"It wasn't supposed to be real," Madame Vivienne wails.

"Seriously?" I stare at her.

"I read Tarot cards and social cues," she bemoans. "It's all harmless nonsense."

"Didn't look harmless the other day," Dusty snorts. "Looked like you had a roomful of pissed off ghosts. Newsflash, honey, those of us who are corporeally challenged don't like being used to fund your hideous fashion choices." She eyes Vivienne's floaty tie-dye dress critically.

"Please." Vivienne turns to me desperately. "You have to fix this!"

"Fix what exactly?" I frown in confusion. "Because I've got to tell you I don't think anything'll fix Dusty's attitude right now. I'm hoping it's just a phase she'll grow out of."

"Don't count on it," Dusty scoffs as she crosses her arms over her chest.

"I'm not talking about her." Vivienne's expression hardens. "I'm talking about the mess you left in my shop the other day."

"Me?" I say incredulously.

"Yes, you," Vivienne glowers. "I never had any problems until you showed up. Now, it's filled with ghosts that I can see! Not just see but hear. I haven't slept properly in days. The shops a mess, things have been flung everywhere. I can't open, and whether you agree with my methods or not, I still have bills to pay."

"I sympathise," I tell her placatingly. "I do, but that had nothing to do with me. The spirits were already there." I turn toward the petulant queen on the sofa. "Dusty tell her."

"He's right. You already had a major infestation before we showed up." Dusty shrugs. "Who you gonna call?"

"Not helping." I mouth at Dusty before I turn back to Vivienne who seems to be vacillating between hopelessness and anger.

"I don't care where they came from or how they got there," Vivienne snaps. "I just want you to put them back."

"That's a bit like trying to stuff yourself into a pair of size four jeans, not happening, honey. May as well just let it all hang out," Dusty says sagely.

"I just want everything to go back to the way it was." Vivienne ignores Dusty and fixes on me with pleading eyes.

"Back to ripping people off you mean." Dusty huffs under her breath, and I roll my eyes.

"Look, Madame Vivienne," I say carefully. "I really don't know what you want me to do. I have no experience with all of this. I can't even fix my own problems let alone anyone else's."

Dusty starts mumbling quietly, and I strain for a couple of seconds to identify the familiar words. "Are you rapping Jay-z's *99 problems*?" I stare at her dryly.

She shrugs. "I'm bored. Can you put the telly on, *Dickinson's Real Deal* is going to be on soon."

"Oh, Dusty." I shake my head slowly. "How far have you fallen?"

"Don't judge me." Her eyes narrow.

"Can you focus here," Vivienne snaps irritably. "I want to know what to do about my haunted shop?"

"Call an exorcist?" I suggest helpfully.

"Look, can you just come back to the shop," Vivienne says slowly, and I know she's trying to reach for her non-existent patience. "It all started when you were in the shop, so maybe you being there will somehow get them to quieten down."

"I don't know," I say skeptically.

"Please," she asks sincerely. "Just try, that's all I'm asking. I don't know what else to do."

"Argh," I groan loudly. "I can't make any promises."

"That's all I..." Her voice trails off as her gaze snags on a book sitting on the coffee table. She snatches it up and waves it in my face, and I'm just about able to see which one it is.

Crawshanks Guide to the Recently Departed.

"Where did you get this?" she demands.

"Your shop," I reply honestly as I snatch it back out of her hands. I know that technically it came from her shop, and, yes, technically if you want to look at it from a certain point of view it may look like I stole it, but I'm actually quite fond of the quirky and humorous how to guide on spirits, and she's not getting it back I decide with uncharacteristic stubbornness. "Someone or something threw it at my head," I explain, "and I still have the egg sized lump under my hair to prove it. I was unintentionally holding onto it as we were bolting out of your shop and away from the potentially homicidal ghosts."

"You didn't pay for it." Her eyes narrow calculatingly.

"And you charged me fifty quid for a reading I didn't get," I counter.

"Fine," she huffs after a moment. "Keep it. I've got loads of copies of it anyway. He was my great great great some number of greats uncle, and out of a print run of a hundred copies, he sold exactly one. Which you're holding in your hands so feel honoured."

"I paid fifty quid for it," I reply flatly. "I'm feeling more over-charged than honoured."

"Are you ready to go then?" She smiles insincerely.

I let out a loud resigned sigh. "What are the chances of you leaving me alone if I say no?"

"None," Vivienne replies simply.

"Thought so." I roll my eyes. "Come on, Dusty, let's go."

"I'm not coming," she replies.

"Why?" I glance over at her as I drop the book back down on the coffee table.

"Because I don't want to." She stares back at me, and I'm beginning to wish I'd never got out of bed this morning. This is not how I envisaged spending my weekend off.

"Look at it this way, Dusty," I say to her. "That place is chockfull of ghosts, maybe there's one there who can teach you how to move things. After all, they seemed to have a field day flinging the furniture and books around when we were last there."

She seems to ponder this for a moment.

"That's true." She perks up. "Okay, I'll go." She unfolds herself from the sofa and smooths down her dress.

"I'll call an Uber," I say, following the pair of them to the door as I grab my jacket and keys.

"I hope it's not the same one as last time." Dusty wrinkles her nose disdainfully. "His car smelled like a week old kebab."

When we arrive at the bookshop, Vivienne unlocks the door and pokes her head inside, hunkering down as if she expects a book missile to be launched at her head at any given moment.

"Okay," she whispers as she steps through and beckons us to follow.

"Why are we whispering?" I whisper, stepping inside.

"Because it's quiet right now, but it doesn't take much to set them off," she murmurs, closing the door quietly.

I look around the shop and it's a mess. The light fixture is swaying ominously from the ceiling, every single shelf in the shop has been emptied and there are books and pages everywhere. I start to pick my way carefully through the snowdrifts of paperbacks covering the floor.

"You know, boo," Dusty says slyly as she totters along beside me. "We're in Whitechapel."

"I had noticed." I glance at her. "And?"

"And a certain hot policeman lives close by."

I stop and turn to look at her.

"I'm just saying." She raises her hands innocently. "That, theoretically, as we're already here and it's going to be dinner time in a few hours..."

"Jesus, Dusty, make your point, don't beat me to death with it." I sigh.

"I just think you should call him and ask him out," she says with aplomb.

"No," I say firmly.

"What?" She shrugs. "What's wrong with asking the man out for dinner? What's the worst that could happen?"

"Dusty," I warn.

"Aww, come on, call the guy."

"Why do you care?" I ask.

"Because I'm miserable," she replies. "All I have left is living vicariously through you, and I figured at least one of us should get to suck a dick tonight."

"Dusty," I hiss, my cheeks burning as Vivienne pretends not to listen, but it's clear from the disapproval lines around her puckered mouth she heard every word.

I look up at a loud thud, and see a book hit the opposite wall. Suddenly, the old fashioned industrial lighting fixtures hanging from the ceiling start to swing wildly, and a loud moaning begins. One by one, spirits begin appearing throughout the room, all from different time periods, different walks of life, a multitude of ages, genders and ethnicities. Some are talking loudly but quite amicably and some are arguing. A scuffle breaks out between a few of them, books are still being thrown across the room and the noise level is building.

"Oooh." Dusty's mouth curves slowly, and I track her gaze over to see that it's snagged on a tall, dark haired, heavily muscled man wearing a rugby uniform. "I'm going to go and talk to that one," she declares with a smirk.

"What the hell am I supposed to do with this lot?" I mutter to myself as Dusty slips through the crowd toward the shy looking gentle giant.

"You need to be firm with them," a female voice speaks up from close by. I glance down and see an old woman with iron grey hair pulled into a neat bun at the nape of her neck and wearing a 1930's style dress and cardigan. She's sitting quite calmly on the sofa and knitting something large and shapeless.

"Pardon?" I frown.

"They're like unruly children." She nods toward the chaos throughout the shop. "They just need a firm hand is all."

"Why don't you do it?" I ask as I eye two spirits who are now wrestling on the floor.

"Because." Her needles clack soothingly as she smiles up at me with a twinkle in her eye. "That's not what I'm here for, Tristan."

"Tristan?" I jolt in shock. "How do you know my name?"

"Because it's you I'm here to see, dear," she says kindly, like a little sweet grandmother. "Now, send the others on their way, and then we'll talk, but mind they clean up their mess first. This kind of behaviour is not really acceptable, and it gives the rest of us a bad name."

"What exactly do I do?" I stare a little wild eyed at the milkman who seems to be having a heated debate with someone who looks like he belongs in a glam rock band. The next thing I know punches are being thrown.

"Just tell them very firmly that they have to leave," she says. "Be firm."

"Be firm." I nod, muttering to myself, "Okay, I can do this... be firm... be firm."

I release a breath and raise my fingers to my lips, letting out a very protracted and very shrill whistle. Suddenly everyone stops, and every single eye turns to me.

Be firm... be firm... be firm... I chant quietly.

I open my mouth, but to my horror nothing comes out. For what seems like an eternity, they all stand staring at me with slightly bored expressions, and for one ridiculous moment, I'm reminded of being forced to sit on a cold, hard floor during junior school assembly while the head mistress droned on about God knows what.

My thoughts slingshot to my junior school headmistress, Mrs Hall. She was utterly terrifying, like a villainous grown up from a Roald Dahl book. She would wear fiercely starched, pleated kilts and woollen tights, and a thickly knitted round necked jumper with a frilly Peter Pan collar tucked neatly over it all year round, even in thirty degree heat. Her grey streaked ash blonde hair was cut in a no-nonsense bob and sat sharply at her jawline. She would wear it ruthlessly slicked back with a thick plastic Alice band, but the thing you always noticed when she spoke was her sparse wiry chin hair, which was so long she could've probably flossed her teeth with it.

When she said jump you didn't ask how high because you were already dangling from the standard issue light fixtures.

Okay, I mentally crack my knuckles, time to channel my inner Mrs Hall. Holy shit, that's not a phrase I ever thought I'd hear myself say.

"Alright, everyone," I shout loudly, injecting it with every single ounce of school board invested authority I can muster. "Clean up this mess and leave immediately."

They stare at me for a moment.

"Now!" I say firmly, feeling weirdly authoritative.

A low mutter begins to ripple through the assorted mish-mash of spirits, but to my utter amazement, they turn around and start disappearing through walls and doorways. At the same time books, and fixtures and furniture start flying through the air reordering themselves and settling neatly back on the shelves. It was like Mary Poppins had snapped her fingers. I stand staring in amazement until the last person has disappeared and the last book is back in place before I glance down at the old woman who is still knitting serenely on the sofa, humming to herself.

"Very nicely done, dear," she mutters, not looking up. "It was a little bit drill sergeant though, next time you might want to soften the edges a bit."

"Bit too *Full Metal Jacket*?" I muse.

"I have no idea what that is," she tuts. "Now, come sit down, dear. I'd like to speak with you about your friend."

"My friend?" I blink. "Do you mean Dusty? Wait a minute... where is Dusty?"

I turn around scanning the now immaculate room. Vivienne is standing behind the counter with wide eyes as she clutches a mug in one hand and a bottle of Jameson's in the other.

"Dusty?" I call out, "Dusty?"

There's a sudden giggle, and one of the bookcases rocks against the wall. Suddenly, two bodies tumble to the floor in a mad tangle of arms and legs. I look down at Dusty with one eyebrow raised. She's flat out on her back with the handsome dark haired rugby player on top of her, her long legs splayed out either side of him. They both look up at me, and I can see Dusty's lipstick smeared all across his mouth and down his neck, the bright fire engine red colour almost matching his flaming cheeks.

"Uh." Dusty smiles up at me innocently. "So good news... turns out I can touch other ghosts."

"Congratulations," I offer.

The rugby player climbs awkwardly to his feet, reaching down to help Dusty up.

"Thank you, Bruce." She winks at him, blowing him a kiss

as he flushes cutely again and turns to disappear back through the bookcase.

"You look like your mood has improved," I observe.

She grins at me and chuckles as her gaze lands on the old woman. "What's up with Grandma Walton?" she asks as she settles on the arm of the sofa, crossing her legs elegantly.

"Actually." The old woman looks up from her knitting. "My name is Evangeline.... Evangeline Crawshanks."

"Crawshanks?" I repeat in surprise. "Are you related to Cornelius Crawshanks?"

"He was my uncle." Evangeline nods.

"Wait a minute," I say suspiciously. "Were you the one who threw that book at me?" I ask, rubbing the phantom spot on my head where it had made impact.

"I was trying to get your attention before you ran out the door."

"Maybe you should have tried calling my name?" I frown.

"Maybe you should learn to duck." She smiles in amusement.

"Why did you want to speak to me?" I ask in confusion.

"I know what happened to you that night," she tells me seriously. "I know you died."

"Yeah, but not for long," I reply defensively. "They revived me."

"No." She shakes her head as she continues looping her stitches expertly on her needles without even looking. "You weren't brought back, you were sent back."

"What?"

"It wasn't your time, Tristan," she says gently. "But they sent you back with a purpose, with a gift."

"A gift?" I repeat slowly in dread, a nasty realisation trickling down my spine like clammy sweat. "You mean this... this... being able to see dead people isn't temporary? It's not going to go away?"

"Sorry, dear, some gifts are non-refundable," she chuckles.

"But I don't want it." I scowl in annoyance. "Surely there's some fine print or something, can't I just get store credit or a gift card instead."

"Tristan, we don't always get what we want," she says softly as her needles clack together continuously. "But sometimes... just sometimes, we get what we need."

"I don't understand." I frown.

"I know, dear," she coos. "But you will in time. For now, you have to help your friend resolve her unfinished business. She won't be at peace until you do."

"And what unfinished business is that?"

"That's for you to figure out." She smiles.

"And how am I supposed to do that?" I ask incredulously.

"That's what the book is for dear," she says in that annoying calm tone.

"What? Cornelius's book? Wouldn't I be better off with something that was actually written in this century?"

"I thought he was a fake?" Vivienne pipes up from the counter.

"Far from it," Evangeline answers as she looks up and fixes Vivienne with a firm stare. "And don't think we won't be discussing how you've been running my daughter's book shop for the last twenty years, young lady."

"Your daughter?" Vivienne swallows.

"Yes, dear, you're my great great grand-daughter, and after I've sent Tristan and his friend on their way, you and I are going to have a very serious discussion about your future."

Vivienne's eyes widen, and she lifts the bottle of whiskey to her lips and starts to glug the fiery liquid copiously.

Evangeline clucks her tongue in disapproval, and setting her knitting down on her lap, she makes a little sweeping gesture with her hand, and the bottle shoots out of Vivienne's hand and settles across the room on a very high shelf.

"That's really not very lady-like, dear." She shakes her head and lifts her needles, resuming her knitting as if there had been no interruption.

"Oh my god, you have got to teach me how to do that." Dusty stares at Evangeline in awe, and the old lady shoots her a little conspiratorial wink.

"Now, where were we?" Evangeline hums. "Ah, yes, Uncle Cornelius. He had a very hard lot in life and was ridiculed by many of his peers of the time. They were very caught up in their shiny new toy called Science, which didn't leave much room for spiritualism or mediumship. I'm afraid he took it quite hard. His gift was real alright, and he may have been a little eccentric but he knew a thing or two about spirits. Of course, he was also inordinately fond of Absinth and laudanum, but the trick with his book is working out which bits are real and which were..." She hums delicately... "Written under the influence shall we say."

"But why do I need his book?" I ask.

"Because, Tristan, it will help you to learn not only how to help your friend but to navigate your gift." Evangeline smiles serenely as if she hadn't just turned my world upside down.

13

Tristan

I stand on the end of the street looking, I imagine, a little shellshocked.

"Well," Dusty says mildly. "That was interesting."

"I don't suppose you have any idea what your unfinished business might be, do you?" I ask hopefully.

"Trying to get rid of me already?" The corner of her mouth twitches.

"You know what I mean." I blow out a slow breath. "I feel a bit..." I shrug helplessly.

"Don't sweat it, boo." Dusty waves a hand.

"Don't sweat it?" I repeat. "She basically just told me they didn't want me in Heaven or the afterlife or whatever and sent me back with ghost vision to spice up my life a bit."

"No." Dusty grins. "What she said was it wasn't your time, plus ghost vision sounds pretty awesome, kinda like a superpower."

"Really? When was the last time you saw a superhero who looked like me?" I gaze down at my long skinny body.

"I've got two words for you," Dusty says smugly. "Tom Holland."

"Ah," I reply.

"Cute, nerdy, sweet as pie." Dusty ticks an imaginary list off her fingers.

"I really don't think anyone would say I was sweet as pie." I wrinkle my nose.

"I bet Inspector Gorgeous probably would given half the chance." A slow smirk curves her mouth. "Speaking of which, I think you should call him and ask him out to dinner."

"I..." I hesitate my brows folding into a frown.

"What?" Dusty asks. "I don't get why you're so reluctant. Every time you and Inspector Delicious are orbiting each other, us mere mortals almost get incinerated by the heat. It's obvious you want him, so what's the problem?"

"It's not the sex." I frown. "Sex I can do, it's all the other stuff."

"Other stuff?" Dusty blinks. "Do you think he has like a sex dungeon or something?"

"No." I huff out an unintentional laugh. "I mean all the dating, relationship stuff. I'm so bad at it, it's not even funny. Guys start out thinking I'm all cute and adorably awkward, like a puppy at Christmas, then inevitably New Year rolls around and the novelty wears off when they realise I'll crap on the rug and chew the furniture."

"You crap on the rug?" Dusty laughs. "Not on the first date I hope."

"It's a metaphor," I reply deprecatingly.

"Tris, honey, I really think you're overthinking this," she chuckles somewhat sympathetically. "How do you know he's not into your brand of weird? They say there's someone out there for everyone. Maybe you just need to take a chance. I mean what's the worst that can happen?"

"Uh, I could embarrass myself horrifically, and he'll never speak to me again," I answer.

"Or." She huffs in amusement. "You'll fall madly in love, get married and live happily ever after going to police auctions and buying collectable vintage medical murder weapons, or whatever it is pathologists and detectives do in their down time."

"That's disturbingly specific." My eyes narrow.

"Oh, for God's sake will you just call him." Dusty rolls her eyes.

"Fine, fine." I pull out my phone and scroll through to his number, hitting connect. I raise my phone to my ear and feel the blood flood my veins in an adrenalin fuelled rush as I listen to it ring the other end. After what feels like an eternity, I'm about to hang up when it answers, and I hear a familiar voice that makes my gut twitch.

"Tristan?" I can almost hear the pleasure in his voice. "I was just thinking about you."

"You were?" I blurt out.

"You sound surprised," he answers curiously.

"I er... I was..." I clear my throat and start again. "I was just wondering what you're up to. I mean do you have plans?"

"Nope, free as a bird, although I have to admit that even if I did have plans, I'd cancel them for you."

I chuckle softly. "I don't really know what to say to that," I admit.

"What can I do for you, Tristan?"

I almost have to repress the shiver that ripples down my spine. That deep, inviting rasp, the delicious Northern burr, and the way his voice curls around my name intimately takes my mind immediately to a place that involves him naked in my bed wrapped around me until all I can do is think and breath nothing but him.

"Tristan?" He asks after a moment's silence. "Where did you go just then?" He chuckles deeply as if he knows exactly where my mind went.

"I'm in the neighbourhood and wondered... you know, if you like a challenge and your personal liability insurance is all up to date, if you want to try having dinner with me, as in you know... a date."

"Yeah, I got that." He laughs lightly. "Your dating experience has been that eventful, huh?"

"That's one way of putting it." I smile. "I have been known to accidentally almost set my date on fire with the ornamental table candle or get them thrown out of certain venues and once even almost broke one of my date's ankles while attempting to dance... and I use the term dance very loosely. It was more like a cross between the electric slide and an orthopaedic back injury."

I hear his loud belly laugh at the other end of the line, and everything inside me lights up like the Eiffel Tower at night.

"I'll take my chances," he replies with delight radiating from his voice.

"Okay, well, don't say I didn't warn you." My cheeks warm.

"Where are you?" he asks.

"I'm in Whitechapel, at the end of the street from the second-hand occult book shop, where I ran into you last time," I tell him.

"I'll be there to pick you up in ten minutes."

"Okay." I flush again.

"Oh, and Tristan?"

"Yeah?" I reply hesitantly.

"I'm really glad you called," he says softly and hangs up, which is just as well because I have no response to that. There's a helpless knock in my chest, and I idly wonder just how much danger my heart is in.

"There," Dusty says smugly. "You're practically glowing, boo. It's like I've sprinkled you with magic fairy dust."

"I am not." I flush again. Dammit, I hate that my emotions are always written all over my face.

"Well, as Patrick says in *To Wong Foo*, sometimes all it takes is a fairy." She winks as she starts walking back toward the alley that leads to the bookshop.

"Hey!" I frown. "Where are you going?"

"Sorry, honey." She twirls effortlessly, walking backwards as she watches me with a smile. "There's no way I'm riding third wheel, so you're flying solo tonight, boo."

"But where are you going?"

"I'm going to see if I can find Bruce." She winks, turning toward the alley. "Don't crap on his rug!" she throws over her shoulder, laughing loudly as she disappears.

"Very funny," I mutter to myself as I turn back toward the road, breathing slowly to calm the nerves currently tap-dancing an upbeat staccato in my belly.

I try not to pace, instead I lean up against one of the short black metal posts sealing off the back alley from drivers and allowing for pedestrians only. I try for a kind of studied nonchalance, but really, I don't think I'm pulling it off. My palms feel sweaty, and I'm now second guessing whether I should've gone home and changed my clothes for something nicer.

I don't have long to lament my current fashion choices as a familiar Peugeot pulls up to the curb and I head over. Suddenly, I let loose a quiet and nervous giggle because all I can picture is that scene in *Pretty Woman* when Julia Roberts struts up to the car in thigh high boots to the encouragement of Kit De Luca telling her to work it baby, own it...

Jesus, maybe Dusty is right, and I do watch too many movies. I need a new hobby... or a better social life.

Danny's door opens and he unfolds himself from the car, turning toward me with a smile, and I almost have to stop myself from sighing out loud like a lovesick teenager with their first crush. But I can't help it, he is so gorgeous, and Dusty was right, he really does look like Taron Egerton.

"Hello, Tristan," he greets and a shiver runs down my spine at that deep voice.

"Hey," I reply shyly.

I watch as he opens the door for me, his smile relaxed as I slide into the passenger side. My heart's pounding as he rounds the car and climbs in the driver's side, and I wonder if they'll ever be a time when I don't feel this nervous excitement around him.

"Where are we going then?" he asks.

"Do you like Italian?" I reply and he nods. "There's a place about ten minutes from here, that I haven't tried, Tavolino's. It overlooks the Thames just past Tower Bridge and is supposed to have incredible views of the river. I booked a table while I was waiting for you, but if you'd rather go somewhere else?"

He reaches over and stills my hand, which was busy twirling my scarf in knots as I spoke.

"It sounds perfect," he says simply.

"Okay." I release a slow breath, fumbling for my phone and pulling up directions to the restaurant on Google maps.

Danny nods as he pulls the car away from the curb and heads down the road. He makes polite small talk as we head out of Whitechapel toward the Tower of London and over Tower Bridge. When we finally find somewhere to park, we head down on foot to the riverside terrace taking in the sights.

This has always been my stomping ground, and as a London boy born and bred, my dad and I would always spend every weekend exploring little hidden parts of our city either on foot or by tube, and never with any kind of plan, just heading wherever the breeze blew us. I forget that this is all still really new to Danny as he takes in the sights around us.

As we walk companionably side by side, I have this over-whelming desire to slip my fingers in his and hold his hand. I don't know what's up with me because I'm not usually this needy, but there's something about him that just makes me want.

By the time we reach the restaurant and give my name for the reservation, I'm a bundle of nerves. I feel awkward and underdressed. I'm second guessing every single decision I've made since the moment I got up this morning that's led to right now.

We're led to our table, and I can feel the heat of Danny's body close to mine as we weave through the restaurant. His hand on the small of my back guiding me, sends sparks shooting up my spine, and I don't think he's aware he's even doing it. I'm trying really hard not to look at him as every time I do, I have this insane urge to climb the man like a tree, wrapping myself around him like a capuchin and surgically attaching my mouth to his.

We stop at our table, which is small and intimate, with a gorgeous view overlooking the river, although we won't be able to see it much longer as the light is failing, but we'll be able to see Tower Bridge lit up from here, which I hope Danny will enjoy. Maybe the view will detract from my rusty dating skills.

I slide onto the padded seat, unwrapping my scarf from my neck as Danny takes the seat opposite me, but somehow, I manage to overbalance, and in the process of righting myself, I smack my kneecaps on the underside of the table. The table wobbles, and one of the empty wineglasses tumbles into the other, the fragile glass cracking and sending a few errant shards skittering across the pristine white tablecloth.

"Guess you weren't kidding about the liability insurance," Danny chuckles as the server hurries forward and cleans up the damaged glasses.

"Well, that's a new record." My face is burning miserably with embarrassment. "Usually, we're at least ten minutes into the meal before I break anything or injure someone."

"Hey," Danny says softly, reaching across the table for my

hand, and as our skin touches, I feel warmth radiate up my arm.

"Tristan." He smiles genuinely. "It doesn't matter. I like you..." His blue eyes lock on mine filled with sincerity. "Just the way you are."

"Oh my god," I mutter. "It's just like *Bridget Jones's Diary*. All we need now is for you to have a fight in the middle of the restaurant with Hugh Grant."

"Does that make me Arsey Darcy then?" Danny grins.

"You've watched it?" I smile widely.

"Can I tell you a secret?" he whispers with amusement dancing in his eyes, and I nod, unconsciously leaning in, absolutely captivated by him. "I'm a bit of a film nerd," he confesses, and my heart just melts.

"Me too!" I exclaim in surprise.

He breaks our gaze and looks up as the server hands us menus and lists this evening's specials. We order a bottle of wine, and the server disappears giving us time to peruse the menu, but I don't even open it. I'm too fascinated with Danny.

"What sort of films do you like?" I ask eagerly, not often meeting a fellow cinephile.

"Pretty much anything," he replies, thinking about it. "I've watched a lot of the classics, *Citizen Kane*, *Casablanca*, and I don't mind films with subtitles. I still think the Dutch version of *The Girl with the Dragon Tattoo* was the best. I've watched horror but it's not really my genre. I love anything based on a true story."

"Oh my god, me too!" I beam. "Did you see *Woman in Gold*?"

"With Helen Mirren?" he replies. "Of course, it told the story of the seminal case which brought about the beginning of the art restitution laws after the Nazi theft of countless works of art, and of course, Ryan Reynolds." Danny winks. "In one of his rare serious roles is brilliant, plus he's always beautiful to look at."

The more Danny talks, the more I can feel myself melting into a gooey pile of hopeless adoration. I feel like one of the looney tunes characters with hearts shooting out of my eyes right now.

"I love the *Blind Side* too," Danny adds as he picks up his glass of water and sips, and like a crazy stalker, my eyes drift to his throat as he swallows.

"Sandra Bullock so deserved that Oscar." I nod. "I love all her films, except maybe *Hope Floats*, so we won't talk about that one, but *Practical Magic* with Nicole Kidman, and oh, did you see *Miss Congeniality*?"

"Michael Caine was hilarious in that." He grins.

The server returns with the wine and new glasses, and there's a brief break in our conversation as we order. I just pick the first thing I see, not really bothered about the food as I'm so entranced with the beautiful man sitting opposite me. I resist the urge to sigh, trying to rein in the massive crush, which at the moment is expanding like a balloon with every word out of Danny's mouth.

It's so effortless with him, I think in wonder. Not only the fact we have something in common but that he doesn't make me feel somehow less like all of my other dating disasters. They either just rolled their eyes at my general lack of grace and social skills, making me feel as if they were tolerating me in public because they wanted to get me into bed or flat out made fun of me.

Danny's not like that. He's so gorgeous and warm. His smile makes my belly tremble and my heart thud faster. He's so laid back and easy to be with, an unruffled calmness about him. He's perfect and a part of me... clearly the self-sabotaging part, can't help but wonder what he sees in me.

"So, do you watch a lot of TV series too or is it just films?" he asks easily as he picks up the wine and pours me a glass.

"Some." I sip the wine and hum in pleasant surprise as the

notes and flavours roll across my tongue. "Lately, I've been watching more, especially since platforms like Amazon and Netflix have introduced all their original projects. Now that the TV & Film market aren't controlled exclusively by the big studios, there's so much more diversity. I loved Netflix's *Stranger Things* and Amazon's *Good Omens*."

"I haven't seen that yet," Danny muses as he picks up his own glass, sipping slowly.

"Which one?" I tilt my head as I watch him.

"Both." He sets his glass down.

"That is a tragedy of Greek proportions." My eyes widen comically. "That's it, it must be remedied immediately. You should come over to my place, and we'll get snacks and binge watch them."

I realise what I've said even as the words spill from my lips. It's only then I realise that's a really coupley thing to do. Most of my dates have only been interested in getting me back to my place and getting me naked as quickly as possible, and here I am suggesting we practically snuggle under a blanket on my sofa like we're having a teenage sleepover.

"Hey." Danny nudges my foot under the table to draw my thoughts back. "I'd love that."

"Really?" I ask quietly.

"Really, really." He grins.

"That's from *Shrek*." I laugh in delight.

"DreamWorks and Disney aren't just for kids." He winks.

"Dusty always says I'm too obsessed and that I need a new hobby other than Netflix." I roll my eyes, and he pauses, his wine glass lifted halfway to his lips as he studies me consideringly.

"What?" I ask, suddenly feeling self-conscious as he sets his glass down without drinking.

"I was just wondering," he replies slowly. "Do you realise you still refer to Dusty as if she's still here."

"Oh." I inwardly grimace at my mistake. Sometimes I don't stop and filter my words, and I really should. I'm going to have to learn if what Evangeline Crawshanks says is true and I'm stuck being able to see dead people. I'll need to learn to stop referring to them in the present tense, even though to me they still are.

"She must have meant a lot to you," he says softly.

"Yeah." I gulp another mouthful of wine. It's not exactly graceful, but I don't really know what to say to that. "How's the case coming along?"

"We're still pursuing leads." He shrugs. "We've got some video footage we're looking at, but there is a hell of a lot of witness statements to go through. It's slow going at the moment."

I nod slowly.

"Can I ask you something?" He looks thoughtful. "Just one question, and then I promise no more shop talk."

"Okay," I agree a little warily.

"Well, considering how well you knew Dusty." He absently toys with the base of the wine glass, moving it a fraction of an inch across the tablecloth. "We've got her diary that we found in her dressing room."

"Oh?" I reply as nonchalantly as possible as I take another sip of my wine. At this rate, I'm going to be half pissed before the meal arrives.

"Yeah," he exhales thoughtfully. "It seems Dusty had a standing appointment every single Friday at 1pm, every week without fail and the diary entries go back at least six months. I was just wondering if you knew anything about that?"

"No." I frown, wishing Dusty was here so I could ask her. "I'm sorry, I don't. Did the diary entry give any other clue?"

Danny shakes his head. "No, just the letter R and 1pm."

"R?" I glance at him sharply.

"Does that mean anything to you?" he asks.

"At the funeral." My eyes narrow as I cast my mind back. "There was an arrangement of flowers, very expensive and rare, black calla lilies. I remember because they were so striking that they stood out from all the other arrangements and because the card had no message on it, just the letter R."

"Hmmm." Danny scrapes his bottom lip thoughtfully with his thumb nail. "I'll have to contact the crematorium and see if I can find out what happened to all the cards from the flowers. Maybe I can track down which florist the flowers came from."

"Cynthia's Bud & Bloom," I reply.

"What?" He blinks in surprise.

"I recognised the little CBB insignia in the corner of the card," I explain. "There's a specific funeral home the mortuary works with quite closely, and Cynthia does a lot of their flower arrangements, and I know she specialises in rare flowers."

Danny's mouth curve's slowly as he watches me. "Maybe you should've gone into the police force."

"No, thank you." I shake my head with a grin. "I couldn't deal with people all day long, I don't have the temperament for it."

"I appreciate the help," Danny replies. "It may turn out to be nothing, but something about those diary entries is..."

"Is what?" I ask curiously.

"I'm not sure yet." He scratches his chin as he stares at me obviously gauging how much information he should share. Finally, he sighs. "Between you and me?"

"Sure." I nod.

"There was a hotel key card tucked into the pages. It had no identifying marks on it, so we haven't been able to track down which hotel yet."

"You think she was meeting someone in that hotel room... the mysterious R?" I muse. "You think she might've been having an affair?"

"It's possible." Danny shrugs. "She was, by all accounts, single and pretty unapologetic about how she lived her life."

"That's Dusty alright." I frown. "She's not the type to sneak around, wasn't the type..." I correct myself, swearing slightly under my breath, stupid present tense.

"That's my impression of her too," Danny agrees. "So, it would stand to reason that whoever she was meeting might be the one insisting on discretion. We've been going over her bank statements and phone bills. There was one number to a burner phone she called every Friday shortly before 1pm, that same number called her the night she was killed. About two hours before she died, and there's video footage of her taking a call, then leaving the room visibly upset."

"I see." I lick my lip and tug it between my teeth, following Danny's gaze as it locks on my mouth, and I swear I see a flash of heat in his eyes before it's quickly masked. "What about the bank statements, are there any hotel bills?"

"No." Danny drags his gaze away from my mouth, and I do a little internal happy dance, feeling only marginally bad considering we're currently discussing Dusty's murder.

"Dusty never paid for the hotel," Danny tells me as he picks up his glass again. "But there were large deposits made into her bank account each month. We're trying to track down the source at the moment, but they started around six months ago at the same time as the diary entries. According to several of her friends and co-workers, she also regularly received expensive gifts, which were delivered to The Rainbow Room."

"You think she had a sugar daddy." I guess as I study his face.

"It fits." He nods. "Possibly someone older, wealthier, someone who gave her money and expensive gifts that she met up with in private regularly. Someone who valued discretion. Someone I think was very likely either in the closet or..."

"Married?" I finish for him. "Makes sense. You think this 'R' person had something to do with Dusty's death?"

"I don't know." He shakes his head. "Given the video footage that has come into our possession there's a very strong possibility we might be looking for a woman, or rather a drag queen, but there's something about this 'R' that just has my hackles rising."

We both look up, our conversation abruptly broken off as the server approaches, laying our plates carefully on the table and asking us if we need anything else. Once she's gone, I turn my attention back to Danny.

"Anyway." He picks up his fork. "Enough about the case, I've waited for a chance to get to know you properly since the first moment I laid eyes on you."

"Oh." I smile. "Would that be the moment I was choking to death?"

"You certainly know how to get a guy's attention." He grins.

"That's me." I snort. "Shameless."

It's so easy being with him. The food is delicious, the lighting inside the restaurant is soft and romantic, the conversation flows, and I marvel at how effortless it is. His attention is focused solely on me like I'm the only man in the room, and it heats my skin and makes me ache for more, for him.

When we finally look up, it's getting late, our plates are empty, and the table cleared. He hasn't had as much of the wine as I have because he's driving, but I feel warm and relaxed, something I've never felt on a date before.

I wonder, not for the first time, if Dusty is right and there's someone for everyone. If it's just a case of waiting for your person to show up and turn your world upside down, or in my case, turn up and wheel in a corpse that turns your world upside down. Either way, I'm glad Danny came into my life, and now I've had a taste I want more. He's like a tube of Jaffa cakes, you can never have just one.

"Look at that," Danny mutters, gazing out the window.

There's a riverboat heading back down the Thames, obviously one of those dinner and dancing cruises that circulate up and down the river, and it's lit up like a Christmas tree.

"It's pretty," I say as I watch it sail indolently past the window.

"We should do that." Danny turns back toward me. "If you'd like? Do you mind being on the water? Some people don't like it."

"I love being on boats," I tell him enthusiastically. "One day I'd like to take a cruise to see the Fjords and the Northern Lights."

"I'd love to see the Northern lights." Danny sighs as he finishes the last of his coffee and sets the cup aside. "The Borealis have always fascinated me ever since I was a kid."

I watch him, a small smile playing across my lips as I try not to imagine the two of us on a cruise together curled up on the deck beneath the glowing neon lights streaking across the starlit sky and fail spectacularly. I want that, all of it. I want a date on the Thames on a dinner boat, I want to travel to Norway and watch the Aurora Borealis, but more importantly I just want more of Danny, naked preferably, and as soon as possible. I want to run my tongue over every inch of his...

"Tristan?"

"Sorry, what?" I blink, trying to focus when I realise he's just said something.

"I said, would you like anything else?" He smiles in amusement.

Yes, you...naked... on top of me...

"Oh, no," I reply, hoping my face isn't as red as I think it is right now.

"Just the bill, thank you." Danny turns to the server I hadn't even noticed was standing there.

"Would you like to take a walk down by the river?" I ask

needing the cool air before we get back in the car and do something reckless like crawl on top of him and kiss him stupid.

He settles the bill, even though I was technically the one to ask him to dinner and therefore should've paid, but he insists, and I can't say no to him. We head out of the building, stepping out into the night. The river terrace looks so pretty. The city really comes alive at night, and it's a sight I never tire of. Danny takes my hand as easily as if we've been doing this for years, and we stroll slowly alongside the balustrades, watching the light from the street lamps reflecting against the dark, oily waters.

We stop about halfway down as Danny stares up at the brightly lit Tower Bridge in awe.

"Wow." He breathes.

"Yeah." I shiver. "It's a beautiful sight."

He looks down at me as my teeth start to chatter. It's colder than it looks, especially along the river's edge, and I'm still wearing my jacket from earlier on in the day when the temperature was a lot milder.

"Come here," he says softly, drawing me in front of him, so my back is pressed to his chest.

He opens his heavy woollen overcoat and wraps the sides around me, enfolding me in his strong arms like a cocoon. He rests his cheek against my hair, swaying slightly as he holds me.

"Better?" he asks after a moment, realising my body has stopped shivering from being buried in his arms and layers of coat with the heat of his body pressed against my back.

"Yes, thank you," I hum, and I don't think I've ever been as content as I am in that moment, and for the first time in forever, I don't feel so alone.

Danny sighs as seemingly content as I am. Another brightly lit barge trails sluggishly past us on the river, and we continue to watch the bridge.

"This is one of the moments I'd be content to live in forever," Danny mutters against my hair.

"Do you miss Leeds?" I ask curiously.

He thinks about that for a moment. "No," he finally answers. "I guess a part of me misses the familiarity, but there was nothing left there for me, not really. Not even my family in the end."

I feel him tilt his head, and as I look up, I can see the lights of the river reflected back in his eyes.

"I'm really glad I came to London," he mutters. "Because it brought me to you."

I turn slowly in his arms until my chest is pressed against his, he carefully rearranges his coat making sure I'm still wrapped up warmly in his arms as I gaze up at him. I rise up on my toes and press my lips to his. For the barest hint of a second, we both still, relishing the perfect moment that our bodies press together and lips meet. Then he tilts his head, parting his lips as his tongue traces the seam of mine. My heart is pounding so hard that I'm sure he can feel it against his chest as I open my mouth and let him taste me.

A deep groan vibrates up my throat as his tongue slides against mine, and I get my first hit of the wild, addictive taste of him. My arms snake around his waist beneath his coat, pressing us together harder. His tongue plunges into my mouth, eating at me with a single-minded intensity.

Holy hell, the kiss goes from gentle exploration to raging inferno in point zero two seconds, do not pass go, do not collect two hundred pounds, and go straight to jail because this kiss is hot and dirty and should be illegal on several different continents.

Who knew the strait laced police inspector could kiss like a god damn porn star? I think my brain might have short circuited because the next thing I know I'm moaning and grinding my hard dick against his. Feeling a small damp patch in my pants, I've never been so close to the edge so quickly before. If he keeps this up, for the first time in my life, I'm pretty sure I could come from a kiss alone.

For one glorious, wild moment, I'm so tempted to slide my hand down, to cup that hard cock rubbing deliciously against mine. I want to lower his zip and slide my hand inside, wrapping my fingers around the thick hard length of him. Concealed beneath his coat on the almost deserted terrace no one would know what we were doing. I'm so desperate for him that had we been somewhere much more private, I'd already be on my knees for him, swallowing down his cock and tasting his precum on my tongue.

The thought makes me groan and kiss him harder as we rub against each other. I'm about to follow through with my insane plan of jacking him off in the middle of a public tourist trap when a sudden ringing jerks me back to reality. I stagger back gasping for air, and as the lust clouded fog begins to lift from my mind, I realise it's my phone that's ringing.

I take another step back, needing the distance to function properly after he'd taken me apart so thoroughly. I fumble in my pocket for my phone, breathing hard and trying not to stare at his swollen lips.

"Yes," I say breathlessly, closing my eyes as I try to will the thundering of my heart to settle back into its normal steady beat. "This is Tristan, what's wrong? What's happened?"

I listen for a moment as the person on the other end of the line speaks rapidly and my heart begins to sink.

"What's he done now?" I ask quietly, and even I can hear the dejection in my voice. I listen for a few moments while they respond, and I blow out a slow frustrated breath. "Yes, of course, I'll be there as soon as possible."

I hang up the phone and stare at it blankly for a few seconds while my brain tries to realign itself.

"Tristan?" Danny's voice breaks me out of my blank stare, his warm hand resting gently on my arm. "What's wrong?"

"I..." I swallow hard, pulling back again as his hand drops back to his side, and his brow falls into a frown. "I need to go. I'm sorry to rush off like this. I had a really great time, but I need to call for an Uber and..."

"Tristan." He catches hold of me gently again. "Tris, just stop. If there's somewhere you need to be urgently, I'll take you. Just tell me what you need."

I look up at him, into those big blue eyes and feel my heart beat slow. He's so calm and steady, and I wonder for a second if I'm crazy to actually be seriously thinking about sharing this with him. The one part of my life I've kept secret for the last six years from everyone who knows me.

"Tris." He cups my face so tenderly, his thumb brushing my jaw and where his touch had almost incinerated me with its heat only moments before, now there is comfort, a bone deep comfort I don't think I've ever felt before.

"It's my dad," I whisper.

Danny doesn't ask any more questions but simply nods and takes my hand, leading me back toward his car.

14

Danny

I'm worried about Tristan as we get back in the car. He seems so absent. The wild passionate man who had almost scorched me to my core as I'd held him in my arms was gone. Those green eyes, which had burned like a primordial world being formed, where now filled with a kind of hollow resignation, and his plump and delicious lips were now set in a grim determined line.

This isn't my Tristan. I shake my head to clear my thoughts for a second. He isn't my Tristan yet... or maybe he is, because one thing I sure as hell know is that in that moment as he'd kissed me, he'd fucking owned me in a way no one else ever had. The connection between us had blazed white-hot for a blistering second, and I honestly wouldn't be surprised if I were to find the words Property of Tristan Everett branded on my soul.

I jam the keys in the ignition and switch the heating on full blast when he starts shivering again.

"Where are we heading?" I ask.

"Sunrise Care Home in Shadwell," he says quietly, and although I'm surprised at his answer, I don't say anything and simply type it into my phone and let Google maps find the directions.

Clipping my phone to the holder on the dash, I ease out onto the road and head toward Shadwell, which isn't far from Whitechapel. We remain in silence for the drive, and I'm not sure he's going to tell me anything when he suddenly speaks.

"Do you remember me telling you my parents were older when they had me?"

"Yes, I do," I say gently.

"They were a lot older," he says as he stares out the window into the dark streets passing by. "I wasn't just a miracle baby for them. I was a change of life baby for my mum, and my dad was already ten years older than her. But it didn't matter, despite their age they still did all the things with me that younger parents would've, and after Mum died, Dad made sure I never felt ignored or unloved. He was always making up these crazy adventures for us. Every weekend when he wasn't working, we'd set off to somewhere new, never with a plan, we'd just set out and see where we ended up."

"He sounds great," I say, and I mean it, although not having a clear plan and strict itinerary is my idea of hell and leaves my tidy organised soul with the cold sweats, I'd have given anything to have had that kind of attention from my father. Well, any attention to be honest.

"He was," Tristan says so quietly that I almost miss it.

"Was?"

He draws in a slow breath. "He has advanced vascular dementia."

"Tristan, I'm so sorry," I tell him, feeling that the words are too inadequate.

He shrugs. "It is what it is."

"Is this usual? The care home calling you in late at night?" I ask with a frown.

He shrugs again. "It's not the first time, and it won't be the last. Sometimes Dad gets..." He pauses for a moment. "Out of sorts. If they can't settle him, they call me. Although he doesn't recognise me most of the time, I think somewhere deep down part of him still knows I'm familiar to him because I can usually get him to calm down."

"So, you have to travel from Hackney to Shadwell in the middle of the night... alone... without a car?" I sum up, not liking the idea at all. I guess it's the policeman in me. Tristan may think he's safe enough, but I've seen too many bad things for me not to worry.

"He's my dad," he says simply.

"Is anyone helping you with him?"

"Only child, remember?" He sighs. "My parents didn't have any siblings, and my grandparents were long gone before I was even born."

"Tristan," I begin, but he shakes his head, and I know he doesn't want to talk about it anymore.

"You can park around the back," he says as we arrive at the home. "The main entrance will be locked, but they know I'm coming and usually let me in the staff entrance."

I pull into the nearest parking space to the small staff entrance and turn the engine off.

"Thanks," Tristan mutters, not quite meeting my eyes. "And sorry." He opens the door and climbs out.

"Tristan, wait!" I unclip my seat belt and climb out, rounding the car and stepping close to him as he watches me silently.

Now that I'm standing in front of him, I'm not sure what to say or do. I want to hold him, I want to wrap him up in my arms and take away all the pain and frustration I see in his eyes, but I can't. I don't know him well enough yet, and he might not even want that kind of comfort. He might just be wanting me to get the hell out of here and leave him to deal with this in private, but I can't seem to walk away, not yet. Maybe it's just the way

I'm built. I can't turn from anyone in pain without trying to help.

"Look." I scrub my hand through my hair as he watches me with an unreadable expression. "It might not be my place. We're only just starting to scratch the surface of whatever this thing is between us but..." I blow out a breath. "I hate seeing you upset. I want to help if you'll let me. If you don't want to do this alone, I'll come with you, or if you don't want me with you, I can wait out here in the car and make sure you get home safely after."

"You can't wait." Tristan frowns. "I could be hours yet."

"I'll wait," I tell him gently.

I watch as he turns to stare at the door, unconsciously folding his lower lip between his teeth in indecision, and after a moment, he exhales loudly.

"You may as well come with me," he finally says and heads toward the door.

The car locks with a quiet beep and a flash of lights as I follow him. He speaks quietly into the intercom, and I hear a muffled response followed by a loud buzz as the door unlocks.

He doesn't say anything as he holds the door open for me, and I step through into a narrow corridor. It has a decidedly hospital feel to it, with blue sheet vinyl flooring and magnolia walls interspersed with generic art prints.

The door closes behind us with a clang, and I follow along behind Tristan who seems to know where he's going as our shoes squeak loudly against the rubbery floor in the utter stillness of the late hour.

As we come to the end of the corridor, there's a small woman in a carers uniform waiting. She looks to be in her early fifties with short ash brown hair, and a brief glance at her ID clipped to the breast pocket of her white tunic reveals her name is Lois.

"Tristan," she greets him with a sweet hug, rubbing his

arms gently. "I'm so sorry to have to call you, love, but he's been like this for hours and isn't settling. It's getting so late, and he's disturbing the other patients."

"It's okay, Lois." Tristan offers a small smile, but it doesn't quite reach his eyes. "I know the drill."

"And who's this?" She peeks over his shoulder, and her eyes lock on me assessingly.

"This is Danny," he introduces me, and she reaches out to shake my hand. "We were just out having dinner."

"Oh no." She looks chagrined. "We've interrupted your date."

"It's okay." Tristan shakes his head. "We'd finished eating and were just taking a walk along the river."

If she notices the beard burn Tristan's sporting on his chin and jaw from our incendiary level make out session, she's at least polite enough not to mention it.

"Still." She sighs. "We held out as long as we could before calling you."

"It's okay, Lois." He grasps her hand gently, and one thing I'm learning about Tristan is that even when he's hurting, he focuses on those around him and tries to soothe them rather than himself. I wonder just how long it's been since Tristan had anyone to care for him, to put his needs first.

"Where is he?" Tristan asks the petite woman.

"He's in the day room. We can't even get him to move to his bedroom," she says apologetically.

"Okay." He takes a deep breath and shrugs his shoulders, stiffening his back as if he's preparing to go into battle. "Take me to him."

We set off again through the maze of corridors, which are brightly lit, rather generic and devoid of character, and smell faintly of disinfectant. I hear a raised voice and shouting before we've even reached our destination. We come to a huge communal room filled with chairs, sofas, and tables. There are large windows either side of the door, presumably so at any given moment the staff can keep an eye on the residents.

Given the level of noise, it comes as no surprise when I see an older gentleman in his pajamas and slippers hurling cushions and toppling chairs as he paces the room shouting nonsensical words. Standing behind him wearing a carers uniform is a slightly overweight man with a bulging paunch tucked tightly into his belt and a balding head. He stands and watches Tristan's dad calmly with his arms crossed.

"You should probably wait out here," Tristan tells me quietly, giving a quick glance in my direction. "He's pretty agitated and you're a stranger."

I nod as he slips through the door into the room. Lois remains out in the corridor with me as we both watch through the window. Tristan is approaching his dad with his hands raised and palms outstretched in a non-threatening way, and I can't hear what he's saying above the shouting.

"It's such as shame," Lois mutters.

"What's he saying?" I ask, frowning and still trying to make out the words.

"Nobody knows." she shrugs. "Mr Everett has vascular dementia with a secondary language disorder. The damage to his brain has affected his language centres, and he's not really capable of rational speech anymore. He used to be a professor you know."

"Did he?" I muse, staring at Tristan who is slowly approaching his dad, still speaking in low hushed tones.

After a moment, he stops shouting and is just shifting his weight from foot to foot, wringing his hands and looking everywhere but at Tristan who reaches out slowly and takes one of his dad's hands, stroking it soothingly and leading him to the sofa before guiding him down onto it. His dad looks up at him, and I can see from here those same vivid green eyes that his son has. He stares silently as Tristan continues to speak. I hear Lois draw in a sharp breath and see the other carer step closer as Mr Everett raises his hand and strokes the side of Tristan's face as his mouth curves into a smile.

For a second, it seems like Tristan has reached him, and my stomach relaxes for the barest hint of a second until I watch in horror as he pulls his hand back and cracks Tristan so hard across the cheek his head snaps to the side, and Lois winces beside me. I jolt and move toward the door, but she stops me sharply.

"No." She stares at me seriously. "Don't go barreling in there, you'll only make it worse."

"But he hit him," I grind out angrily.

"I know." She raises her hand placatingly. "I know but Charles is in there, and he'll make sure he doesn't seriously hurt Tristan."

I turn back to the window and see that the burly man, named Charles apparently, is leaning over the back of the sofa, bracketing Mr Everett's arms gently but firmly against his sides while Tristan holds his dad's hands tightly in his lap, continuing to speak to him in low tones.

"I know it's hard to see, but it's not unusual," she explains. "They often lash out unexpectedly."

"Has he hit Tristan before?" I ask heatedly.

"Like I said," she replies patiently. "They often lash out, but they don't mean to. They don't understand. Conditions like Mr Everett's often manifest as aggression and inappropriate behaviour. We all end up with bruises more often than not. That's part of the job we do."

"Your job not his," I growl.

"It's true," she concedes.

"Why?" I breath heavily as I turn to Lois. "Why do you keep doing this to him? Why do you keep dragging him in here?"

"Because Mr Everett's dementia has deteriorated to extremely severe. He's almost at the limit of the medications we can give him, and we can't restrain him. Not only would he end up hurting his fragile body but it's cruel, and he doesn't understand. For some reason Tristan is the only one he still responds to... look." She nods toward the window, and I frown in confusion. Tristan's dad is now cuddled into Tristan's side like a kitten, his head leaning on his shoulder, his arm around Tristan's waist as they lean back into the sofa. Tristan is talking softly, and his dad is listening.

"He doesn't know that's his son and can no longer communicate, but I think there's a part of him deep, deep down inside that still recognises Tristan. Maybe it's because of the bond they forged after Tristan's mother passed away," Lois murmurs as she watches them. "It was always just the two of them against the world."

"You speak as if you know them well," I reply.

"I've known Tristan for the past three years, ever since his father was brought to us," Lois explains. "I've gotten to know him pretty well over these late nights. He's the sweetest, most genuine person you'll ever meet." She sighs. "He's shy and doesn't always feel comfortable around people, or even in his own skin for that matter. He's so lonely. I can see it. That boy needs someone to love him. All he has is moments like this, where for a brief second they connect."

"He doesn't have much longer left, does he?" I ask reading between the lines and seeing the sympathy in her eyes.

She shrugs. "With dementia, once it's reached this level of severity, it's difficult to gauge. He could have a month, he could have six... he could slip away in his sleep tonight. There's no way to tell, but what I do know is that Tristan and his dad are on borrowed time. You think we're passing the buck and making him do our job for us but that's just not true. What we're doing is giving them moments like this because in the end that's all Tristan will have."

I turn back to watch Tristan, and my heart aches when I watch how tenderly he cradles his father, even with a painful red welt on his cheek where he's been hit. He just keeps talking endlessly in a soft, warm soothing voice. After a few more minutes, his dad yawns loudly, and Tristan glances over to Charles who nods in return. Together they carefully move, pulling Mr Everett up so he's standing. Tristan, still speaking, wraps his arm around his dad, guiding his shuffling steps. They exit the day room and turn down the corridor. Tristan, once again knowing where they are going, continues to speak, and as Lois and I trail along in their wake, I listen to Tristan's smooth voice.

"This is the land of Narnia," said the Faun, "where we are now; all that lies between the lamp-post and the castle of Cair Paravel on the Eastern Sea. And you - you have come from the wild woods of the west?"

As I listen in fascination, I realise he's not just talking about random things to fill the silence, he's reciting a story from memory. *The Lion, the Witch, and the Wardrobe* unless I'm mistaken.

I'm so caught up in the story that I almost stumble when Tristan stops and opens a door, leading his dad inside. I peer in but don't cross the threshold. It's a bedroom, simply decorated with a bed, a chest of drawers, a wardrobe and a deeply cushioned chair. The walls are filled with framed pictures and photos of Tristan, his dad and a woman who is presumably his mother. I'm itching to step inside and take a closer look, but it feels too rude and intrusive. Instead, I step back and watch as Lois switches on the beside lamp, filling the room with soft light.

Pulling the covers back, Tristan lowers his father to the bed, kneeling down and removing his slippers and carefully tucking them underneath. He settles his dad gently into bed, smoothing the covers over him and brushing his hair back from his forehead tenderly as if he were a child. Mr Everett's eyes are already closed, and his breathing has evened out. I can't help the clenching of my stomach as I watch Tristan lean forward and kiss his dad's forehead gently.

"Goodnight Dad," he whispers. "Love you lots like jelly tots."

He steps out of the room, looking up at me for the first time since we arrived. Unable to help myself, I move closer until our bodies are almost touching, like he's my own personal centre of gravity. I place my fingertips under his chin, gently tilting his face to examine at the sharp red handprint.

"Here," a voice speaks up behind me, and as I turn, I see Charles holding out an ice pack.

"Thanks." I nod taking it and pressing it gently to the swelling at the side of Tristan's face, and he doesn't even wince.

"He didn't mean to," Tristan whispers with a frown.

I tilt his chin again until he meets my eyes, holding the ice against his face gently. "I know," I murmur.

I lean in and brush my lips across his as light as a fairy wing. It's brief and has none of the earlier heat, instead it's meant to comfort without words because I know from the look in his eyes, he's too emotionally wrung out to talk.

Lois steps out of Mr Everett's room, clicking the door shut behind her and stroking Tristan's shoulder comfortingly. "Go on home and get some rest, love."

He nods, placing his hand over the ice pack at his cheek, and I release my grip on it, taking his hand instead. With a brief and subdued farewell, we leave the home, neither of us speaking as we head out into the car park, and I settle Tristan into the car. By the time I'm pulling out onto the almost silent road and heading back toward Hackney, Tristan is leaning against the window staring out at the passing streetlights as he presses the ice pack to his pale face.

"Do you always read him *The Lion, the Witch and the Wardrobe*?" I ask, finally breaking the silence.

"It's one of our favourites," he murmurs, lost in thought. "After Mum died, I was too scared to sleep," he continues to speak softly. "I was convinced Dad was going to die too, that I was going to wake up and find him like I found Mum."

"Jesus, Tris." I breathe heavily. He hadn't told me he'd been the one to find her.

"My dad built a fort on the floor of my bedroom made with sheets, blankets, duvets and every pillow we had in the house," he tells me as he continues to watch the streets passing by in a shadowy blur. "He set up a nightlight inside. It was one of the ones with shapes cut out that spun around like a carousel, casting shadows of stars and moons and constellations up onto the tented sheets above us. We slept in there every night for six months, and every night he'd read me stories, but the Narnia ones were my favourites; *The Magician's Nephew*, *Prince Caspian*, and *Voyage of the Dawntreader*, that one was my favourite. We read them so many times, I know every single one word for word. He seems to respond best when I recite them for him. It calms him down, and for a brief second, I hope he remembers."

"Tristan," I whisper, overwhelmed by this sweet and complex man beside me.

"Turn left here. Just at the end of the street, this is me," he instructs.

I pull up to the curb and park, looking up at the narrow Victorian terrace with the green front door.

I climb out of the car as Tristan steps up onto the pavement next to me. For a moment, we stand on the silent street watching each other as he toys with the melting ice pack uncomfortably.

"Danny, I..." He breaks off and frowns as he looks behind

me. I turn in time to see a net curtain in the downstairs bay window twitch abruptly.

Tristan sighs loudly. "You may as well come upstairs. I don't really want to have this conversation with an audience," he says, eyeing his nosy neighbours window in tired frustration.

He steps up to the front door and unlocks it quickly. We head up a steep, narrow staircase that creaks alarmingly beneath my feet, which is not surprising with a house that's well over a hundred and fifty years old. Now that we're inside, I can see that, like most of its counterparts, this old terrace has been converted into two flats, one up one down. I'm guessing Tristan's is upstairs as we reach the top landing, and he unlocks his door.

He flicks on the lights and tosses his keys down on the table where there is a large bowl of odds and ends. The keys, however, miss the bowl entirely and slide across the table, dropping to the floor with a loud clatter. It's followed by a meow, and a large grey tortoise shell cat hops down and starts rubbing against my legs, purring loudly. I reach down and pet him or her, I'm not sure which, but my gaze remains firmly fixed on Tristan who's removed his coat and scarf and tossed them haphazardly onto the back of a chair.

"Danny." He breathes deeply. "I really enjoyed our date earlier tonight, but I don't think it's a good idea to be starting something between us right now."

"And why is that?" I ask, although I'm pretty sure I can guess the answer.

"I let you come with me tonight because you needed to see," he replies with a troubled scowl.

"To see what exactly?" I say calmly.

"To see what my life is, to see what you're getting yourself into. It's obvious I'm attracted to you, and I think we can both agree we've got unbelievable chemistry, and for a while I thought maybe this time... things could be different... that I could be different." He shakes his head. "But the truth is my whole life is surrounded by death and sadness. I spend my days with the dead and my nights hauling myself out of bed and dragging myself across London to deal with my dad who's often violent and doesn't even know who I am most of the time. You can't have a normal life with me."

"What's so great about normal?" I ask.

"Danny." He sighs. "You don't want me and all the hang ups and baggage I come with."

"I told you before, Tris," I reply earnestly. "I like you just the way you are, and what the hell is normal anyway? Because if you're talking complicated and filled with obligation, you can file my life into that category right alongside yours. I can't guarantee I'm not going to get called out in the middle of the night on a case or put in a dangerous situation that I might not come back from. Life with a Scotland Yard detective isn't for everyone. There are times when I'm hurting from the things I've seen or the people I've failed, or I'm frustrated or struggling with a system that's over stretched and undermanned and bound by so much red tape you could hold a parade."

Tristan's brow folds.

"My point is," I continue. "Life isn't normal... it isn't perfect. It's messy and painful and why we take joy where we can find it, even if it's only in small snatches. I know we haven't known each other long, but I really think we've got a chance at something good between us, something that makes the bad a little easier to bear."

"Sometimes," Tristan whispers so quietly I almost miss it. "I wish my dad had died. I wish he'd just slipped away peacefully like Mum did. The man I knew, the dad I loved more than anything is gone. He's not even a shadow of the man he used to be, at least then there would be something I'd recognise, something I could hold onto. Now, he's a completely different person. He lives in the prison of what's left of his brilliant mind, angry and confused, and he hurts me." His voice breaks on the last word, and my gut clenches. "But he's still my dad. What sort of person wishes their dad was dead? It makes me a horrible person."

"No," I tell him softly. "It makes you human."

"I..." His voice cracks, and I can see the wet sheen of unshed tears glazing those beautiful green eyes of his, and I take a step toward him. "Don't," he breathes out sharply.

I can't help it, and it's killing me to see him hurting and not offer the comfort he so desperately needs but keeps denying himself.

"Don't," he whispers again brokenly as the first tear slides down his cheek, but as I reach for him, wrapping his trembling body tightly in my arms, his arms snake around my waist, his hand grasping onto my coat desperately, and as he buries his face in my chest, the first sob breaks loose.

It absolutely destroys me to hear him cry, deep wracking sobs that he's held in for far too long. All the pain and hurt and loneliness is painful to hear, and all I can do is hold him tighter to keep the pieces of him from flying apart. I rock him gently in my arms, crooning softly in his ear, nonsense words, soothing and comforting as I stroke his hair and kiss his temple.

Finally, exhaustion wins out, and he quiets, slumping against me bonelessly. He feels so tiny right now, so fragile even though I know he's anything but. I'm in awe of his strength and resilience, but right now, he needs to be the one being cared for. I bend and lift him into my arms. He doesn't even fight me, he just holds on, burying his hot tear-stained face in my neck.

The flat is so small that it's doesn't take a map to locate his bedroom. I carry him inside, setting him down on the edge of the bed as I bend to remove his boots. Urging him to his feet, I strip off his jeans and turn down the bedding as he climbs in.

"Danny." His voice is a hoarse whisper as he reaches out and grabs my arm. "Stay, please."

Nodding silently, I kick off my shoes and remove my coat, climbing into the bed behind him and drawing him into my body so he's spooning against my chest. I wrap my arms around him, and holding on tightly, we both descend into a deep, contented sleep.

15

Tristan

I wake to find the bed empty. For a moment, I wonder if I imagined last night, but as I roll onto my side and press my cheek into the pillow it smarts. Blowing out a resigned breath, I push the covers off me and climb out of my warm cocoon, fumbling for my glasses on the bedside table. Pushing my unruly mop of hair from my eyes, I pad out into the kitchen, pausing briefly to check my reflection in the mirror. The swelling on my cheek has gone down and leaving just a faint smudge of a bruise, which isn't too bad, hardly even noticeable.

My stomach growls loudly, and my head's pounding from crying last night. I reach up into the kitchen cupboard for the paracetamol and grab a glass of water. I still can't believe I broke down like that in front of Danny. We'd had the most wonderful date, in fact the best date of my whole life. Granted, the bar wasn't set very high, but we'd talked, we'd laughed and discovered we have a lot in common starting with our shared and obsessive love of movies.

Even our personalities shouldn't mesh as well as they do. I'm inherently messy and chaotic, and my anxiety often causes me to second guess everything, not to mention my deeply ingrained penchant toward being unsociable, whereas Danny is neat and orderly, methodical, and open and friendly to everyone. We're a paradox and shouldn't work but somehow, we do.

Being with him is so easy, and I don't find myself fidgeting or watching the clock, or constantly having to think about the words coming out of my mouth. I'd relaxed, without even realising it. It had been perfect, and the moment he'd wrapped me up in his coat against the cold wind, holding me close to his body, as we'd watched the lazy slide of the river and the bright lights of Tower Bridge had been one of the most perfect moments of my life.

Then there was the kiss... holy moly mother of God, that kiss. I swear I can still feel a phantom tingling in my lips even now. I keep wondering what would have happened if we hadn't been interrupted by that phone call... but we had.

Now, Danny's had an up close and personal front row seat to the one part of my life I don't share with anyone. He'd been so understanding even when I'd tried to tell him I thought we should take a step back.

I like him, like really like him, so much that I'd started to fantasise about what a real relationship with him would look like. Intimate dinners, long walks holding hands, going to the movies and having someone to dissect the plot lines with. Long cozy evenings snuggled on the sofa with a glass of wine, but more than that, someone to talk to, someone to ask how my day was, someone to share funny and embarrassing stories about work with. As soon as I'd pictured it, I wanted it. Wanted it more than I've ever wanted anything in my life, and for two glorious seconds, I'd let myself believe.

Then reality came crashing in and with it the realisation that I can't drag him into my life and the mess it currently is. My dad, my job, Dusty... Christ, Dusty, how am I supposed to explain I'm suddenly Haley Joel Osment and I see dead people? That's just asking for an extended stay at a mental health facility. Worse still, what if I don't tell him the truth? How the hell am I supposed to hide it from him? People are already starting to think I'm weird... okay, well, weirder than usual. Whenever I'm talking to Dusty, they just assume I'm talking to myself.

I blow out a frustrated breath. I'm so bloody confused. I want Danny, it's that simple. I've never wanted anything before that was just mine, but I'm scared it's going to go wrong, and I'll end up alone again. That's if he even still wants to date me after arriving back here last night and me telling him we shouldn't be together, crying my eyes out all over him, then practically begging him to stay the night. Poor guy probably snuck out as soon as I passed out and eased up my death grip on him. Talk about mixed messages. I wonder if I'll even hear from him again.

I set the empty glass in the sink and turn around, leaning against the kitchen counter when my gaze falls on a tall take out coffee cup and a paper bag. I cross the kitchen and see the words DRINK ME on the side of the coffee cup, and likewise I find EAT ME stencilled on the paper bag with a black marker. I pick up the cup and flip off the lid. It's cold but it's a flat white, and my usual morning coffee order. Smiling to myself, I stick it in the microwave to re-heat and take a peek in the bag to find a light, fluffy pastry. There's also a folded note beneath it.

Sorry I didn't wake you before I left, but you looked so cute snoring, and I figured you could use the sleep after last night. I've been called into the station for a few hours, but I'm hoping you'll want to see me later. Danny x

I can feel the slow smile creeping across my face even as my belly warms. I read the note through several times even after the microwave has dinged to let me know my coffee is now once again piping hot and ready to take some layers of skin off the roof of my mouth.

"You look like you had an interesting night," a familiar voice rumbles across the other side of the kitchen.

Dusty is leaning up against the doorway, smirking as she takes in my smile, the fact that I'm wandering around in nothing but my boxers, the same t-shirt and sweater I was wearing last night and a pair of mismatched socks.

I turn toward her, and as she gets a good look, her smile drops. She strides across the kitchen... okay, wobbles across the kitchen, and I decide we really need to do something about the one shoe issue.

"What the hell happened?" she growls indignantly. 'Who hurt you? Was it him? Did he hit you? Because I don't care if he's a cop or not, I swear I'll go full on the Conjuring all over his arse."

"Dusty." I smile softly, ridiculously touched at her concern for me. "It wasn't Danny, he wouldn't hurt me." And even as I say the words, I know absolutely that they're true.

"What happened, boo?" she demands. "Tell me who it was."

I let out a resigned breath because there really is no way around this and given that she's around me ninety nine percent of the time until I've solved her unfinished business and helped her move on, she's bound to find out about my dad anyway.

"Tristan?"

"It was my dad," I confess slowly, and her eyes widen momentarily then soften in sympathy all the while still holding a hint of anger. "He didn't mean to."

"Honey, that's what they all say," she replies bitterly.

"Well, in this instance it's true," I defend him. "He has dementia and is in a home. Sometimes he lashes out at whoever happens to be near him. It wasn't even aimed at me personally, and he doesn't realise he's doing it."

"I'm sorry, boo," she says after a moment, hopping up on the kitchen table in front of me and crossing her legs as she leans back on her hands, her body naturally adopting the most appealing pose. I don't even think she's aware she's doing it, it's just an innate part of who she is. "What happened?" she asks.

"I went out to dinner with Danny." I move across the kitchen and grab my coffee from the microwave, peeling off the lid and blowing on it.

"And?" she asks impatiently.

"And." I sag against the counter as I pick up the pastry and take a big bite. "We had an incredible time and an even more incredible kiss."

"Awww," Dusty croons as she flutters her heavy lashes. "My little Tristan's growing up so fast."

"Shut up." I laugh as I ball up the pastry bag and throw it at her. It passes straight through her and bounces uselessly off the wall.

"What happened next?"

"We'd gone for a walk along the river and were pretty much making out." I pick up the coffee and take an experimental sip.

"Omg, in public!" she gasps in mock horror.

"I know, right?" Usually, I'd never kiss a guy in such a public place, that's just asking for trouble. People don't tend to appreciate guys kissing in front of them. I shake my head as I think back to that kiss. "I think I may have just lost my mind for a moment, either that or he just kissed all the common sense straight out of me. I've never been kissed like that before. I couldn't think about anything but him, and all I wanted was my mouth on his, nothing else mattered."

"Hmmm," Dusty hums in pleasure. "Boo, those are the best kind of kisses. I told you you're a lucky boy. Inspector Hot Lips is just yummy."

"Anyway, we got interrupted when the care home my dad lives in called. He was getting agitated, and they couldn't calm him down. So, I had to head over there and deal with it. In the process of settling him down, I got hit. It looks worse than it actually is, but Danny brought me home."

"Wait, he stayed with you?" Dusty clarifies. "He didn't just drop you off?"

I shake my head. "He stayed with me," I murmur. "He brought me home after, and I don't know but something inside me just snapped. I can't remember the last time I cried like that. The poor guy had me wailing hysterically all over him, but he just held on..." I look over at her. "He held me, Dusty, all night. Just tucked me into bed and spooned me until I fell asleep."

"Well," Dusty says after a minute. "I hate to scare you, boo, but I think you may have found a keeper."

"Do you think so?" I ask carefully, hating the raw vulnerability thudding in my chest.

"What do you think, boo?" she asks gently.

"I don't know." I chew my lip. "I think it could all too easily slip into... something."

"I'm glad, Tristan," she says genuinely. "You deserve someone special."

I flush in embarrassment, not liking the focus on me. "What about you? Did you go and find Bruce?"

"Sure did." She winks. "And you would not believe what that man is packing in those tiny shorts. Seriously, it must be like the Tardis in there."

"Really?" I blink. "I mean, not about the size..." Flushing in embarrassment, I start again. "I know you said you can touch each other, but can you actually feel... you know."

"Honey, all I can tell you is that his impressive equipment works the same as it did when he was alive if you know what I mean." She wiggles her eyebrows. "Made my jaw ache."

"Oh, um." I'm betting that my face is burning so red it resembles a gas giant right about now.

"TMI?" She snorts.

"A little bit." I laugh helplessly. "But that's good right? I mean it won't get so lonely if you can actually physically interact with other spirits."

"I suppose." Dusty sighs. "Maybe, eventually."

"What do you mean?" I frown in confusion.

"His body may work the same as when it was alive but mine doesn't." She waves a hand up and down herself. "I'm still trapped looking exactly as I did at the point of death. I can't change anything."

"But he can?" I scratch my jaw thoughtfully. "How does that even work?"

"I don't know." Dusty shrugs. "Evangeline, the old lady ghost in the shop, well, she was trying to explain it to me, but it all sounded so complicated. To be fair, I kept getting distracted by Bruce's arse in those really tight shorts. I mean have you seen the size of his thighs?"

"Dusty, focus." I sigh. "What did Evangeline say?"

"I don't know, just that I was caught in some kind of death cycle or feedback loop or something. Basically, I was killed before my time. Apparently, we're all born with an invisible expiry date, and our job during our lifetime is to get from A to B. If we die before our contract is up it creates a...a... crap, I really don't know. You'd be better off speaking to her. All I know is I'm in limbo, and until my death is resolved, I'm stuck like this."

"Kind of like you're buffering," I muse. "Like your internet connection's cut out and you're just stuck with that little circle icon that just goes round and round."

"Fuck, I don't know." Dusty frowns. "The only thing I know how to do on a laptop is look up porn and shop."

"Does she think solving your murder will snap you out of it and allow you to move on?" I ask.

"I guess." Dusty shrugs. "I mean, she just kept using the phrase unfinished business, and what's more unfinished than not finding out who killed me and why?"

"Maybe there's something in the book." I go back to chewing my lip thoughtfully.

"Which book?" Dusty frowns in confusion.

"The Crawshanks one, the guide to the spirits," I clarify.

"Great," she mutters sourly. "So, my future ability to orgasm is going to be dictated by a hundred year old drug addict's book of stoned out nonsense."

"We might as well just have a look." I go in search of the book, picking it up off the coffee table. "There might be something in here that can help."

"It's next to useless." Dusty flings herself down dramatically on the sofa. "You heard what Evangeline said, he was off his face half the time. It's going to be practically impossible to figure out what information is real and what's not."

"It's worth a try." I open the book and start scanning through the pages.

"Hey!" Dusty perks up as if a sudden thought has occurred to her. "Do you want to see what Bruce showed me?"

"I don't know," I reply suspiciously. "Do I?"

"Get your mind out of the gutter." She laughs as she sits up and leans over the coffee table.

I watch as she draws in a breath, cracking her knuckles loudly and wiggling her fingers before leaning forward and poking at the stack of paperback novels on the table. Her finger passes straight through.

"I don't think I want to know where he's been teaching you to poke your finger," I mutter.

"Shush." She scowls. "I'm trying to concentrate."

"On what?" My brows raise questioningly. "How to become the undead world Jenga champion?"

"I'm not undead," she mutters, staring at the small tower of books like it's a personal insult as her finger passes through once more. "I'm all the way dead."

"Uh-huh." My eyes narrow as on the fifth try the book stack falls and scatters across the table and topples over the edge. "Did you just..."

"Yep." She beams. "Moved it myself."

"Oh, Jesus." I close my eyes briefly. "You can move stuff now?"

"Not all the time." She shakes her head. "Like you saw, it takes practise and concentration, but Bruce says that with time I'll get stronger and should be able to move things more easily."

"So, you can interact with and change your environment, you just can't alter anything about yourself?" I muse as I look back down at the book in my hands and flip through the pages. "This is ridiculous," I huff after a moment. "It's the equivalent of trying to build Ikea furniture using Chinese instructions. Why couldn't we be given a proper instruction manual?"

"Don't ask me." Dusty shrugs.

"Listen to this." I lift up the book. "Thrice is the number three, and three is thrice, thrice the triad is a triangle and its sides number three..."

"Wow," Dusty says impassively. "His elevator really didn't go all the way to the top, did it?"

"There's more." I laugh and continue to read. "And it's sides number three, if three is to tri and tri is a triangle, which is half of a star, and a star has three primary points."

"He really likes the number three," Dusty says wryly.

"It sounds like he's hitting the Laudanum pretty hard at this point. That stuff was pure opium and alcohol, and I reckon he's pretty smashed by now. Listen..." I clear my throat and continue, "Has three primary points. Of speaking in the metaphysical, three is of paramount import, for the spiritual realms number three. Purgatory, Limbo and Heaven. Three is a spiritual number, therefore when in the presence of a spirit shall it knock three times."

"What?" Dusty frowns. "You lost me at purgatory."

"Basically, he's saying if there's a spirit around, they'll knock three times," I sum up.

"What a load of bullshi..."

Her voice is suddenly drowned out by three loud knocks,

and she shoots up from the sofa. "What was that?" she asks, eyes wide.

"I think it came from the front door," I reply, my voice barely above a whisper as we both slowly turn toward the door.

"Are you expecting anyone?" Dusty whispers.

"No, and why are you whispering?" I whisper back. "Are you expecting anyone?"

"Because you're whispering." She shakes her head. "And don't be ridiculous, why would I be expecting anyone?"

"I don't know, maybe you gave Bruce the address?" I whisper.

"Bruce doesn't leave the bookshop," she mutters, still staring at the door as if it was an electric fence and there was a T-Rex on the other side.

"Why?"

"Something about a portal." She shakes her head.

"Seriously?" I blink, turning my head to look at her. "What like a magic portal?"

"I don't know," she hisses. "I had his dick in my mouth at the time."

The three knocks pound against the door again, and we both jump.

"You should get that."

"Me?" I squeak. "Why me?"

"Because it's your flat," she snaps. "And I'm dead."

"Exactly." I stare at her. "You can't exactly get any deader, so can't you beam to the other side of the door or something?"

"This isn't bloody *Star Trek*," Dusty hisses.

"Urgh, okay, fine." I suck in a sharp breath and edge toward the door, clutching Crawshanks Guide to my chest like the world's most useless shield.

I'm almost to the door when the banging comes again, this time followed by a familiar voice, and I instantly relax, blowing out a combination of relief and laughter.

"Hey Tristan, your downstairs neighbour let me in," the muffled voice explains.

"I really am going to have to have words with him about letting random people in," I grumble as I yank the door open.

"I'm random people, am I?" Chan pouts prettily.

"I'm sorry, I didn't mean you, Chan," I apologise, staring at Dusty's best friend. She looks as stunningly immaculate as she did the last time. "Please, come in." I step back, glancing at Dusty who's laughing over our paranoid stupidity.

"Happy Halloween, Tristan, darling." Chan air kisses my cheeks as she saunters confidently into the apartment.

"Oh." I blink. "It is Halloween, isn't it?" My brain hasn't currently processed beyond it's Sunday.

"What happened to your face, honey?" she asks in concern, and she lifts one gloved hand to my jaw and tilts my head slightly to study my bruised cheek.

"Long story." I shake my head.

"But you're okay?" she enquires genuinely.

"I'm okay." I smile, touched by her worry for me. It's really very strange going from being on my own ninety percent of the time to suddenly being surrounded by people who are sincerely interested in me and my well-being. "What can I do for you, Chan?"

"I have something to show you." She pulls her phone from her pocket. "Ruby managed to lift this from Ari's computer. I know for a fact he's already passed it to the police, but I want you to see this."

I lean in curiously as she brings up video footage of a blonde drag queen in some sort of corridor.

"I don't know what I'm looking at, Chan." I frown. "Who is she? And where was this taken?"

"I don't know who she is." Chan shakes her head. "She's not one of us, and this is the backstage corridor at The Rainbow

Room and leads directly to Dusty's dressing room. It was taken about twenty minutes before Dusty's murder."

I hear a sharp breath behind me, then feel Dusty's presence as she leans over my shoulder to stare at the screen.

"Chan's right, she's not one of ours." Dusty stares at the screen studying the person who may have been responsible for her death. "I don't know who she is." Dusty glowers. "But there's something familiar about her."

"Dusty says she doesn't know who it is either." I dutifully repeat the information to Chan.

"Dusty's here now?" She looks across to me and I nod.

"She says that she looks familiar though," I add.

"I think there's a very good chance she killed Dusty," Chan says, her eyes turning flinty. "And I can prove it."

"How?"

She flips to another video file and hits play. It's time stamped thirty minutes later and shows the same drag queen, only this time exiting the corridor. At the last moment, she turns back to look behind her almost as if she'd heard something.

"This is hardly proof. It's circumstantial at best," I counter.

"Look closer." Chan flips back to the first video. "In this one, she's not wearing a necklace." She flips to the second video and replays it. "In this one, she is."

"So she picked up a necklace." I shrug. "That's not enough to convict someone of murder."

"The thing is." Chan breathes quietly. "That's Dusty's locket, and I know for a fact she was wearing it an hour before she died. She always wore it; she never took it off because it was her mum's."

"Are you sure?" I ask, looking up at Dusty whose hand has once again moved to her neck and is unconsciously stroking the bare skin at her collar bone.

I'd noticed her doing the same thing on several occasions.

I'd just thought it an unconscious habit, but she was doing it because she was no longer wearing her locket. Which meant if she's trapped looking exactly the way she did at the moment of death, she couldn't have been wearing the locket when her heart stopped.

"The post-mortem," I whisper in realisation.

"What about it?" Chan asks.

"When I carried out Dusty's post-mortem, I noted a very fine ligature mark at the back of her neck. It was very thin, almost like a friction burn, and only marked the back of her neck and not the front, which ruled out any suspicion of strangulation, but also because the mark was too thin and shallow to have caused any real harm. It's only now I realise that it's consistent with a thin chain being ripped from her neck. The killer probably tore the chain from her neck in the struggle moments before she died."

"Dusty." Chan closes her eyes, pressing her hand to her sternum as if to ease the pain.

I stare down at the still image of the person who probably murdered Dusty, and I'm filled with anger at the life she cut short. Dusty didn't deserve that, and the unfairness of it all is choking me. This isn't about resolving Dusty's murder so she can move on and my life can go back to normal. It's about getting justice for Dusty, it's about doing what's right, and in that second, I make a life altering decision.

"We need to find her," I state emphatically, leaving no room for arguments. "This is personal now. We need to find her and make sure she answers for what she's done." I stare at Dusty and then at Chan.

"Do you mean that?" Chan asks carefully.

"Yes, why?"

"Because I have a theory," Chan replies. "You know that Dusty was offered a Netflix original series charting the highs and lows of a drag artist?' I nod. "Well, what I'm sure you don't know is that she wasn't the only one up for that series. It was between Dusty, and another drag artist from a rival club."

"Who?" I ask curiously.

"Jubilee Jinx," Chan replies.

"She sounds like a fucking My Little Pony," Dusty mutters dryly.

"Who is she?" I ask Chan.

"She's fairly new, and she performs at Angelz in Islington," Chan answers. "The night Dusty was murdered Jubilee and a couple of her bitches, Suzie Q and Roxy Ru, were seen at The Rainbow Room, no doubt checking out the competition. Ruby said she saw Jubilee and that she was certain she was wearing a blonde wig that night."

"And you think this might be her?" I ask, peering back down at the security footage.

"It's hard to tell. I've only met Jubilee once, and the video doesn't have a clear shot of her face, but you can see the drag queen in the footage has a birthmark or maybe a small tattoo on her shoulder."

"Okay." I frown, not sure where she's going with this.

"It just so happens that Angelz has a Halloween themed night tonight, everyone's going to be in costumes or masks. So, hypothetically speaking, if someone was to pay a visit to said club and just so happen to search Jubilee's dressing room for, I don't know, say a missing locket, or to confirm that Jubilee does indeed have a birthmark on her shoulder..." her eyes widen innocently.

"What exactly are you suggesting, Chan?" I stare at her, watching as her gaze sweeps up and down the length of my body slowly before coming to rest on my face.

"How do you feel about shaving your legs?" she asks with a smirk.

Stage 5

Acceptance

16

Tristan

"This is such a bad idea." I fidget in my seat.

"Tristan, will you sit still," Chan murmurs in concentration. "You're going to end up with a wonky line and try to stop blinking so much."

"I'm sorry, I can't help it. I'm not used to the contact lenses," I reply. "And I've never worn make-up in my life. I'm going to look stupid. I don't think I have what it takes to pull this off."

"I think you're underestimating yourself, honey." Chan finishes perfecting the eyeliner and tossing it back on the dressing table before picking up a tube of mascara.

I'm still not entirely sure how Chan talked me into this. Not going to the club in Islington to see if we can identify the drag queen in the video footage, I'm all up for that. I want to find Dusty's killer as much as she does. I mean the part where she managed to talk me into letting her dress me up like her own personal doll. I've never really considered wearing any kind of make up or feminine clothes. I've never really bothered with my appearance at all, which is why I stick to my DM's, jeans and a vast array of t-shirts and plain sweaters.

Now, I find myself in one of the dressing rooms at The

Rainbow Room, sat demurely on a plushly cushioned stool in front of a dressing table lit by dozens of stage lights and overflowing with more make up than the counter at Harrods, and I'm wrapped up in nothing but a short silk kimono robe with freshly shaved legs.

"Look down, honey," Chan instructs softly. "But don't close your eyes."

I do as she says and hear her let out a loud sigh. "Look down with your eyes, Tristan, not your whole head."

"Sorry." I smile, unable to help myself. I correct my head position and cast my eyes down, partially lowering my eyelids so she can continue to apply the mascara.

My gaze skims over her, and I can't help but be impressed with her costume. It's a skin-tight latex cat suit that zips from groin to throat, if it was zipped to her throat, instead she has it lowered enough to tease with a decent amount of subtle cleavage. Her boots are pointed with needle thin heels and stretch all the way to her thighs. Her jet-black silky hair is poker straight and smoothed back from her stunning face in a high ponytail, which falls all the way down to the small of her back, and on her head sits a pair of pointed cat ears. She looks just like Eartha Kitt, sexy, feline and a little dangerous.

I don't know how she pulls it off. She's so effortlessly elegant while being undeniably sexy. I just feel awkward.

"What's wrong, honey?" She slides the mascara wand back into the tube and screws it tightly shut.

"I don't know about this, Chan," I confess. "Everyone at that club is going to take one look at me and know I'm a fraud."

"You're wrong, darling." She lifts my chin so I'm looking at her. "Being a drag queen, or a female impersonator, or just someone who enjoys wearing make-up and feminine clothes is something each of us feels inside. We each have our own styles, and how far we go is down to us individually. There is no one size fits all. Some of us go to the extremes and some just dance around the edges. There's no right or wrong way to do this, and no expectation of what you should look like, just how you feel."

"Look." She tilts my face so I'm staring at myself in the mirror.

My eyes widen, and I can't help the gasp that escapes my lips. She hasn't gone full drag like I thought she would, instead she's covered the faint bruising to my cheek, given my natural brows more shape and definition instead of covering them, and making them higher. The eye make-up is stunning, smoky greys and dark colours that make my green eyes pop, and the inky black eyeliner and thick mascara instead of false lashes make my eyes look somehow enormous. There's a light dusting of blusher across my cheek bones along with something that makes them shimmer. My lips look full and kissable, plumped up with a tinted gloss rather than thick lipstick.

Rather than go with a wig, she's embraced my thick, wild curling dark hair, adding gels and sprays to add volume. The result is like something out of a *Mid-Summer Night's Dream*. I look like a little fae creature designed for mischief and sin and ready to trap you in the faery realms. I don't realise it but my mouth curves into a smile.

"Stop thinking about what other people will say and tell me how you feel," Chan whispers.

I think about it for a moment, staring at the ethereal creature blinking back at me with huge eyes, and I search deep down inside myself.

"I look pretty," I whisper.

"Yes, you do." Chan's soft hand smooths down my back, flowing against the silk of the robe. "There are no rules here, Tristan. You can be anything or anyone you want to be, the only person you have to be true to is yourself."

I turn to gaze into her dark eyes. "Thank you, Chan."

"Sweet boy." She brushes the pad of her thumb over my chin. "You are going to break hearts looking like you do."

I glance across the room to Dusty who has been uncharacteristically quiet while we've been here. I find her tucked away in the corner, perched on a chair staring at nothing in particular. The look on her face breaks my heart, and I know how hard it must be for her to be in here. This was not only her dressing room but the room where she was murdered.

"Doesn't it bother you, Chan?" I turn back and ask. "Being in here?"

"Yes." She sighs. "It does but also it's the one place other than Dusty's flat that I feel closest to her. None of the other girls wanted this dressing room after what happened to Dusty, and it hurts to know that she took her last breath in this room. It kills me that she was all alone."

I look up to see Dusty watching Chan with sad eyes.

"If it helps," I tell Chan. "She doesn't remember her murder."

"It does a little." She sniffs blinking rapidly so the tears don't fall and ruin her make-up. "I just miss her so bad."

A tissue box shoots across the dressing table sliding to a stop in front of her, and she sucks in a sharp breath, her eyes widening in shock. I guess believing Dusty's there, despite the fact she can't see her, is very different from knowing she's there.

I glance up at Dusty who's now standing beside Chan.

"You're getting better at that," I tell Dusty who gives a small smile.

"Strong emotions just like Patrick says." Dusty winks.

"I should write a book," I mutter. "*Navigating the Afterlife according to Patrick Swayze Movies.*"

"Dusty was always a big Patrick fan." Chan laughs and sniffles as she plucks a tissue from the box and carefully dabs the tears from the corner of her eyes.

"We will find out who hurt her," I tell Chan, reaching out and laying my hand on her shoulder in comfort. Usually, I would go out of my way to avoid unnecessary contact with other people. With Chan, it feels so natural, and I want to ease her pain.

Chan nods, reaching up as she pats my hand. "You should get changed." She glances at the clock. "We need to get going soon. Ruby said she'll cover all my numbers tonight, but I want to slip out before Ari sees me and Brandy starts causing trouble."

"Okay." I blow out a breath as I rise from the stool.

Chan rummages through the outfits on a nearby rack and pulls out a black dress and hands it to me. I slip behind the oriental silk screen and hang the dress on a hook. There's a full length mirror mounted on the wall and a small stool.

"Here." Chan pokes her head around the corner and hands me a pair of shoes. "These should fit you, and they're wedges and much easier to get your balance in the first time around."

I nod and take them off her, sitting down on the stool and sliding my feet into them and wiggling my freshly painted toenails. Although I don't plan on making a habit of this, I have to admit, it'd felt nice having Chan curled up on the sofa with me painting my nails. I glance down at my shiny black finger-nails, and I kinda like them.

Shaking my head with a smile, I reach down to buckle the shoes. They're wedge platforms in black suede with a series of thick straps that crisscross my feet and wind around my ankles. Once they're firmly buckled in place, I try standing experimen-tally, wobbling slightly, and feeling ridiculously tall. Turning around to face the mirror, I wobble again, and I'm forced to reach out and steady myself. If I make it through this evening without breaking my ankle, it will be a miracle.

Taking a nervous breath, I unbelt the jade green kimono, which Dusty insisted matches my eyes. I let it slide from my shoulders, taking in my body in the mirror. My chest is hairless, not because I've waxed but because I just don't grow that much hair, even on my face. My body is slim to the point of being skinny regardless of how much I eat and with the wedges on my feet it makes my legs look impossibly long, but what I'm really staring at is that instead of my usual boxers I'm wearing a pair of black lace knickers. I turn slightly to get a good look at the back. They ride up my bum almost like a thong, and the thin lace frames the tops of my buttocks lovingly. They're not uncomfortable though, they feel... sort of sexy.

I can feel my face heating as I turn back around and stare at myself once again. My cock and balls are nestled into the lace, making it bulge slightly in front, and the material feels nice against my sensitive foreskin. Like the nail varnish, I kinda like it. I'm feeling pretty conflicted about it, like I'm not supposed to, but Chan said there are no rules, no right or wrong, only how I feel.

I feel... sexy, like it's a little secret under my clothes no one knows about. For a brief moment, I wonder what Danny would think if he saw me in them, would he think they were sexy? Or would he be turned off? I shake my head and try not to think about him because the last thing I need is a boner, and there's no way these knickers would be able to contain that.

I reach for the hanger and pull the dress off, unzipping the back and lowering it over my head and letting it fall down the length of my body. It fits perfectly as I smooth it into place. It's a black skater dress, which is so short it barely covers my bum cheeks. It's got cute capped shoulders and a tight waist that flares out into a flirty little skirt. Chan picked this one rather than something tight fitting so I wouldn't have to tape the way she does. We also decided to forgo any kind of padding, instead going with my natural shape. Chan says we're aiming for waif-like super model, and I think with a huff, supermodel my arse. I have to admit it does look cute, but I'm still worried about what other people will think. More importantly, what will Danny think?"

I reach behind me for the zip, and I've just got it tugged

halfway up my spine when I realise it's going to take the skills of a contortionist to get it all the way without some assistance. I'm about to call out for Chan when I hear a loud and determined knock at the door, followed by the clip clip of Chan's heels as she crosses the room to open it.

"Where is he?" Danny demands.

"Well, hello to you too, Inspector Hayes." Chan smirks at him as she leans against the doorframe with one arm blocking the entrance to the dressing room.

I can see their reflections in the full-length mirror propped in the corner of the room, and I watch as Danny's eyes quickly take in Chan's costume.

"You got a license for that outfit?"

"Well, aren't you just the sweetest thing?" she purrs in amusement, and Danny sighs in resignation.

"Where's Tristan?" She moves aside and allows him to enter while I remain hidden behind the silk screen, trying to pull the zip up on the dress. "Tristan?" Danny calls out, casting his gaze across the room.

"I'm right here," I reply. "I'm just getting changed. I'll be right out."

"I got your message," he growls, and my dick twitches at the sheer hotness of the timbre of his voice.

"You sound cross," I say mildly.

"I am bloody cross," he replies. "What are you thinking going into a potentially dangerous situation just the two of you?"

"That's why we called you," Chan answers sarcastically. "So we'd have a big manly man around to protect us."

"Cut the crap," he snaps back. "You shouldn't be anywhere near that club if there's any hint that one of the performers is a suspect. You should've reported it and left it to us to deal with."

"We did report it," I reply wading into their heated argument. "We told you."

"The fact is," Chan adds. "That you catch more flies with honey than vinegar if that's the saying. You and half of Scotland Yard barrelling in there asking questions would have them closing ranks and clamming up quicker than a nun's knees. Tris and I can slip in there in costume and with masks, and no one will be any the wiser. We can take a quick look, do some recon, then let you and the boys in blue handle the rest."

"It's still too dangerous," he replies stubbornly.

"Told you he'd be pissed," Dusty adds, even though neither Danny nor Chan can hear her.

"Danny," I tell him firmly, the breath almost whooshing out of me as I finally manage to pull the zip up. "We're going whether you like it or not. I promise we'll be careful, but Chan's right, we're less likely to be noticed than a bunch of police officers. I knew you wouldn't be happy if we kept you in the dark, so we figured you could tag along as my date."

"Tag along as your date?" he repeats slowly, pinching the bridge of his nose. "Tristan, will you please come out? I can't have this conversation with you behind a screen."

"No." I stare nervously at my reflection in the full length mirror in front of me.

"Why?" he asks.

"Because you'll laugh." I sulk. "I look silly."

"No, you don't, honey," Chan calls out softly. "Now, come on out and show us how stunning you look."

"That's easy for you to say you always look perfect." I pout.

"That's sweet of you," she laughs. "Now, get your cute arse out here before I send your man behind there to sling you over his shoulder and carry you out."

Dusty pokes her head around the screen and stares at me, her mouth curving into a wide smile. "I knew that dress was perfect for you, boo. You look amazing."

"Fine," I grumble, edging around the screen tentatively. Not just because of the nerves, but because I don't want to fall off the heels I've never worn before in my life.

I round the screen and step into the room. Dusty is standing beaming at me beside Chan who lets out a cry of utter delight and claps her hands enthusiastically. I take a nervous breath and risk a glance at Danny.

His eyes are wide, his mouth hanging slightly open, as his gaze slowly and painstakingly trails the length of my body from my face to my toes and back up, lingering on my legs for a moment before reaching my eyes, and my breath catches in my throat at the heat I see there.

"You look good... great." He clears his throat, his cheeks flushing as he raises his hand and rubs the back of his neck. "You look great."

"Thanks," I murmur, turning to glance at Dusty and Chan who are standing side by side with their arms crossed and wearing identical smug smiles.

Danny lets out a long sigh. "Are you really set on doing this?"

"Danny." I step closer to him. "I need to do this for Dusty. I feel like she's not at rest, that she can't be until this is solved. It's like she won't leave me alone." I turn my head a fraction of an inch to see that Dusty is now standing beside me, her face inches from mine as she grins.

"I suppose I'd better tag along then." His mouth curves as he looks at me. "As your date..."

"Thank you," I tell him earnestly. "I know you're worried and you want to protect me, but I need to do this."

"Fine," he concedes. "But you have to agree that if at any point I feel you're in danger, either of you—" He turns to Chan to include her. "You'll leave immediately."

"I promise." I nod.

"Chan?" He looks to her.

"Fine, whatever." She rolls her eyes, turning back to me. "Now for the finishing touches."

She settles a headband with a small pair of Maleficent horns on my head and then helps me into a pair of small black feathered wings. Lastly, she ties a lace mask over my eyes.

"There, perfect." She turns to look critically at Danny. "Guess I'm just going to have to work with what I've got." She hums.

She sashays up to Danny, eyeing his dark coloured suit and white shirt. "I can make this work." She nods, yanking on his dark coloured tie and loosening it slightly before unbuttoning his collar, then she reaches up and ruffles his hair to make it all messy as if he's dragged his hands through it continuously.

"There," she declares. "If anyone asks, you're John Constantine. Just try to look like a broody supernatural detective that's just been dragged out of Hell."

"I can do that." Danny grins. "You haven't seen the amount of paperwork that goes with my job. Hell's where I spend most of my days."

Laughing, I wobble slightly on my heels and reach out to steady myself, knocking down a costume from a hanger. Without thinking, I turn and bend over to retrieve it. It's only when I hear a strangled noise from behind me that I remember I'm wearing an incredibly short skirt.

I risk a glance up to see Danny looking very red faced and breathing rather unevenly, but before I can apologise, Chan laughs warmly, taking the costume from my hands and straightening me up.

"Just remember, honey, don't show anyone the goodies." She winks. "Unless you mean to."

17

Danny

My dick is hard, and my palms are sweaty. I swallow tightly and try to count to ten, willing my body under control. What the hell's wrong with me? I never lose control like this. My eyes are still glued to Tristan, his legs go all the way to his ears, and they're so long and smooth, and with very little effort I can imagine them wrapped around my hips as I pound him into the mattress, or even better wrapped around my head as I bury my face in his groin and swallow his cock, hearing him moan my name and grip my hair.

Damn it... not helping the situation...

Is it hot in here? I reach up and tug at my already loose collar with one finger. I'm sure I'm sweating, maybe I'm coming down with something, or maybe it was the shocking glimpse of those tiny lacy boy shorts lovingly cupping Tristan's curvy arse. Christ, I swallow hard. His legs had parted just enough for me to see his balls hugged by the lacy fabric, and a bolt of pure lust had shot straight to my cock.

This is all a bit confusing. My dick may be fully on board, but my brain is struggling to catch up. My instant and startling reaction to seeing Tristan wearing lace underwear has caught me completely off guard.

I already knew he was nothing like the type I usually go for because the men I usually end up in bed with are of a similar shape and build to me. Tall, broad, athletic, likes a pint or two, into watching football. Tristan is completely unlike anyone I've ever gone for, and it just feels right. My gaze once again drops to that skirt, and it's deliciously easy to imagine bending him over that table, flipping his skirt up and sliding those sexy lace panties over the curve of his arse. I wouldn't take them off completely, I'd nudge them just under his cheeks, cupping his balls as I slide my cock into...

Fuck... need a distraction ASAP...

"Shouldn't we be going then?" I cough, raking my hand through my hair as my stomach clenches, and my dick twitches again.

Do not think about bending Tristan over...

"We should definitely go." Chan nods. "Before Ari chews me out over not working tonight."

"Okay then." Tristan blows out a breath and takes a wobbly step toward the door.

"Are you going to be alright in those things?" I frown in alarm.

"I'll be fine." Tristan waves off my concern as he opens the door, but as he steps through, there's another wobble followed by a yelp, and he disappears with a loud crash. "I'm okay..." a small, muffled voice comes from the corridor.

I turn to look at Chan and she just shrugs.

It's surprisingly easy to get into the club in Islington. Chan has now also donned a mask, this one black latex to match her outfit, which just covers her eyes and the bridge of her nose.

The club itself is pretty much on par with The Rainbow Room, with a similar layout and size.

The Halloween party is already in full swing as we make our way to the bar. I grab myself a beer and a cocktail each for Tristan and Chan. My brows raising slightly as Tristan asks for a straw with his.

"Are you sure that's a good idea?" I frown. "That'll just get you drunk quicker, and I don't want you breaking an ankle in those shoes."

"Safety precaution." He smiles. "Do you not remember what happened last time I had a cocktail?" he yells above the music.

I grin, as I lean in close to his ear, my voice still loud enough for him to hear. "There are easier ways to get my mouth on you other than performing CPR."

He laughs again, and I take a swig of my beer, looking toward the stage where all the Angelz drag queens seem to be dressed up as Zombie Cheerleaders and performing a mash up of Michael Jackson's Thriller and The Yeah Yeah Yeah's, Heads will Roll.

"They're not bad." I lean back as I glance around.

"I suppose," Chan scoffs. "If you're into Glee rip offs."

She stares at the stage for a moment, her eyes narrowing through the crowd.

"Can you see her?" I ask.

She stares for a moment longer. "There," she finally says. "Third from the right."

"Got it." I nod.

"You and Tristan see if you can find a way backstage and get close enough to see if she's got a tattoo or birthmark on her shoulder."

"What about you?" I frown.

"I'm going to see if I can find out which dressing room is hers," Chan says.

"I don't think that's a good... idea," I finish, but it's too late she's already disappeared into the crowd, which swallows her up like a rolling tide.

"Where's she gone?" Tristan leans over and asks.

I shake my head, there's no point trying to explain over the level of the music, not without risking someone overhearing. Instead, I take his hand, and once he's set his empty glass down, I lead him to the packed dance floor in front of the stage. His eyes widen as he realises where we're heading, and he tugs on my hand to stop me.

"I can't dance," he leans in and shouts in my ear.

I pull back and stare at him. "Trust me?"

His eyes dart to toward the gyrating bodies in front of the stage, and he swallows hard. I know this is hard for him being in such a crowded place with so many people and way out of his comfort zone, but I also know he's determined to see this through for Dusty.

He nods slowly. I can feel his hand gripping mine so tightly it's almost cutting off the circulation, and I'm not entirely certain if it's because he doesn't want to stumble and fall in those heels amidst the tight press of bodies or because he really doesn't want to dance.

I pull him in close, pressing his body to mine and breathing him in. "Relax." I press my mouth close to his ear and feel him shiver against me. "Dancing is just like sex, let go and let your body feel it."

He lets me lead him, and I lift his arms, draping them around my neck as my hands slip down to his hips, pulling him in closer, so you couldn't get a sheet of paper between our bodies. After a few moments, we're moving and grinding to the music, and I'm so tempted to lower my head and press my lips to his and devour his mouth but I don't. I have to remember why we're here, even if he makes me want to throw every rule out the window.

I turn him in my arms, so his back is pressed against my chest as we sway together. I lean down and press my mouth to his ear. "Tris, can you see that exit over there to the edge of the stage, it's just a heavy black curtain."

He nods slowly, and I can see his gaze is fixed on it. "We're going to head over there slowly, and when no one's looking, we're going to slip through, okay?"

He nods again. We edge across the crowded dance floor under the guise of dancing until we reach the edge of the stage. We press into the shadows, feeling the music pulsing and vibrating through our bodies this close up. I lean into him briefly so that to anyone who happened to glance in our direction they'd think we were just making out.

Once I'm certain no one's looking, I lift the edge of the heavy stage curtain and push him through, slipping in behind him. Although it doesn't change the volume of the music significantly, the lighting shifts. Gone are the intermittent strobes and the brightly flashing neon colours of the dance floor, instead it's a dim muted light the stagehands can move about by.

Tristan looks around curiously at the stacks of props, backdrops and huge overhead platforms, ropes, and lighting rigs.

"It's just like *Phantom of the Opera*." He grins.

"You like musical theatre?" I ask curiously as we sneak further backstage.

"No, I like Gerard Butler," he snorts. "You know, the 2004 movie? I must have a bit of a dark side though. I mean you can forget the hero Raoul, I'm all about the Phantom. Seriously, if Gerard had been serenading me with the *Music of the Night,* I'd have climbed him quicker than Quasimodo scaling a stone gargoyle on top of Notre Dame."

"Have you ever been to Paris?"

"No." He shakes his head. "It was one of the places Dad and I always talked about visiting but then he got sick. Maybe one day though." He shakes his head. "Anyway, what are we doing here?"

"Chan is looking for Jubilee's dressing room, so we're going to stalk her backstage and see if we can get close enough to confirm whether or not she has a mark on her shoulder."

"It's all so clandestine." He grins. "I feel like James Bond."

"I think it's more like Zak Efron in Baywatch." I glance down at the dress and heels, and he laughs.

"Wait," he whispers, pulling me into an alcove as a couple of the performers head off stage to make a quick change. "Is that her?"

"I think it might be," I whisper back. "Let's get closer." I take his hand, and we edge along the backdrops. "Dammit, where did she go?"

The music suddenly changes out on stage, and there's a loud grinding sound behind us. I look up and grab Tristan, lifting his slight weight into my arms as I turn sharply and press him into the wall, shielding him as one of the large, heavy backdrops slides toward us so a new set can move forward onto the stage.

"What was that?" Tristan asks breathlessly, held in my arms and pinned to the wall with my body pressed intimately between his spread legs.

"Set change," I reply. "The backdrops are on runners, and they shift to change scenery throughout the show, I guess."

"Okay." He flushes as he feels the hardness of my cock pressing against his. "Um, I think you can put me down now."

"I can't," I admit, suppressing a groan when he wriggles against me, making my cock harder.

"What? Why not?"

"Because the backdrop is pinning me," I reply. "I can't move until they shift the set again."

"Shit," he murmurs. "This is just like when Han Solo and

Princess Leia got trapped in the garbage compactor and nearly got crushed to death."

"Well, you can relax, Princess." I chuckle. "The backdrop is on runners and can't go any further than it already is. We may be temporarily trapped but it won't crush us."

"Guess we're stuck," he murmurs staring into my eyes.

"Guess we are," I mumble in return. My hands graze the backs of his bare thighs, shifting his weight.

He props one foot on the framework of the backdrop so I'm not holding as much of his weight, but all he succeeds in doing is canting his hips and pressing even more intimately into my dick. He sucks in a breath, and I watch as his pupils dilate.

"Danny." He breathes heavily as he pushes his eye mask up to the top of his head so I can see him more clearly.

Whatever the hell Chan did to his subtle but sexy eye make-up makes his green eyes pop, and his mouth is slick with some sort of cherry gloss, plumping his lips up and making it look as if he's been sucking cock.

"Damn!" I press closer, my mouth hovering above his, almost skimming those perfect lips. "You're so fucking beautiful."

He closes the distance, pressing his mouth to mine on a long, serrated groan and rocking his hips and grinding his hard dick against mine. His tongue is in my mouth, his fingers tangled in my hair and everything around us ceases to exist.

"Fuck... Tristan," I gasp out against his lips.

"Yes," he moans. "That sounds like a brilliant idea, you should definitely do that," he pants as he grinds against me trying to use the friction to ease the ache in his dick.

"Please, Danny," he begs against my mouth as he humps and rides against my cock, and it's the fucking sexiest thing I've ever heard.

Jesus Christ, my balls are so tight they're aching as my fingertips slide underneath his skirt and toy with the edges of his lace knickers. "These are driving me fucking insane," I pant hoarsely.

"Do you like them?" He breathes between kisses. "I've never worn them before, but they feel so good against my dick and balls."

Fuck me, I nearly come in my pants right there and then, which I haven't done since I was a teenager. How does he do this to me? How does he take me apart like this with nothing more than his kisses and words?

"I want my mouth on them," I whisper against his lips. "I want to lick and suck your cock through the lace, and I want to watch you soak them with your cum."

He moans into my mouth, and I slide one finger beneath the lace, stroking his balls teasingly. His legs wrap around me tighter like he's trying to climb me like a tree. I trace my finger backwards, skimming over his hole and teasing the puckered and sensitive skin there until he shivers.

"For fuck's sake, get a room you two," a harsh whisper breaks our trance. I pull my fingers away and break the kiss looking up to see Chan leaning around one of the curtains. "Tristan, put your mask back on," she hisses.

"Oh, um, sorry." He pulls his mask back down over his eyes.

"If you two have quite finished, I found the dressing room." She flicks her head. "Come on, let's go."

"Um..." Tristan wrinkles his nose apologetically. "We can't."

"What?" Chan frowns. "Why?"

"Because we're kind of stuck," I answer.

"Accidentally glued your dicks together?" Her brows rise sardonically.

"Not exactly." I shake my head. "When the sets shifted, we got pinned by the backdrop."

"Oh, for the love of..." She rolls her eyes and creeps toward us. "Hang on a minute."

She looks at one of the catches holding it in place. "Get

ready to move quickly," she warns as she flicks the catch up and gives the backdrop a shove. It glides forward sharply on well-oiled runners, and there's a clang and a crash, followed by loud yelps of distress.

"Move quickly before they catch us." She giggles wickedly, and we hurry back through the way she came. Glancing to my right quickly, I see a flash of the stage and a huge pile up of bodies where the chorus line have gone down like a line of dominoes. Chan gives another delighted cackle and drags us into a corridor.

We follow her blindly as I keep a tight grip on Tristan's hand, through several twists and turns until we come to a plain door with the number 3 on it. She listens quietly for a moment, then opens the door and shoves us unceremoniously through.

It opens into a small, cluttered dressing room, not unlike Dusty's, with a huge brightly lit table littered with make-up and accessories. Racks of clothes, shoes, and wigs are stacked everywhere.

"Okay, be quick," Chan says. "We don't have long."

Tristan and I dive for the drawers, while Chan roots through the jewellery boxes on the table. After about ten minutes of fruitless searching, we've all come up empty handed.

"Shit," Chan swears, and as the word leaves her mouth the door handle rattles and swings open.

A tall, broad drag queen marches in, her eyes wide with shock and outrage. She's changed out of the zombie Cheerleader costume and is now wearing a tight sequinned dress with a matching bolero, which unfortunately covers her shoulders so we can't see if she has a mark, but something about her doesn't sit right. I'm sure, she's much taller and broader than the drag queen in the security footage. My gut's telling me it's not the same person.

"What the fuck are you doing in here?" she demands in a deep voice.

"Oh, you know," Chan says breezily as she stands between me and Tristan. I watch as she wraps her arm around his waist and drops a kiss on his lips before she turns to me and does the same. "We were just looking for someplace private to party." She winks suggestively.

"Well, not in fucking here, you're not," Jubilee growls. "Do you know who I am?"

"No." Chan smirks as insultingly as possible, even though she damn well knows who she is. "I don't know, sorry. Are you one of the cleaners?"

Jubilee's face turns a rather interesting shade of puce. "Get the fuck out of here before I have you thrown out," she demands.

"Alright, we're going." Chan holds up her hands. "Don't bust your girdle."

"You bitch." Jubilee lunges for Chan.

I step in between them while they squabble and try to grab at each other over me. Chan manages to grab her bolero and yank the sleeve down revealing an unmarked shoulder.

"Shit," Chan hisses as I pull them apart.

"Ladies, that's quite enough," I tell them firmly. "Come on." I turn to Chan and Tristan. "Let's go."

"Yeah, this place is so lame." Chan smirks. "We should try The Rainbow Room, way classier than that train wreck of a floor show."

Jubilee growls and launches herself at Chan again, but I shove them out the door and slam it closed behind us and leaving, what sounds like, Jubilee launching her shoes at the other side of the door in outrage.

"Go!" I order Chan firmly, reaching for Tristan's hand.

We aim for the nearest fire exit and step out into the cold

night. Chan lets out a long frustrated breath and tilts her head back staring at the stars.

"It's not her, Chan," I tell her sympathetically.

"I know," she breathes out in defeat. "Shit, back to square one."

18

Tristan

It's late by the time Danny parks at the curb in front of my flat. We'd dropped Chan home first as she wasn't in the mood to go back to The Rainbow Room. Dusty seems to have disappeared too since we left Islington, and although I briefly wonder where she's got to, I know she'll show up sooner or later.

I take Danny's hand as he helps me out of the car, trying modestly not to flash the entire street my lace knickers. It's really not as easy as it looks, especially as I'm still teetering on the platform wedges Chan made me wear, and I'm surprised I haven't broken my neck yet. Although, I have to admit it has given me the excuse to hold onto Danny all night.

I try to stifle a yawn as I step up onto the pavement. I'm tired and I have to get up for work in the morning. I don't know what the time actually is, but I'm pretty certain we're heading into the early hours of the morning. I should really thank Danny for the ride home and head to bed. Except I don't want to, at least not alone. All I keep thinking about is when Danny had me pressed against the wall, my legs wrapped around his waist as he slid his hand under my skirt and teased my balls while his tongue was in my mouth.

I may just spontaneously combust if I don't get another taste of him.

"So." He stands in front of me casually with a smile tugging at the corners of that talented mouth of his.

"So." I smile back shyly.

"Monday tomorrow," he remarks casually.

"Hmm, work." I nod.

"Yeah," he agrees. "Probably should call it a night."

"It is getting late." My mouth twitches.

"So." He smiles.

"So," I return, feeling a lovely little hum of anticipation low in my belly. There is no way we're not on the same page here.

We stare at each other a moment longer.

"You... uh... want to come up?" I ask casually.

"I thought you'd never ask." He grins as he lifts me off my feet.

My legs automatically wrap around him, and my arms snake around his neck as I lean in. I'm just about to plant my lips on his when a movement behind him catches my eye. Peering over his shoulder, I see the curtain twitch. Behind it, not hiding very stealthily to conceal his snooping, is my downstairs neighbour in blue and white striped pajamas, his eyes narrowed and lips pursed in disapproval no doubt by A. what I'm wearing and B. the fact that I'm wrapped around a very sexy policeman who I hope is about to do very bad things to me.

Danny glances over his shoulder to see what I'm looking at, and the curtain twitches again.

"Ah, maybe we should take this inside," he says rather responsibly.

He turns and heads down the diamond patterned tile path to the front door, still carrying me, and I can't help myself, maybe I've been hanging around Dusty too long, but I wink and blow my neighbour a kiss as Danny chuckles.

Once we reach the door, I fumble for my keys and manage to unlock it while Danny seems to show absolutely no inclination to put me down.

"Are you seriously going to carry me over the threshold?"I ask as the door swings open.

"It's that or a trip to A&E," he chuckles. "I don't trust you on those steep, narrow stairs in those shoes."

"I suppose you may have a point." I smile down at him. "These things should require you to have a provisional license before attempting to wear them for the first time."

He laughs as he kicks the door closed behind us, and I flip the lock. He carries me up the dark, narrow staircase and reluctantly sets me on my feet on the upper landing so I can unlock the door to my flat.

I flip the lights on as I invite him in, and he glances around curiously at my home. Last time we were here, I'm guessing he didn't take in the surroundings much as I was clearly upset at the time.

"Been here long?" he asks.

"A few years," I toss over my shoulder as I head towards the kitchen, chucking my keys into the bowl on the kitchen table.

"It's nice," he replies as he follows me into the kitchen.

"It's not much." I glance up at him as I pick up the kettle and head over to the sink to fill it. "But it's home, and we don't need much room."

"We?" He raises a brow questioningly.

"It's just me and Jacob." I set the kettle down and flip the button, reaching into the cupboard for mugs, which is a bit of a weird feeling as I'm wearing heels and don't really need to stretch like I usually do.

"You have a roommate?" he asks casually.

"No," I chuckle, and as I do, there's a loud mewl and a huge fur ball brushes past Danny, rubbing up against his legs, his tail swishing, and I can't really blame my cat. I'd love nothing more than to rub myself over every inch of that man. "Danny, Jacob Marley, Jacob Marley, Danny," I introduce them.

"You have a cat named Jacob Marley?"

"Don't ask." I shake my head with a smile as I turn around and lean back against the counter, the coffee momentarily forgotten.

I watch as Danny leans down and gives Jacob Marley a slow stroke from head to tail as he purrs loudly, and I mean the cat not Danny. Although admittedly, I'd love to stroke Danny and see if I could make him purr, or even better, growl.

When Jacob Marley finally decides he's had enough pets, he turns to look at me. Now, if cats could do a double take, I'd swear blind that's just what my cat did. He eyes me suspiciously as if he can't quite figure out why I'm dressed the way I am. Then with a regal sniff of dismissal, he turns, tail raised high in the air, and swaggers back out of the kitchen.

"That's a hell of a strut," Danny states in amusement.

"Oh yeah, he's full of attitude," I huff, watching Danny as he strides across the kitchen toward me.

He places his hands on the counter either side of me, caging me in. His mouth inches from mine as he watches me.

"Do you want coffee?" I swallow, my mouth suddenly dry.

"I don't want coffee." His gaze snags on my mouth as I lick my lips slowly.

"What do you want?" I ask breathlessly.

"You," he says simply as his mouth crashes down on mine.

I'm not sure which of us groans, maybe it's both of us. All I know is that the kiss goes from zero to sixty in less than a second. I let go of the counter to wrap my arms around his neck, and as I do, I catch one of the empty mugs, sending it sailing majestically across the kitchen. I barely register the crash as it hits the floor and smashes. I'm way to busy tangling my fingers in his hair as his tongue plunges into my mouth, unable to get enough of the hot and wild flavour of him.

I let out an embarrassingly needy whine as his palms skim the backs of my bare thighs, sliding under the dress and grabbing on as he lifts me effortlessly onto the counter. My head falls back and thuds against the cupboard loudly as he releases my mouth, and I drag in a desperate gasp of air. His lips devour my neck, leaving me trembling, my skin pebbling with the intensity and my nipples hardening.

"These," he gasps as his wide palms snake around my hips to cup my arse cheeks, squeezing them tightly through the lace. "Fuck me, these..." he growls again. "I never thought I'd be turned on by something like these, but you're so fucking sexy. The thought of you in these lace knickers has been driving me crazy all night."

"I... you... um... uh." Okay, so no words for Tristan then. His hands and mouth have apparently reduced me to an incoherent mess. "Please," I pant, there an actual word, although I'm not exactly sure what I'm pleading for. I just know that I want it desperately.

He pulls me off the counter, and before my brain has a chance to catch up, he flips me around and bends me over it, knocking his foot between my feet and forcing me to spread my legs. I groan loudly as he peels off the black feathered angel wings I'm wearing and tosses them carelessly behind him. I arch sinuously as he strokes his palm down the length of my spine before grasping the zip of the dress and lowering it so slowly that the only sound in the room is our harsh breaths and the ponderous creak of the zip as each tooth unlocks. Once the zip reaches the end, somewhere just above the curve of my buttocks, he places his warm hands inside the gaping material and pushes it aside to reveal the ridges of my spine.

I'm dying slowly I think to myself as he places hot, wet open mouthed kisses to my naked back. I groan loudly as his hands skim once again up my thighs, this time dragging the skirt of the dress up and folding it over my arse. I almost whine when he leans back, but as I turn to look over my shoulder, I can see his hot blue eyes fixed on my bum as he toys with the edges of the lace.

"I've been thinking about this for hours," he says hoarsely. "What you would look like bent over for me in these sexy knickers." He leans forward, his body curling over mine, his breath hot against my ear as his hand slips between my thighs, and his palm rubs across my balls and my dick nestled in the sheer fabric.

I can't help the reedy cry of sheer need as he pulls his hand away. He reaches around my body and slides his hand into the front of the knickers where the head of my hard cock is already trying to escape and fists my dick with a firm grip.

I cry out again, unable to stop the rocking of my hips as I ride the tight tunnel of his fist. His other hand reaches up and wraps around my throat, not enough to restrict my breathing or hurt me in any way, just enough to hold me in place and to give the slippery and dangerous feel of someone else being in charge of my pleasure.

"Do you like this?" he growls in my ear, and I feel the precum slicking my cock as he pumps up and down slowly. The wedges I'm wearing put me at the perfect height and angle so that I don't have to raise up onto my toes to offer myself to him. For a crazy moment, I want him to just rip those knickers down to my knees and shove his cock in me, pounding me hard until we both come in a sweaty, exhausted mess, but equally, I don't want this to be over too quickly. I want to savour every moment.

"Yes," I gasp as he strokes me.

It's so intense, feeling him surrounding me, building the pleasure in my body until I'm trembling. Suddenly I feel the tell tale tingle in my balls, and I shove him back, turning abruptly and forcing him to break his hold on my cock as I breath heavily.

"Too close," I gasp. "I don't want to come yet."

He's panting as much as I am, and as I look down, I see his dick tenting the front of his trousers. I want him so badly it's almost painful. I've never felt this kind of all-consuming desperation with anyone else before.

I throw myself at him, wrapping my arms around his neck and latching my mouth to his and devouring him. The full weight of me colliding with him, sends him off balance, and he stumbles back with his arms wrapped around me. With a smack, we crash into the kitchen table, sending it grinding across the floor, the wooden legs screeching loudly in protest. It hits the kitchen wall and gouges out a lump of plaster, which rains to the floor. Danny falls back onto the table, one arm wrapped around me protectively as the other falls against the surface of the table to get his balance. His hand catches the glass bowl, which is full of odds and ends, sending it crashing to the ground in a tumble of broken glass, keys, elastic bands, safety pins and God knows what else.

I practically climb on top of him, grinding our dicks together as we kiss frantically, moaning at the delicious friction. His hand fists in my dark curls, dragging my head back as he feasts on my neck.

"Danny," I pant pulling back until I'm standing gazing down at him splayed out across my kitchen table like an offering to the Gods.

Fuck, he's gorgeous. I reach down and grab one of his shoes yanking it off and tossing it over my shoulder. There's a loud clanking of plates, and I'm willing to bet it landed in the sink.

"Oops," I snigger as I pull his sock off.

He yanks me forward on top of him and takes my mouth again, and the forward momentum of my body makes the table lurch again, this time sending a chair toppling over with a clatter. I loosen his tie and unbutton his shirt, losing my patience halfway through and ripping it open, sending little buttons pinging everywhere like tiny missiles.

Humming in appreciation, I skim my fingers through the fine blonde hairs fanning across his hard chest before latching onto the flat disc of his nipple and sucking hard. He grunts and fists my hair again. My fingers are already busy unbuckling his belt and pulling it through the loops of his trousers, dropping it to the floor. He barely has time to register me ripping open his trousers and freeing him before I slide down his body and swallow his cock.

Crying out loudly, his hips bucking at the sudden hot, tight suction forces his cock deeper, making me gag slightly, but it doesn't stop me. I suck his cock like my life depends on it, and the salty and addictive taste of his precum bursts across my tongue. His moans and gasps are like a symphony as I take him right to the edge.

Grabbing my hair, he pulls my mouth off him panting as he grips the base of his cock to stop himself from coming.

"Bed," he growls as he pushes himself up from the table and snatches me up, hauling me into his arms as my legs wrap around his hips. "Now!"

"Mind... the... glass..." I gasp between kisses. "On... the floor."

Somehow, he manages to navigate us across the floor, which has now become a minefield, while wearing only one shoe and sock. We stumble out into the hallway, knocking into the wall. We only manage to make it a few steps before he shoves me up against the wall, our cocks rubbing lusciously together, his wet with my spit, mine slick with copious amounts of my precum.

The dress, which is still loose at the back, is hanging off my shoulder, and he yanks it down and wraps his lips around my nipple, suckling as he rocks against me, shoving me further up the wall. My shoulders catch the picture mounted on the wall behind me, dislodging it from its hook and sending it crashing to the floor.

"Need to fuck you so bad," Danny groans against my skin.

"Then... take me... to... bed," I pant out.

He pushes away from the wall still holding onto me as we stumble to my room. We tumble to the bed, and there's a loud and rather alarming cracking sound as the end of the bed gives way and hits the floor while the top end remains attached to the legs and headboard, leaving us laying on a sort of mini ski slope.

I snort and laugh loudly.

"Are you okay?" he looks up and glances around.

"Yes." I grin.

"Sorry about the bed," he chuckles against my mouth.

"I needed a new one any way," I murmur as he kisses me again.

He pulls back, grabbing the hem of the dress and yanking it up and over my head, leaving me in nothing but the strappy wedge shoes and the black lace knickers, which are now lewdly bunched under my stiff and aching prick.

"Fuck, you look sexy," he growls as he rips his tie up and over his head, tossing it carelessly. He yanks off his other shoe and sock, stripping quickly out of the rest of his clothes until he's gloriously naked. My mouth is watering as my gaze trails the length of his body to his rock hard cock. The flushing head weeping with moisture that I just want to lap up with my tongue.

"Danny, please." I squirm under his intense gaze.

He lifts one of my feet slowly and unbuckles the strap around my ankle, sliding the shoe off and kissing the arch of my foot. He repeats the action with the other, kissing my ankle and then following a slow and torturous route up my calf to my inner thigh. His fingers hook in the edge of the knickers and draw them down my legs, leaving me as naked as he is.

My mouth hangs open slightly as I watch him lean forward and lap at the liquid pooling at the tip of my slit before he suckles the head into his mouth. I fall back against the mattress with a groan as he swallows me down, his hot mouth working my aching dick. He feels it twitch sharply in his mouth, and I suck in a breath as he tugs my balls, tearing his mouth free.

"No," he whispers harshly. "Don't come yet."

"Then fuck me," I hiss impatiently, and the bastard chuckles.

"Get the lube," he instructs, and I reach behind me, my arm hanging off the bed at an awkward angle as I fumble for the drawer in the bedside table. I yank it open a little too forcefully and feel the handle snap off in my hand as the drawer clatters to the floor.

"Fuck," I groan, tossing the useless handle as I roll over onto my stomach. Danny's rubbing against my back as I search the wreckage of the drawer. "Stop distracting me," I half groan, half laugh as his throbbing cock slides back and forth between my arse cheeks.

"Can't help it." He kisses the back of my neck.

I manage to grab a condom and the bottle of lube, tossing it on the bed as he straddles my hips, keeping me on my stomach as he pumps the lube onto his fingers, rubbing them together to warm it. I bury my head in the sheet and give a long, low serrated groan as I feel his fingers massaging my hole, loosening my entrance before he's sliding one finger deep inside me. I hiss at the momentary burn, after all it's been a while, but as he slowly works it in and out and by the time he adds a second finger, I'm moaning and humping the mattress, trying to get some relief.

"Danny, please," I whisper desperately as I turn my head to look at him.

Danny

His witchy green eyes lock on me in the dim light of the room, and I can't look away. It's like he has me completely under his spell, which is apt considering its Halloween. My slick fingers are buried deep inside the hot, tight heat of his passage as he rides them desperately, grinding his aching dick into the mattress.

My own cock is throbbing unmercifully, but I need to make sure he's ready. He's so tight, and I don't want to hurt him, but Jesus, I want to fuck him so badly. I've never wanted anyone the way I want him.

The sexy little pants and whimpers from his lush swollen mouth are driving me crazy, and I don't know if I can hold back much longer. I slide my fingers from his hole and grope across the sheets for the condom packet, ripping it open blindly. I drop to the bed on my back and roll it down the length of my dick, snapping it into place as he watches me, his eyes like hot green glass.

Before I have a chance to reach for him, he scrambles across the bed, launching himself eagerly across my body as I grab him and twist so I can roll him underneath me.

Unfortunately, we both fail to take into consideration the fact that the bottom end of the bed is now on the floor and creating an incline. We both roll down wildly, the bedding tangling around us as we hit the floor with a muted thud, bundled up in his quilt like a burrito. There's a second of stunned silence and then we're both laughing loudly. I'm trying to disentangle us from the quilt, and he's grasping my face, kissing my mouth even as we're both giggling like idiots.

"This is a new position," he sniggers. "I've never tried a sex pancake roll before."

The laugh rips from my chest before I can stop it.

"It's new," I grin. "Do you like it?"

"Very ground-breaking." He pants out a laugh as he grinds his dick against my thigh.

"More like bed-breaking." I seal my mouth over his again as he huffs a laugh against my lips followed by a groan.

I've never experienced anything like this. How can I be having fun and be filled with humour, and yet at the same time feel this soul-destroying desperation, like if I don't have him, I'm literally going to die. It feels like the two should cancel each other out. It's like we're caught in some weird paradox.

I finally shove the quilt off us and roll over as he straddles my hips.

"Danny." He breathes heavily looking at me from underneath slow, slumberous eyelids. "Now."

I slide my hands up his thighs, gripping his arse cheeks and spreading them as he reaches down and grips my cock, angling it upwards. I suck in a sharp breath as I feel the head pushing at his entrance.

He lets out a long, slow moan as he slides down a fraction, fucking himself onto me in shallow thrusts as his rim stretches to accommodate the intrusion. We're both panting heavily, our breath the only sound in the room as I grip his arse so tightly, I'm sure my fingerprints will be bruised into his skin come morning.

He lets out a loud groan as he slides the rest of the way, taking me to the hilt. I still for a moment, my heart hammering in my chest and resisting the urge to thrust up into the hot, damp heat of him.

"Fuck," I hiss, my voice shakier than I'd like.

He leans back, canting his hips and changing the angle, rolling sinuously as he begins to ride me. I can do nothing but throw my head back, grasping the bony ridges of his hips as he takes me.

"Tris," I moan loudly, and I rock into him.

Before long, we're both making an obscene amount of noise, the floorboards creaking beneath us, and the occasional scrape of the bed being shoved out of position as we knock against it.

"More, Danny," Tristan gasps. "I need more."

I lift him off me, throwing him face down on the incline of the bed and lifting his hips so he's on his knees. Fisting my cock, I thrust back inside him as he groans loudly, setting a brain rattling pace as I pound into him. His hands grasp and scratch at the bedding, fisting the material tightly as the fitted sheet pings from the corner of the mattress.

"Argh, harder," he cries out.

"Fuck," I hiss, and in that second, I know I'm never going to be able to get enough of him. I could be buried balls deep in him until the end of time and it still wouldn't be enough.

"I'm... going... to... come..." he pants haltingly in time to the pounding staccato of my cock.

I pull out quickly and he whines in protest.

"Wha..." He looks over his shoulder.

"I want see your face when I make you come for the first time," I growl as I roll him over, sliding my arms under him and moving him higher up the bed. He spreads his legs in invitation, and I slide back into the welcoming grasp of him as he wraps his legs around me tightly.

"Danny, please," he begs, fisting my hair. "Make me come."

I hook his legs over my shoulders, canting his hips as I slam into him. He cries out as I peg his prostate almost continuously, but before I can get my hand around his dick, his passage tightens around my cock deliciously, and he erupts, coming so forcefully it streaks up his abdomen and chest, almost hitting his chin.

I lean in and lick a stripe of it, pressing my lips to his even as I taste the flavour of him. Two more battering thrusts and white-hot lightning bursts down my spine. I shoot deep inside the condom and wishing I could feel him bare, marking him as mine in the most primal way possible.

Our hearts are pounding as we both come down from an impossible high. I release his legs carefully, and he winces at the soreness in his hips from this position. As he stretches out, I have enough presence of mind to tie off the condom and drop it in the bin next to the remnants of the bedside drawer, which is spilled across the floor, before flopping back against the ruins of the bed on to the bare mattress covered in sweat and cum. I pull Tristan in close, needing to feel his skin against mine. I've never been much of a cuddler before, but right now, I can't think of anything better than holding the man I've just shared the most mind blowing sex of my life with.

"Sorry about the bed." I wince as I gaze around at the carnage we've wrought between us, and I can feel Tristan chuckle against me.

"I'll deal with it tomorrow," he snorts sleepily. "Along with the rest of it."

"We," I correct him. "We'll deal with it tomorrow," I tell him, thinking back to all the things we've probably broken or damaged in the kitchen in our haste to get to each other.

"I like the sound of we," he murmurs, and I can tell he's succumbing to exhaustion.

"Sleep, love," I rumble as I wrap my arms around him and yawn. Not realising the endearment as it rolls off my tongue with far too much ease.

We only manage to sleep for a few hours before I'm awoken by the muffled vibration and accompanying ringtone of my phone. I haul myself carefully off the broken bed, fumbling for my trousers and grabbing my phone out of my pocket just as it rings off.

Frowning as I recognise the number, I listen to the voice-mail intently before shooting off a text message and dragging my boxers and trousers back on. I manage to find my shirt, but there's only a few buttons left on it and the seam is ripped. I also can't find my sock as I pick up my solitary shoe, remembering the other one is in the kitchen somewhere.

"Where are you going?" Tristan mumbles reaching across the bed, his warm sleepy body a temptation wrapped in the wrinkled sheet.

"I have to go into work," I tell him softly, dropping down beside the bed.

"It's too early." He rolls onto his back, cracking one eye open as he props himself up on his elbows, and fuck if I don't want to crawl straight back into bed with him and pick up where we left off before we passed out.

"I know it's early." I smile. "But I'm about to do the walk of shame with no socks and a ripped shirt. I need to go home first and change."

"Why do they want you in so early?" He yawns again.

"Tris." I brush an errant lock of hair from his temple. "They think they've found the murder weapon."

I watch as his sleepy eyes widen.

"Dusty's murder weapon?" he asks, and I nod. "What? Where? How?"

"I don't know." I shake my head. "I don't have any of the details yet."

"Okay," he says quietly, his pretty face crumbling into a frown.

"Hey." I tuck my fingertips gently under his chin and tilt his face up so I can see his eyes. "Trust me, as soon as I have answers, I'll tell you."

He nods in resignation as I lean in and take his lips. It's a mistake. As he parts his lips and his tongue tangles with mine, I want to just roll him straight back into the wreck of his bed and make him come again, gasping loudly with my name on his lips.

But I can't.

I need to get home to shower and change then I'm needed at The Yard. As tempting as he is all warm and rosy and naked, I have to go.

"Tris," I whisper against his lips. "I have to go."

"No," he protests. "Just five more minutes."

I grin against his mouth, utterly delighted by him.

"I. Need. To. Go." I punctuate every word with a kiss.

"Fine." He pouts.

"Hey." I nip his swollen lips. "I'll be back later, okay?"

"Okay." He smiles shyly, his cheeks flushing with pleasure and invitation.

"Stop it," I groan as my dick twitches.

"Stop what?" He smiles innocently.

"You know exactly what." I give him one last peck on the mouth, then I head out of the room, giving him one more glance as he snuggles back into what's left of the bed with a smile on his lips.

19

Tristan

I hear the front door slam, and I flop back against the mattress on the broken bed, splayed out like Da Vinci's Vitruvian Man, the wrinkled sheets tangled around my hips barely covering anything. I know I have a really stupid smile plastered on my face as I stare up at the ceiling. A loud sigh of happiness escapes and I giggle. Still, no one's around to hear me, right?

Wrong...

"Holy shit! What happened in here?" I hear Dusty's wild exclamation from the doorway to the bedroom, and I barely lift my head to see her gazing at the complete devastation that used to be my bedroom. "Darling, I don't know whether to be impressed or call an exorcist."

My head drops back against the bed, and I chuckle loudly. From the corner of my eye, I see Dusty climb onto the bed and lay down next to me so she's also staring at the ceiling.

"Finally got your pipes cleaned then?" She smirks.

"Classy," I deadpan.

"That's me." She grins. "I'm a classy bird. So, tell me." She glances over at me. "Has he got a huge cock?"

I turn to her and blush. "I feel kinda weird laying here talking about this while I'm naked and covered in lube and dry cum."

"Hey, honey," she chuckles. "I'm about to spend eternity with my dick taped between my bum cheeks, there's no judgement here."

"Where did you go last night after the club?" I look over at her.

"I stayed with Chan," Dusty says quietly. "I know she can't see or hear me, but she's struggling, and I can't bear to see her in pain. I miss being able to hold her."

"Dusty," I say seriously. "No matter what happens, I'll make sure Chan is okay."

"I know you will, sweet boy." She smiles softly at me. "You know of all the mortuaries in London I could've woken up in, I'm glad I woke up in yours."

"Me too," I reply quietly as I roll over onto my side and prop my head on my hand. "Dusty, can I ask you something personal?"

"Sure," she says quietly as she stares over at me.

"Danny said he found something in your diary," I say as she watches me. "You had a standing appointment every Friday at 1pm marked by the letter R, and there was a hotel key card tucked in the pages. Plus, at the funeral there was an arrangement of black calla lilies, and the card was also signed R... were you... were you having an affair?"

Dusty stares at me wordlessly for another moment before turning her attention back to the ceiling and sighing slowly.

"His name was Ronald," she finally answers with a frown. "We'd been meeting up once a week for about six months."

"Was he a sugar daddy?" I ask curiously. "Danny said you were receiving payments every month, and the others at The Rainbow Room said you received a lot of gifts, expensive ones."

"My god what a lot of gossips." She pouts in annoyance.

"Dusty," I say sincerely. "You can trust me. This isn't about gossiping it's about trying to find out who murdered you."

"I know." She blows out a loud resigned breath. "It's just a sore spot."

"Were you in love with him?"

"God, no!" Dusty huffs a laugh but there's no humour.

"What happened?" I ask softly.

"His name's Ronald Fletcher, he's in financial services and works at Canary Wharf. He saw one of my shows and took a liking to me. Ron." She sighs. "He swept me off my feet in the beginning. He was older and very attractive, and who doesn't like being lavished with gifts? He spoiled me, not just financially but with his attention. It was flattering, a man like that paying me so much attention and the sex was hot."

"Was he out?" I wonder aloud.

"Not exactly." Dusty shakes her head. "I didn't think he was in the closet, but he was careful. We had to be discreet whenever we met up and couldn't be seen together in public. I never asked him outright, but we didn't exactly have long meaningful conversations. We'd meet up and fuck, and he'd spend an obscene amount of money on me. I never really questioned it. I wasn't really interested in his world of dry corporate banking, and he was a widower. I figured he was bored and lonely, and I was a way to fill that void without any strings."

"I take it things changed?" I surmise from the tone of her voice.

"It was fun at first, and the first few months passed in the blink of an eye, then about four months in, things began to change. He started getting demanding and clingy. It started to cross the line from something fun to something that was beginning to make me feel really uncomfortable, so I started to pull back. I tried to stop him from giving me money, and whenever he'd deposit it in my account, I'd instruct my bank to return it. I didn't have an address to send the gifts back, so I'd donate them. I tried to tell him to stop, that it was over and that I didn't think we should see each other anymore, and that's when the letters started."

"Letters?"

"Yeah," Dusty replies sourly. "Not just letters, flowers, cards, emails, text messages, and he'd stalk my social media."

"He was stalking you." I frown. "And you didn't think this was worth mentioning?"

"Because it wasn't him." Dusty shakes her head. "I've seen the security footage. It isn't him in that corridor right before I was killed."

"Are you sure?" I chew my lip thoughtfully.

"There's no way in hell Ron would dress up in drag, and besides, he's completely the wrong build and body type for the person in the footage."

"Doesn't mean he wasn't involved somehow." I scowl.

"Maybe," Dusty replies quietly.

"When was the last time you spoke to him?" I ask.

Dusty turns to stare at me carefully. "The night I died," she admits finally.

"What?"

"I told you. I remember arriving at the club," she explains. "I was sitting at the bar with Ramone and the ladies having a drink when he called me."

"What did he say?"

"He was..." She draws in a breath. "Upset... he thought the reason I'd broken things off with him was because I'd found out he lied to me."

"About what?" I ask in concern.

"His wife." She frowns. "Turns out he's not a widower at all, and the whole time he was meeting up with me he was cheating on her."

"Dusty," I whisper.

"I know." She covers her face. "As if I didn't feel sick enough over the whole situation, I found out I was breaking up a family."

"Not you, Dusty," I say fiercely. "You didn't know, so this is on him. He made the decision to cheat, he made the choice to lie. That's not on you."

"I felt so disgusted. I'm a lot of things." Her mouth tips down. "But I have one unbreakable rule, I never sleep with married men, it's not my style."

"What did you say to him when he told you?" I ask, my stomach starting to churn.

"He told me he was leaving his wife so we could be together." Her lips twist in disgust. "I told him that was never happening. I wasn't interested."

"Was he angry?"

"He was furious. He said he'd already told his wife." Dusty sighs. "I told him that was his problem. I'd already told him we were over weeks before I even found out his wife was still alive and that he was still married to her."

"Did he threaten you?" I ask in concern.

She shakes her head. "That's just it, he didn't. He took a moment and calmed down, then he apologised for his outburst and said he'd give me a couple of days to think it over."

"Think what over?" I frown.

She shrugs. "I told him there was nothing to think over, that we were over and that wasn't going to change. I didn't want to see or speak to him again. Then I hung up and blocked his number, not that it would've stopped him. He probably would've just bought a new phone."

"Dusty," I whisper. "You should've said something."

"Why?" She scowls. "Why the hell would I tell you about the married guy I was sleeping with that turned out to be a creepy, obsessive stalker. He wanted to be with me not kill me."

"For people that unstable it's a very fine line," I say seriously.

"I already told you it's not him on the security footage," she says stubbornly.

"But it could be his wife," I state emphatically, and she snorts. "No, think about it, what if it isn't a drag queen we're looking for. What if it was just a woman all along? You said yourself, Ronald told his wife he was leaving her."

"Why come after me though?" She frowns. "She didn't even know me."

"She knew you'd been sleeping with her husband for six months," I remind her.

"But I didn't know about her."

"I'm betting Ronald didn't bother explaining that to her," I muse.

"Then she should've clubbed him to death instead," Dusty says angrily.

"We need to tell Danny," I say gently to Dusty. "And let him investigate them both."

"This is so humiliating," Dusty bemoans.

"I know it is," I agree. "But if they are responsible for your murder, are you really going to let them get away with it?"

She huffs out a breath. "I kept everything," she says quietly.

"What?"

"I kept everything," she repeats. "All the letters, notes, emails, voice messages, and I even kept recordings of all our conversations in the last month, it's all saved in my iCloud."

"Why?"

"Because I was going to go to the police. I was also going to file a restraining order," Dusty admits slowly. "I held off for ages because I felt bad. I knew he was trying to keep his sexuality under wraps, and me filing a restraining order would have brought a lot of attention to him. I didn't want to do it, but he was forcing my hand."

"God, Dusty." I breath heavily. "That's even more motive to

keep you quiet and make the problem go away. Where's all the proof you collected?"

"It's at my flat in a hat box on top of my wardrobe," she replies.

"Okay." I say as my alarm goes off on my phone, and I quickly switch it off. "Here's what we're going to do, I'm going to take a shower and get dressed, then call into work and take the day off. Alan's back in, and he owes me for covering for him. I'll call Danny and tell him to look into Ronald and his wife, then I'm going to call Chan to meet me at your flat. She's got keys, hasn't she?"

Dusty nods mutely as I wrap the wreckage of the sheets around me to head to the bathroom.

"Why are you doing this?" she asks so quietly I almost miss it.

I stop and turn toward her slowly. "Because I care about you, Dusty. We may have met under unconventional circumstances but we're friends, and I don't have that many."

"I think you have a lot more than you think, Tristan." She watches me softly.

"I'm going to make sure they find out who hurt you, not because I want to get rid of you, but because it's the right thing to do, because you matter."

"Thank you," she mutters, and I nod, leaving her to her thoughts on my broken bed as I wander into the bathroom.

By the time I step out of my front door and onto the street, I'm filled with determination as Dusty ambles alongside me with her usual lopsided gait. However, what isn't usual is her silence. I've never known Dusty to be so withdrawn, and even though I haven't known her long, I'd like to think I know her well due to the enforced 24/7 proximity.

Pushing the worry aside for the moment, we walk side by

side in companionable silence. The weather has turned blustery, the chill autumn wind churning up the dry leaves in a myriad of bright colours. Tucking my coat in around me tighter, I pull my phone from my pocket to call Danny, but after a few rings it goes to voicemail.

"Hey, Danny, it's Tristan. I have some information for you about Dusty's appointment with R. His name is Ronald Fletcher, he works in the financial industry at Canary Wharf. They got involved about six months ago, and he told her he was a widower but that wasn't true. She found out his wife was still alive, and they were still together. He got too intense for Dusty, and she tried to call it off, but he kept stalking her, sending her letters, note, cards, emails. She kept them all, and they're hidden at her flat." I draw in a slow breath casting a quick glance at Dusty, who is still quiet, her mouth turned down and her gaze not meeting mine. "Danny..." I say in a low voice. "He called Dusty the night she died and told her that he was leaving his wife for her. Even though she told him no and that it was over, but he'd already told his wife. I think he didn't just tell her he was leaving her. I think he told her about Dusty... Danny, what if she's the one who was in the club that night? Anyway, I'm meeting Chan at Dusty's flat, and we'll bring all the evidence to you."

I hang up the phone a little glad I didn't have to do that face to face and could just leave a message. I still wasn't a hundred percent sure how I'm going to explain my newly found and very detailed information of Dusty's involvement with Ronald Fletcher. At least this way, I've postponed the questions a while longer.

Pulling up the Uber app, I order a car, and before I know it, we're pulling up outside Dusty's flat in Shoreditch. Dusty was still worryingly quiet, and as soon as the car drives off, leaving us standing on the pavement, I turn to her.

"Do you want to talk about it?" I ask and she shakes her head.

"There's nothing to say," she mutters. "Nothing that I haven't already told you. It's just so humiliating."

"Dusty, you didn't do anything wrong, this isn't on you," I tell her as we head into the building.

"Whatever." She frowns. "Let's just get this over with." She pauses, staring at the door to her flat.

"You haven't been back since..." My voice trails off mid question when I see the sadness in her eyes.

"Since I died," she says quietly.

"You don't have to do this, Dusty."

"Yes, I do," she murmurs. "This isn't my life anymore, and I have to be able to let it go."

She's breaking my heart, the pain and loss I can hear in her voice, the longing in her eyes. It's not fair. They took everything from her, her future, her friends, her family and now her home. It only makes me more determined to see that they're brought to justice, and the proof buried in this flat is going to help Danny build a case against them.

I raise my hand and knock firmly, and after a few moments the door opens and Chan is standing there, her eyes red rimmed and her eyeliner smudged slightly from where she's obviously been crying. I don't stop, don't think, for me, the least demonstrative person in the world, I simply step forward and wrap her in my arms. She buries her face in my shoulder and just breaks. Her cries tearing at my heart as much as Dusty's had, but there is no way for me to offer Dusty comfort other than words and justice. Chan is a different matter.

I manoeuvre her into the flat and close the door behind us with a quiet click, stroking her hair comfortingly. I dare not look at Dusty right now, knowing she's feeling her friend's pain as well as her own.

"Sorry." Chan pulls back sniffling. "It's hard being here. I should've started sorting through all her stuff and packing it up already, but I just couldn't face it, so I paid up an extra month's rent."

"You don't have to do this alone, Chan." I stroke her arm comfortingly. "When you're ready, I'll help you."

"Thank you." She wipes her nose on a piece of screwed up tissue.

"Why don't you take a minute," I tell Chan sympathetically. "I'll grab the hat box with the letters in."

"No, it's okay." She takes a deep shuddering breath. "I have to face it sooner or later. Besides, I want to know what that bastard was doing to my best friend."

I glance up at Dusty and see her lips pinch into a thin line, and I know there's something she's not telling us.

"Did you know that Dusty was seeing him?" I ask Chan, still watching Dusty who refuses to meet my gaze.

"I knew she was seeing someone. I didn't know who and I didn't press for details. Dusty wasn't one for married guys. She has a strict moral compass when it comes to stuff like that, plus she doesn't like complications." Chan shakes her head. "You don't know how much I wish I'd pressed her for details. We were always so careful about making sure each other was safe, and when she needed me most, I failed her."

"No, you didn't," I say softly.

"No?" Chan says bitterly. "I was there in the club that night in my dressing room while she was two rooms away dying all alone."

I watch as Dusty steps close and takes a deep breath almost bracing herself as she lifts her hand and touches the back of Chan's head, stroking the length of her long, silky hair. Chan gasps and touches the back of her head.

"Can you feel that?" I ask Chan, and she nods mutely with wide eyes.

"Tell her what I'm saying," Dusty says quietly.

"She wants me to tell you what she's saying," I explain to Chan.

"I didn't tell you what was going on with Ron because I didn't want you to worry, but I would've, when it got to the point I was going to involve the police. I never would have kept that from you," Dusty speaks, her gaze fixed on Chan, and I dutifully repeat it word for word.

"I never thought it would come to this, but I want you to know, I don't remember dying, and it doesn't matter that I was alone. Chan, you have been the most important person in my life since we were six years old. I can tell you now with absolute certainty, that even though I don't remember those final few moments, my last thought would have been you. So, you have to understand, that even though you weren't sitting there holding my hand, you were with me right at the end."

I again repeat Dusty's words, the sadness burning the back of my throat, and my heart aching as Chan's eyes fill with tears.

"Come on." I take Chan's hand, shooting Dusty an understanding smile. "Let's grab this box and get out of here."

She nods mutely and we head into the bedroom. I'm struck with how much I can see Dusty in here. It's filled with bright fabrics and pop art, dozens of different textures as feather boas hang from a silk screen, fluffy pillows on a chaise longue and racks of clothes and shoes, not unlike her dressing room at The Rainbow Room.

I watch as Chan reaches up and lifts a large round hat box down from the top of the wardrobe, which is decorated with a Parisienne design. We both drop down onto the end of the bed and set the box between us, gingerly lifting off the lid.

"Jesus Christ," I mutter.

Not only is the box bigger than I imagined but it's almost filled to the brim. Notes, cards, letters, candid photos of Dusty taken at the club, so, so many photos. It's easy to see that this man was not only obsessed with Dusty but that he'd been spiralling for some time.

"Dusty," I gasp as I look up at her.

Her lips are pursed, her eyes filled with shame and embarrassment.

"Why didn't you tell me it got this bad?" Chan breathes in horror as she flips through a couple of the notes.

Dusty, we're meant to be together...

I'm never going to let you go...

You belong to me...

She reads aloud, and with each one, my stomach churns tighter and tighter.

"Dusty?" Chan looks up, even though she can't see her, turning to me for answers.

"Let it go, Chan." I shake my head. "What's done is done. What's important now is that we get all of this to Danny, so he can start building a case against Ronald Fletcher."

She opens her mouth, about to respond when there's a loud knock at the door to the flat.

"Are you expecting anyone?" I frown.

"It's probably just the building manager," she replies, dropping the notes back into the box and placing the lid back. "He needs to speak with me about clearing Dusty's stuff out."

"You get that then." I nod. "I'll bring the box."

She gives me a weak smile as she lifts herself from the end of the bed and clips out of the room on tall, elegant heels.

"She's blaming herself," Dusty mutters as she watches Chan go.

"I know." I sigh. "It will take time."

"I should've said something," Dusty says quietly. "This is all my fault."

"No, Dusty." I stand abruptly. "None of this is your fault. You're the victim here."

"I don't want to be a victim," she snaps, her eyes filled with pain and sadness.

"I know," I say softly. "But we can't change the past, all we can do is make sure you have justice."

Knowing that Dusty isn't in the mood to talk anymore, I lift the hat box, tucking it under one arm. I'm just heading out of the room when my phone rings, and I drag it from my jeans pocket. Seeing Danny's name flash across the screen, I hit connect as I step out of the bedroom and raise it to my ear, but before I can utter a single word, I freeze finding myself staring down the barrel of a gun.

Stage 6

WTF?

20

Danny

"Benny?" I look across the table to the kid in front of me. He looks so worried, but then again, I'm not surprised. My colleagues dragged him in for questioning before I could suggest a more neutral place. He's not being charged with anything yet, but he's a definite person of interest considering the murder weapon which killed Dusty Le Frey was found hidden at the bottom of his locker at The Rainbow Room.

"Inspector Danny," he replies. "Where's Tristan?"

"He's not here right now." I shift in my chair, wishing I was back at Tristan's flat snuggled up against him naked instead of stuck in a freezing cold interrogation room at the arse crack of dawn questioning a sweet kid with Downs Syndrome that I don't believe for one second harmed Dusty.

"Why am I here?" He frowns in confusion. "Did I do something wrong?"

"No, Benny," I say softly, making a mental note to kick the arse of whoever jumped the gun and dragged Benny in when I could've quite easily asked him these questions in his home where he'd have been more comfortable. "Benny, you're not in any trouble," I tell him carefully. "I just need to ask you a few questions, then you can go home, okay?"

"Okay." He nods as his representative stares at me coolly.

"He shouldn't have been brought in at all," she says angrily. "You haven't pressed any charges and you didn't give us any notice. As a vulnerable person we need to make sure his rights are not infringed upon and that he's not being coerced into giving a false statement indicating any guilt on his behalf."

"Mrs Lovell?" I glance down at the paperwork in front of me to make sure I've got the name right. I look up and she nods sharply. "Mrs Lovell, I'm not here to coerce Benny into any kind of coached statement. I'm simply looking for the truth, that's all. Although the murder weapon was found in his locker, I am aware that Benny never keeps it locked and as such, can be easily accessed by anyone. Any evidence against him is purely circumstantial. I don't believe he had anything to do with Miz Le Frey's murder, but I need to ascertain how it came to be in his locker."

She nods again sharply, and I turn my attention to Benny.

"I didn't hurt Dusty." His eyes fill with tears. "I love her."

"Hey," I say gently, I know I should maintain a professional distance, but I can't help it, the kid just tugs at me. I reach across the table and squeeze his hand comfortingly. "Benny, I don't think you hurt Dusty. I know how much you loved her."

"I miss her." He sniffles.

"I know." I nod in sympathy. "But, Benny, I could really use your help catching the person who did hurt Dusty. What do you say? Will you help me out?"

"Yes, Inspector Danny." He wipes his nose on his sleeve, and I beckon one of the uniformed officers behind me to go and find a box of tissues. "I don't know who hurt her though," Benny adds.

"I know." I lift a sealed evidence bag containing a trophy that comprises of a long slim trunk with a football sitting on top of it surrounded by stars. I set it carefully in front of Benny so he can see it clearly. "Can you tell me what this is?"

Benny stares down at it thoughtfully.

"It's my football trophy." He frowns in confusion. "Why do you have my football trophy?"

"We think someone hit Dusty with your trophy, it has her blood on it. We found it hidden at the bottom of your locker wrapped in an old sweatshirt, can you tell me how it got there?"

I watch as Benny shakes his head.

"I left it in Dusty's room, so she could see it," he says quietly. "My team won, and I wanted to show her. I put it on her dressing table."

"When was this?" I ask.

"The day she died." He frowns. "I had to go home. I don't work late. I come in during the day to clean," he says sniffing again. "I left it for Dusty to see when she came in, but when I went into her room the next day, I couldn't find it."

There's a quiet tap at the door and as I look up, I see one of my colleagues beckon me into the corridor.

"Okay, Benny, thank you." I stand up. "Will you excuse me for a moment."

I step out into the corridor and shut the door behind me with a quiet click.

"Danes." I nod to the officer.

"Sir," he replies. "His story checks out. We've reviewed the full security footage for that day for the corridor leading to the victims dressing room. You can clearly see the kid taking the trophy to the room and returning without it at about 4pm and at least six hours before the homicide took place. We also have several witnesses that saw him leaving The Rainbow Room at about 5.30pm. He was driven home by one of the other employees. Even though he has his own flat and lives alone, it's in a warden assisted building. Security footage and witness statements put him in the common room playing Monopoly with another resident at the time of the murder. That, plus the fact, we only found the murder weapon because we had an anonymous tip called in, it just seems a little too convenient."

"And you couldn't have checked all this out before you dragged the poor kid in here and scared him half to death?" I ask angrily.

"Sorry, sir." He shakes his head. "I didn't think it was a good idea to bring him in, but it wasn't my call, it was James. He pulled rank, was convinced the kid was involved somehow."

Although I hadn't been here long, I knew PC James Turnbull was an arsehole.

I clench my jaw tightly. "I'll deal with James. For now, make sure Benny gets home safely."

He nods in agreement. "Also, Maddie is looking for you, says she has something."

"Okay, tell her I'll be there in a moment." I turn and slip back into the room, not bothering to sit back in the uncomfortable metal chair. Instead, I move closer to the kid.

"Benny, I want to thank you for your help. There's an officer waiting outside who's going to take you home now," I tell him.

"Okay." He nods. "Did I help?" he asks hopefully.

"Yes, lad." I nod. "You did." I offer him a small smile and turn, but his hand on my arm stops me.

"I have something for you, Inspector Danny." He reaches into his pocket, and I watch curiously as he retrieves a tattered sheet of stickers. He peels one off and sticks it to the lapel of my suit jacket, smoothing it down a few times until he's satisfied its stuck firmly. I glance down and grin, it's a Sheriff's badge. "There." Benny nods. "It will help you catch the bad guys."

"Thank you, Benny." I smile genuinely. "I'll check in on you soon, I promise."

I head back out into the corridor toward the stairs and head up a level to the offices, pulling my phone from my pocket as I walk briskly. I'd felt it vibrate in my pocket during the interview but let it go to voicemail. I can't help the smile that curves my lips when I see I've had a missed call from Tristan.

I've been trying not to think about him ever since I left his place this morning, but it's impossible not to. The way he moaned and cried out when I was buried deep inside him. The taste of him on my tongue, the way he'd wrapped himself around me as if he never wanted to let go. He felt so small and vulnerable tucked into my side as I'd held him in bed, except I know it's a bit of a misnomer, he's slim and willowy, nothing like I've ever experienced before, but he's also incredibly strong in every way that matters both physically and emotionally.

I pull up his voicemail and listen, my focus sharpening when I realise exactly why he called me. I hang up the phone and walk between the banks of desks looking for Maddie, one of the other investigators, churning over everything I've just learned from Tristan.

"Danny." Maddie waves me over as she stands beside one of the junior officers as he taps away on a keyboard.

"What have you got?" I ask as I approach. "Danes said you were looking for me?"

She nods. "The bank payments into Dusty Le Frey's account, we've managed to track them back to the source. They originated here in London from a small independent financial firm in the city named Banks-Chappell Investment & Finance Brokers."

I scratch my chin thoughtfully as I think back to Tristan's message.

"Got a list of employees?" I ask.

"Sure." She looks down at the officer as he starts typing again, flicking between screens. "Who are you looking for?"

"Ronald Fletcher," I tell her.

"Got him," the officer interrupts. "Ronald Fletcher, he's the owner and CEO."

"The owner?" I reply solicitously.

"Who is he?" Maddie asks me.

"The mysterious R from Dusty's diary," I reply.

"He's the one she was meeting up with, the sugar daddy?" Her eyes narrow as she stares at the screen. "She was having an affair with him?"

"According to my source she didn't know he was married, he told her he was a widower. I'm guessing he sent her money through his business expense accounts so his wife didn't find out."

"Slimeball." Maddie sniffs in distaste as she turns to the kid at the computer. "What do we know about this Ronald Fletcher?"

He begins tapping away furiously, flipping through screens so fast I can't keep up.

"Ronald Fletcher, age fifty-two, married to Helen Fletcher, formerly Banks-Chappell," he begins reeling off facts. "Looks like Ronald's company was originally founded by his father in law, Harlon Banks-Chappell. When he passed away, he bypassed his only daughter and left the company to his son in law Ronald, lock, stock and barrel."

"Ouch." Maddie winces. "That's got to sting. We got an address?"

"Mayfair." He looks up and Maddie whistles.

"Okay." I nod. "Looks like it's time to go and have a little chat with Mr & Mrs Fletcher. You tagging along?" I ask Maddie.

"And miss the chance to snoop around a place in Mayfair? Hell yeah!" She grins. "Wait until I tell Sonia about this."

"You're not supposed to gossip with your wife about random cases." I smile.

"Yeah, yeah." She shoves me playfully. "It's not like I tell her any details."

I shake my head in amusement as she grabs her coat. "After you, Inspector." I step aside and let her move past me."

"Why thank you, Inspector. Want to go make some rich people cry?" she asks impishly.

"I'd love to." I grin. "You want to be good cop or bad cop this time?"

"Bad as always." She winks.

By the time we're in the car heading into central London, I've filled Maddie in on the information Tristan supplied.

"So, you think the wife was the one caught on the footage?" Maddie muses. "I mean, I get it, you find out not only that your husband is stepping out on you but that he's using your daddy's company, which should have been your inheritance, as his own personal piggy bank to pay for his mistress. Yeah, I'd be pissed too."

"There's a big leap from being pissed at your husband to dressing up in drag to sneak into a club and batter someone to death with a football trophy." I tap my fingers against the wheel.

"Always the good cop," she snorts. "It's still motive."

"And I'm not in any way disputing that," I reply. "He's got plenty of motive too. There's nothing to say he wasn't the one dressed in drag sneaking down that corridor."

"Either way it stinks." Maddie wrinkles her nose.

"No argument here." I pull in and park the car, glancing up at the white brick residence with an elegant black front door, flanked by Greek style columns. Coming from Leeds, the youngest son of a coal miner, properties like this still bemuse me, like I can't quite believe people actually live like this outside the confines of film and TV.

Maddie clucks her tongue as her sharp gaze takes in the private residence of Ronald Fletcher. We'd already tried his offices, only to be informed he hadn't been in the office for weeks. We climb the three steps to the front door and knock on the huge brass knocker. After a few moments, the door opens ponderously, and I blink in surprise, there's an honest to God butler standing there staring at us expectantly and wearing a ruthlessly pressed black suit and a Windsor collared shirt. He didn't seem to be in any rush to greet us, merely stood waiting for one of us to speak.

"Good morning." I nod a little awkwardly. "We're looking for Mr Ronald Fletcher."

His eyes quickly dart down, taking in our attire and seemingly unimpressed. "Mr Fletcher is not available at present," he finally replies, his voice, his accent so sharp you could cut glass with it.

"I'm afraid we're going to have to insist," I tell him bluntly as I show my ID. "Inspector Danny Hayes, Scotland Yard. This is my colleague, Inspector Madeleine Wilkes."

"We can either speak with him here, or we can drag him down to the station." Madeleine smiles pleasantly.

"Very well." The butler, who didn't offer his name, steps aside and allows us to enter. "Mr Fletcher is currently in the main parlour, but he is... slightly indisposed at present. I hope you'll make your enquiry brief."

"We'll see," I mutter as we step inside the cool and cavernous foyer. A staircase coils up and to the right. Curiously, it has a chair lift parked at the bottom and a heavy metal rail curving up the length of the stairs. We bypass the small round table in the centre of the foyer upon which is an expensive arrangement of black calla lilies in a Waterford vase. The significance of the flowers is not lost on me, as I know for a fact Ronald Fletcher sent an identical arrangement to Dusty's funeral.

We cross the highly polished tiled floor and enter a doorway to the left that opens up into an elegant parlour with high backed cream-coloured sofas, which look a bit uncomfortable to be honest. Not the sort of sofa you can kick back on with a couple of bags of Doritos and watch *Downton Abbey*.

As my gaze scans the room it falls upon a hunched figure

slumped in a chair looking more than a little dishevelled and clutching a half empty decanter of brandy.

"Mr Fletcher?" I enquire as Maddie and I cross the room, but he merely grunts and looks up, his eyes bleary and bloodshot.

"Mr Fletcher?" Maddie tries, but he simply stares at us and lifts the decanter, slurping messily from the wide lip.

"I'm afraid you're not going to get much sense out of my husband at the moment," a smooth cultured voice speaks from behind us.

I turn to look and see an elegant middle-aged woman with mousy brown hair and light brown eyes. She's wearing a navy-blue sheath dress and a single strand of pearls, looking perfectly put together. However, my gaze wanders over the wheelchair she's sat in, and from the looks of her painfully thin and emaciated legs beneath the skirt of her conservative sheath dress, she has been for quite some time.

"Mrs Fletcher?" I ask as I step closer, and she nods.

"Please, take a seat, Inspector?"

"Hayes," I supply for her. "And this is my colleague, Inspector Wilkes."

"Very well." She tightens her lips and nods toward the high backed sofa. "Please, take a seat and then you can tell me exactly what it is you want with my husband."

"Thank you, ma'am." I take a seat and realise my initial assumption was right, this sofa is about as comfortable as sitting on a stack of plywood. I shift slightly as Maddie takes a seat next to me.

"What can we do for you, Inspectors?" she asks politely.

"We had hoped to speak with your husband," I begin, glancing at the man in the corner who's so ripe I could probably get inebriated from the fumes coming off him.

"Yes, well." She glowers at him. "I think you can see that's not going to happen."

"Is he like this often?"

"Inspector Hayes," she says briskly, smoothing out an imaginary wrinkle in her skirt. "Please, do me the courtesy of being candid. I don't much care for chit chat."

"Very well." I nod, glancing at Maddie who inclines her head in agreement. "We're here to speak with your husband regarding his relationship with a drag artist known as Dusty Le Frey. I have evidence to suggest they had an intimate relationship."

She turns to glare at her husband. "Another one, Ronald?" she says bitterly.

"Forgive me." I draw her attention back to me. "I was under the impression that he'd told you about the affair."

"No." Her mouth wrinkles in distaste. "A few weeks ago, on the afternoon of the 21st, he told me he was leaving me. He didn't give a reason, he simply stated that he could no longer live this farce that was our marriage."

"And you didn't question why?" Maddie asks suspiciously.

"Frankly, I was relieved," she scoffs. "I was young and naive once, and I believed in sweet words and hollow promises. I thought, like many of those men my husband has since been involved with, that he loved me. He didn't, he never has. He's too selfish to love. He married me and charmed my father right out of my rightful inheritance, and since then, it's been a never-ending cycle of him pursuing these... persons. My husband has a predilection for men in case you hadn't noticed, more specifically, female impersonators, and this Dusty person is just the latest in a long line of humiliation."

"Why did you stay with him?" I ask.

"I was going to leave him once," she says reflectively. "But then I was involved in an accident, and this chair is the consequence. After that, there was simply nowhere for me to go. I resigned myself to this life as long as he remained discreet. However, this really is the last straw." She glances over at him speculatively. "As soon as he sobers up, I shall be contacting my solicitor to begin divorce proceedings. If you have any evidence of his infidelity, I would appreciate it if you could share those with my legal team."

"I will of course pass your request along," I inform her politely. "However, as this is an active investigation that might not be possible."

"What exactly is this Dusty person accusing him of?" Her gaze narrows. "Is he after money?"

"No," I reply coolly. "She..." I correct her. "Is not after anything. She's dead. This is a murder investigation."

"What happened?" She frowns.

"That's what we're trying to figure out. She was found bludgeoned to death on the evening of the 21st ^{of} October," I answer. "You said, Mr Fletcher informed you on the 21st that he planned to leave you?"

She nods. "Afterwards, he disappeared into his study to make a phone call. I don't know who he spoke to, but he didn't come out of the study all evening. Cramer found him passed out drunk in there around 10pm, he put him to bed where he remained all night. He sobered up the next day but then something changed." She frowns. "He crawled inside a bottle and has been there ever since. I've never seen him drink for this length of time. He hasn't worked, has barely changed his clothes." Her nose wrinkles in disgust. "I'm not even sure of when he last showered."

"I'm betting he found out about Dusty's death, that's what triggered the drinking binge," Maddie muses. "He's mourning her."

"Please," Mrs Fletcher snorts. "You have to love someone to mourn them, and he's incapable of love. I know my husband. He's like a petulant child when he doesn't get his own way. Once he sobers up, he'll be chasing someone else."

"Maybe," I murmur as I stare at the guy who's now snoring

lightly, his mouth hanging open and a thin thread of drool hanging from the corner of his lip. On a good day, I can see that he'd be considered a very attractive man, but at the moment, he just looks bloated and broken. My brow creases slightly in thought as I turn back to his wife. "Who's Cramer?" I ask. "You said he found your husband passed out drunk in his study at about 10pm?"

"That's right." She nods. "You're welcome to ask him yourself. Cramer is our butler. I myself checked in on Ronald a few times during the night."

"That was generous of you." Maddie's eyes narrow. "Considering he'd told you he was leaving you only hours earlier."

"Or maybe I was hoping he'd choke to death on his own vomit and save me the bother of a divorce." She glares back. "As much as I'd love to see my husband in prison, which to me would be as satisfying as divorcing him and leaving him destitute, he couldn't have killed this Dusty person. If he was killed on the evening of the 21st, then I can tell you that Ronald was here all night. He couldn't have killed him."

"Her," I correct again, and seeing her look of confusion, I add, "Couldn't have killed her."

"Inspector Hayes," she says coolly. "It's bad enough I have to dissect the humiliation of my marriage in front of you, so I'm certainly not going to argue semantics with you. I'm very sorry that this person met with an unfortunate end. I'm even more sorry they had the misfortune to get tangled up with my husband in the first place, but he was not responsible for the murder."

I release a quiet breath, she's right. If the butler was pouring Ronald Fletcher into bed around 10pm, which is around the time of Dusty's death, it definitely rules him out. Likewise, with Helen Fletcher confined to a wheelchair she also couldn't have been in that corridor leading to Dusty's dressing room that night. We've hit another dead end, and it makes me want to growl in frustration. However, maintaining my air of professionalism, I rise from the sofa and offer Mrs Fletcher my hand.

"Thank you for your co-operation, Mrs Fletcher."

She nods as she shakes my hand. "Inspector Hayes, Inspector Wilkes." She glances briefly at Maddie.

I turn toward the doorway, and as I do, my attention snags on a framed photograph resting on top of a narrow side table. I step forward, my eyes glued to the image. Reaching out I pick it up and turn toward Mrs Fletcher.

"Who's this?" I lift the picture.

"That's our daughter, Kaitlin," she replies in confusion. "Why?"

I turn my attention back to the photograph. It's of a young woman with the same mousy brown hair and light brown eyes as her mother. In the picture, she's wearing a strapless evening gown, and right there on her shoulder is a large birthmark.

"Mrs Fletcher, where is Kaitlin now?" I ask.

"She said she had to go out, that she had an errand to run. She'll be back for dinner as usual."

"She lives here?" I state, my mind racing as the pieces slot into place.

"She does as a matter of fact," Mrs Fletcher replies. "Kaitlin has..." She hesitates for a moment. "Emotional difficulties. We thought it best she remained here with us."

"May we take a look at her room?" I request as calmly as possible.

"I don't think that's appropriate," she replies evenly and folds her hands in her lap.

"Mrs Fletcher," I tell her firmly. "I can get a warrant, but it will be quicker with your permission. Your co-operation in our investigation will also go a long way toward your request for access to the evidence pertaining to your husband's indiscretions," I add, my eyes flicking to Ronald who is still passed out drunk. "Trust me when I say there's more than enough there for you not only to be granted a quick divorce but to take him to the cleaners while you're at it."

Her mouth purses as she stares at me consideringly, clearly torn between protecting her daughter's privacy and the chance to be rid of her no good husband.

"Cramer," she calls out loudly, and I'm sure from the hard look in her eyes that we're about to be shown the door. "Show the Inspectors to Miss Kaitlin's room," she instructs the butler as he enters the room.

"Very good, ma'am." He nods. "If you would be so good as to follow me."

"Thank you." I nod to Mrs Fletcher as we pass her.

Cramer leads us up the curving staircase and along the hallway to a large, airy room. Maddie and I stop abruptly, staring as we take in the room.

"Well, this isn't creepy at all," Maddie murmurs. "How old would you say the daughter is?"

"Late twenties, maybe early thirties," I mumble, still staring.

It looks like a room that would belong to a six year old. It's painted baby pink with a four-poster bed dominating one wall and mounted with frilly lace curtains tied with pink ribbons. The bed itself is stacked with pillows and dolls...

There are dolls everywhere. Lined up on shelves, sitting in a rocking chair beside the window, and along one of the other walls, sitting on a low table is a huge Victorian style dolls house.

"Fuck," Maddie whispers. "I'm going to be having nightmares about this room for years."

"Come on." I step further into the room as Cramer disappears, and the door clicks ominously closed behind us. "We need to search the room before Kaitlin returns."

"What exactly are we looking for?" she asks.

"Dusty's locket for one," I reply as I open the nearest drawer and start rummaging through it. "And anything else that will tie her to The Rainbow Room and the murder."

Maddie heads toward the wardrobe and opens the door as I continue to look through the chest of drawers. After several long minutes of searching, I find a trunk pushed right under the bed. It takes a bit of squirming and some careful manoeuvring, but I manage to retrieve it and set it on the bed. It has a small padlock on it, which I tug at uselessly. Glancing around, I pick up a small bobby pin from a dish on the dressing table. A little wiggling and the lock clicks open. I glance up at Maddie who's watching me with a raised brow.

"Mis-spent youth." I grin. "And several older brothers."

She chuckles but the laugh dies on her lips as I flip the trunk open.

"Jesus Christ." Her eyes widen as I pull out a curly blonde wig and a green sequinned dress, the exact outfit the person in the video footage had been wearing, and sure enough, underneath it, on top of a pile of other stuff, is a gold locket.

Dusty's locket.

I pick it up and turn it over in my palm, looking up sharply when I hear Maddie's gasp.

"Danny." Her eyes are wide, and she looks like she's holding a stack of large sized photos. "You should look at this."

I take them as she hands them across the bed, and my stomach clenches in horror. A cold sweat has broken out at the back of my neck as I turn through photo after photo... of Tristan.

"What the hell?" I breathe heavily. In some of the pictures, I'm with him. One taken through the window of the coffee shop in Whitechapel on our first date. One of us on the riverside terrace outside the restaurant kissing passionately. "She's been following him for weeks." I frown. "But why?"

"Look at this." Maddie tosses down an ID along with Dusty's funeral order of service.

"She was there." I realise, picking up the ID, which has her photo, a fake name, and the logo for a catering company. "Brambles's Catering." I think back. "I'm sure they're the ones who catered Dusty's wake at The Rainbow Room."

"Um..." Maddie looks at me a bit sickly. "Didn't Mrs Fletcher say that Dusty wasn't the only one her husband had an affair with?"

I nod, and she throws down a small stack of funeral order of services. I pick them up and scan through the names and photographs on the front. They all look like drag queens.

"I don't think Dusty was the first problem of her father's that she made 'disappear'." Maddie stares at me.

"Shit," I mutter. "We need to pull the details on all of these, see if any are unsolved murders. These deaths all need to be looked at again."

I move the stack of photographs of Tristan, and one slips out, drifting to the bed. I pick it up, and my heart starts to pound. It's a picture of him and Chan standing talking outside The Rainbow Room, but there are big, angry red slashes across both of their faces in marker pen.

"Danny?" Maddie says worriedly, and I look down at the half empty box of bullets in her hand. "I think Kaitlin might have a gun."

I drop the stack of photos I'm holding on the bed and scramble for my phone. Finding Tristan's number with shaky fingers, I hit connect. I swallow hard against the sudden and inexplicable panic churning in my gut as the phone rings. I need to get him someplace safe until we can get Kaitlin into custody. Finally, just when I think it's going to go to voice mail the call connects, but he doesn't answer, instead I hear a cold female voice.

"Drop the phone," she instructs slowly, then the line goes dead.

21

Tristan

"Drop the phone," a cold voice instructs, and given no other choice, I do so and watch as she stamps on my iPhone, smashing the screen. "The box too."

I set the box down on the ground still staring at the woman. She's about my height, with mousy brown hair and light brown eyes, and she's wearing a conservative dark grey dress with a matching blazer and sensible heels. There's nothing remarkable about her, but I get the feeling I'm looking at the woman who was in the corridor that night.

"You're the one who killed Dusty," I accuse before I can censor the words out of my mouth.

Chan sucks in a sharp breath, and I edge toward her, reaching for her hand and drawing her behind me protectively.

"What the actual fuck?" I hear a startled exclamation, and as my gaze deviates slightly to the right, I see Dusty standing right next to the woman, studying her face up close seeing as the woman can't actually see her. "Shit." Dusty scowls after a moment. "She's Ronald's daughter... Katy something... no wait, Kaitlin. I'm sure it's her. Ronald used to keep a picture of her in his wallet."

"You're Ronald Fletcher's daughter?" I exclaim in surprise. Well, that I didn't see coming. I didn't even realise he had a kid, well... grown up kid. She looks to be in her early thirties.

"How did you know that?" she demands, punctuating the air with little stabs of the gun.

"Um..." I grimace. Okay, how to explain to a psycho with a gun that you can see dead people? Yeah, I can't see this ending well.

"I know who you are too, Tristan Everett, and you." She swings the gun toward Chan. "Li Chan. I've been watching you ever since the funeral."

"You were at the funeral." Chan frowns.

"Of course, I was." Kaitlin smiles sweetly. "The funeral is always the best part. All those people, so sad."

"You've done this before." I realise with a sick sinking feeling in my gut. "You killed Dusty, but she wasn't the first, was she?"

"Nope." Kaitlin smiles wickedly. "It's not the first time I've cleaned up Daddy's mess."

"But why?" I ask.

"Because he was going to leave us," she replies as if the answer should be obvious. "And now he won't, now he'll stay, and I'll take care of him while he's grieving. Just like he grieved the others."

"He knew about the others?"

She shrugs. "Not all of them, but some. I was very careful to make them look like accidents or suicides. Dusty was a mistake. She wouldn't drink the cocktail I'd made especially for her. She would've just slipped away like the others, but she wouldn't." Kaitlin sighs. "All she had to do was drink, but she was so stubborn. I really didn't have a choice."

"Why take her locket?" Chan asks angrily.

"Because I wanted it," Kaitlin states as if she were a child who'd just taken another kid's Barbie doll. "It was pretty." Then she shakes her head as if it doesn't matter. "I knew it would make Daddy sad, but it's okay because he has me to love him."

"Oh, honey." Chan stares at her. "We've all got daddy issues, but yours are edging into *Game of Thrones* territory."

"You don't know what you're talking about," Kaitlin snaps. "He loves me. I take care of him, just like I took care of Mum."

"What do you mean?" I ask warily.

"Mum was going to leave too," she says frankly. "But I made it so she couldn't. I'm sorry she got hurt, but it's really better this way. Now I can take care of her too, and she can't ever leave me."

"Jesus Christ, this is one fucked up family," Dusty scoffs.

"What did you do to your mother?" I ask unable to help myself.

"I cut the brakes on her car." Kaitlin shrugs. "I didn't want her to leave."

"*Psycho,*" Chan mouths to me, tilting her head toward the woman with the gun.

"Wow, whatever happened to baby Jane?" Dusty says slowly as she stares at Kaitlin. "The lights are on but no one's home if you know what I mean."

"But I don't understand." I shake my head, frowning. "What do you want with me and Chan? Why follow us?"

"Not her." Kaitlin's eyes narrow as she trains the gun on me. "YOU."

"But why?"

"Because I overheard you talking at The Rainbow Room, and you said the drag bitch that was fucking my dad was haunting you."

"I'm pretty sure that's not what I said," I reply blandly.

"Is it true?" she demands, pointing the gun at me in agitation.

"There really is no good answer to that," I answer. "And what does it matter? She's dead, you killed her."

"But she'll haunt me, she'll be mad, and she'll come after me." Kaitlin's eyes dart around restlessly as if Dusty could be anywhere, ready to leap out at her, rather than standing right next to her with her arms folded across her chest tapping her foot in annoyance.

"What's your plan here?" I ask, holding my hands up non-threateningly.

"I'm going to kill you, of course, silly." She shakes her head. "Pay attention. She's angry because I killed her, but if I kill the two of you, it will make it all go away."

"Sorry." Chan frowns in confusion. "You lost me at I'm a psycho nut job... blah blah blah gonna murder you."

"Not helping," I mouth at Chan.

"Chan is her best friend, so she'll have someone to keep her company and you're the only one who can see her, so if I kill you. It all goes away." She explains as if it's the most logical thing in the world.

"Honey, I think you've got a real shot at that insanity plea," Chan agrees.

"Okay, so that's all settled." Kaitlin cocks the hammer on the gun and aims it at me first. "Do you have any last words?"

"Yeah," Dusty snorts. "Your arse looks fat in that dress."

"Wait, wait, wait," Chan yells. "Just wait a minute, okay? You don't want to shoot us here."

"I think I do." Kaitlin ponders the question. "You both need to die, and then that drag queen, Dusty whatever her name is, won't be mad at me anyone."

"I'm pretty sure I will." Dusty glares at her.

"No, wait." Chan stops her again as she moves the gun to Chan. "Look where you are, honey. You're in the middle of a busy block of flats. Anyone can hear the gun shot. What you want is to take us somewhere quiet, somewhere no one will know."

"What are you doing?" I hiss, then I feel a tugging on my

back pocket, and I realise Chan has managed to slip her phone into my back pocket. She gives me the barest hint of a wink. "Why don't you take us back to The Rainbow Room," she suggests. "At this time of the morning, it will be empty. No one's usually in until early afternoon, even the cleaning staff. The building is completely self-contained. No one will hear anything."

Kaitlin seems to consider her words. "It does have a nice sense of symmetry to it. If I kill you in the place where Dusty died, do you think it will appease her?"

"What do you think this is, ancient fucking Peru? You can't sacrifice people to appease me," Dusty growls at her. "If you hurt them, I swear to God, I'll haunt you until the end of fucking time."

"Okay, yes." Kaitlin decides. "The Rainbow Room, I have my car, but I have the gun so one of you will have to drive."

"I will," I tell her quickly. "Chan can't drive in those heels, and I have a licence."

It's true I do have a licence, but I haven't been behind the wheel of a car since I took my test years ago. There's not really any need when public transport is so accessible in London, plus the small fact, which I won't admit, is that I'm a simply appalling driver, but hey, what's the worst that can happen? With any luck we'll get pulled over by the police, that is if I don't accidentally kill us first.

"Alright move." Kaitlin waves the gun in the direction of the door.

It's really shit luck that we manage to make it down three flights of stairs of a council tower block in the middle of Shoreditch without running into one single person. I mean really, where's a nosy neighbour or a random drug dealer when you need one?

I'm surprised the wheels are still on Kaitlin's pristine little Fiat 500 when we make it to the parking spaces. She unlocks the car and waits for me to get in before shoving Chan into the back seat and sitting next to her. Poor Chan. Cramped is an understatement and with legs as long as hers they're practically folded around her ears as Kaitlin presses the gun to her side.

"No funny business," she tells me as I watch her in the rear view mirror. "Or I shoot her."

I nod slowly. "I'm just going to adjust the seat, okay?"

"Be quick," she tells me, and I squirm in my seat, readjusting it to the right leg room and carefully pulling Chan's phone from my pocket. It's a good job I was obsessive enough to memorise Danny's number. I type it in as surreptitiously as I can while making a show of adjusting the mirrors and hit connect. Dropping it in my lap and covering it with my sweater, I hope to God that Danny is on the other end listening. I look up to where Dusty is sitting in the front passenger seat beside me, and she nods.

"Come on, move!" Kaitlin snaps, and I start the engine.

"I don't usually drive," I say calmly as I rather awkwardly reverse out of the space in jerky movements, almost hitting a concrete bollard.

"Jesus Christ, boo." Even Dusty gasps. "Are you sure you can drive?"

"I'm just a bit rusty," I say, hoping Kaitlin will think I'm talking to her not Dusty. "I'm sure it'll all come back to me. Although you might have to give me directions to The Rainbow Room," I say loudly. "I don't live around here so I'm not familiar with the best route."

"Down to the end of the road and turn left," Kaitlin instructs.

I'm a sweaty, shaking mess by the time we arrive at The Rainbow Room with a clear reminder once again of why I choose not to drive in London. I think the cyclists alone have just shaved twenty years off my life. I park around the back, close to the building where the rear entrance is located. We climb out the car warily, and as Kaitlin herds us toward the door, glancing around to make sure we're not seen, I feel Dusty lean in close to my ear.

"As soon as you get inside, boo, it'll be dark," she tells me quietly. "I'll try and distract her, you and Chan run."

I cast my eyes to the right, catching her profile as she nods, and I reach out lacing my fingers through Chan's. She turns to look at me enquiringly, and I mouth the word 'run' and stare at the door pointedly, hoping she gets my drift.

Her brows furrow and I'm not entirely sure we're on the same page here. We just need to stay alive long enough for the calvary to hopefully show up in the form of my sort of boyfriend and his police buddies.

"Now what?" Kaitlin hisses as we approach the door, and she sees the keypad.

"Relax," Chan says calmly. "I know the door code."

We step up to the door with Kaitlin behind us still pointing the gun at our backs. Chan punches in the code, and I open the door and step through, keeping a tight hold on her hand. The second we step into the darkness, there's a blast of cold air, and Kaitlin stumbles dropping the gun.

"RUN!" I shout to Chan, yanking on her hand.

She doesn't need to be told twice, she kicks her heels off and takes off, towing me alongside her, not daring to let go. I follow along blindly in the dark not knowing where the hell we are or where we're heading, but Chan does. She knows this place like the back of her hand. We run flat out through the maze of twists and turns. Somewhere behind us, I can hear Kaitlin. I know by now she's retrieved the gun and is pursuing us. I can only hope she gets turned around and lost in the darkness of the club.

Chan drags me down a corridor and into the backstage area, which is lit by very dim emergency lighting. It's only just enough to make out backdrops and props, and lighting rigs. We wind through them, then through the curtains and onto the side of the main stage, but as we do, the main area is flooded with light, causing us both to stumble as our eyes adjust.

We scramble across the stage and down the steps to the dance floor. We've just about made it across to the nests of tables and chairs, which have been stacked and pushed aside so the floors can be cleaned, when a loud shot rings out, and we hear the sound of breaking glass. We skid to a halt when Kaitlin appears from behind the bar and crosses the floor to stand directly in front of us.

"Thought you could lose me, did you?" she asks coolly. "I spent weeks scoping this place out so I could figure out the best way to get to your friend without raising suspicion. Did you really think I didn't know my way around, or where the lights were?" Kaitlin glares at us. "Enough games." She raises the gun and points it at us. "You're going to die now, the only question is, which one first?"

As we stand there breathing heavily, I hear a strange sound, kind of like the light tinkling of a glass wind chime. My eyes roll slowly up to the ceiling, and my mouth falls open. There, straddling the chandelier as if she were Miley Cyrus riding a wrecking ball is Dusty. Her dress hiked up around her hips, one glittery stiletto braced against the glass as she calmly unscrews the ceiling bolts of the enormous glass chandelier.

I can't help myself as an incredulous slash horrified slash nervous giggle bubbles up from my lips at the sheer ridiculousness of the situation.

"What are you laughing at?" Kaitlin demands angrily, pointing the gun at me.

"Duck," I say with a helpless giggle.

"What?" She frowns in confusion.

"Duck," I repeat as the bolts clatter to the floor loudly, and seconds later, the Chandelier plummets to the ground directly over Kaitlin.

There's a loud crack that ricochets through the air and a punch of icy cold air that takes both mine and Chan's feet out from under us. The glass behind the bar explodes behind us as a bullet misses us by millimetres and takes out an expensive looking bottle of booze. Chan and I go down in a tangle of arms and legs, hitting the ground hard enough to knock the air from our lungs.

I see Dusty hovering over us protectively, her eyes filled with concern.

"You're getting better at that," I tell her.

"Strong motivation, boo." She winks when she sees we're both okay.

I glance over to the wreckage of the chandelier, and all I see is two feet peeking out from underneath.

"She looks like the Wicked Witch of the East after Dorothy's house drops on her," I remark. "I wonder if she's okay?"

"That bitch killed Dusty, she deserves everything she gets," Chan growls. "If I could, I'd drop a fucking house on her without thinking twice."

Suddenly, the doors slam open, and an armed police unit burst in noisily.

"Oh, look," I say observationally. "The police are finally here."

"Budget cuts." Chan nods. "What are you gonna do?"

I snort as I look at her, and we both start laughing hysterically on an adrenalin overload.

"Don't look now, boo, but your Prince Charming is here." Dusty smirks.

I glance up and see Danny running across the floor, his face an absolute picture of fear filled concern as he sees me splayed out on the floor.

"Tristan!" He skids across the dance floor and crouches beside me, checking me over for injuries.

"I'm fine by the way," Chan adds dryly.

Danny hauls me to my feet, and once I'm steady, he reaches down for Chan and helps her. Before I can get a word out, he's back to running his hands over me as if he can't believe I'm generally unharmed. Except for the frisbee shaped bruise I'm sure will be decorating my arse after Dusty threw the pair of us to the ground with enough force to take down a heavyweight champion.

"Danny, I'm okay." I smile as he fusses over me like a mother hen. I look up at him and open my mouth to reassure him, but before I can say anything more, his arms wrap around me, pulling me in tight, and his lips crash against mine. I forget everything around us, it all melts away into the background, and I feel safe. For the first time in my life, I feel... whole.

I blink and pull back as I hear the sound of a throat clearing. I look around Danny to see a small, compact red-haired woman smiling at me and offering her hand.

"I'm Inspector Maddie Wilkes, soon to be this one's partner on the job once they make it official." She hikes a thumb in Danny's direction. "I'm guessing you're his boyfriend, or well on your way to being. You two should come over for dinner and meet my wife, Sonja."

"Um, thanks." I blush as Maddie turns to Chan.

"Chan," she introduces herself and shakes the Inspector's hand.

"I don't suppose either one of you want to tell us just what the hell happened here?" Maddie says looking around.

Chan and I look at each other, and she nods to me.

"Okay." I take a deep breath. "The short version." I point to the chandelier, which has several officers gathered around it tending to the unconscious woman under it. "That's Kaitlin Fletcher, daughter of Ronald Fletcher, the one who Dusty was seeing. Kaitlin has a rather unhealthy fixation with both of her parents, her father in particular. I think she has the kind of relationship with him that even George RR Martin wouldn't

285

touch with a bargepole. She murdered Dusty to stop her father from leaving her and her mother. She's also killed other former lovers of her father. I believe she was also responsible for an accident in which her mother was hurt. She confessed to cutting the brake lines on her mother's car."

"She then decided she was going to kill both myself and Chan because she's not playing with an entirely full deck, if you know what I mean. She's convinced that Dusty will haunt her if she doesn't appease her spirit by killing the pair of us. She's been stalking me for weeks and turned up at Dusty's flat as we were retrieving the evidence of her father stalking Dusty. She smashed my phone and Chan convinced her to not shoot us at Dusty's flat but instead bring us to the club in order to buy us more time."

"Which is kind of brilliant when you think about it. Like that scene in *Harry Potter and the Order of the Phoenix* when Hermione tricked Professor Umbridge into the forbidden forest thinking that Dumbledore had built a secret weapon against the Ministry of Magic, spoiler alert if you haven't seen it. But there was no weapon and Hermione was leading her into the forest so that the centaurs could take Professor Umbridge, kind of like the police showing up here, although you were late. Not that I'm comparing you all to a mythical half man half horse. Anyway, when we got here, we ran to try and get away from Kaitlin, and luckily she missed when she shot at us and then a chandelier fell on her."

"Stroke of luck," Chan says with an entirely straight face. "What are the odds?"

There is absolute silence as Maddie and Danny both stare at me.

Danny blinks slowly before pinching the bridge of his nose. "Jesus, I actually understood all of that."

"That was the short version?" Maddie adds before glancing across the room. "Danny, the paramedics are here for Kaitlin."

"Okay." He nods. "Don't go anywhere, I'll be right back," he tells me firmly as if he's worried to let me out of his sight.

"Wow." Chan turns to me. "That was a hell of a mouthful."

"Bet you say that to all the boys." My mouth twitches, and she laughs.

"Tristan, there is no one in the world quite like you." She smiles warmly as she leans in and plants a kiss on my lips. It's sweet and sincere and filled with friendship. "I'm going to go and give them my statement now but promise me one thing."

I look at her expectantly.

"Don't be a stranger," she says softly.

"I won't," I reply genuinely.

She turns to walk away, but she only gets a few paces when she stops and turns back, glancing around me. "And Dusty," she adds. "I love you, but when my time comes you better be waiting for me because we're going to throw one hell of a party."

"Count on it," Dusty mumbles, and even though Chan can't hear her, she turns and walks away.

I turn back to Dusty. "Well, we did it," I say pensively. "We solved your murder, brought your killer to justice and you got to say goodbye to Chan."

"Yes, I did," Dusty murmurs, staring out across the busy dance floor at all the police and paramedics.

"Dusty." I draw her attention back to me. "Why are you still here?" I ask softly, and when she doesn't respond, I have my answer. "Solving your murder wasn't your unfinished business, was it?" She shakes her head slowly. "You've known all along what your unfinished business was, haven't you?"

She lets out a slow resigned breath. "Come with me, Tristan."

I turn and follow her backstage and along the corridor, which I now know leads to her dressing room. I let us both in, and she directs me to the cupboard where her body was discovered.

"Down there." She points to the floor. I pull out a couple of plastic storage boxes filled with costumes and accessories and find a hidden compartment in the wall. Reaching inside, I pull out a shoe box. Looking up at her I see her nod, so I open the lid, and my breath catches in my throat when I see the contents. I look up at her again.

"Please," she whispers.

We hurry back out into the club, and I can see Danny looking for me. As his gaze locks on mine, he visibly relaxes.

"What is it?" he asks when he sees my solemn expression and the shoe box tucked under my arm.

"I need your help with something," I tell him.

"Anything." He pulls me aside, away from a couple of officers so we can have some privacy. "What do you need?"

"I need you to drive me to Tadworth in Surrey," I reply.

"Tadworth?" he repeats, and I nod. He stares a me for a moment, and I'm pretty certain he knows exactly where in Tadworth I need to go. "Okay." He finally nods. "Let me tie up a few loose ends first."

I hover around the edges of the room, giving my statement when required, watching as Kaitlin is loaded into an ambulance. They think she's suffering with some broken ribs, a broken collar bone and a minor concussion, but as far as I'm concerned, there aren't enough broken bones in the world to make up for what she did to Dusty and the others. I don't care how emotionally fragile she is or whatever the excuse is. I'm just glad she'll stand trial.

When Danny finally finishes up and leaves his partner Maddie to it, we head out to his car with his fingers firmly entangled with mine. He doesn't seem to care that his colleagues can see. It's like he's claiming me and damn if that doesn't give me a little warm fuzzy feeling in my belly. I know it can't be easy being openly gay in the Metropolitan police force, but I kind of like that he refuses to hide me.

An hour later, we drive into the large village of Tadworth in Surrey, just south-east of the Epsom Downs. We park up in the drive of a tidy little two bed mid-terrace in warm coloured brickwork. I stare up at the house as I climb out of the car, Dusty by my side. She hasn't spoken since the club, not since she showed me the shoe box I have safely tucked under my arm as if it were the crown jewels.

Danny rounds the car and joins me, and together we walk up the path to the dark green front door, Dusty trailing behind reluctantly.

I straighten my back and swallow as Danny reaches up and rings the bell. A moment later the door opens slowly, and a man in his sixties appears. His hair is thinning and brushed neatly to the side, and he's wearing a buttoned up cardigan over his neatly pressed shirt and trousers, and on his feet are a pair of tartan slippers.

"Yes?" he says softly. "May I help you?"

"Mr Boyle," Danny says politely. "I'm Inspector Danny Hayes, Scotland Yard, and this is Tristan Everett. We'd like to speak with you about your son, Dustin."

He stares at us with an unreadable expression for a long moment. "I suppose you'd better come in then," he says finally, stepping aside and allowing us to step into the hallway. "Take your shoes off, please," he says, and we both do as he requests, placing our shoes neatly by the door, our feet sinking into the soft, plush dove grey carpet as he leads us through into the sitting room.

"Would you like a cup of tea? Or perhaps a coffee?" Mr Boyle asks, and as we shake our heads, he sits down on a comfortable looking burgundy patterned sofa. Indicating the two matching armchairs for Danny and I to sit in. I'm still aware of Dusty hovering on the outskirts of the room as I take a seat, arranging the shoebox neatly on my knees. I glance around the tidy and scrupulously clean room, taking in all the school photos mounted on the wall. With several more framed photos lined along the polished sideboard covered with a doily. I stare at the photos unable to see my friend in the skinny, freckled boy with gaps in his front teeth as he beams for the camera.

"Mr Boyle," Danny begins gently. "The Metropolitan Police Department would like to inform you that we have found the person responsible for the death of your son."

I watch as he stares at Danny, and the only sign of any outward emotion is a tiny little tic in his jaw.

"Who was it?" he asks after a moment.

"A young woman. I'm afraid I can't disclose her name at this time. She has both mental and emotional problems and it seems that your son was not the only person she may have harmed," Danny informs him dutifully. "I know it's probably little comfort to you now, but she will stand trial, and we are confident we'll have more than enough evidence for her to be held to account for her actions."

Mr Boyle sits silently listening to Danny's words as he stares at a picture on the mantle of Dusty holding a football like it's a ticking time bomb.

"It won't bring him back though, will it," he mumbles. "I haven't spoken to my son in ten years, and now I never will."

"Mr Boyle," I say softly, drawing his attention, and I see a flicker of emotion in his eyes. "I'm here because I knew Dusty very well. I was a friend of hers." I see his eyes flicker again as I refer to Dusty as her. I know it's difficult for him to reconcile the boy he knew with the identity Dusty ultimately chose, and I'm willing to bet that was the cause of the friction between them.

"He was such a good boy," Mr Boyle says quietly. "He was kind and funny. He had so much of his mother in him. There was an innate sense of fairness in him, and he didn't suffer fools gladly. Losing his mother was hard on us both. I never loved anyone after that. It was always my Lorraine for me. I only ever wanted what was best for Dustin, but all that other stuff... I didn't know how to handle it. His mother would've known, but I never knew the right things to say or do. I didn't understand it, but I wanted to. I wanted to be close to him, but every time I opened my mouth, the wrong things came out until we just didn't know how to talk to each other anymore." He swallows hard. "I've replayed that last conversation we had over and over in my mind, the things I should've said but didn't, and now? My son died thinking I didn't care, thinking I was angry with him."

"Mr Boyle." I draw in a breath. "I have something for you. Something that Dusty wanted you to have."

He looks up at me as I pass him the shoe box. He stares at it in his hands for a moment before lifting the lid and setting it on the coffee table.

"What is this?" he asks in confusion.

"One hundred and twenty six letters," I tell him. "And every single one of them for you. Dusty wrote to you every single month for the last ten years you were apart. She wanted to keep you in her life even though she didn't know how to bridge the gap between you, so she wrote to you even though she didn't post them. Every month she'd tell you what she'd been up to, what was going on in her life, funny stories, anecdotes, things that made her happy, things that made her sad. If you want to know Dusty, know who she really was, it's all there right in front of you. All you have to do is read."

I watch as his face crumples like a piece of paper, and a ragged sob tears from his lips. He tries to stifle it, but in the end, he just buries his face in his hands and sobs, great glugging, heart wrenching sobs that tear at my heart. It's one of the most painful sounds I've ever experienced, hearing a parent weep for their child.

I stand and cross the room, grabbing a couple of tissues

from a nearby box as I plant myself next to Dusty's dad and hand them to him, rubbing his back soothingly.

"Dusty loved you, so much," I tell him. "But she's also stubborn and sheer bloody minded." I smile, unable to bring myself to look at Dusty in case I start crying too. "She has so much of you in her too. She didn't know how to talk to you anymore than you knew how to talk to her."

"And now it's too late." He sniffles. "I can read his letters, but he'll never know how I feel."

I give him a small understanding smile.

"Mr Boyle," I say softly. "Close your eyes."

"What?"

"Trust me." I nod. "Close your eyes and take a deep breath."

He closes his eyes and takes a stuttered breath. "Now, imagine Dusty was right here in front of you." I watch as Dusty sinks to the carpet, kneeling in front of her dad as she reaches out and takes his hands. "Now, tell Dusty how you feel, say it out loud. All those things you wish you could've said but didn't."

He takes another breath as his hiccuping sobs quieten.

"Dustin," he whispers, keeping his eyes closed. "I never understood you, never understood the things you needed. The things that made you... you. I should've tried harder, but it wasn't because I didn't love you. I wasn't angry with you. I was angry with myself for not knowing the right things to say. I'm sorry that we argued the last time we saw each other. I'm sorry that we both said things in the heat of the moment that we can never take back or make right, but I want you to know that I love you just the way you are. Whether you're Dustin or Dusty, you're my child, and I will always love you, and I will always be proud of you."

I look over and see the silent tears streaming down Dusty's cheeks as she listens to her dad's words. Reaching up, she traces her fingers, with their long glittery red nail polish, down his pale cheeks tenderly, and even though he still has his eyes closed, Mr Boyle lets out a slow sigh filled with peace.

"I love you too, Dad, always," she murmurs softly. "I'll say hello to Mum for you."

Dusty's hands drop from his face, and she turns to look at me, her eyes filled with grateful tears, and her mouth curving into a smile.

"Thank you," she mouths slowly as she disappears.

EPILOGUE

Tristan

It's been days since Dusty crossed over, and I still don't feel right. Maybe I'm coming down with something I think to myself... or maybe I'm just missing my friend I silently admit. The flat feels empty, and I don't have any enthusiasm for anything. Even Jacob Marley is mooning about the place.

I miss Dusty.

I can feel my bottom lip sticking out in a pout as I stand in front of my wardrobe, pulling out another shirt and tossing it on the bed behind me. This is ridiculous. I've never had a problem dressing myself before, yet here I am, standing in my jeans and Doc Martens naked from the waist up all because I can't decide on a shirt. I've never cared what shirt I've worn before as long as it's clean.

"This is ridiculous," I snap as I grab out the first shirt my hand touches. I go to pull it over my head and sigh, letting my hands drop, still clutching the shirt. "I miss Dusty." I say miserably out loud.

"Well, that's nice to hear," a familiar voice speaks from behind me, and I spin around so sharply I almost whip myself in the face with my shirt.

"Dusty!" I gasp in shock as I stare at her.

Gone is the crumpled gold lamé dress, odd shoe, and bloodstained wig. The ruined make-up, which had given her the look of an eighties rock icon, is now immaculate. I stare at her outfit, which can only be described as a 1960's Pan-AM flight attendant. Her blonde wig is now a bell-shaped beehive with a blunt fringe and flicked ends. On her head, perched at a rather jaunty angle, is a small cap, which looks a bit like an upside down ashtray, in pale blue to match the buttoned-up jacket and prim skirt. A small silk scarf is tied at her throat, and she's wearing killer black stilettos and white cotton gloves with her hands folded demurely in front of her.

"Tah-dah!" She lifts her hands. "They let me come back."

"W-why?" I stare in stupefied shock.

"See this?" She taps her chest with a white gloved finger, and I see a little pair of golden wings pinned to her breast like a set of pilot's wings. "I'm a spirit guide." She grins.

"A spirit guide?" I repeat.

"Well." She rolls her eyes. "A spirit guide in training... sort of." She grins again. "I'm here to guide you."

"You're... here to... guide me?" I blink slowly.

"Are you just going to repeat everything I say?" She fists a hand on her cocked hip. "Yes, honey." She glances down at the shirt hanging limply in my fingers. "And right now, I'm going to be guiding you straight back to your wardrobe. Boo, you cannot be seen in that travesty of a shirt, in fact you should burn it."

Dusty flicks her hand casually, and the shirt is suddenly torn from my fingers by an unseen source.

"Learned a few new tricks." She winks.

Nope, I can't deal with that conversation right now.

"Dusty... seriously... why are you here?" I ask in confusion.

"I told you," she says gently as her gaze softens. "I'm here for you. If there's anyone in the world who needs a bestie it's you,

295

and I'm here to fill that role until you find your happily ever after."

"What if I never find it?"

"Then I'll wait for you." Her mouth curves. "And when Chan joins us, the three of us will wander off into the afterlife together and see what trouble we can get ourselves into."

I smile at her and the heaviness that I've carried since I was at her father's house finally lifts.

"Of course," Dusty continues. "That happily ever after might be closer than you think."

"What?" I frown in confusion as the doorbell rings.

"Go answer the door, boo." She smiles as I snag the first shirt I can and tug it over my head, grabbing a hoodie off the nearby chair and slipping my arms into the sleeves.

I open the door and find a delicious looking detective in jeans and a sweater, his heavy coat unbuttoned and looking gloriously windswept.

"Hey." He smiles leaning sexily against the door frame.

"Hey," I reply. "You want to come in?"

"Actually." He flushes and glances down to a basket tucked at the side of the doorway. "I have something I want to ask you." He rubs the back of his neck awkwardly.

"What?" I tilt my head curiously as I watch him. Danny is one of the most confident and self-assured men I know, and to see him so nervous is unusual.

"I... uh... well we haven't had much of a chance to talk or see each other over the last few days while I've been tying up the case against Kaitlin Fletcher, and I thought, well, I wanted to know... thought I might ask..."

"Yes?"

"Doyouwanttobemyboyfriend?" he rushes out, his cheeks adorably pink.

"Sorry?" I raise my brows. "Do I need to learn to speak Danny?"

"Well," he chuckles. "It's only fair, after all I learned to speak Tristan."

"Ask me again." I smile widely.

He sighs loudly and rolls his eyes. "Do you want to be my boyfriend?" I grin at him, and he grimaces. "Bit too Junior school?"

"Yes, but it's perfect." I beam as I reach out and grasp the chunky cable knit of his sweater and pull him in closer, looking up into those beautiful blue eyes. "And the answer's yes... so... do you want to be my boyfriend?" I ask.

"Yes." He grins down at me as he leans in and takes my mouth.

I slide into the kiss like it's made of thick syrupy molasses. It's filled with warmth and comfort, filling all the lonely dark spaces inside me, and making me glow from the inside. He pulls me closer to his firm body, devouring my mouth, and it feels like I'm adrift at sea, just floating wherever the tide takes me. I could happily kiss this man for the rest of my days without drawing a breath, but in the end, my relentless curiosity wins out, and I pull back.

"Okay, I'll bite." I smile. "What's in the basket?"

"A picnic." He smiles back, still holding me and giving a little playful sway as he brushes a lock of hair back from my temple.

"A picnic?" I laugh. "Danny, it's November."

"I know." He shrugs bashfully. "But they've got a pop up cinema in a Victorian warehouse in Bethnal Green. They're showing a double feature of *The Illusionist* and *The Prestige*. I thought we could take some pillows, a blanket and a picnic, and pretend to watch Hugh Jackman while we make out."

"Sounds perfect," I reply softly.

I feel a gust of warm air pass me, faintly tinged with a delicious perfume, and when I look past Danny, I see Dusty standing on the staircase. She's changed her outfit again. No longer dressed as an airline hostess, she's wearing her signature blonde wig, and it's huge and backcombed with curls and waves spilling down her back. Her slender body is encased in a very short, fire engine red fringed dress with thin straps. Her lips are also siren red, and on her feet, she has red gladiator sandals with five-inch heels and laces all the way up her calves.

"Don't wait up." She blows me a kiss. "I'm going out."

I almost ask her where she's going, but then I remember Danny is still standing right next to me.

"I'm going to find Bruce." She winks at me and answering my unspoken question. "Not taped anymore," she mouths as she points downwards, and I chuckle quietly to myself. "Oh, and by the way," she says conversationally. "When I was on the other side, Patrick said to say hello."

Patrick? She couldn't possibly mean...

"So, you going to grab your jacket then?" Danny asks dragging my attention away from Dusty who has disappeared again.

"Sure." I smile, stepping into my flat and grabbing my coat, keys, and wallet.

For a second, I just stop and smile to myself. Got my best friend back and a gorgeous boyfriend who gets me. I guess Evangeline Crawshanks was right, sometimes you don't get what you want, sometimes... just sometimes... you get what you need.

CRAWSHANKS GUIDE TO THE RECENTLY DEPARTED

The Three Ghosts of Christmas

Crawshanks Guide to the Recently Departed
The Three Ghosts of Christmas

WHEN THE BELLS TOLL ONE

Tristan

"Don't move," Danny chuckles into my ear as I groan into the pillow and shift my hips.

"Please," I half whine, half pant, shifting again as I feel the rumble of his chest against my back. "You're so mean."

He's been edging me for what seems like hours and has every single nerve in my body vibrating like a plucked string. I want to come so badly that I think I may actually die if he doesn't give me a good hard pounding soon.

"You're such a tease," I whisper on a long serrated groan as he leisurely pulls out almost to the tip and then slides back deep inside me silkily.

"You like it though," he murmurs in my ear.

Bastard. He's right, I do love it when he takes me to the very edge of reason where pleasure is madness and nothing else exists except the primitive drumbeat of blood pounding through my veins.

I push back, getting my hands underneath me and pushing myself up from the mattress. He rolls off me with a chuckle and onto his back, those violet blue eyes watching me intently as I growl and throw my leg over his hips straddling him. I lean forward and pin his hands above him.

"Tristan." He grins. "I love it when you get all authoritative."

"I'll show you authoritative," I promise. "As soon as soon as I figure out where you've hidden your handcuffs."

"That's a gross misuse of police equipment I'll have you know," he rumbles in his deliciously low northern burr, his eyes twinkling.

"I'll show you misuse of police equipment," I murmur as I fist the base of his cock, still slick with lube and sink down on him, watching as his eyes roll back in his head, and his hands grip my hips now that I'm in charge.

I set a fast pace, rolling my hips as I ride him, an air of desperation whipping through me. My dick is aching, and my balls tight with the need for release. Danny's head falls back, his neck arching as he grips my hips harder, grinding me into him so his cock roots deeper, pegging my prostate on every thrust.

"Danny," I cry out loudly, gasping for breath. "I need to come."

He sits up, and I wrap my arms and legs around him tightly, my mouth hungrily latching onto his as he cups my arse cheeks and urges me to ride his dick harder in his lap. He's grunting and groaning against my lips as my tongue tangles with his.

White-hot lightning shoots down my spine, and my toes curl as I let go and come so hard I have little flecks of reflective light swimming in front of my eyes. I can hear the whoosh of my pulse pounding in my ears. Danny gives one last hoarse cry, and I can feel the base of his dick pulsing as he comes inside me.

"Fuck," he gasps, pressing his lips to mine on a panting breath. "How does it keep getting better?"

"Practice." I grin as I pull back and look at him. "At least we didn't break the bed this time."

He huffs a laugh against my lips. His gorgeous face is kind of lost on me at the moment as I don't have my glasses on, and his features are slightly blurry, but the one thing I can see are those crystal eyes staring at me intently.

"What?" I sweep a stray lock of blonde hair from his forehead.

I swear he opens his mouth as if to say something, but he pauses and shakes his head.

"What?" I ask again.

"Nothing." He smiles softly as he lifts me slightly.

He slides out of me, and I flop down onto my lovely new bed and reach over to the bedside table, grabbing the roll of toilet paper. I rip off a long stretch and toss it casually over to Danny as I clean up the cum from my stomach. Balling up the tissue I lob it toward the bin, groaning when I miss. Climbing out of bed quickly I grab the tissue off the floor and stuff it into the bin before jumping back into bed, burrowing under the covers. Now that my body temperature is cooling, the room feels freezing.

Danny chuckles again, pulling me into his arms and tucking the blanket around me all the way up to my chin, and it's like I've been enveloped in a cocoon. I let out a deep sigh of contentment as he runs his fingers slowly through my wild bed hair. Unable to help myself I yawn, it's been a long week.

It's Christmas Eve and I finally have a few days off to spend with Danny. I've been looking forward to this all month, but the excitement of my first Christmas with Danny is tempered by the guilt I feel.

This will not only be our first Christmas together but the first proper Christmas either of us has had in years. For Danny, he'd tried to avoid the constant disapproval and awkwardness with his family by working every Christmas day. For myself, I may not have been at work, but I was always on my own. I'd go and visit Dad in the home for a few hours, but beyond that I was always in my flat on my own with my microwave Christmas dinner and a tin of Quality Street while watching the Queen's speech... okay you've got me. I didn't watch the Queen's speech.

"Tris." Danny's low husky voice pulls me from my thoughts. "It's not too late to change your mind you know."

"I know," I murmur as he traces lazy circles on my back beneath the covers.

I shouldn't be surprised he knows what's bothering me. I've struggled with it all month. This is the first time I'm going to have a real Christmas since Dad got sick.

I just wanted one day, one special day with Danny to make some good memories. We've got presents under the tree for each other, and our only mutual stipulation was that we had to buy really silly things to make each other laugh. I've got a present from Chan, and even a present from Madam Vivienne, which when you shake it sounds remarkably like a box of biscuits. I also have a bottle of wine from Dusty's dad, who I've kept in touch with.

Danny and I even have a turkey, which we're going to attempt to cook, despite the fact neither of us can cook worth a damn. We also bought a box of Christmas crackers, which I don't usually bother with as it's only me.

There's just one problem. I made the decision not to go see my dad on Christmas day but visit Boxing Day instead. I feel like I'm being incredibly selfish, and I don't know what to do. His nurse told me to take the day for myself, and she promised they'd take good care of him, but the guilt is killing me.

"We can still go and see him tomorrow. We can run down there first thing tomorrow morning and still be back in plenty of time to sacrifice... I mean cook the turkey." Danny continues to stroke my back. "You don't have to wait until Boxing Day."

"I know." I snuggle into him with a smile playing on my lips. "I just really wanted to make some new memories of Christmas day."

"And we will." He leans in and kisses my mouth softly. "Besides, we've got plenty of years ahead of us to make memories."

"You think so?" My smile widens.

"I hope so." He kisses me again. "Why don't you sleep on it and make a decision in the morning."

"Okay," I whisper, leaning over to switch off the light and snuggling back down into the warm cocoon of his arms, our naked bodies pressed together as the peaceful darkness lulls us into sleep.

"Psst... psst... psst... oh, for Fuck's sake, Tristan wake up!"

I open my eyes blinking blearily into the darkness and fumbling on the bedside table for my glasses. Tapping my phone gently, the screen lights up casting a dim light, and I see Dusty kneeling beside the bed.

"Dusty?" I whisper, glancing over my shoulder to make sure Danny is fast asleep.

"Don't worry, he won't be waking up, he sleeps like the dead." Dusty rolls her eyes.

"I thought we agreed the bedroom is off limits when Danny stays over," I hiss.

"Sorry, boo, but I'm under strict orders." "Orders?" I blink in confusion. "From who?"

"The... uh... Upstairs Management," she whispers.

"Who?"

"The Upstairs Management," she points vaguely to the ceiling as she stands, and I get a good look at her.

"Dusty, why are you dressed like Mariah Carey?" I push my new glasses back up my nose as they slide down again, and I make a mental note to remember to get them adjusted. That, or make sure not to crush them during wild bouts of sex so that I end up having to get them replaced twice in one month.

"What?" She does a flirty little twirl. "Don't you like it?"

She's wearing a red velvet Santa dress trimmed in white fur. The skirt barely skims her bum cheeks leaving miles and miles of legs on display that end in cute little black ankle boots. She's still wearing her signature blonde wig, but it's got little Farrah Fawcett flicks framing her face and a Santa hat pinned at a jaunty angle.

"You look incredible as always." I yawn so widely my jaw cracks.

"Anyway, stop distracting me." She waves her hand impatiently, giving a flash of gold glittery nail polish. "We're running out of time."

"For what?" I frown. "It's the middle of the night."

"Well, I don't know exactly who's in charge up there." She points upwards again. "But they sent me with a message."

"What sort of message?" I ask suspiciously. "And why couldn't it wait until breakfast?"

"Tonight, you will be visited by three spirits," she begins.

"What?" I reply dryly.

"Expect the first, when the bell tolls one."

"You're totally ripping off Charles Dickens right now, you know that right?" I blink slowly.

"Where do you think he got it from?" She huffs and fists a hand on her hip. "Seriously, boo, haul your cute arse out of bed and go and have a wash and get some clothes on. Trust me, you do not want to meet this particular ghost with your hot boyfriend's dried spunk on you."

"Actually, it's mine." I grimace and Dusty snorts. "Must've missed a spot."

"Hey, I'm not judging, honey." She shakes her head. "We've all done the loo roll run and showered in the morning, but trust me, this spirit, you're going to want to be clean and presentable for."

"That sounds very ominous."

"Trust me?" She smiles, fluttering her eyelashes, and I growl quietly as I climb out of bed.

"Last time I did that I ended up getting kidnapped by a nut job with daddy issues and a gun," I murmur sourly, already missing the warmth of Danny's body.

"Love you too." She grins as I stride toward the bathroom completely stark naked. I've given up trying to keep any form of modesty around Dusty. She'll just randomly appear perched on the end of the bathtub while I'm showering and strike up a conversation. She didn't have many boundaries when she was alive according to Chan, but now she's dead, she seems to have none at all.

I can't face a shower in my freezing cold bathroom at quarter to one in the morning, so I quickly strip wash in the sink and dry myself. I nip back into the bedroom and pull on my pyjamas, an old gray hoodie of Danny's, which I refuse to let him have back, and a thick pair of fleece socks.

These old Victorian houses are pretty draughty at the best of times, but tonight it's freezing. Zipping up my hoodie and debating on whether or not to grab a beanie I pad out of the bedroom looking for Dusty. I've just reached the living room in the pitch black darkness when I freeze. I hear the ponderous chime of a grandfather clock signalling the hour of one, which wouldn't have been so strange... except I don't have a grandfather clock.

I'm standing there pondering what to do when a dim light catches the corner of my eye. Turning slowly in the direction of the kitchen I hear the faint strains of Wham's *Last Christmas* playing on a tinny sounding old radio.

I shuffle forward curiously on silent feet, and as I approach the kitchen, the light gets brighter. I can hear the familiar and comforting sounds of pots being set on a cooker and plates being laid on the table... but above it all there's a female voice humming.

I step into the room and my heart stops. When I finally speak, my mouth moves but there's almost no sound.

"Mum?"

THE GHOST OF CHRISTMAS PAST

Tristan

"Mum," I whisper almost unintelligibly.

She turns and smiles at me, and everything shifts inside me. I'm filled with warmth and love, and peace.

"Tristan." She smiles. "Sit down, poppet, I've made your favourite."

I glance around the kitchen, but it's no longer my kitchen we're standing in. We're in the kitchen of my childhood home. The one that was sold when my dad had to go into care. Everything is exactly how I remember it. Right down to the freshly scrubbed Aga in place of a cooker and the egg holder shaped like a clucking hen.

I look at the pots of prepared vegetables sitting ready on the top of the Aga, and the turkey dressed and sitting in a deep tray on the worn countertop. I slide into my usual chair at the small, round kitchen table as Mum wipes her hands on her frilly home-made apron.

The music subtly changes to Slade's *Merry Christmas Everybody*, but I'm not paying it any mind. All my attention is fixed on the warm, loving woman as she sets a small plate and a glass of milk on the table in front of me. Leaning forward to kiss the top of my head affectionately, just like she always did, and the familiarity of the gesture brings a lump to my throat and tears to my eyes. If this is some kind of dream, I'm not sure I want to wake up.

"Merry Christmas, Tristan, love." She smiles as she takes the seat opposite me. Lifting the chipped rose print tea pot and pouring herself a cup of tea.

"Merry Christmas, Mum," I whisper. "Eat up, love." She nods at my plate, and as I look down, I see she's made me chocolate spread on toast, just like she used to when I was a kid.

"Mum." My voice breaks even as the word slips from my lips. "There now, poppet, don't fret." She leans forward. "We have time."

"I don't understand." I swallow thickly and blink back the tears. "Why are you here?"

She smiles indulgently as she tilts her head and watches me. "I'd've thought that was obvious, pet,' she replies. 'I'm here to show you the past." She pats my arm comfortingly.

I'm vaguely aware of what she's saying, but my gaze is rooted to the spot on my arm, or rather the tingle in my skin from where she touched me. The small hairs are raised beneath the sleeve of the hoodie, and I feel like I'm buzzing with static electricity, and there's also a strange metallic taste in my mouth.

"You can touch me?" I reply in shock. "But how?"

She smiles again, the kind of loving, indulgent smile you give a four year old that tells you two plus two equals a ham sandwich.

"It's a very special night," she whispers. "The usual rules don't apply. Come on." She stands and reaches for me. "There's something you need to see."

I stare at her hand for a moment before tentatively reaching for it. I brace myself, expecting it to pass straight through her like Dusty, but I'm met with warm, solid flesh and the scent of *Timeless*, the Avon perfume she used to wear.

I smile up at her as she squeezes my hand, and I lift out of the chair, crossing the kitchen toward the living room. In front of the bay window is a scraggly looking plastic Christmas tree covered in bright baubles, rainbow fairy lights and strands of silver angel hair. A pile of half unwrapped presents are scattered around the base on the garishly patterned carpet. From the ceiling hangs tinsel garlands and honeycomb shaped stars and bells, but I'm not looking at the ceiling. I'm looking at the floor in front of the old gas fire where my dad sits comfortably cross legged with a baby no more than ten months old.

"That's me," I whisper as I stare at the kid, or rather myself.

My legs are chubby, and I'm wearing some kind of romper suit. My hair is the wild bed hair I still have, and I'm drooling quite happily on a Mr Clever bib. My dad is smiling at me as he patiently builds a tower of brightly coloured bricks for me to knock down.

But that's not what has my attention either. There sitting on the floor beside us, is an old woman in a grey pleated skirt and pale pink jumper. Dad doesn't seem to be able to see her, but the baby version of me keeps looking directly at her, babbling incoherently, and offering her a spit festooned block to which she smiles serenely and shakes her head, at which point I obviously get bored and lob the block I'm holding at the tower, knocking it to the ground and clapping my hands enthusiastically.

I turn to look at my mother questioningly as she stands beside me.

"That was your grandmother on your father's side, Granny Nell," she remarks conversationally as if she hasn't just introduced an old woman who died ten years before I was even born.

"I don't understand." I frown.

"Just look." Mum nods.

I turn back to the living room, and everything blurs and shifts. This time I'm looking at an older version of myself. I'm maybe seven years old. I'm sitting on the sofa by the same old Christmas tree, which is looking even more worn with age, but beside me on the sofa is a young man wearing a military uniform, and the younger version of me is quite happily reading him a children's book.

"You always were an advanced reader." Mum smiles.

"Um, Mum, who's the dead soldier I'm reading Winnie the Pooh to?" I ask incredulously.

"Oh him,' she muses. 'That's your Great-Uncle William, he died at Dunkirk, poor lamb, like so many soldiers taken too soon and so far from home, in 1940 I think it was. He was your grandfather's oldest brother."

"Uh, that doesn't really explain why I'm reading him stories about a stuffed bear that likes honey." I frown.

"Tristan," she says softly as I turn to look at her. "You still think after everything that has happened to you in the last few months, that it's some kind of fluke. That some strange freak of science landed you with the ability to see the spirits of the departed but... the simple truth is... you were always able to see them."

"Then why don't I remember any of this?" I shake my head in confusion. "Memories of childhood fade," mum says sadly. "But for you it was something more."

She turns her attention back to the living room, and I follow her gaze. The tacky Christmas decorations are now gone. Rain is hammering against the window, the skies outside are storm laden, punctuated with ugly slashes of grey and black. The room is filled with grown-ups talking in hushed tones, huddled together in small groups and all of them wearing unrelieved, black and sombre expressions.

My eyes automatically drift to the corner of the room where

I see a young version of myself wearing a black suit and a white shirt. My hair oddly subdued, and my glasses taped together at the bridge of my nose. There's a spirit sat next to me talking in low, hushed tones, but the younger me doesn't see her. He sits staring blankly with a paper plate laying forgotten in his lap, containing an uneaten ham sandwich, a couple of half burnt sausage rolls and a handful of crisps.

"You shut yourself away," mum says sadly. "After I..." She sighs softly. "You were never the same boy. You withdrew into yourself, closed yourself off from everyone around you. Your dad was the only one you let in. When you stopped listening to the spirits, they simply stopped talking, and as time passed, you forgot them."

I turn to mum, my heart thudding painfully in my chest and my throat burning.

"Why?" I finally manage to choke out. "Why did you leave me?"

"Oh, Tristan." Her eyes are filled with sympathy. "It was just my time. It was like... falling asleep."

"But I needed you." I blink as the tears roll down my cheeks.

"No, you didn't." She smiles softly. "You had a different path to walk. I know it's difficult to understand because you still feel the hurt and loss of the child that you were, but everything happens for a reason, even if you can't fathom what that reason may be."

"Even if that reason is cruel?" I reply bitterly.

"Even then, I'm sorry to say." She nods. "Tristan." She reaches out and cups my cheek. "My darling boy, my miracle baby. We didn't get as long together as either of us would have wanted, but I am so grateful that I was chosen to be your mum. I loved you so much. Love like that doesn't stop or vanish simply because the person isn't there anymore."

She wraps her arms around me tightly, and for the first time in twenty years, I hug my mum. The smell and feel of her is so heartbreakingly familiar to me, even after all this time, that it hurts as much as it soothes.

I jerk in her arms as I hear the clock begin to strike the hour.

"No!" I pull back and dash the tears away frantically with the back of my hand. "I'm not ready."

"Yes, you are, sweetheart," she replies softly.

"Will I see you again?" I ask desperately.

"Tristan." She smiles. "Silly boy... I never left."

The clock strikes two and the room around me swirls and disappears.

THE GHOST OF CHRISTMAS PRESENT

Tristan

I blink and I'm standing in my living room, in my flat, staring at the full lush branches of the fir tree Danny and I decorated together with Star Wars themed baubles.

My hands are still trembling, and I sniff loudly, wiping away the tears as my mind tries to comprehend what I've just experienced. I'm just drawing a shaky breath when I hear a throat clearing behind me. I turn slowly and stare at the man standing in the doorway of my living room. He's wearing a rugby kit, and he has dark hair and a sweet bashful face even though he's built like a wrestler. He's wearing a Santa robe hanging open at the front with a circle of tinsel on his head rather than a wreath, and he looks like he belongs in the chorus line of a kid's nativity play in that outfit.

He clears his throat again, obviously bracing him for something, and his cheeks flush as he begins to speak.

"I am the ghost of Christmas, look upon my presents," he announces, and I hear a hushed whisper from the other side of the doorway. "I am the ghost of Christmas..." he listens to another loud whisper. "Present. I am the ghost of Christmas present, look upon me." He spreads his arms expansively.

"You've seen me like, never. Come in and know a better man." There is another whisper, and he frowns. "What?" he whispers out the side of his mouth, unconsciously leaning toward the doorframe.

Suddenly, a hand pokes out with suspiciously glittery nails and waves a small stack of flash cards, which he takes with a faint frown.

"You have never seen the like of me before," he reads tonelessly from the first card, and I really do feel like I'm watching a junior school Christmas production. I can't help the smile tugging at the corner of my lips. "Come in and know me better, man." He spreads one arm theatrically. "I have aught to teach you, and may you profit by it..." he reads as he tugs on his robe. "Touch my robe... for we have much to see, and the night grows snort..." He squints closer at the card. "Short." He corrects himself and suddenly turns back to the door frame whispering loudly. "Are you sure about this? it really doesn't make sense."

There's another whisper, and he rolls his eyes. Turning back to me, tossing the flash cards over his shoulder, he steps forward with his hand outstretched as they flutter to the floor behind him.

"Hi, Tristan, isn't it?'" He shakes my hand, and I marvel at the warm, solid feel of him, almost wincing at the firm grip he has. "I'm Bruce, Dusty talks about you all the time." He grins.

"No, no, no!" Dusty scrambles from behind the doorframe with my cat Jacob Marley winding circles around her legs. "You're not supposed to break character. You're supposed to be the Ghost of Christmas bloody Present."

Bruce turns back to me with a chuckle.

"I thought you never left the bookshop?" I ask curiously.

"I don't." He shakes his head. "I have a job to do there, but tonight's a special night."

"What job?" I tilt my head as I study him.

"That's what I'm here to show you." He grins. "Will you come with me?" He holds out his hand again.

"Okay." I smile, taking his hand as he turns to Dusty.

"Are you coming, babe?"

"No." She sulks. "I'm not allowed. I'll wait here."

Bruce chuckles again and leans down pressing a sweet kiss to her pouty lips.

"Well, at least I've got you for company, JM." Dusty reaches down and strokes Jacob Marley, sending him into paroxysms of delight because he can finally touch her as he rubs against her legs and purring loudly in utter bliss.

"Let's go then." Bruce gives my hand a little tug and everything around us blurs and shifts. When our surroundings solidify, we're standing in a dark frost-coated back alley in Whitechapel and directly in front of us is Madame Vivienne's book shop. The sign offering the purveyor of otherworldly nonsense has been removed from the window. It seems the ghost of Evangeline Crawshanks has some very definite ideas about what is and isn't an acceptable way to make a living. Other than that, though, very little about the book shop has changed.

Bruce tugs on my hand again and we both walk straight through the door. I stumble at the sudden noise and scene that greets me. The normally quiet bookshop is a hive of drunken disorderliness. There are spirits everywhere wearing paper party hats and gulping from cocktail and pint glasses. There's some dancing going on, lively conversations, raucous laughter and even a few drunken brawls breaking out.

"What in merry hell is this?" I murmur, my eyes trying to take in everything at once.

"Do you think we don't celebrate Christmas too?" Bruce grins. "Just because we're dead, doesn't mean we don't know how to have a good time. This is our annual office Christmas party."

"No kidding," I mutter as he guides me through the crowd. I'm bumped and jostled constantly. It's very strange suddenly being able to be touched by ghosts, and I kind of hope it's just a temporary thing.

"Tristan!" A sweet voice rings out, and I turn to see Evangeline Crawshanks perched on a chair with her trademark knitting in her lap. Her needles clacking continuously.

"Evangeline." I smile. "Merry Christmas."

"Merry Christmas," she replies with a sweet grandmotherly smile. "Well, I won't keep you, I know Bruce is on a timetable and the next shift is in a minute."

"What does she mean?" I ask Bruce as he tows me through the rest of the crowd toward the back room.

"You'll see." He smiles enigmatically.

We walk through another door, which leads to a tiny little box shaped storeroom. The floor is old, scratched exposed floorboards, and the wallpaper is peeling. There are stacks of old books and musty cardboard boxes everywhere.

"What are we doing in here?" I frown in confusion. "There's nothing here."

"Don't be so sure." Bruce grins, taking my hand and pulling me straight through the wall with the yellowed floral wallpaper. I blink slowly as we come to a stop in a completely different room. I say room, but it's huge, and there's no way this would fit into the bookstore.

"Don't think so hard." Bruce shakes his head. "You'll give yourself a headache. Let's just say that this place exists within the confines of the bookshop, but the physical laws of size don't apply because it's not part of the physical realm."

"What is this place?" I breathe wonderingly as I stare.

"It's an in-between place."

"A what?" I frown.

"The spot in the wall we just walked through was an old doorway, which had been blocked up. It originally would have led to a small courtyard out the back of the shop until they built the new building behind. The doorway was covered over but it still remains beneath the plaster and wallpaper. The Victorian's believed door-ways were in-between places, which allowed spirits to pass through, one of the few things they were actually right about."

I look around the massive space we find ourselves in. There's a small, circular raised platform in the centre of the room, and directly in front of it is a thick red line painted onto the stone floor.

To the right of the empty platform is a long queue of spirits, and at the head of the queue is a large desk surrounded by chipped metal filing cabinets and wire trays. The desk is piled high with stacks of paperwork, and in the middle sits a pencil pot and an old-fashioned typewriter, but it's the person behind the typewriter that interests me, a portly middle aged woman with pale almost greyish skin.

Her pale pink tipped fingers are clacking away at the type-writer, pausing every few seconds to whip the roller back into place with a loud zing. From what I can see of her above the desk she's wearing a knitted argyle vest over a frilly beige blouse with a scalloped collar and bow. Her red painted lips are pinched into the perpetually dissatisfied pout of a civil servant. Her hair is backcombed into an enormous iron grey beehive, with tiny little corkscrew curls sticking out above her ears. She's wearing blue eyeshadow applied thickly all the way to her brows and a pair of dark rimmed cats' eyes spectacles from which a gold chain is hung.

"Who's that?" I whisper.

"That's Doris." Bruce shakes his head. "Don't get on her bad side."

"NEXT!" Doris yells, and I watch as an old woman hobble forward. "Name?" Doris asks in a bored tone.

"Vera Langston," the old lady replies so faintly that I have to strain to hear her voice.

"Paperwork?" Doris holds out her hand, still staring down at the typewriter as she taps the keys with one hand.

"I don't have any," Vera replies softly.

Doris stops typing and slowly raises her gaze to the old lady, her mouth thinning tightly, revealing the puckers lines around her lips. She removes her glasses, allowing them to fall against her chest, suspended by the arms on the thin gold chain. She sucks her teeth and clucks her tongue in disapproval before whipping the piece of paper out of the typewriter and handing it to Vera.

"Fill this out," she tells the old woman sternly. "Back of the queue."

Vera takes the paper and slowly begins to shuffle down the line, her bedroom slippers making a little wisping noise against the hard floor.

"NEXT!" Doris yells as she rolls a fresh piece of paper into the typewriter and begins pecking away at the keys once again. This time a large man sidles up to the desk with a jovial smile beneath his thick moustache.

"Paperwork?" Doris holds out her hand and takes the sheet of paper he offers her. She stares at him suspiciously as she retrieves her glasses, which are draped against her ample bosom, and unfolds them slowly, once again perching them on the end of her nose as she begins to read.

"Alan Armitage?" She peeks over the top of her glasses as he nods his head vigorously. She dips her gaze back to the form. "Age 63?" He nods again. "It says here, coronary artery blockage and massive heart failure." Alan nods again a little ruefully. "Should've listened to your wife when she told you to ease up on the fried breakfasts." He nods sagely as she lays the paper on the desk and retrieves a large metal stamp. She slaps it against the form with a loud clunk, leaving the word

APPROVED in big red letters before adding the form to a huge pile at the corner of the desk.

"Step up to the platform, keep your arms and feet inside the line unless you want to be disincorporated. Next shift is in five minutes," she intones blandly. "NEXT!"

"What is this shift everyone keeps talking about?" I turn to Bruce curiously. "You'll see, keep watching."

"YOU!" I glance up to see Doris staring at me from across the room. "You're not dead, you don't belong here." She points a bony coral tipped finger at me.

"It's okay, Doris." Bruce waves a hand easily. "He's with me. This is Tristan Everett.

"Everett, eh?" Her eyes narrow as she studies me for what seems like forever before finally sucking her teeth loudly again, which she seems to do once she's come to some sort of decision. "He'll need to fill in a copy of form B-732QR/N3, sub paragraph N62 dash A396..." She purses her lips and her eyes narrow further. "In triplicate."

"Don't worry, Doris, I'll take care of it." Bruce nods.

She harrumphs quietly. "NEXT!"

"Lois Pottersworth." A skinny, nervous looking woman steps up and waves a piece of paper.

Doris grabs the form and skims over it before stamping it and adding it to the pile.

"Step up to the platform, keep your arms and feet inside the line unless you want to be disincorporated. Next shift is in five minutes," she repeats. "NEXT!"

Suddenly, I can hear a vast roaring sound, like an approaching tube train heading through a tunnel. The floor begins to vibrate beneath my feet, and I'm blasted in the face with a whoosh of air. I blink in shock and stare at the huge stone archway that has appeared on the platform. At its centre is a diaphanous curtain flapping ponderously as if caught by a light breeze.

I watch as Alan steps up to the platform with a wide smile on his face.

"Mum!" he yells happily, lifting his arms up as if he were a child about to be scooped into his mother's arm. His feet lift off the floor, and he floats toward the opening and disappears through the curtain in a flash of light.

"What the?" I frown.

"It's the veil." Bruce nods. "The gateway between life and death."

"What's the shift?" I ask in confusion.

"It's an alignment thing." He shrugs. "The gateway appears in shifts, every hour for fifteen minutes then disappears again."

"Oh, I see." I turn to look at Bruce. "Why are you showing me this?"

"Because we're on the same team here, Tristan," he explains. "We both help lost souls. Some of them, like Dusty, have unfinished business and can't leave until they've resolved it. Others don't have any unfinished business, but they're just not ready to leave. They walk the earth until they decide to cross over, then we bring them here."

I frown and stare down at my fluffy socks, my mind churning.

"They're not going to leave me alone, are they?" I look back up at him. "Am I going to have to do this for the rest of my life?"

"No." He smiles kindly. "It's your choice. It's always been a choice. You can just ignore them and go back to your life the way it was."

I think back to how lonely and dull my life was before I met Dusty, and because of her I met Danny and Chan. Now I have friends and I'm happy.

Bruce's mouth curves as if he knows what I'm thinking. "It's all about free will, but..." He glances upward. "They have a habit of rewarding the right choices."

I huff out a laugh as the loud chiming of the grandfather clock begins again.

"Oops, nearly out of time." Bruce claps me on the back. 'It was nice to meet you properly, Tristan. Stop by the bookshop anytime you have questions."

I open my mouth to speak but everything around me blurs and shifts.

"Don't forget to fill out that form..." A faint voice swirls into nothingness and as my surroundings solidify, and I find myself standing in the mortuary next to the clean, empty stainless steel table and standing on the opposite side is... Morgan Freeman?

THE GHOST OF CHRISTMAS FUTURE

Tristan

"Uh..." My mind is drawing a complete blank as I find myself staring at Morgan Freeman dressed exactly like he was in Bruce Almighty when he played... "OH MY GOD!" My eyes widen.

"You can just call me the Ghost of Christmas Future," he chuckles.

"Aren't you supposed to be like, eight feet tall with bony hands and a black hooded shroud?" I murmur nervously.

"Have you been watching The Muppet's Christmas Carol again?" He smiles.

"You're not Morgan Freeman, are you?" I swallow tightly.

"No." He grins. "But I'm told that humans find his voice and his countenance soothing."

"Are you really...." The three-letter word dances on my tongue, but I can't bring myself to say it without fainting.

"I have many names," Morgan says smoothly, dragging his hand along the edge of the table as he looks around the huge, tiled room. "So, this is where you work."

"I um..." My brain seems to have stalled.

Morgan chuckles again. "Relax, Tristan. I'm here for a

conversation, nothing more, nothing less. You can't do it wrong."

"UUU...aa." Okay, I can make vowels sounds that's good. Now if I could just get some consonants in there that'd be great.

"Why don't I start?" Morgan says with a smile. "How are you, Tristan?"

"I... I'm good..." I squeak.

"Excellent." He beams. "Now, we've thrown a lot at you recently. A lot of things have changed in your life and are going to change in the future, but you can't know where you're going until you know where you've been. That's what all this was about." He holds his hands up. "I know it was hard for you when your mother came home to us."

I nod mutely.

Morgan glances around the room again. "Tell me what you enjoy most about your work, Tristan."

"I... I like figuring things out. It's like a puzzle to solve," I reply, thrown by the sudden change of topic.

"But it's more than that isn't it?" Morgan says. "What did you tell Danny when you first met him?"

"That I wanted to give the families of the deceased answers," I murmur thoughtfully.

"Exactly, you wanted to ease their pain." He nods looking directly at me. "You wanted to help them."

"I suppose."

"Dealing with the departed is no different than dealing with the living." He shrugs. "It's a calling, one you responded to admirably with your friend Dusty."

"Wait?" I frown. "Was that a test?"

"Call it an audition." Morgan shrugs. "Many are born with the potential but ignore it or squander it. You did neither. Even when you didn't want to, even when you weren't sure, you still did the right thing, and how did it feel?"

"Good, I guess." I shrug.

"Tristan, I'm not here to make you do anything you don't want to," Morgan says. "But it's something to think about. Which brings us to where you're going from here."

He points to something behind me, and as I turn, I'm no longer standing staring at the Victorian tiles of the mortuary, I'm now sitting on a bench alongside Morgan staring out at a cemetery. Not too far from us, I can see a recently filled in grave, and I can see myself standing looking down at it with Danny standing behind me. His arms wrapped around me gently. We're both dressed in black and surrounded by an ocean of wreaths and flowers.

"Dad?" I whisper. I don't need to look at the gravestone to know whose funeral it is.

"He doesn't have much time left," Morgan says quietly. "His task is almost complete, and then he'll come home to us too."

"What task?" I ask.

"It's not for you to know." Morgan shakes his head. "You have your own path to walk, but I want you to know that when his time comes there won't be any pain. He'll simply fall asleep."

"I thought I was ready." I swallow hard. Feeling the edges of panic fluttering in my chest. "I'm not ready to lose him."

"No one ever is." He smiles kindly. "But there's time yet, not a lot but some."

I draw in a shaky breath.

"Come, walk with me." He stands slowly.

I push up from the bench and follow him along the narrow footpath, winding between the gravestones and leaving the image of Danny holding me behind us. I watch as Morgan pauses and reaches down, plucking something off the ground, and when he turns it over in his hand, it's an old penny with King George IV stamped on the back. "What is it you say?" Morgan muses. "See a penny pick it up, all day long you'll have good luck?"

"Something like that," I murmur.

I turn my head sharply as something flickers in the corner of my eye, and my breath catches in my throat. There's a huge shadow, it almost looks like it's wearing a shroud and a deeply cowled hood. It undulates through the air like its swimming underwater, weaving back and forth over the fresh gravestone and scenting the air.

"What's that?" I breathe in shock.

"Oh, him?" Morgan glances in the wraith's direction absently. "He doesn't really have a name, but he's been here since the beginning though. Probably best to not get too close."

"What is he?"

"Not your concern," Morgan tells me firmly.

I glance back to Me and Danny in the distance and frown.

"What?" Morgan asks.

"Do you think I should tell him? Danny, I mean," I wonder aloud. "About the things I can see... the ghosts. Do I tell him the truth?" I turn and ask Morgan directly.

"Sorry." He shakes his head. "That's something you'll have to figure out for yourself. Free will, Tristan. It's both a blessing and a curse. You're the only one that can make that call."

"I don't know," I mumble. "Everything's still so new between us. I guess I'm not sure how much crazy he can take."

"I think he may surprise you." Morgan grins.

"What am I doing here?" I stop and turn to Morgan.

"That's for you to figure out, Tristan," Morgan says softly. "Soon, you will be faced with a choice. One path will lead to devastation and the other to peace and contentment."

"No pressure then." I frown. "I don't suppose you want to give me a clue?"

"Sorry." He smiles slowly. "I can't give you any help that would influence you in any way... Free will, remember? All that pesky fine print. The Archangels are sticklers for detail. They do love their bureaucracy."

"How do I know I'm making the right choice then?" I sigh.

"Trust your gut."

"That's it?" I repeat. "Trust my gut?"

"Hasn't steered you wrong yet." He grins.

"Tell that to Dusty. According to her, my gut has made some questionable fashion choices," I reply dryly.

"That's why we sent her back to you."

"To re-organise my wardrobe?" I blink.

"To bring colour to your life," Morgan says with a smile. "You were living in black and white, but now you get to experience everything in glorious Technicolour." He watches me closely. "And although she won't admit it, she needs you as much as you need her." He glances up at the cloudy sky. "Well, time's up, and this is where I leave you."

He takes my hand, and my whole body feels like it's tingling from head to toe with static electricity, even my hair is standing on end. He turns my hand over and places the penny in my palm.

"For luck." He smiles. "I'll be watching you, Tristan Everett."

And once again the grandfather clock begins to chime and everything around me melts and disappears.

ALL I WANT FOR CHRISTMAS IS YOU

Tristan

I roll over, yawning widely and stretching to find the bed next to me empty. I glance up, grabbing my glasses off the bedside table as I tap the screen of my phone and see it's only 8.15 am. Wondering where Danny is, I shove the covers off me and am greeted with an indignant mewl.

"Oops, sorry, Jacob Marley." I fumble with the covers and find a furry face and an accusing pair of eyes. "I didn't see you there."

I watch as Jacob Marley struts up the bed, slapping me purposefully in the face with his tail before settling down on my pillow with a sniff of disapproval and going back to sleep. Feeling thoroughly chastised, pretty amused and full of affection for my grumpy cat, I pad out of the bedroom. My sock covered feet make no sound as I head into the kitchen.

I stop for a moment, my heart melting as I watch Danny. He's pulling a couple of slices of toast from the toaster and setting them on a plate, which is on a tray, along with a little shot glass with a sprig of mistletoe in. There's also a mug of steaming coffee and a glass of orange juice.

"Hey," I say softly as I cross the kitchen, wrapping my arms around his waist and hugging his back. "Whatcha doin?"

"I was trying to be incredibly romantic and make you breakfast in bed." He turns in my arms and wraps me up in his embrace as he ducks down and brushes a soft kiss against my lips. "Even though you were snoring and drooling a little... it was cute."

"You're spoiling me." I grin up at him.

"That's the whole point," he murmurs as his fingers tangle gently in my hair, and he kisses me again. "Merry Christmas, Tristan," he whispers against my mouth.

"Merry Christmas, Danny." I kiss him back, sighing in contentment as I pull back and rest my face against his broad chest.

Danny gives the best hugs. It's like being completely surrounded by him in a safe, little, warm cocoon as he gives a little sway and kisses the top of my head.

"Why don't you go back to bed," he rubs my back. "And I'll bring this to you."

"As tempting as that sounds, that's not happening," I say ruefully as I pull back further and stare up at him. "Jacob Marley has planted a flag on my pillow and claimed it as his territory. The only way I'm getting back in that bed is a full frontal assault across enemy lines."

Danny chuckles and nods toward the table. "You'd better take a seat then."

I settle down in one of the chairs, frowning slightly as the song changes on the playlist that Danny's set up on his phone. Wham's *Last Christmas* comes on, and a flicker of a memory tugs at my mind.

"What is it?" Danny asks as he sets the mug of coffee in front of me.

"Nothing." I shake my head. "I just had the strangest dream last night about my mu..."

I glance down as he sets a plate in front of me.

"Chocolate spread on toast?" I murmur.

"I know." He shrugs.

"Not what I was originally planning for breakfast, but when I woke up this morning, I had a craving for chocolate spread on toast. Which is really weird when you consider I probably haven't had that since I was a kid. Then I looked in the cupboard and you had a jar of chocolate spread still in date."

"I didn't buy that." I frown.

"You must have." Danny retrieves his own plate and slides it onto the table as he takes a seat. "Unless it was Jacob Marley." He grins. "Because I didn't."

"Must've forgotten," I mumble, taking a bite of the toast and smiling as I think back to the dream about my mum.

The song on the playlist changes to Slade's *Merry Christmas* as Danny takes a sip of his coffee. "After we're done, I thought we could get dressed and head over to Sunrise to see your dad," he says conversationally as he chews his toast.

"But, what about our pyjama day?" I say quietly as I look at him.

"We can change into our PJs when we get back." He grins. "Or if you're that set on it, we could always wear our PJs to the home, we'd fit right in with the residents."

My belly warms and my eyes soften as I watch him.

"You know you'll feel better if you see him," Danny says gently. "We can massacre the turkey when we get back."

I reach across the table and link my fingers with his. "How did I end up here, like this with you," I say wonderingly.

"Lucky ice cube." He grins around a mouthful of toast.

I snort quietly as I sip my coffee.

"Anyway." Danny chews his last mouthful of toast and gets up from the table, dropping his plate and mug into the sink. "I'm going to take a shower." He glances up at the clock mounted on the wall. "At this time of the morning there shouldn't be too much traffic. If we time it right, we'll arrive just after your dad's had his breakfast, and we can take him his present."

He bends down to kiss me, and overwhelmed with affection for this sweet man, I grab his face and latch on, kissing him deeply and tasting coffee and chocolate.

"Thank you." I pull back slightly, still cupping his face in my hands. He opens his mouth to say something and then stops. "What?"

"Nothing." He smiles and shakes his head. "It can wait." He drops another quick kiss on my lips. "Don't be too long. We have a turkey awaiting execution."

I watch as he ducks out of the kitchen, and I smile, sighing deeply as the happiness floods every molecule in my body.

I finish my breakfast quickly, but as I cross the kitchen, something drops out of the pocket of my hoodie and hits the ground. Setting my plate and mug into the sink alongside Danny's, I reach down and pick up the small metallic item, turning it over in my palm. It's an old George IV penny, and I rub my thumb over the tarnished copper surface and smile, as a feeling of awareness prickles along my skin, raising the hairs on the back of my neck.

"Hey!" Danny's muffled voice carries through the flat. "Bet you a fiver we can both squeeze in this tiny shower!"

I grin and grab the sprig of mistletoe from the shot glass as I shove the penny back into my pocket before bustling out of the kitchen.

"Do you think it needs a post-mortem?" Danny asks seriously as he clutches the small fire extinguisher in his hand.

I snort, staring down at the charred carcass welded to the tin. "It didn't look like that in Jamie Oliver's tutorial on YouTube," I remark casually.

"I'm pretty certain he said roast gently on gas mark 5, not incinerate on gas mark 9." Danny replies sagely.

"Yeah, noted for next time," I nod, still holding my hands up and wearing the brand new oven mitts, which are now burned and charred to match the turkey.

"Is there any hope for the potatoes?" Danny asks.

I remove the oven mitts and pick up a knife, prodding one of them experimentally. "Hmm, they appear to be cremated on the outside and raw on the inside." I shake my head.

"Rest in peace," Danny intones sombrely, and I can't help but giggle.

He sets the fire extinguisher on the table and pulls me into his arms, with laughter in his eyes. Planting a kiss on my smiling lips. "Pot Noodle, then?"

I laugh again, but just as he leans in for a kiss, there's a loud knock at the door.

"I'll get it," Danny laughs as he releases me.

A few moments later, I hear Chan's voice, and I smile, looking up as she steps into the kitchen with bags of MacDonald's. "Auntie Chan to the rescue, I had a feeling you might need... good fucking god." She stares down at the blackened, congealed mess in the tray. "What the hell did that turkey ever do to you?"

"Merry Christmas, Chan." I grin. "You're lifesaver."

"I know, darling." She winks and blows me a kiss as Danny appears behind her carrying several large carrier bags.

"What's all this?" I ask as she sets the MacDonald's bags down on the table.

"Provisions for our Christmas movie marathon. See here, exhibit A." She waves a hand in front of herself. "Pyjamas as requested."

I glance down at her in amusement. She's wearing a pink fluffy onesie with Princess Chan written across the chest in a curly silver script, and on her feet, she has five inch silver stiletto's.

"And Exhibit B." She rummages in the bags. "Frozen cocktails." She pulls a bendy plastic children's straw out of the bag and hands it to me. "Better safe than sorry." She winks as I stare at her dryly, and Danny barks out a laugh. "I also got snacks. I call the Cadbury's Roses, and I'm not sharing them."

She empties out the bag on the counter and tucks the tin of chocolates under her arm, grabbing a couple of pouches of frozen cocktail and one of the MacDonald's bags as she sails into the living room.

"Ooh, I call dibs on the Terry's Chocolate Orange." I snatch up the small square box gleefully.

"Hey!" Danny frowns. "Why do I get left with the After Eight mints?"

"Oh, baby." I wrap my arms around him and lay a kiss on his sulky mouth. "I'll share my chocolate orange with you." The laughter dies on my lips at the intensity in his eyes.

"I love you," he says suddenly.

"Boy, you really do take your Chocolate Oranges seriously." I smile.

"I'm serious, Tristan," Danny says. "I think I'm in love with you."

"You think?" I whisper.

"I think about you all the time," he says. "It makes my stomach feel all warm when I come home to your place after work and know I'm going to see you. I get this really goofy look on my face when I'm thinking about you according to my work colleagues,

I talk about you all day, like to the point where they've seriously considered locking me in one of the holding cells, and when we lie in bed at night and I'm holding you, I feel like..."

"Feel like?"

"Like there's nowhere else I want to be," he finishes, slightly embarrassed.

"Sounds like love to me," I whisper as I reach up and touch his face. "I think I love you too, by the way, in case you were wondering."

He smiles as he pulls me close, his head dips down, and as his lips touch mine, I sink into his kiss. My heart thuds in my chest, filled to bursting with happiness.

"Danny," I whisper against his lips as he continues to kiss me.

"Yes," he murmurs.

"You're crushing the After Eight mints." He snorts loudly and pulls back, tossing the box of chocolates he'd been holding on the table.

"Come on you two," Chan calls loudly. "Your Big Mac's getting cold."

Grinning at each other we grab up armfuls of snacks and the other bag of MacDonald's before heading into the living room.

I stop and smile as I see Chan in the armchair with her feet propped on my coffee table as she shoves a mouthful of fries in her mouth and then takes a slurp of some blue coloured slushy cocktail. Perched on the arm of the chair next to her is Dusty in a pair of leopard print silk pyjamas and fluffy stiletto slippers. She blows me a kiss as she curls around Chan, even though Chan can't see her.

Danny and I settle on the sofa together as I pick up the remote control and Danny unpacks the food.

"What are we watching first?" I ask flipping through the channels.

"Uh, Die Hard!" Chan answers with an implied duh, as if the choice should be clearly obvious. "It's not Christmas until you've seen Bruce Willis all dirty and bloody on top of Nakatomi Plaza."

"A sentiment I happen to share." Danny grins as he pops the top on his beer and hands me a burger, settling back with his arm around me.

"Okay." I smile happily. "Die Hard it is."

Want more Tristan, Danny and Dusty?

Don't miss Book 2!
Dead Serious Case #2 Mrs Delores Abernathy.
AVAILABLE NOW!

ABOUT THE AUTHOR

Vawn Cassidy is the MM pen name of author Wendy Saunders. She lives in Hampshire in the UK with her husband and three children.

She writes Supernatural and Contemporary Fantasy Fiction as Wendy Saunders and Romantic Suspense as WJ Saunders.

With Dead Serious she returned to her Supernatural roots and her love of all things ghostly and preternatural with a good healthy dose of humour.

So if you want to get in touch feel free, she's always lurking around on social media, or you can sign up to her mailing list here and also visit her website

www.vawncassidy.com

ALSO BY VAWN CASSIDY

Crawshanks Guide to the Recently Departed

Dead Serious Case#1 Miz Dusty Le Frey

Dead Serious Case#2 Mrs Delores Abanathy

Belong to Me

Book 1 Suddenly Beck

Book 2 Definitely Deacon

Book 2.5 Forever Finn (Novella)

Printed in Great Britain
by Amazon